ROBERT RIOUX

Idol Pursuits: Debut

First published by Rioux Inc. 2023

For more information contact: rpriouxbooks@protonmail.com

Library of Congress Control Number: 2023950931

Second edition

ISBN: 979-8-9888565-0-4

This book was professionally typeset on Reedsy.
Find out more at reedsy.com

To Ngan, with enduring love

Contents

Acknowledgments

First and foremost, I wish to express gratitude to my wife who makes everything possible through abundant patience and a huge heart. Special thanks also to Susan Chang for her expert advice, Dianne Bangle, Red Warner, and Barry Klusman for their tireless encouragement, and to muses throughout the ages for inspiring generations.

1

A PLACE IN THE WORLD

Bathed in sunlight, with expansive views of the neighboring metropolis, Grace found the St. Ignatius University campus to be the loveliest she had ever seen. Perched on a bluff overlooking Marina del Rey, the panorama before her stretched from Topanga State Park and the Malibu shore to the Hollywood Hills and downtown Los Angeles. Its prime location allowed the school to embrace the city's restless energy while serving as a peaceful haven from its more frequent and pervasive irritations.

Echoing its foundation as a Jesuit institution of higher learning, the grounds, richly adorned with tree-lined walkways and abundant green spaces, adopted the overall form of a cross. Centered on two broad pedestrian avenues intersecting at an expansive plaza near the campus' heart stood the most important administrative buildings. Lining each mall were the primary colleges: Liberal Arts, Education, Performing and Fine Arts, Film and Television, Science and Engineering, and Grace's second home of late, the Business school.

The architectural pièce de résistance was the Sacred Heart

Chapel. Commanding a prominent spot overlooking the lush lawns of the Sunken Garden, the magnificent Spanish Gothic structure stood at the tip of the cross. Visible from both the campus entrance and the city below, the house of worship relished its status as the university's iconic public symbol.

Grace often visited the palm-adorned bluff-side path surrounding the chapel, preferring to stop there on her way home after class. If lucky, she'd find an unoccupied bench as a momentary resting place to unwind from the stress of studies. Her favorite moments came when soft breezes wafted from the ocean, carrying penstemon and morning glory scents.

All plans for visiting this spot were derailed one September afternoon when the fussy teacher's assistant from Economics approached, clutching a piece of paper and shouting her surname. "Ms. So," he said. Grace, who had been listening to "Rum Pum Pum Pum" by f(x), struggled to remove her earbuds in time to acknowledge the address.

"Yes?"

"Are you in contact with Heather Moon, by any chance?"

"Is something wrong?"

"Professor Harding wants to know. If she drops, this form must be signed and returned by Monday."

"Heather's dropping Economics?"

"That's what I assume. She's missed classes, skipped tests, and is behind on two assignments. You used to sit by her."

"I'll see what I can do. She hasn't been feeling well lately."

* * *

Though Heather's Playa del Rey apartment was just ten minutes from campus, Grace had never paid it a visit. This was ironic, considering their prior close relationship before college, but when her friend had asked for space, Grace obliged. That request had grown more challenging as their meetings and messages dwindled to a trifle. The TA's report was concerning. Indeed, the final straw. Something had to be done, even if it meant invading her friend's privacy more than she would have preferred.

Grace located the apartment and knocked. A mussy-haired girl in square-rimmed glasses answered. She frowned in disappointment.

"Does Heather live here?" Grace asked, ignoring the girl's icy reception.

"Living isn't the first word that comes to mind," she responded. "If you're inquiring whether an entity by that name refers to this address as her domicile, then yes."

"Well then, might the Heather entity be present…uh, presently?" Grace winced at her own lame attempt to impress through mimicry.

"She's sleeping," said the girl, continuing with her stone-faced demeanor. "There's no point in coming back, though. Nothing will change." She opened the door wide and returned to the couch, unmuting the television. Grace concluded it was the closest thing to an invitation she'd be getting and stepped inside. The apartment was furnished with mundane yet functional home products. Browns, yellows, and oranges dominated the aesthetic. The lack of shoes piled in the entryway betrayed the house's custom.

Grace waited for permission to proceed, but the roommate was engrossed in a daytime talk show and failed to notice. A forceful throat-clearing was required to regain her attention. "Oh, her room is at the end of the hallway," the roommate said.

"If you're not out in fifteen, I'll call search-and-rescue."

Before Grace reached the hallway entrance, the girl shared an unsolicited observation. "You know, I was thrilled when Housing told me my college roommate would be a K-pop singer. I never in a million years expected such a train wreck." Grace nodded but inquired no further.

The knock on Heather's door yielded no response. Grace struck harder. Not a peep. She turned the handle. Unlocked. A peek inside revealed a dingy room reeking of stale air and resembling a mausoleum more than a bedroom. It took considerable effort to push the door open. A heavy object had fallen at its base, blocking its path. A sliver of light clipped past the opaque curtains to penetrate the gloom. Grace could hear low breathing in the darkness. She groped around for a light switch but bumped a picture frame instead, nearly dislodging it from its hook. With the faint illumination as her guide, she braved the cheerless space. A slippery substance encountered along the way made her grateful she wore shoes.

To her surprise, Grace reached the window without breaking her neck. She ripped the curtains open, flooding the room with bright light. The scene that emerged was disheartening. She considered shutting them again. Detritus covered every inch of floor space and furniture, especially the bed and its environs. Countless plastic bags, food wrappers, dirty dishes, books, papers, and vast piles of clothing littered the room, resembling the aftermath of a looting disaster. The closet contained a few hangers, all bereft of garments. The empty beer cans and soju bottles would have made a dedicated recycler's eyes water.

Opening the windows as wide as they would go, she allowed fresh air to enter the space for perhaps the first time in weeks. A pile of clothing and blankets stirred on the futon. One tug at it revealed Heather, her face almost unrecognizable, bloated with dark bags under her eyes. The sudden exposure to sunlight and circulated air caused her to shrink away like a vampire ejected from a crypt. Heather reached for the first item she could grab, a red pullover sweater, and buried her head in it. "Turn off the light!" It wasn't a request.

Grace pulled the sweater away and tossed it into a distant corner, far out of reach. She pinned her friend's arms to the futon, forcing her to adapt to the new conditions. "Heather, this has gone on long enough."

"I'm tired. Let me sleep."

"You missed how many classes? You don't return messages. This is not normal. People are asking. And look at this pigsty! You used to be meticulous."

"I'm busy."

"Give me a break. When was the last time you left this room?"

"I..." Heather turned her face away in shame.

Grace pulled the girl into an upright position and hugged her tightly. The compassion she displayed prompted her friend to sob. "Look, I understand you're still hurting, but you can't throw your whole life away because of one moment."

Heather took comfort in the words of support. "I...you know...I'm..." She was too embarrassed to finish.

"Go ahead, you can tell me."

"I'm three weeks late."

Grace's eyes widened. She swept the hair from her despondent friend's face. "Have you tested?"

"Not yet."

"Who's the guy?"

Heather appeared chagrined and avoided eye contact.

Grace's belly knotted at the realization. "You have no idea."

"Are you slut-shaming me?"

"No. Listen. If I thought for a second you enjoyed this lifestyle, I'd be the first to cheer you on," Grace said, grabbing both sides of Heather's head and forcing her to pay attention. "But I know you. This is not what you're about. When we first met, you were unstoppable."

Heather slapped Grace's hands away and crashed onto the bed. "I'm trash. It's about time I admit it."

Grace had reached the limit of her patience. "You know what's trash?" she implored, ripping the remaining bedding off Heather's body. "This attitude of yours." Grabbing one arm, she dragged her friend off the futon.

"What are you doing?"

"You're getting cleaned up. God, you weigh a ton." Grace couldn't recall Heather's weight ever exceeding 45 kilograms during training. Those days seemed like a lifetime ago.

Despite the unexpected burden, she made it as far as the bathroom door. Heather, now resigned to the intervention, stopped resisting and stood on two feet. Grace plugged the bathtub drain, opened the faucet, and poured copious amounts of salt and soap into the water. "Take a good long soak. I'll make it nice and hot. You'll feel better. When I return from the store, you're taking a pregnancy test, then we'll detoxify this landfill together."

* * *

Light from the diner pierced the darkness like a beacon. Shea's was a stalwart eatery for locals and one of the few 24-hour places operating on the far east end of Santa Monica's Pico

Boulevard. After an evening scrubbing Heather's room while commiserating over hot tea, Grace suggested a late-night excursion to de-stress. Waking up for her early Consumer Behavior class would be challenging, but she didn't want to miss this critical opportunity to positively alter a friend's life.

Built in the 1930s, the curved glass façade of Shea's had become iconic. Its cherry-wood counters and stools contrasted with the jade-green wall tiles. Stainless steel appliances lined the rear wall, while subtle architectural details evoked a bygone era of Los Angeles' Streamline Moderne past. The restaurant, within walking distance of her parents' house, was a favorite of Grace's. She hoped its relaxed vibe would put Heather in a receptive mood for what she had to say.

A white, blonde male was wiping the menus as they entered. The only other patron, a Black man in a dark blue suit, sat on the opposite leg of the L-shaped counter. "I Can't Tell You Why," by the Eagles, played over the sound system. Grace ordered an omelet with green onions and tomatoes. To disapproving looks, Heather chose a slice of marionberry pie with no ice cream. "I promise I'll start my diet tomorrow," she said. "Allow me one last indulgence."

"At least you're not eating for two."

"I'll be more careful from now on."

"You scared me. I've never seen you like that."

Heather's expression was dour. She avoided looking at Grace as she spoke. "I downloaded that new dating app. At first, it was like a high. I could pick any guy I wanted, knowing he'd be mine by the night's end. I felt powerful. Desirable. Loved. Yet the illusion slipped away as I gorged through one encounter after the next. I realized they were using me as much as I was using them. It became so meaningless. So pointless. The last guy I was with even had the gall to search for a new date while I was getting dressed. That's when it hit me. I felt so cheap, so worthless. It broke me."

"Have you sought help?"

"A little." She paused. "You could help, can't you?"

"I'm an excellent listener."

"No. I mean, consider going to therapy for me. I used up my free sessions at the counseling center and can't afford any more."

Grace wanted to appear receptive, but the request baffled her. "How would *my* therapy in any way help *you*?" She considered it a moment longer. "And how could you possibly be out of free ones already? The semester's barely started."

"You're not using them, are you?" Heather appeared dead serious, but Grace understood from experience that looks could be deceiving. Her friend excelled at straight-faced humor. "Think about it. I'll write my problems down; you'll present them as yours. Afterward, just relay whatever advice they give."

Grace looked at Heather. "I honestly can't tell sometimes if you're joking or not, but regardless, yeah, that's gonna be a no from me dawg."

"Give me your ID then. I doubt they'll check."

"Heather, therapy is long-term. I'm talking about the here and now."

"I'm feeling much better, thanks to you."

"For how long? A month? A semester, tops? Call me skeptical, but I doubt you're cured after one close call."

"I'll concentrate on school. My dad will be thrilled."

"Forget him. The way you beg for his approval. It's masochistic."

"I want him to be proud of me."

"I distinctly remember you saying that about 37-G Entertainment, and look how that turned out."

"Don't compare the two."

"Listen. You don't need therapy. I'll tell you right now what's wrong."

Heather lifted one eyebrow. "Go ahead, then. Explain me to me."

"When you channel your energy into something positive, you're superhuman. Remain idle, though, and you melt away like butter on the grill. Sometimes, I think you like it that way."

"Why would I like that?"

"Because you're afraid."

"Of what?"

"Success."

"That's ridiculous."

"Is it? We both watched people with a fraction of your talent become idols. Why? Because they believed in themselves. They weren't afraid to make the most of their limited gifts."

"I believe in myself."

"Do you? Because all I'm seeing is a scared little girl who holds herself back."

"I'm a team player."

"You still don't get it. Your talent inspires people. When you give up, you disappoint those who count on you most."

Heather sat with shoulders slumped toward the counter. It took many long minutes before she spoke again. "What we had in Korea, that's not an option anymore."

"We'll find an alternative."

"I'm good at one thing."

"Then try a new way."

Heather enunciated each word in a sing-song voice to emphasize her point. "Hello. We don't live there anymore."

"You're making excuses."

"Grace. Come on. How can you be so dense? I can't be a K-pop idol in L.A."

"Who says?"

"Um, reality."

Grace assessed the restaurant's two occupants. "Hey, are either of you named Reality?" Both men dismissed her as possibly drunk and remained silent. "See, Reality doesn't care."

"I'm not soloist material."

"Well, start a group then."

"You're telling me to start a K-pop group with no money, no agency, and two members?"

"I'm not telling you anything. You want this. Admit it." Grace watched her friend patiently. It took a good long while. Eventually, however, she detected a slight change in Heather's face. One that suggested an adjustment in demeanor.

"Come to think of it, people start bands all the time."

"Of every variety," Grace agreed.

"Why not K-pop?"

"Why not?"

As Heather's enthusiasm grew, words came tumbling forth. "I honestly thought I could forget what happened there, but it's been eating at me ever since. My lifelong dream was within reach, and I..." In an instant, her positivity vanished again. "Oh, who am I fooling? Where would I start? It's impossible."

Grace, sensing that she had laid enough groundwork, was ready to launch her plan. "Funny you should mention that.

Look what I found." Extracting a business card from her bag, she placed it on the counter between them, using a dramatic flourish to emphasize its importance. "I was at Art of the Cinema on Tuesday when I found these on the bulletin board and took one."

Heather snatched the card and read it aloud, "Film/Recording Arts major seeks talented musical act for a collaborative endeavor. Serious inquiries only. Contact Steve Shepard at blah, blah, blah." She held the notice next to her head as if it were a protest sign, one eyebrow raised in disbelief. "That's it?"

The coffeemaker signaled the end of its cycle. Despite the hour, the smell of freshly brewed java made Grace long for a cup. She frowned at Heather's reaction, then pointed at one sentence: "You conveniently skipped the part about a possible cash prize."

Heather snapped the card on the counter like a losing poker hand. "You're serious about this, aren't you?" The server stopped working long enough to assess the outburst. Satisfied it was none of his business, he returned to cleaning. "I figured you were just humoring me," Heather said, now in a softer voice. "After all we went through?"

"Yes, I am serious. Look how hard we worked, and what do we have to show for it?" Grace leaned closer, tapping her finger on the counter to emphasize her words. "Nothing. That's what. Absolutely nothing. This time will be different. This time, we'll do it our way."

"Why would this guy pick us? He doesn't sound Korean."

"He's white, actually."

"There must be plenty of other candidates. Besides, we don't even have a group."

"Come on. It's L.A." Grace raised her eyebrows, waiting for Heather to pick up the dropped hint. "You've heard of K-town? Hollywood? The entertainment capital of the world? Do these terms ring a bell? Use your imagination."

The server came by to collect dishes, but sensing the depth of their conversation, slinked away without touching them. "I don't know," Heather concluded. "I wasn't expecting to hear this tonight."

"Don't you miss performing?"

Long moments passed with Heather staring into space before answering, "Like you wouldn't believe. But is K-pop viable outside of Korea?"

"Wouldn't you love to find out?"

A half-hour passed where they spoke little. Grace waited while Heather played with her napkin. An elderly gentleman in a white fedora entered, ordering a Reuben sandwich and a root beer. He regaled the Black man with tales from his merchant marine days. Two lost socialites dressed for clubbing popped in long enough to get directions to Main Street.

In time, Heather broke the reverie. "We should go. I have class in the morning." Grace tried to hide her disappointment. She was hoping for at least one tangible outcome from this effort. They walked back to Grace's parents' house, speaking in low whispers, arm in arm.

Any lingering doubts about the success of her mission evaporated moments later. While driving away, Heather shouted through the open car window. "He'd be stupid not to pick us."

Grace smiled. "Attagirl," she mumbled to herself.

For the rest of that night, Heather communicated her sweeping vision through a series of text messages to Grace. Their exchange went like this:

3:13 A.M. Heather: I want to try a hybrid concept. Half band, half dance unit. Crazy, I'm sure. But it's been done before. Once.

3:14 A.M. Heather: We need to find X more members who can sing, dance, play instruments, and fit the idol image. Won't be easy. Three doable. *Love* to get five, though.

3:16 A.M. Heather: Step One. Hire manager. Find gigs.

3:22 A.M. Heather: Step Two. Raise money. Necessary evil.

3:23 A.M. Heather: Step Three. Record an EP. Imagine!

3:23 A.M. Heather: Step Four. Get on streaming, at least. Hope for radio. HOPE FOR RADIO!!!

3:36 A.M. Heather: Don't know about you, but I'm thinking this might actually work.

3:55 A.M. Heather: Are you getting any of these messages??? Why so quiet???

4:03 A.M. Grace: I'm excited too, Heather, but have you noticed the time by any chance?

* * *

While walking past the Theater Building fountain later that afternoon, an ebullient Heather bounded into a groggy Grace. Despite mildly regretting ever mentioning the band idea, Grace listened intently. In truth, after all the doom and gloom of the last few months, she loved seeing Heather's enthusiasm. Would it persist, though? she wondered. Or would this prove a temporary diversion?

"I've been thinking about the members," said Heather. "We should start with people we know. Do we know anyone?"

Grace, who had struggled to stay awake through Statistics, shifted her focus as best she could onto the question at hand. Shaking her head as if rattling free some spare thoughts, she responded, "We do. Remember Sun-hee Ahn?"

"From Giga Music? Yeah."

"Well, she left the agency. Why? I don't know. But she's enrolled at UCLA now. We could try her."

"She sings *and* plays keys. We've got to get her!"

"There's no harm in asking. I'll DM her."

Two days later, Grace sat with Heather on the steps overlooking the Sunken Garden at SIU. They shared a snack of hummus and carrot sticks as a long-haired, rasta cap-wearing guy raced by on a Segway. He towed a wagon carrying a friend who reclined on a stack of pillows while licking an ice cream cone.

"Remember, in grade school, when we tried so hard to be like everyone else for fear of being bullied?" Grace asked. "Now in college, you see people like that doing their own thing and think, 'Dang, those guys got it all figured out.'"

Without acknowledging her friend's observation, Heather asked, "Any luck with Sun-hee?"

"She hasn't responded."

"Regardless, it seems likely we'll need to run auditions at some point. I looked into reserving a room."

"Will it cost anything?"

"Not on Sundays."

"Okay, book one, and I'll green-light the casting notices—" Grace stopped mid-sentence and stared at the student commons. "Oh, my. Do you see what I see?"

Heather cast her eyes in the same direction. Students

scurried like ants across the crisscrossing paths connecting the northern dorms to the bustling heart of the campus. Despite the throng that was so typical of a mid-semester weekday, it was clear to whom Grace was referring. A petite, youthful girl of East Asian descent walked across their field of view. Short in stature like Heather, she possessed a small frame, relatively broad in the shoulders and tapering to a slight waist and understated hips. In her right hand, she carried a hardshell instrument case.

"Manna from heaven!" Heather exclaimed.

"That's what I'm thinking."

"Looks too young to be in college. Do you think she's Korean?"

"I bet she is, but there's one way to make sure." Grace sprang down the steps on a course to intercept their target. As she approached, the girl glanced in her direction without pausing and kept walking. Grace greeted her in Korean, "Annyeonghaseyo."

The youthful student decelerated and faced her greeter, looking wide-eyed and unsure what to do next.

Hearing no response, Grace offered a second greeting, this time in Japanese. "Konbanwa." The young woman reacted with even more bewilderment and settled for a halting attempt at broken and accented Korean. To end the poor victim's misery, Grace said, "Don't worry, I speak English."

Relief clear on her face, the new girl laughed. "I'm sorry, I'm learning Korean, but reading it and speaking it are two different things. I get so nervous and tongue-tied." Her voice, betraying a subtle drawl, was delightful and small, mirroring the same adolescent vibe evident in her looks.

"That's okay. You don't need to apologize. I saw you passing by and thought I'd introduce myself. I'm Grace So."

The girl smiled. "You speak Korean well." Grace found the comment amusing since she had only used one Korean word thus far. By this point, Heather had joined them, giving a thumbs-up for Grace's sole benefit. She mouthed, 'she's cute' behind the girl's back.

"I'm American but lived in Korea for five years," responded Grace without acknowledging Heather. "You?"

"The opposite. I was born in Korea but adopted as a baby by a family from Oklahoma. Harper, Oklahoma, to be exact. That's where I grew up until I moved here for college."

Heather seized on that moment to interject her own introduction. "Hi, my name is Heather Moon," she said, stepping to the girl's side and extending a hand in greeting. "So, you're a student here? You appear so young."

"That's what everyone says. My curse, I guess." The new girl blushed and accepted the offered hand. "My birth name's Ha-eun, by the way, but people call me Erin. My full name's Erin MacLeay."

"Hello, Erin. I'm glad we met."

"Me too." The shy one's eyes diverted as she continued forward. "Listen, I don't want to seem rude, but I can't be late for rehearsals. I play bass in a Britpop Revival band, and this is only my second practice."

Heather, still positioned behind their target's back, gestured as if they had just won a jackpot.

"Britpop, you say?" Grace smiled and laced her arm through Erin's. Wasting no time, Heather soon joined them, taking the opposite arm. "Do you mind if we walk with you, Erin MacLeay from Oklahoma? We have an idea we'd like to propose."

2

IS THERE A CATCH?

Heather felt like a secret agent skulking outside the entrance to Amorphous Records. As she spied through the window, a call came in from Grace.

"Wanna work on songs tonight?"

"Love to, but I'm in Hollywood tracking down a potential addition to our group."

"Heather Moon taking the initiative. This, I like."

"The more I think about it, the more I want to prove this idea possible."

"That's the spirit. So, who's the target?"

"I was watching dance cover videos on YouTube the other day when I ran across a pretty good local act. One member, in particular, struck me as either an amateur with natural talent or someone who'd been formally trained."

"Go on."

"Anyway, upon further research, she debuted with a K-pop group a few years ago. Have you heard of WeR5?"

"That name sounds vaguely familiar."

"They had a modest hit called 'Hummingbird.' Disbanded

eventually. Not clear on the rest."

"What's her specialty?"

"That's the best part. She's a drummer!"

The girl's birth name was Min-ji, but she used an alias in the States. Over the past week, Heather had sent many direct and indirect messages. None were returned. Lacking other options, she was inclined to take a more aggressive approach. On impulse, Heather drove to Hollywood to investigate in person after Philosophy class was canceled unexpectedly.

James Blake's "Where's the Catch?" blared on the record store's sound system as she entered. Heather approached the retail counter where a bearded, white, hipster-looking fellow sorted through a stack of documents. "Is Mindy here today?" She asked loudly.

Instead of giving her a blank stare as she half expected, the guy responded without making eye contact, "On break. Try back in 20."

With time to kill, Heather wandered among the store's treasures, marveling at the sheer amount of stuff. She targeted new releases, reasoning that it would be best to start in familiar territory. Vinyl wasn't exactly her thing, but she thrilled at the thought of accidentally stumbling upon a hidden treasure buried deep within the record bins. Album graphics especially piqued her interest. The eye-catching examples on display evoked the elaborate packaging that encased most K-pop CDs. The visuals and supplementary materials were often complete works of art in their own right.

About thirty minutes into her visit, she was greeted by a soft voice with a slight accent. Heather instantly recognized Mindy, who loomed over her by several inches. Her luxurious locks had grown out since the YouTube videos, and she had matured some. Still, the girl's mixed-race heritage gave her a unique countenance that was hard to confuse with anyone else's. Despite wearing a simple outfit of jeans, a black vest, and a white blouse, her hourglass figure was conspicuous. Mindy exuded an undeniable sexiness while retaining a type of wholesomeness that has long been stock-in-trade for K-pop idols.

Heather turned on the charm. "You don't know me, but I'm Heather Moon. I've been messaging you."

Abruptly dropping the polite customer service demeanor, Mindy cut her off, switched to Korean, and responded tersely. "How did you get my deets?" She pointed over her shoulder at the guy staffing the retail counter. "If you're the one who left those messages on Instagram, I'm not interested in your project. Stop bothering me. I have work to do." She walked away without saying another word.

Unfazed by the rejection, Heather decided to stick around until closing. The wait was excruciating. Although the corner of Hollywood and Vine sometimes proved exciting, spending three hours solo on a weeknight felt interminable. Returning to the store, she watched the neon lights flicker off as the staff closed shop for the night.

Five minutes later, Mindy exited and made her way to the parking lot. Her eyes rolled when she spotted Heather waiting. "You again."

"I'm motivated."

"Delusional, too," Mindy said, facing her follower directly. "Look, I'm not sure what you want from me, but my K-pop days are over. Got it?"

Heather remained undeterred. "Then why are you doing dance covers?"

Mindy's face flushed with color. She smiled guiltily. "Because it's fun, and I don't have to follow anyone's rules. That's why."

"We're not an entertainment company. I'm tired of their crap too. Just listen to my pitch. Okay?"

Mindy looked away and fidgeted as if she were having a tantrum. Suddenly composing herself, she said, "Here's the deal. I haven't eaten yet. There's a place nearby I go sometimes. You have until they close to change my mind; then I'm going home."

Heather smiled.

"And you're buying."

"How did you end up here?" asked Heather as she sipped her blood-orange aqua fresca at the restaurant. Empty plates that once contained shared orders of grilled-fish mini tacos, tempura asparagus, and herb salad littered the table between them.

"I wanted to get as far away as possible to clear my head, and L.A. was the most viable option," said Mindy. "I'm recognized here but rarely bothered. Actually, I made it two months this time until you came along."

Heather let the dismissive comment slide. "Is that why you go by Mindy?"

"People here tend to react better to English names, I've concluded." She averted her gaze as she spoke. "Why? What's your Korean name?"

"Heather is my only name. I used it even in Korea. Your surname is Japanese, though. Ito?"

"My father is half Japanese, half Korean. He met my Ukrainian-American mother when she was teaching English in Seoul. How's that for a mix? Where am I supposed to fit in? I'm not Japanese enough for Japan, Korean enough for Korea, and here I'm considered too whitewashed to be truly Asian and too Asian to be truly American."

"Sounds familiar," said Heather. Not wishing to change the subject, but growing anxious at the approaching deadline, she pushed the issue at hand. "I watched WeR5 videos. Your group was talented. Shame it didn't work out."

"It's a crappy business. You were lucky to leave when you did."

"I wouldn't go that far."

"It was only a matter of time. You'd have gotten screwed too."

"You'd be surprised."

Mindy analyzed Heather's face as if reading her thoughts. "Oh, so you do know what I'm talking about," she said with a grimace. "What's your sputter, lemon butter? Why so anxious to get back in?"

"Let's say unfinished business."

"Ah," Mindy said slyly, waving a finger in the air. "See, I can tell. You're hiding something, like everyone else in this town."

Heather admired the girl's keen awareness. "I'm aware there's a dark side to this industry, Mindy. We both saw things we'd probably rather not dwell on. But it wasn't all bad. You remember what performing in front of your fans was like, don't you?"

"I avoid reflection. It's easier."

"You could make a difference, you know? I want to build a group bigger than the sum of its parts, whose members trust each other and are willing to pull in the same direction. If I didn't think it was possible, I wouldn't ask."

"I find your naïve optimism endearing."

"That wasn't at all condescending." Heather finished her drink. She was beginning to lose patience with the recalcitrant prey. "What is your plan, anyway? All I see in your future is dance cover videos and retail. Most people don't have the dedication to push like you did. Where did your ambition and work ethic go?"

"Tell me what ambition and work ethic got me. A headache. That's all."

"Our group will be young. You'd be our unnie. We'd listen to your advice."

Mindy didn't retort right away. She pondered the possibility for a moment. "Sounds rather hopeless."

"It's not. Besides, what do you have to lose at this point? Meet with us and see how it goes. If you don't like it, walk away. No hard feelings."

A taciturn server came to drop off the check and collect the empty plates. "We'll be closing in 10 minutes," he said before stepping away.

"Time's up. What do you say?"

Mindy reclined in her chair and let her arms drop to her sides, swinging them gently as the long minutes passed. "Part of me is tempted to stick around just so I can say I told you so when this idea of yours fails."

Heather hid her disappointment but chose to accept the statement for what it was. "Maybe it'll prove different this time."

"Look, I appreciate the invite, but that lifestyle holds no value for me anymore. Good luck, though. You'll need it."

* * *

The next afternoon, after stopping by the university's book-store to buy a lesson guide, Heather returned to her apartment. The smell of oven-fresh cookies greeted her nose when she stepped inside. "Smells good," she shouted towards the kitchen.

Roommate Kylie poked her head around the corner. "My turn bringing snacks to mock trial tonight. I utilized the mix I found in the cupboard. Hope you don't mind. Oh, a package came for you. I put it in your room."

A toaster-oven-sized box sat on her bed, thoroughly covered in packing tape and Korea Post stickers. Her mother usually overdid things, so cutting through the protective layers took a few minutes. The box revealed a bounty of goodies, including her favorite brand of low-carb konjac snacks. Despite much searching, she couldn't find them in the States. The gift, in total, made her heart leap. Sweet potato balls, diet jellies, and instant tteok-bokki; the box was packed. A few personal items from her old bedroom were also included. The brief note read:

Heather,

I sent some of your favorite things in case you were feeling homesick. How's school going? Your brother did well in the Suneung. Your father is so proud and thinks his scores will get him into Seoul National University. He's also applying to Stanford. Wouldn't that be wonderful? You'd both be in the same state. Keep working hard. We miss you.

Mom.

Among the items her mother had sent was a photograph of Heather holding the acceptance letter from St. Ignatius with her parents standing behind her. Her mother, Ji-woo, smiled, while her father, Dae-hee, stood stiffly, not frowning, but not precisely happy either. *Actually, that's pretty good from him*, she thought to herself. The photo was taken at Chuseok last year while she was still training at 37-G. Back then, college was a backup plan. At least to her, it was. She remembered the visit clearly.

"Help! Police! A stranger's in our house!" shouted Heather's brother Andrew as he sat before the TV playing *Kingdom of Legends*. His torrid pace of enemy slaying had ceased long enough to assess her before returning to his virtual castle siege.

"Hardy-har," said Heather, leaving her shoes in the tiled foyer and stepping onto the pristine wood floor in stockings. "Is Mom home?"

"Kitchen."

Ji-woo emerged, looking exasperated. She took one look at her daughter and smiled. "Did you get the songpyeon?"

"I stopped by the shop near Bangi station. There was more left than expected." She collapsed her suitcase's lift handle, unzipped its front pocket, and wrested a mangled plastic bag full of holiday rice cakes to present to her mother. "They got a little smushed. Sorry."

"Your father went to pick up your uncle's family. They're excited to see you again. You were a child last time we all spent the holiday together. And you've not even met your cousins."

"When will they get here?"

"Not until late, I imagine. The traffic from Goyang is terrible tonight. You can see them in the morning if you feel like sleeping early."

With multiple cooking appliances operating at once, the apartment was balmy. The scent of freshly cut vegetables and heated cooking oil permeated the room. Heather's base of operations stretched across the kitchen table. As Ji-woo handed over trays of sliced lotus root and sweet potatoes, Heather dipped them into an egg and flour batter. Once appropriately coated, she placed the savory cakes on an electric griddle, flipping each once until both sides were crispy golden-brown. It took a while to establish a good rhythm, but her delectable jeon-making operation was now flying.

"It's not like we live far away. You can't visit more than twice a year?"

"Between school and rehearsals, I get three or four hours of sleep as it is. That's with the dorm only five minutes from the agency. The thought of adding a long subway ride on top of it—"

"I have to get used to you being gone, I guess. Especially with college on the horizon."

College. Heather knew that sensitive subject would inevitably arise during the holiday weekend. All efforts to devise a deflection strategy had failed. She opted to address the matter head-on. "Yeah, about that."

Sensing a distinct lack of enthusiasm, Ji-woo stopped slicing to face her, waving a cutting knife as she spoke. "Your father's expecting you to go to university. You've been accepted and everything."

"I mean, can't it wait? At least until I know for sure."

"Know what for sure? This is non-negotiable, Heather."

"My agency is debuting a new girl group soon. That's what

rumors say."

"Rumors," her mother said. "You can't put your life on hold for rumors."

"I've been working towards this for years. What's the rush? College will always be there."

"Your father has it all planned out. Since he's paying for it, you must follow his schedule. Surely you can see the value?"

"She's scared she'll fail," her brother said, unexpectedly appearing in the kitchen doorway, interrupting their conversation. Heather stuck her tongue out at him, but not before he used the distraction to steal three pancakes from the cooling platter.

"You brat! At least take the ugly ones." She watched helplessly as he slipped away from view with his ill-gotten booty.

"We had an agreement," Ji-woo said as she returned to slicing. "We'd let you attend the agency through high school as long as you kept your grades up."

"And I have."

"But high school's almost over."

"Most idols debut around my age. Why would I leave now?"

"Good luck convincing your father of that. He's been more than patient."

Heather replaced the stolen jeon with fresh ones from the griddle. "Appa doesn't take my dreams seriously. Not for one minute."

"He has his reasons. Try to see through his eyes."

"And with that, I won the grand prize," Heather said, beaming at her relatives who sat around the table. "The first one to do so in K-pop." After sharing the tale of her recent triumph at

37-G, she assessed the reactions of those who had gathered for the annual feast. Uncle Tae-sung and Aunt Hyo-sonn offered strained smiles. Ji-woo glanced at her father, whose expression remained blank. Heather's two young cousins played with wooden blocks on the floor, oblivious to the conversation. Andrew seized the opportunity to mock his sister with facial gestures. She chose to ignore him. "Anyway, the galbi feast was amazing. Best meal ever! Everyone at the agency was so grateful."

"Your mother works hard to make the meals she does," her father said.

Heather looked at her mother with alarm. "Oh, I didn't mean anything by that, Umma, I'm just saying. Masheesuhyo!"

"It's okay, I understand." Her reassurance sounded disingenuous.

The block tower her cousins were building came crashing down. Dae-hee looked annoyed at the disturbance but didn't admonish them. "Andrew's on track to finish at the top of his class!" he said, changing the subject in his favor. A surge of enthusiasm greeted the news.

"Oh, that's wonderful, Andrew! Congratulations," her uncle said.

"That boy will run a company someday. Just you wait," added her aunt. Heather had difficulty envisioning that outcome unless, of course, there was a sudden demand for CEOs who were also avid gamers.

"Will you stay here or go abroad?" asked Uncle Tae-sung of Andrew.

"I'd prefer he aim for a California school when the time comes," stated Dae-hee, answering on his son's behalf. "But we have another to send off first." Heather chafed at the renewed attention.

"So, what are your plans, Heather?" her aunt asked.

"Keun eomoni..." She stopped short of responding, unable to find the exact words to please all occupants at the table.

Andrew exploited her hesitation by volunteering a suggestion. "I hear there's a shortage of tomato pickers." The outburst of laughter that resulted shook the table.

"Andrew," scolded her mother. "That boy. I don't know what gets into him sometimes." Heather had a few ideas, but wasn't keen to share them.

"I'm sure she has better options. Right?" Aunt Hyo-sonn's mild defense failed to mask her amusement. Heather reached for the japchae to take her mind off the humiliation. The scent of garlic stir-fried noodles with beef and vegetables reminded her of childhood. Simpler days.

"I was hoping my daughter would take an interest in medical school, but that dream died years ago."

"You wanted that, Appa," protested Heather.

"Maybe a law degree, then," Uncle Tae-sung asked. "Have you considered that?"

"Not my strong suit." She glared at Andrew, who was still chuckling at her torment.

"No, of course not," Aunt Hyo-sonn said.

"I'm thinking a business degree would work for her," continued Dae-hee. "Finance or management, for example."

"An excellent idea. How about that, Heather?"

Hoping acquiescence would bring the discussion to a rapid end, she opted for the path of least resistance. "Sure. Why not?"

Unfortunately, Appa wouldn't let it drop. "Don't forget why you're there," said her father.

"Yes. School. Got it."

"No. You're there to excel. It should be easy where you're going."

His comment confounded her. "What's that supposed to mean?" she shrieked, unable to contain the emotion in her voice.

"Heather," scolded her mother. "Mind your formalities."

"Of course, Umma." She tried to remain calm, but her father habitually knew what buttons to push. "What are you implying?"

"Your brother took studies seriously. He can choose from the top universities worldwide."

"I applied to the one school I wanted to attend."

"That's because you don't challenge yourself."

"Do you have any idea how hard I worked these past few years?"

"Is that what you call it? Work?"

"You have no idea what it takes."

"Singing is not a stable career, Heather. I was willing to humor your mother for a while, but it's time to grow up. Take college seriously and get a proper job when you graduate."

"Oh, boy. I can't wait to sell ball bearings."

Her mother eyed Appa with concern but remained silent as he spoke. "Precision metal components have afforded us a comfortable lifestyle. The income is paying for your college, don't forget."

"I'm sure you won't let me."

Deciding that she'd rather watch a hippo take up gardening than spend another moment at this demoralizing gathering, Heather imagined herself vanishing in a puff of smoke. The holiday was ruined before it had started. Even if she could speak her mind without fear of reproach, she recognized that her words would fall on deaf ears. It seemed pointless to voice frustrations about the industry's fickleness and how success depended on luck as much as hard work. Her father understood these truths quite well, yet expressing them would only worsen matters. Heather had many thoughts, but uttered few.

With one day left before Heather returned to the agency, her mother demanded she sift through old boxes slated for the discard pile. The closet space desperately needed attention, and she hadn't touched those belongings in years. Most of it was junk. Toys and books were set aside for donation. Ancient school projects were destined for the recycling bin. However, much of her childhood artwork was preserved, particularly those that still held merit or evoked specific memories. A box of worn-out colored chalks reminded her of the elaborate sidewalk illustrations she had created as a child. Passersby often commented on the lovely depictions of smiling flowers and generous sun rays.

One ambitious project followed a family excursion to California's Antelope Valley Poppy Preserve. Inspired by the occasion, seven-year-old Heather promptly set to work on her epic masterpiece the next day. Stretching along both sides of the street, the illustration was massive, depicting hundreds of poppies. Her orange and green chalks were reduced to nubs when it was finished. The driveway itself featured an elaborately framed message of well-wishing in bright explosions of color. Bursting with pride, she eagerly awaited her father's return from a business trip. So excited was she to witness his reaction that she camped out on the lawn, setting out a folding chair just for that purpose.

To her dismay, he simply ignored it when he arrived. Instead of admiring the drawing as expected, he drove straight onto the driveway, parking on top as if it never existed. *Maybe he didn't see it*, she thought. "Welcome home, Daddy. Do you like my drawing?"

He looked at the driveway and just then noticed the art stretching down the entire block. "Our neighbors will call the police if you keep this up." Rounding the vehicle's rear, he stopped long enough to read the few unobstructed words. "Heather, how could you be so careless? What on earth is wrong with you?" He pointed at what she had written. "Since when do you spell nice with an S? Change it immediately. I don't want people thinking my daughter's an idiot." Without another word, he went inside.

Alone on the pavement, the child washed away the error with her tears.

"Did you hear me? I asked a question." Roommate Kylie stood at the bedroom door, holding a plastic container of freshly baked cookies. "Should I leave some for you?"

Heather displayed her konjac snack bag. "No, thanks. I'm fine."

3

MISFIT TOYS

An ocean away, and two seasons removed from Seoul's Giga Music, Ahn Sun-hee had launched a new adventure. Though her idol training had ended in failure, the experience convinced her to pursue music more fully. Towards that end, she applied to UCLA's School of Music and was accepted.

Sun-hee's first day of college elicited equal amounts of excitement and terror. Her decision to study abroad only intensified those feelings. To make matters worse, she was facing them alone. Limited finances discouraged her parents from tagging along. Besides, she was on the threshold of independence. What sense was there in prolonging it by a couple of days? In retrospect, that approach seemed foolhardy. She could have used their support right about now.

Despite having wheels, her luggage was unmanageable. The mistake of packing all the heavy items in one enormous suitcase became apparent. Logic suggested that the most durable bag could withstand a heavier load. The thought that she'd have to handle it alone never crossed her mind. Appa dealt with the package at Incheon, and the LAX shuttle driver had loaded it into his van. Now that she was independent, the overweight baggage was beyond her capacity to maneuver up the dorm's steep ADA access ramp.

Sun-hee abandoned the idea of pulling it by the handle. Pushing it required bending over, which made her feel self-conscious. The suggestive pose drew the unwanted attention of two boorish males who sat nearby, one with brown hair and the other blonde. They watched with great interest.

By using maximum effort, Sun-hee nudged the bag. Unfortunately, this caused a wheel to lodge in a pavement crack. Repeated attempts to extract it failed. The exertion exhausted her. She fell to her knees in defeat. The brown-haired onlooker seized that opportunity to ridicule. "Ha, that's how I like my women, on their knees." He and the blonde friend shared a laugh.

Sun-hee rolled her eyes in disbelief. She had hoped college would produce a better quality male, but those expectations seemed premature. These boys had arrived straight from high school, seemingly intent on retaining their immaturity for as long as possible. She considered ignoring them, but saw a chance to turn the situation in her favor. "A gentleman would offer his help," she responded. The tone of her voice lacked any resentment.

"Well, I ain't your servant," the boy retorted.

"Oh, certainly. I understand."

Her agreeable reaction disarmed him. The brown-haired kid's mouth fell open. He expected more of a fight. "Good. Glad we got that straight," he said.

"Please explain, though, what you mean by liking women on their knees."

The two friends chuckled again. Their laughter continued until they realized that Sun-hee was seriously expecting an answer. Brown Hair was now at a loss for words; his smile went missing. "Oh, you know," he said, cheeks flushed. His blonde friend elbowed him in the ribs as if encouraging a more substantial response.

"No, I don't," she responded, mustering as much exaggerated innocence as possible. "Would you mind explaining your joke to me? I'm sure it was funny."

"It's, like…" Brown Hair stammered. "You know, like, women being on their knees to…"

"You mean push my luggage?"

"No!" The boy was squirming now. "Like…" He turned to his friend for support but wasn't getting any. Now feeling ill-at-ease, the blonde kid looked for an exit, hoping to leave before the circumstances worsened. "Dude, gotta run. See you in class." With that, he left his mouthy associate behind to deal with the mess.

"I'm afraid I still don't understand," said Sun-hee, pressing the advantage.

"Well, you see…" the boy's face turned bright red. "Oh, forget it. It wasn't that funny anyhow."

"If you say so," she said, feigning disappointment. "I better get back to moving then."

"Yeah, okay," said the kid, standing up.

"Before you go, though, do you think you could push this for me?" She pointed at her oversized bag as if summoning a porter.

Now eager to display some semblance of decency after his earlier poor form, Brown Hair responded, "Oh yeah, sure. No problem."

The exhilaration of attending university in a foreign country wore off after four weeks. Sun-hee met plenty of fascinating people at orientation and spent many happy hours exploring the campus and its surrounding neighborhoods with them. Making friends was ridiculously easy at first since everyone was new and eager for companionship. But these engagements soon turned superficial. She sensed her cohorts were unlikely to stick around once they found more compatible colleagues. Sure enough, three weeks in, her pals offered frequent excuses to cancel their plans. As she settled into a predictable routine, she missed Korea.

"Umma, I want to go back," she told her mother. Sun-hee had purchased a calling card to phone home without spending a fortune. Video chat wasn't an option. Her mother disliked going online.

Chan-sook responded with a sigh. "Sun-hee'ya, you just arrived."

"I know, but it's harder than I thought."

"Of course. UCLA's an excellent school. Did you think it would be easy?"

"Not school. That's fine. It's...everything else."

"Like what? Is someone bothering you?"

"No. People have been welcoming, but you know how I get around strangers."

"Give it more time. You'll make friends. What about your roommate? Isn't she nice?"

"She is," Sun-hee responded, taking an extra breath, "but she has her own group, and they're into different things. Besides, I doubt their idea of fun is babysitting a shy foreigner."

"Well, you need to work on that."

She opened her dorm room window to get some air and enjoy

the magnificent view of the stately campus. A co-ed soccer game was in progress on the nearby athletic field. Runners tested each other on the track. A flag squad rehearsed a routine in the far corner. "I miss your cooking, Umma."

"Surely they have Korean food there."

"I can barely afford a bowl of noodles, though."

"We're unable to send any more money right now, and besides, we paid for a meal plan. Aren't you using it?"

"I am, but Korean options are limited."

"Well, you can't expect all the comforts of home, especially since it was your idea to study abroad."

"Umma, I know. You've reminded me so many times."

"Part of maturing is learning how to adapt. It won't be easy, but you'll be better for it. Isn't there a group you can join?"

"I went to some Korean club events."

"Did you meet anyone?"

"None were the creative type. We didn't have much in common." Sun-hee heard tapping sounds coming from her mother's end of the line. "What are you doing?"

"Your aunt Ri-na is having us over for dinner tomorrow, and I'm making a dish to bring. Soo-min and Myung miss you. Your sister especially admires you."

"I wish we weren't so far away."

"Did you respond to that girl who posted on your profile page?"

"What girl?"

"The idol trainee."

"You mean Grace? Not yet."

"Well, that's your problem. You say you want more friends but aren't willing to meet halfway."

"It's hard."

"It isn't. You're being difficult." A loud thunk followed by a rattle suggested whatever her mother was working on had fallen over. She made no mention of it. "There's always a pathway," she continued. "Sometimes, the way is hidden, and you have to find it. She's doing a music project, right? I thought you'd be interested."

"She goes to a different school. The bus takes an hour. I feel trapped on this campus."

"Can't you use the metro?"

"Ha! I wish it was like Seoul's, or even Busan's. I can walk to Westwood. After that, my options are busses or nothing."

"Well, Sun-hee'ya, I'm telling you, your father and I are in no position to get you a car. It's costing enough to send you to school as it is. Besides, you don't drive. Repay us by working hard and getting good grades."

"I'm trying, Umma."

"Okay, you're trying. That means you'll stay then?"

"Yes, Umma," she said meekly.

"You can do it. You're stronger than you think."

"I don't feel very strong right now."

"You have your own way of showing it. Learn to trust that."

Sun-hee reflected on the pile of piano music sheets on her desk. "I have to go. Practice time."

Following the call, the girl stared at her phone for several minutes. The screen remained dark as she contemplated options. She wasn't sure what Grace wanted. They were acquaintances only who'd met twice on various idol projects. Perhaps she was just reaching out to reconnect. Sun-hee figured she could muster enough energy to handle that much. Would it hurt to say hello back? At least they had one thing in common.

* * *

"Mindy, can I see you for a moment?" Bearded supervisor Brad stood in his office doorway, wiggling an index finger. This has to be bad news, she concluded. While navigating the rows of music bins at Amorphous Records, Mindy contemplated her recent job performance. Nothing alarming stood out. Maybe it was that argument she had with Cynthia two weeks ago? That annoying employee quit the following day, though, casting doubt on its relevance.

The door closing behind them signaled the meeting would cover more than rescheduling. "What's the haps, Paps?" she asked, attempting to lighten the mood, at least for herself.

"Let's talk about job performance," said Brad.

"I reorganized the entire classical section on my own. Nobody else wanted to touch it."

"Not that. I'll cut to the chase. I've been talking with the owners, and we both think you'd make a great assistant manager." Mindy fell silent. Brad had subverted her expectations. "So, whaddaya think?" he asked.

"It pays more, right?"

"Sure, after a mandatory training period. I must warn you, though, that increased pay brings increased responsibility. Your hours will be longer and not as flexible."

"I see."

"That's okay, right? You've never mentioned having any commitments."

That's me, Mindy thought to herself, *The Original Miss Goldbrick.* "No, yeah. I guess I don't."

"So, is that a yes?"

She considered the offer without waiting too long. The extra money would ease her ongoing debt crisis. That was for sure. "Yeah. Let's do this."

The worst part about staff scheduling, Mindy soon discovered, was the incessant bargaining. After 90 minutes of crafting what she considered a perfectly fair order of business, fellow employees ripped her painstaking output to shreds within minutes of posting. Some gave her the evil eye for failing to cater to their every whim. The negotiated changes demanded a constant stream of new schedule postings. Despite these hassles, she knew that familiarity would make this particular task easier over time.

Bookkeeping proved a more significant challenge. Mindy wasn't bad with numbers, per se, but keeping track of every dollar going in and out became overwhelming. Finishing these responsibilities left her with just under half an hour before closing. She still had to stock the shelves with new merchandise before going home.

While filing pressings of De La Soul's *3 Feet High and Rising LP*, a customer shouted at her, "Hey, I know you!" Mindy looked up at the unfamiliar Asian male in his mid-20s who stood in an adjacent aisle. "Weren't you in that Fox Force Five band or something?"

"You must have me confused with someone else."

"No, I'm pretty sure it's you. The drummer, right?" Mindy tried to ignore him, but the guy wouldn't give it a rest. "Wow, times must be tough in K-pop if you ended up here."

"I have a lot to do. You need anything?"

"No. Just curious, is all. Can I take your photo?"

"Please don't"

Disregarding her plea, the guy pulled out his smartphone

and snapped a quick one before scooting out the front door with a wide grin. Mindy felt certain that a hundred K-pop gossip sites would feature the image within an hour.

That evening, out of curiosity, she considered contacting her old bandmates to discover what they were doing. After much consternation, she opted against direct communication and instead searched their social media postings. This proved a smart move. Even accounting for hype inflation, her colleagues seemed to have achieved success. More than she had, at least. Three remained in the music industry (behind the scenes). The fourth was a mid-level manager at an upstart telecommunications firm.

Mindy assessed her own life in the wake of WeR5's breakup. She liked her job and co-workers at the record store well enough. They seemed to like her. Was this career worthy though? If not, what else could she do? Heather was right about one thing: What happened to her ambition? As tough as K-pop was to survive, she never once felt directionless in that world. Amorphous was the first job Mindy landed upon arriving in the U.S. Now, they wanted her to play a more significant role in the operation. Ten years could pass in a flash if she chose comfort over aspiration. What options would remain then? She tapped her contacts list and stared at Heather's number. Six times did she reach her thumb towards the dial button before pulling back. The seventh time she hit it.

Mindy assessed the quartet seated with her at a table in a quiet corner of The Lair, the university's main cafe. Heather, she knew from the Amorphous Records meeting. The girl possessed all the hallmarks of classic Korean beauty, that much was certain: a slender face defined by a v-shaped jawline, small lips, cherubic cheeks, and a slight puffiness beneath her eyes that emphasized youthfulness. In this setting, though, the singer seemed to take a back seat to Grace, the confident one. The pair had trained together at 37-G, which was impressive enough in its own right, but how they ended up in L.A. remained a mystery. She'd have to investigate that intriguing morsel sooner rather than later.

The other trainee was Sun-hee from Giga Music. She spoke little and seemed shy, but presented herself assuredly, suggesting there was more to her than met the eye. Then there was the youngest one, Erin. She was in college, too, but acted more like a middle-schooler allowed to sit at the big kids' table during Thanksgiving. The group was a mixed bag, but she'd seen worse in her day.

"I was hoping to set a rehearsal for this evening but couldn't find space," said Grace. "In the meantime, I thought we could meet and get oriented." The first order of business was introductions. Each of the girls took turns sharing something of her background. Most of the information she could have gleaned just by observing. The one exception was Sun-hee, who felt compelled to share an interesting story about her mother.

"Umma loved to make Western recipes, and we often ate au gratin potatoes growing up. I always called them old rotten potatoes, which made my mom laugh. She thought it was a slip on my part and never corrected me. I never admitted to her that I was intentionally getting it wrong."

Mindy found this admission surprising. "Why would you do that?" she asked.

"Because Umma was going through a stressful period back

then. I rarely saw her laugh. Whatever I could do to lighten her mood, I did."

Mindy wasn't sure why, but something about Sun-hee's story put her at ease.

Heather presented her vision for the band. The hybrid approach was appealing. She'd always been a wonderful dancer, but WeR5 had strictly been a band. That she'd now be able to explore both sides of the equation stoked her enthusiasm. Skepticism pulled the idea back to earth, though. The chances they could pull off one concept, let alone both, seemed slim. At least they were trying, however. For that, she gave them points.

Grace followed up by establishing the goals and expectations. Mindy paid careful attention but found the address lacking. "Okay, but there's one overarching problem we have here," she noted after Grace's presentation. "We lack an agency. Convince me this is anything more than a hobby."

Grace frowned at Mindy's frank assessment. "You're right. We are independent. But the bright side is we can do things our way. No silly rules stopping us."

"But the bigger problem remains. No agency, no money. No money, no future. What's the plan to address that?"

Grace glanced at Heather, who took the gesture as permission to respond. "We've identified key goals to gain valuable prize money while increasing our exposure."

"That *sounds* nice, but what goals specifically?"

This time, Grace responded. "You're all familiar with *Soundscape Magazine?*" Heads nodded in unison. "Besides tracking music charts, they also run the *Soundscape Showdown.* Have you heard of that?" The girls assessed each other but admitted no familiarity with that event. "It's one of the biggest and oldest band competitions in the country. Winning would provide a significant boost to exposure. Many record company executives attend. The prizes are substantial."

Girls chatted excitedly, seeing this moment as both a splendid chance and a daunting test. All except Mindy, whose skepticism continued. "Excuse me, but doesn't it strike you as a little foolish to pin all our hopes on winning a contest? Isn't that a little presumptuous? We haven't even played one song yet."

Grace sighed, her lips pinched together. "We have to start somewhere, don't we? We could sit here all night coming up with hundreds of reasons why this will never work, but naysaying won't get us very far."

"The journey of a thousand miles begins with a single step," added Heather. "The thing is, these goals compound the benefits. We must check off a few boxes before qualifying for the *Showdown*. A music video is one. We also need gigs, an EP, and radio airplay. Even if we don't make it into *Showdown*, these achievements will be necessary if we're ever to be taken seriously as a group."

"In other words, the competition will motivate us to get these things done," said Grace.

Mindy still didn't buy into the optimism. "How are we gonna make all this stuff? Do we use smartphones to film videos?"

"Good question. A student filmmaker here at SIU is looking to team up with a band for a music video. Auditions are coming up soon, and our first goal is securing that slot. We'll focus on covers to start, but the plan is to write our own songs."

"Okay, and what else? Radio play? Who's gonna put us on American radio?"

Grace was on the verge of exasperation with the incessant

questioning. "Yes, some problems remain unsolved, but I remind you this group has been together for less than two hours. Don't you think a little patience is in order?" Mindy displayed toughness towards the others; but not without purpose. She pushed them to test their limits.

Heather's concluding speech proved a standout moment. She spoke passionately about prizing teamwork and collaboration. The group's enthusiasm impressed Mindy, yet she had lingering doubts. She gave the band a lifespan of three months before the harsh realities of show business hit them like a ton of bricks.

Despite the reservations, Mindy was determined to give it her all. She didn't want to be held responsible if things went wrong. Who knows? Maybe something good would come out of it in the end. After all, it wasn't like she had endless options.

4

SUNSHOWERS

Grace reflected on their just-concluded audition as the five band members left the Film & Television Building. She felt hopeful. They were the last to sign up and the last to enter. Director Steve Shepard was a student filmmaker in his junior year. He struck Grace as intelligent but a little dorky. He seemed easy to read, open, and honest about his thoughts and feelings. She estimated they had a better-than-average chance of getting picked. Judging from the other acts they encountered in the waiting area, the competition was not stiff. Out-of-tune mishmashes of "Smoke On the Stairway To Sweet Child O' Sandman" still rang in her ears.

Heather, though, lodged a complaint as the quintet approached Grace's beloved 2005 Subaru Tribeca. "Why did you tell him the group's nearly complete?"

"I didn't want him thinking we were closer to the beginning than the end," Grace responded as she placed her guitar case in the back. "Besides, I wasn't the only one improvising on the fly. Made in Heaven? Where did that name come from?"

"What? You don't like it?" Heather stacked her guitar case

on top of Grace's with a lack of finesse that made her wince.

"It's okay, I guess." Grace maneuvered Sun-hee's keyboard and Erin's bass into the remaining space. "But I thought we were collaborating on those creative decisions." While angling the equipment to fit it all in, Grace noticed Mindy still holding her djembe, brought in place of a complete drum kit.

Mindy sighed in resignation. "Nevermind. I'll hold it in my lap."

"I think Made in Heaven sounds nice," said Sun-hee.

"It'll grow on me, I suppose," said Grace. While she preferred another name, it wasn't a hill she particularly wanted to die on. "And since you brought it up, we still have the dance unit to assemble. Are you sure we need seven?"

Heather nodded. "Odd numbers make nicer-looking formations. We'll always have a clear center at any given point."

"We have five now."

"But who will choreograph? We have no dance specialists."

"I was hoping to be done with recruiting by this point. If that's the case, look for Talent with a capital T. Not just any old K-pop fan. Start beating the bushes. I'm not doing this all by myself. Talk to everyone you know." She slammed the hatchback shut. "They should have a strong work ethic, get along with others, and look the part."

"Piece of cake," Heather said teasingly as she snapped her fingers.

"We're going to need a manager before too long, too."

"Where do we find one of those?"

"No idea. I suppose we'll have to advertise. Until then, I'm gonna kiss sleep goodbye."

The inbound phone call went straight to Grace's voicemail

during her Business Ethics class the following day. *"You know what to do, so do it at the beep."*

"Um, Hi, Grace. This is Steve Shepard. You know, the music video guy. Listen, I enjoyed your performance the other day. You have a promising group. I hope it goes well for you. Fact is, though, I decided to go in another direction. Hope you understand. The other band's ready now. See you around campus. Good luck."

* * *

The quintet had spent the last two hours at the Fine Arts Building, shuffling from room to room as availability allowed. Beggars can't be choosers. Surprisingly, they found the best dance studio empty at 5:30 p.m. Their excitement vanished upon learning why. Typically a glorious place in which to work, that space was exposed to direct sunlight in late fall. For some reason, the vertical blinds were stuck that day. Productivity suffered because of the intense heat and mirrored walls, which felt like they could turn into instant death rays. The oppressive heat sapped the group's stamina.

With the persistent need to replenish fluids, Grace issued frequent breaks. During one of these, Heather's insecurities emerged. "I think we should disband," she said while lying in repose on the parquet floor.

Grace sat up straight to assess her friend. She knew well enough to tread carefully in moments like this. Her subsequent words could prove pivotal. "Let's take a moment to think about this first."

"I mean it. I'm not good enough. This will spare us the embarrassment."

"Why do you say that?"

"What have I accomplished? Can you tell me that?"

"You're an amazingly talented person."

"I'm a fraud. My dad made everything possible. I'm just along for the ride."

"Don't let what happened at 37-G define you. They lost their star."

"I can't even win an audition for an amateur video. How am I a star?"

Grace couldn't let her friend suffer alone. If anything, Made in Heaven was a vital distraction and a source of much-needed confidence-building. She had to continue selling the idea, if only for Heather's mental well-being. "You're a star to me. Doesn't that matter?"

Heather's eyes blinked three times in rapid succession. "It does matter."

"Then prove it."

"I'm telling you now."

"Show me."

"How?"

"By turning this group into a powerhouse. We have talent on this squad. Mold us into your vision." Heather sat up as if receiving an epiphany. Grace's suggestion seemed to do the trick. Who knew how long it would last? But she had to keep trying.

With the music video a lost cause, attention had shifted to assembling the dance unit. This was proving more difficult than expected. Other musicians they had invited were only interested in the band unit, which already had the bases covered. Truthfully, Grace considered it a stroke of luck that they found five members with the flexibility to handle both tasks. That good fortune had run out, though. The last two members would have to be dancers. Toward that goal, she was prepared to play a wild card. Once the girls returned to the studio, she primed the pump. "By the way, I invited a guest to rate our performance tonight."

The general chatter stopped as curiosity got the better of the girls. "Are we ready for that?" asked Mindy.

"Vanessa's in my English class. She's the best dancer at SIU. Recruited on a full scholarship."

"Does she speak Korean?" queried Heather.

"She's Vietnamese."

Heather sighed.

"Let's talk to her at least. Find out where she's at." Heather remained unconvinced. "She's good. You'll see. Fair warning, though. She's an acquired taste." Twenty-five minutes later, Grace was making introductions. "Everyone, I'd like you to meet Vanessa Nguyen."

The dance major had her own sense of style. This was clear next to the other three, who took a more conservative approach to fashion. Vanessa was hard to mistake for anyone else. She wore a flouncing, brightly patterned mini sundress under a faded jean vest, black mid-thigh stockings, boots, and a black felt hat. Her long, voluminous black hair was curly, with a single braided strand as an accent. Compared to the others, she had a well-honed physique, molded, no doubt, by countless hours of repetitive movement. She looked fit and powerful without appearing muscular. Lithe and lissome without looking delicate.

"I've seen you around campus but forgot your name," said Erin. "Nice to meet you."

Vanessa smiled weakly, appearing irritated with the formalities, but said nothing in return. Grace explained their overarching goals and described their choreography. She requested a critique of their performance.

"Sure thing. Show me whatcha got." The dance major leaned against the mirrored wall facing the windows, arms crossed. Fortunately, the sun had since dipped behind the trees, so she had a clear view of the proceedings.

A few minutes later, the presentation ended. Grace found their performance pleasing overall, even though they made some mistakes. She expected a favorable verdict. That hope died quickly. Wasting little time, Vanessa snatched her belongings and bolted for the door. The annoyed look on her face spoke volumes.

"Okay, thanks for the offer, but I'm out. See you in class."

"Wait! Where are you going?" shouted Grace.

"At least tell us what's wrong," pleaded Heather.

Vanessa stopped in her tracks to face the other five, who stood with mouths agape in disbelief. "I thought you said this was K-pop," she said with a snarl.

"And?"

"So, what's with all the cheerleader bullshit?"

Muted gasps.

"See, I told you," said Mindy.

"Was it that bad?" asked Sun-hee, crestfallen.

"Oh, my god, are you kidding me?" Her dance bag plopped to the floor with a thud. Vanessa contorted herself into the most clichéd high school cheerleader moves imaginable, overemphasizing them for a humorous effect. "C'mon, my sister in middle school does more interesting stuff than that." Her comic shimmying pierced the tension in the room, causing the girls to giggle. Everyone, except Grace, who remained miffed and contemplating a withdrawal of her invitation.

As Vanessa ceased her gyrations, Heather stepped forward, restraining a laugh. "That's why we could use your help."

Vanessa's expression eased somewhat at Heather's calming tone. "Look, you're decent dancers, but your routine lacks imagination. You need much more than my help." Vanessa assessed with pity the forlorn group before her. Apparently, their hopeless faces did the trick. "Okay, tell you what." After a brief search on her phone, she declared, "I'm sending you a contact."

Grace's phone vibrated a moment later. "Who's Danya?" she asked after glancing at the message.

"Danya Kay. She's the one who's gonna save your ass. As a former Army brat from Camp Henry, she's familiar with K-pop choreography. I'm willing to stick around long enough to see how this goes, but if you wanna keep me, you gotta convince her."

"That's terrific," said Grace.

"One hitch, though."

"Of course, there is." The room went silent as the group awaited Vanessa's caveat.

"She's busy because she's top-notch. Won't be easy to convince. And let me tell you, *Bring It On* ain't going to cut it."

The next day, Grace spoke to Vanessa before English class. If she were expecting superficial platitudes, there weren't any. The dance major's dismantling of every aspect of their performance left her speechless. "Mindy is your best dancer but looks out of shape and was lagging. Sun-hee is good but lacks inspiration. She was going through the motions. Heather tries hard, but I hope her singing chops are enough to make up for the pedestrian technique she displayed. You have your moments, too, but really need to sharpen your movements. Way too sloppy. And don't get me started on that little girl. Where in hell did you find her?"

"You mean Erin?"

"Whatever, she's a lost cause."

"You don't mince words, do you?"

Vanessa frowned. "People say I'm insensitive. But I'm just being honest. If you want someone to blow smoke up your butt, you picked the wrong girl."

"So, is there any point in trying to engage Danya? It sounds like you've already made up your mind."

"Look, I wouldn't even bother if I thought this was hopeless. I'm only trying to help."

"If it's frankness you want, here's my take," said Grace. "Your points are valid. We could use improvement. I just think you ought to find a better way to tell people what they need to hear."

* * *

With the college semester in full swing, available rehearsal space on campus was at a premium. Grace soon learned that the more established clubs had booked meeting rooms well in advance, leaving little to choose from at a moment's notice. Numerous bands had emerged from the incoming freshman class, which placed further strain on facility resources. Lacking any better options that day, she invited the group to her parent's house in Santa Monica, where they set up instruments in the backyard. Their first attempt at an original song was "Celestial." I say attempt because they never managed to finish it. An artificial downpour sent the girls diving for cover halfway through the second chorus. All except Mindy, who insisted on shielding her precious drum kit from the torrent with a nearby tarp while getting doused.

"Who the hell turned that sprinkler on?" asked their drummer in a huff as she stepped away from the mess.

"That's our lovely neighbor, Mrs. Cavanaugh," said Grace. She switched to a sing-song voice loud enough to be audible over the fence. "How are you doing today, Mrs. Cavanaugh?"

An elderly woman shouted back. "Next time it happens, I'll report you to the HOA."

"Thank you, Mrs. Cavanaugh. It won't happen again."

"Why be so nice to her? That was a bitch move she pulled," whispered Mindy, now drying her hair with a sweater.

"Years of experience. Believe me, this is the best way."

Once nerves settled down, Grace's mother, Ha-yoon, delivered a tray of yogurt parfaits and a pitcher of lemonade to the backyard table. Heather looked disappointed, stating her need to leave for a singing lesson. Ha-yoon insisted she take one for the road.

After Heather's departure, the remaining members chatted into the evening. It was an unexpected, but welcome, bonding session. So preoccupied were they with musical matters that few opportunities had arisen for simple conversation. Grace found it comforting until one unwelcome subject came up. During the wide-ranging conversation, the group's curiosity turned to Grace's and Heather's time at the agency in Korea.

"37-G is growing into a big deal," said Erin. "Why would you ever leave?"

Grace frowned. "It wasn't by choice."

"So were you cut?" asked Mindy.

"I wouldn't put it that way either."

"Well, what's the truth then? We have a right to know."

"No, you do. I just don't think it's my place to tell the story. It should be Heather."

"She's been very coy about the whole thing," said Erin.

"And you'll understand why. But Heather's still recovering. I beg you not to push until she's ready."

Erin, Mindy, and Sun-hee exchanged glances. "How bad was it?" Sun-hee asked.

"Like you can't even imagine." That admission plunged the group into momentary silence.

"Did you two meet there," asked Erin. "I've been wondering."

"Did we ever." Grace smiled and let out a chuckle. "Talk about a good first impression. No, that doesn't do it any justice. My introduction to Heather Moon was epic. Truly epic." The group sat back and listened as she recalled the events of that day in minute detail.

"I was told this class had talent. Why am I not seeing it?"

Grace had been warned that her first day of K-pop training would be unusual. That proved an understatement. By mid-morning, word had spread that the trainees were to prepare for a surprise guest. Dongpang Chul, the legendary main singer of first-generation boy band J.em, was visiting Seoul's 37-G Entertainment. This news sent the agency into a tizzy. They canceled rehearsals and shifted the schedule. At noon, four dozen members of the premier class of girl trainees gathered promptly in the third-floor assembly room. Without fuss, they arranged themselves into a tidy set of four lines to greet their visitor. A nervous intensity replaced the jocularity Grace had witnessed during the morning introductions.

Chul's visits exposed trainees to the experiences of a seon-bae who could provide mentorship. While valuable, his sessions had also become famous in industry circles for an unrelated yet more compelling reason. In recent years, what launched as a mere diversion had grown into a tense competition. After each session, Chul offered his students what he called the Three Bowl Challenge. Supposedly, the series of tests was his method of identifying exceptional talent. Its exact purpose, however, remained a mystery, as no idol had ever won. Several came close, but the skill required to pass all three trials remained elusive.

The girls understood that winning the competition would bring considerable esteem to 37-G. Despite recent gains, the company still ranked as one of the lesser entertainment companies in K-pop. While renown was a motivating factor, a more primal desire preoccupied the girls in that moment: food. You see, Dongpang Chul's family also owned one of Korea's most renowned galbi restaurants. His longstanding offer was an all-expenses-paid dinner for the winning agency's entire class. To girls who had, at times, subsisted on little more than raw cucumbers as they observed mandatory weight limits, the prize was more desirable than the Golden Fleece.

The rules of the game were simple. Three colored bowls sat on a table, ranging in order of difficulty from red to green to blue. In each container were wooden chits imprinted with numbers corresponding to designated tasks. Contestants would pick a chit from one bowl, address the challenge, and continue down the line until they had won all three. The game would end on a single failed attempt.

Regardless of their motivations for playing, the girls of 37-G were failing miserably. Ten trainees agreed to try. Merely two passed the Red Bowl Challenge. None had made it beyond that stage. The last contestant, Yoon-suh, resumed a spot amongst her peers, head hanging low in disappointment for failing the Green Bowl Challenge.

"Is this all?" Chul asked. "Is this the best you can do?"

The two oldest members, the unnies, exchanged wordless glances. Class leader Da-som stood and faced Chul. "No, Teacher, there is another."

As if on cue, a figure approached.

The sound of footsteps in the tiled corridor heralded her arrival. Without hesitation, the trainees parted like the sea divinely making way for a prophet. Grace followed their example, unsure of what was happening. The room's atmosphere crackled with energy.

She strained to glimpse the newcomer without being obvious about it. The figure came closer, passing through pools of illumination as she navigated the unevenly lit hallway. Light, dark, light, dark. The measured clacking cadence of her shoes increased in volume. Grace wondered if this trainee was the one she'd heard mention of earlier.

Upon reaching the threshold, the girl stepped into the open space. Trimmed with straight, black, shoulder-length hair, her face was angelic. Elegant. Classic. Even in a setting where above-average beauty was the bare minimum expectation, hers stood apart. Grace imagined she would have inspired the poems and legends of ancient scribes had she lived in their day.

"Teacher, it is my pleasure to introduce our classmate, Heather Moon," Da-Som announced. "We'd be honored if you consider her for the challenge."

Heather stood silently, eyes cast forward, hands clasped

together, arms down. Her baby-blue, sleeveless, square-necked sheath dress, with two thin white stripes under the bustline and another accenting the hem above the knees, was exquisitely tailored. She basked in the attention. Standing poised, only five feet tall, by Grace's estimation, her presence was commanding. Her expression suggested cool confidence.

Chul assessed Heather. It was unclear whether her sudden arrival annoyed or intrigued him. Perhaps both. Without saying a word, he encouraged her to step forward. "How old are you?" he asked as she took a position near the keyboard in the center of the room.

"Eighteen," she responded.

"Your accent. The States?"

"Los Angeles."

When he switched to English, the trainees expressed dismay at being deprived of their exchange. All except one. Neither Dongpang Chul nor Heather Moon knew that Grace, the first-day newbie in their midst, was also an Angeleno and understood every word they said.

"Why would an American come to Korea to be an idol?"

"I wouldn't be the first."

"I could reject you straight away, you are aware?"

"Then, you'd be missing the best."

"How does tardiness make you the best?"

"Being number one necessitates being odd, does it not?"

Chul pondered her answers. His expression revealed no emotion. "Do you take pride in being different?"

"I exist. If that makes me different, so be it."

He took a sip of water from the glass on his table. "Heather." He said, pondering her name. "That is a lucky flower. Do you consider yourself lucky?"

"If I were to name myself, I'd choose otherwise."

"Why is that?"

"Luck runs out when you push it."

He rubbed his chin in thought. "Are you capable of impressing me?"

"The girls have worked hard. I wish to reward them."

A sly grin betrayed his amusement at the curious conversation. "Let's begin," he said in Korean. The assembly sighed in relief.

Chul reviewed the rules as a measure of courtesy, despite his audience knowing them by heart. With formalities over, Heather stepped forward. She reached into the red bowl, extracted a chit, and read its number aloud. "Twelve," she stated, presenting it for all to see.

Chul consulted a predetermined chart and explained the challenge. "I will play brief excerpts of ten different songs. Afterward, you'll have one minute to name the ten artists and titles in the order you heard them. Proceed."

The edited audio clips, separated by brief intervals of silence, lasted a few seconds each. Grace had difficulty identifying more than two of them, let alone ten. As soon as the last clip had played, Chul started the countdown clock at the edge of his table. Its red digits loomed large in the minds of the assembly as they watched the time slip away. The trainees grew concerned. Ten seconds had passed, and Heather had yet to name a single song. Girls sucked in their breath, pondering how their valued ringer could fail them.

Finally, the answers came forth in a torrent.

"'Shut Down' by Blackpink."

"'Very Nice' by Seventeen."

"'Butterfly' LOONA."

"'Drawing the Line' by Royal Pirates."

The anticipation kept building. As Heather delivered her answers, younger trainees applauded. Song names continued to pour forth.

"'Don't Be Shy,' Primary."

"'Don't Believe' by Berry Good."

"'Move' by Taemin."

"'Awoo' by Lim Kim."

"'Senorita,' VAV."

She stopped short with 15 seconds left. Heather had named nine songs, but the clock kept ticking down. Grace looked at her peers, whose faces strained with worry. Had Heather lost count? Five. Four. Three. The seconds melted away.

And then, "'Just Leave' by Wax."

The timer buzzed. Attention turned to Chul, who smiled and said, "Correct."

The applause was generous and enthusiastic. Heather had passed the initial hurdle, the third trainee to have done so that day. Could the class's last great hope progress further?

Chul presented the green bowl. She extracted a chit with the number three on it.

"Turn away from me," he instructed. Heather looked confused but complied without resistance. "I will play for you three musical notes. Without a reference tone, I want you to identify the notes within 15 seconds."

Several trainees whistled in disbelief. "Perfect pitch. That's so unfair," Grace whispered to the girl beside her, who nodded in agreement.

Chul played three notes on his miniature keyboard and restarted the timer. The digits on the clock ticked down.

Once more, Heather waited until seconds remained before

attempting an answer. She repeated the three notes by singing them. Her bright and powerful voice filled the room as if amplified. Then she stated, "E-G-C, the first inversion of a C Major triad."

The timer buzzed, and the trainees looked to Chul for a response.

"Once again, correct." This resulted in more applause. Nobody from 37-G had ever reached this point in the competition. The moment they'd been waiting for arrived: the Blue Bowl Challenge. By then, a handful of agency managers had sensed the building momentum and gathered at the door to watch the rest of the contest.

The rattling of wooden chits around the plastic bowl produced a prolonged, thunderous sound. Heather grabbed one. Four was its number.

Chul referred to his chart once more. The look on his face showed disappointment. "You have poor luck today, I'm afraid."

The trainees grew impatient and demanded details. Chul milked their enthusiasm for as long as he dared before relenting. "I will play the third movement of Bach's Brandenburg Concerto No. 3 for you. Listen carefully. Once it's over, you must answer one question regarding what you heard. Signal when you're ready."

The open-ended description did not satisfy the trainees, but they had little time to protest. Heather cleared her mind. The room fell silent. When she showed her readiness, Chul played the audio track.

Three groups of instruments, violins, violas, and cellos, began their cheerful, energetic race through the music. While only a few minutes long, the Allegro movement sounded complex. Quick notes cascaded through each of the instrument groups. Grace imagined the danceable rhythm to be the embodiment of popular music in its day. At its conclusion, the trainees mumbled in nervous anticipation of the last question.

Chul waited for the room to resettle before describing the challenge. "Play for me the first cello's notes from the 12th measure."

The initial reaction was complete shock, expressed as total silence. A beat later, a general revolt followed. The girls abandoned decorum and expressed their opinions about the contest.

"Ridiculous!"

"That's impossible."

"Teacher, you must let her pull another."

"No wonder nobody wins."

"It's rigged!"

Chul absorbed the criticism, having expected their reaction. Heather, for her part, said nothing as the furor subsided. With the countdown clock off, she closed her eyes and ruminated on the music. The room grew silent. Grace tried to recall the elaborate composition's details, but there was too much to remember.

Several long minutes passed before Heather opened her eyes again. She reached for the keyboard. "The three cello parts are identical at this point," she said, then played six notes.

Something was off-kilter to Grace, yet also vaguely familiar.

Chul grimaced, saying, "That's incorrect."

Groans of disappointment rumbled through the room as the class realized how close they'd come to achieving their goal. Before the discord ceased, however, Grace interrupted. "Excuse me, Teacher," she said in perfect English. The assembly hushed in surprise, especially the two who had assumed their prior exchange was relatively private. "Correct me if I'm wrong, but if you play her response backward, you'll find the answer to your question."

Heather smirked and shot a glance from the corner of her eye at the source of the comment, acknowledging Grace for the first time.

Chul plucked at his miniature keyboard without expression, testing Grace's theory. When the correct passage revealed itself, a smile crept across his face.

"Explain yourself," he demanded in Korean.

Heather responded with a mischievous grin. "You never specified what order I should play them in."

Chul burst into laughter at her answer. "Fair enough. Congratulations. You have won the contest."

The room erupted into howls of ecstasy once the girls realized what had happened. Heather's classmates showered her with endless gratitude. She became an instant legend. Soon, the other K-pop agencies would hear the news as well. Heather had single-handedly enhanced 37-G's reputation. The celebration waned as the managers urged their charges to bid farewell to their guest and return to rehearsals.

While waiting for the elevator, Heather introduced herself. "I hoped to drag that along a little further, but you spoiled it." She delivered her words in English with a coy smile and no trace of malice.

"Those who cannot trust themselves, trust in luck." Grace mused.

Heather wrinkled her nose. "Let's talk tonight at the dorms." Her delivery suggested that the invitation was not open to debate.

Little did Grace realize it then, but she'd eventually mark her life in two distinct phases: that which came before meeting Heather Moon and that which came after.

The sun had set by the time Grace finished her account of that day, and Mrs. Cavanaugh's sprinkler shut off. The extraordinary tale had clearly affected the band members. They listened intently the entire time, never once interrupting.

"That sounds incredible," Erin said. "Still, I don't understand why she's here with us now. No offense, but Heather seems a little out of our league. I'm just saying."

"No dream survives contact with life," responded Grace.

5

LITTLE PINK HOUSES

I t's common knowledge that thousands of aspiring wannabe talents flock to Hollywood yearly to pursue dreams of stardom. For most, the move represents an exciting new chapter in life. For 19-year-old Kwan Jeong and her aunt Ye-jin, the past two years had already irreversibly altered their lives, and landing in Los Angeles brought a sense of closure.

As passengers in a family minivan, they gaped at the row of beautiful houses they passed, awestruck by their beauty. Like the fabric of dreams, each displayed vast green lawns, immaculately tended flowerbeds, and prettily painted exteriors. It thrilled them to realize that the residences they had repeatedly witnessed in smuggled films were genuine. A departure from the drab, uniform, and crumbling structures Jeong grew up with.

Their new reality finally dawned on them when the customs agent at LAX called her June. Her adopted English name seemed as foreign as the strange metropolis she was glimpsing for the first time. This represented another change she would need to adjust to. America had already overturned many of her expectations. They would not be the last. Her head swam with questions.

The city appeared enormous. From the air, Los Angeles stretched to the horizon and beyond. She hadn't known municipalities could cover so vast a ground. Those in China stood much taller. This one was short and squat, like those of her homeland, but it reached to places unseen. Where it ended, she could only guess. The airport's arrivals hall proved to be an unprecedented spectacle, crammed with a vast array of people representing every ethnicity, physique, build, shade, and fashion. If life as a refugee in China expanded her worldview, this experience energized it to an altogether different magnitude. Having grown up in a monoculture, the new situation jarred her, but she also found it invigorating.

June's English remained poor, but she could manage basic conversations. Ye-jin relied on her for everything. Before meeting the church volunteers in the greeting area, they had to navigate the customs process independently, through a forest of bewildering signs. Vast quantities of them pointed in every direction. None were in Korean. Her aunt waited patiently as June studied them, trying to determine where to go next.

"Are you lost?" A stocky Black woman in her late 50s greeted them. The encounter marked the first time June had met someone of her race in person, though she'd seen actors in movies and magazines before. The woman smiled and wore a staff uniform. June's initial instincts, however, bred by years of survival through distrust, led her to assume the worst from anyone offering unsolicited help.

"No," she responded curtly.

Noticing the baggage claim tickets in her hand, the woman provided directions to the luggage carousels, but again, June resisted the aid. "I'm sorry. We have no money."

The attendant looked surprised and laughed. "I'm not interested in your money. Here, follow me." The guide escorted them through the labyrinthine terminal, chatting without pause. Much of what she said flew by incomprehensibly, but the guide's demeanor remained engaging. The woman spoke about her family and job, and asked if it was their first time in America. Why would a stranger be so gregarious unless it formed part of a scam attempt, June concluded? She kept on guard and clutched her documents tightly. Yet, once they had reached their destination, the chaperon simply wished them farewell and walked away, soliciting nothing in return. June felt embarrassed for being so distrustful. She had a lot to learn about this new place.

A half-hour later, standing in the arrival hall with their meager belongings, they spotted their names on a placard. The smiling group of Korean-Americans, a family of four born and raised in the U.S., welcomed them. Their dialect remained unfamiliar. Even though they spoke Korean, they were as difficult to understand as the Black woman. With patience, June could piece together facts about the church's refugee resettlement program. Like the airport guide, they too seemed at ease sharing intimate details of their personal lives. Was this a common trait among Americans, she wondered?

The immigrants declined a dinner invitation despite being famished. "We have no money."

"Don't worry," the family matriarch replied. "Consider it our homecoming gift." This offer confused June, but she accepted it to avoid appearing rude. The restaurant they visited sold hamburgers. The few she'd sampled abroad tasted awful. Despite being jammed with patrons and all tables occupied, the white-and-red-tiled eatery appeared immaculately tidy. A host of staff worked furiously shoulder to shoulder behind the bright red counters. Numbers were called at regular intervals while customers retrieved their orders. The delicious scent of beef patties and onions from the grill exacerbated her hunger.

"I recommend the Double-Double, animal style," the father suggested. By this point, June was becoming more agreeable and took his advice, despite having no clue what he was referring to. It didn't take long to realize her previous encounters with the dish were mere mockeries compared to what she ate that day. Their first meal in their new home proved to be a memorable one.

The curiosities didn't end there. The family explained that they were traveling on a freeway. One, two, three—June had to count each lane; there were so many. Ten on each side, all crammed with vehicles. She wondered how that was even possible. The traffic was chaotic compared to the empty streets of her youth. The father navigated it all effortlessly.

Not everything she saw was pleasant. Brightly colored canopies and lots strewn with garbage occupied sizeable areas under bridges and along roadways. June didn't understand what they were for. She wondered why authorities neglected to clean up the mess, since they presented such eyesores. To her dismay, she learned the canopies (tents they were called) were temporary shelters for those without homes. It worried her how a country with such wealth could allow people to live in such conditions.

The van left the freeway and entered a neighborhood much

different from the ones she had seen earlier. This place was not cheerful. The apartment complexes looked old and utilitarian, more like what she was used to. Lawns, if they existed at all, remained untended. Someone had painted unreadable words along many of the walls and fences. Cars parked on the street were in disrepair. The few trees that grew in spots appeared scrawny and starved of water.

The van stopped before a building with faded grayish paint. Without prompting, the family members helped move the refugees' meager belongings into one apartment.

"Welcome to your new home," said the mother cheerfully. June surveyed the place. It was austere and worn out from years of constant use, but clean and enormous compared to what they'd grown accustomed to. The dwelling was also devoid of furniture. The family presented several gift boxes prepared by church members. Donations included food staples, necessary household supplies, sheets, blankets, dishes, lightbulbs, clothing, and kitchen items. They explained how to use the appliances and reviewed the assistance programs. Aunt Ye-jin's yawn must've betrayed her weariness. The mother apologized for taking up their time, and their greeters departed soon after, but only after reemphasizing their contact information should any need arise.

When the minivan drove away, the newcomers burst into tears. They hugged each other as if their lives depended on it, overwhelmed by the understanding that they had beaten the odds by making it this far. At the same time, they were sobered by their standing in this new world.

"We survived," said June. "We should be grateful for that."

"We have so much work to do," her aunt responded.

6

ACQUIRED TASTES

Heather felt pangs of hunger. Her belly grumbled as if a small but vociferous monster lived inside. Despite being only the second day of her crash diet, it seemed like an eternity had passed since she started. Her energy sank lower than the Mariana Trench. She couldn't think straight. The extra weight she had gained from the beginning of the school year, the 'Freshman 15' as the phenomenon was called, remained unacceptable. She needed drastic measures. A traditional diet took too long. Quick results were necessary.

Determined, she embarked on the 'idol special,' a week-long cleanse of nothing but juice while continuing her usual workout routine. But there was one catch: no water allowed! She intuitively knew the pounds would return without dili-gence, but that was no longer a priority. Her idol training weight remained an obsession. The band could get gigs at any moment, and if this method proved swiftest, so be it.

The thought of sticking to it for an entire week, though, seemed impossible. At the agency, she was constantly surrounded by starving idols. They all suffered, but did so together. Her reality at SIU was a whole different story. Here, enticing food abounded. Parties, dorm room study sessions, well-placed vending machines, multiple restaurants, and the cafeteria that served a cornucopia of culinary indulgences that she had to pass twice every day both to and from class. The brute in her belly grew furious. Ignoring it much longer seemed untenable. Concentrating on schoolwork helped some, but even this approach had limits.

Heather's mind wandered during Professor Shaw's Introductory Economics class. Her only thought was to marginalize his "Thinking on the Margins," lecture altogether. A much-welcomed diversion arrived in the form of a texted conversation with Appa.

3:23 P.M. Dae-hee: Remember we discussed an internship before you left?

3:24 P.M. Heather: I do.

3:24 P.M. Dae-hee: You know Kwan Byung-hoon? He was an associate of mine when we lived in Los Angeles. He came to our house for dinner a few times.

3:25 P.M. Heather: I guess.

3:25 P.M. Dae-hee: You were pretty young.

Yeah.

3:26 P.M. Dae-hee: Anyway I mentioned you were going to school there and he agreed to meet regarding an internship his company offers.

3:28 P.M. Heather: Isn't it a little early for that? I just started.

3:28 P.M. Dae-hee: It's never too early to consider your future. You must seize opportunities as they come.

She struggled to devise a believable excuse.

3:32 P.M. Heather: I planned on getting a part-time job. Internships are unpaid, right?

3:32 P.M. Dae-hee: What do you need money for?

3:32 P.M. Dae-hee: We pay your expenses.

3:32 P.M. Dae-hee: Take advantage of our support.

3:33 P.M. Dae-hee: While you can.

3:35 P.M. Heather: I see.

3:35 P.M. Dae-hee: Mr. Kwan is a busy man. He'll see you as a favor to me. Don't disappoint.

3:36 P.M. Heather: I

"Ms. Moon?"

Looking up, she realized all eyes were on her. The entire class awaited a coherent response. From her.

"Since you have apparently mastered the material," Professor Shaw said with a sardonic smile, "would you kindly share an example of how William Stanley Jevons might have used his marginal utility theory to explain consumer behavior?"

3:36 P.M. Heather: gtg

She turned off the phone. "Um..."

There's that bothersome cafeteria again. An intoxicating aroma emanated from the place. Heather wondered whether they were barbecuing chicken or pork ribs. Or both! Of course, there was one way to make sure. She stopped in her tracks and looked up at the second floor windows. Students chatting while enjoying their meals. Then a jock took an enormous bite of chicken leg. "Well, that answers that question," she muttered to herself. Before her well-honed idol discipline manifested itself and carried her right past the enticement, she heard her name being shouted by a familiar voice.

"Hey, Heather. Wait up!" The smile disappeared from her

face as she identified the caller. Twenty yards down the path in the direction she had just traversed stood a waving Steve, the video director who'd rejected Made in Heaven. She had no interest whatsoever in chatting with the likes of him. Before she could escape, however, he approached.

"Oh, hi," she said bluntly before resuming her walk.

Unperturbed, Steve accompanied her. "We're going the same way. Mind if I join you?"

"It's a free country, I guess."

"I'm Steve, remember? From the auditions?"

"How could I ever forget?" snipped Heather, keeping her eyes locked straight ahead. "So, how's the music video biz?"

He ignored the question. "Maybe Grace told you, but I thought your band was superb. My decision was a tough one."

"I bet you struggled for days."

"I did, actually. Anyway, I'd like to hear you guys play again when you get gigs. You kept my contact info, didn't you?"

"We'll see."

"Are you parked over here?"

"Are you following me?"

"No." Steve stopped at the crosswalk, but Heather walked straight through without hesitation, forcing him to wait for another car to pass before he regained her side. "I thought we'd work on a project together in the future. Wouldn't that be fun?"

She chose not to respond. They continued walking silently. Awkwardly. Steve searched for an opportunity to make a graceful exit.

"That's my dorm over there. Rosecrans. I have to go."

"Don't get lost."

"Nice chatting with you."

Heather made no effort to acknowledge his farewell. For all she cared, he could have genuflected and it would've made no difference. She ambled towards her car, mind wracked with thoughts of starvation.

* * *

Heather and Grace renewed their push to fill out the membership. Vanessa remained an infuriating toss-up. They had yet to contact Danya, the choreographer, as they lacked an obvious strategy to persuade her. Grace argued they'd only get one shot at it, 'so it'd better be good.' Without Danya, they'd have no pull with Vanessa. Regardless, Heather remained adamant that Made in Heaven needed seven members. Towards that end, they held auditions.

The fruits of that labor lay before them, meager as they were. Grace scattered a pile of Polaroids across her dining room table. Heather had proposed photographing each auditionee to better attach names to faces. The strategy proved wise. Primarily amateurs, many attended without headshots. The first order of business was to eliminate those lacking any obvious talent.

"No." Snap. "No." Snap. "No." Snap. "Definitely a no," Grace said. The discards piled up.

"Add these to the reject pile," suggested Heather, handing over two more.

Grace assessed them. "Oh, for sure."

"To be honest, I'm kind of disappointed. There were no clear front runners."

"At this rate, we'll have to hold a second audition or devise another plan."

Grace's mother, Ha-yoon, entered bearing two cups of chrysanthemum tea. "How's it going?"

"Thanks, Umma," said Grace, eyeing the tea placed on the table. "Like a broken-down jalopy. Not sure if we have anything."

"Yeah, it was pretty weird," Heather said. "One girl just broke down and started crying for no reason. Lots weren't even prepared. Two guys even showed up. Gotta give them credit for trying. Some were clueless about K-pop, yet remained determined to try. What else am I missing?"

"That girl's original song featuring the F-word every other line."

"Oh, my," her mom said.

Heather laughed, "Yeah, we'll be sure to consult her when we go gangsta rap. And don't forget the actress who was convinced we were casting for a movie or something. Delivering lines from *Downton Abbey*. That was...interesting."

"And pretty much everyone was surprised to see us. I guess they expected old white men instead."

The phone rang in the other room.

"Well, it sounds like you have your work cut out. Gotta get that." Ha-yoon left them to their task.

"We have a strategic decision to make first." Heather picked out two photos from the pile and showed them to Grace. "Two of the best performers were white. What's our policy on that? With one member who can barely speak Korean, do we add a second?"

"Good point. Too many would handicap us."

"The other thing is body type. This girl, for example," Heather pulled a photo of an Amazon. "Pleasant voice, but much taller and more muscular than anyone else in the group. I hate to say it, but it would make our dances look strange." Heather knew how much K-pop choreography relied on exceptionally well-drilled and coordinated movements. Groups lived and died on their ability to synchronize. It would be quite difficult, possibly insurmountable, if one dancer looked markedly unlike the others.

"Yeah, I felt the same way. There's one more," Grace stated, presenting another photograph. "Julie Walker sang and danced well enough, but she's petite and would blend in better."

"And as a St. Ignatius student, she wouldn't have to travel far. But there's one more. Let me find it." Heather searched through the remaining photos. "Here." She presented another image. "June Kwan. She had the perfect look. Too bad about the live audition. Her video was dynamite."

"Deeply flawed but impressive." Grace took the photo from Heather to assess it again. "Looked like a movie star. And Korean, too."

"But what about that accent?"

"Yeah, no idea. Odd one, though."

"Well, regardless, once she botched the song, I knew it was over. She got flustered and gave up before the dance."

"Clearly a noob," Grace observed.

"Stage fright hits us all at some point, but during a low-pressure audition? That's a red flag. Julie seems the safer bet."

7

SECOND CHANCES

With their Marketing Analytics class over, Grace and Heather walked to their cars in the northeast campus lot. Grace described her call inviting Julie to the group when her friend interrupted. "Quick, turn around." No sooner had Heather spoken than she reversed course and went in the opposite direction.

"Did you forget something?" asked a puzzled Grace, trying to catch up.

"*He's* standing there. I don't want him to see us."

"Who is standing where?" She inquired, looking around.

"Steve! That video guy. I think he's stalking me."

Grace laughed in surprise. "Oh, come on, Heather, you're being ridiculous."

"Well, humor me, at least."

As Grace pondered the preposterous notion that they'd have to walk all the way back to their classroom, a shout rose from behind. "Hey, Heather. Grace. Wait up!" Heather pretended not to notice and kept walking. Grace, however, grew tired of the charade, stopped, and glanced over her shoulder. She used a much louder voice than was necessary. "Oh, look, Heather, it's Steve. Say hello to Steve."

Heather halted a few feet away, accepting defeat. Grace experienced the sharp points of censure on the back of her head as the film director drew near. He huffed as if out of breath. It was hard to tell whether that was from physical exertion or excitement. "I'm so glad to see you two," he exclaimed. "I was going to call, but my news will sound better in person."

"What's up?" Grace asked, hoping to ease the tension.

"I changed my mind. I'd love for you to be in my music video."

Heather and Grace exchanged surprised glances. "What about the other group?" queried Grace.

"After thinking about it, I realized my mistake."

Heather smirked. "Come clean. I'm not buying this sudden change of heart angle."

Steve looked embarrassed. "Okay. I admit I blew it. Please accept my apology. The truth is Radial Elliot put me in an awful jam and need your help."

Heather squeezed her notebook to her chest. "So now we're good enough, but only because you're in trouble?"

"I deserve that," said Steve.

Grace attempted to de-escalate the situation. "Heather, calm down."

"I'm not ready to calm down yet!"

Steve looked pained. "My friend convinced me to go with Radial Elliot. Terrible idea," he said, shaking his hands in distress. "Like you wouldn't believe."

Grace watched the two converse. Their body language revealed some mysterious force at play. Steve displayed every sign of someone smitten with Heather. This was nothing new.

Her bombshell friend often turned guys into quivering lumps of jelly with a simple bat of the eyelashes. What struck Grace as odd was how Heather responded to *him*. After the audition, Heather described his lack of fragility-masking machismo as refreshing while admitting that he wasn't her type. Once Steve rejected Made in Heaven, though, Heather seemed to take the news personally. Now, her face was flushed red. Was this anger, or was something else involved?

Heather appeared open to his pitch for now, but she refused to let him off the hook. "We're not a consolation prize, you know?"

"I...I don't..." Steve seemed stumped for a response.

Grace showed more leniency. "We've been working on some new songs."

Heather remained silent, trusting Grace's strategy.

"Oh, that's great," said Steve. "Can you be ready soon?"

"Sure, no problem."

Heather looked askance, then tossed her head back as if questioning her friend's sanity.

"Oh, you are lifesavers. I'd've lost my studio time otherwise. Is two weeks okay?"

"Of course," Grace said without hesitation.

"Now, who's being ridiculous?" asked Heather in Korean. She smiled at the perplexed Steve, relishing the advantages of multilingualism, and not for the last time.

"What about song choice?" asked Grace while returning to English.

"Whaddaya say we talk over dinner at the cafeteria?" Steve suggested.

"Sounds more fun than homework." The pair proceeded in that direction until Grace realized they weren't being followed.

"Aren't you coming?"

"I have plans."

Heather was fibbing, but Grace knew better than to press the issue. "This is important."

"I trust your judgment."

Grace shook her head. "Okay, but don't blame me later."

Over a dinner of roasted chicken and grilled Brussels sprouts, Grace listened to Steve's account of his decision-making process. "From the moment I left the voicemail, I regretted it. I had a history with Radial Elliot. They were a straightforward rock act that had long been together. I knew what I was getting with them. My music producer friend talked me into taking the safe route, and I listened to him instead of my heart."

"What did your heart say?" asked Grace.

"Keep in mind that I had been in auditions all day prior to meeting you. Let me tell ya, it was a non-stop procession of overdramatic, angsty, and downright pretentious acts that would've exhausted anyone. I was seriously regretting the whole business."

"Why have auditions at all, then?"

"Just a faint hope I'd find something better, I guess."

"But you didn't, apparently."

Steve smiled and stuck a finger in the air for emphasis. "Au contraire. I just hadn't realized it yet. Honestly, I never expected a K-pop act to walk through the door, and I wouldn't have been ready to process what you were offering anyway."

"So what happened with...Radio...Idiot?" She asked, half-forgetting the name.

"Radial Elliot," he said in correction, "though I'm starting to like your version better. I got an early morning wake-up call informing me that the band had broken up. Irrevocably."

"What caused that?"

"Girl trouble, of course." He blushed and corrected himself. "No offense intended."

"Naturally."

"To make a long story short, basically everyone in the group was cheating with each others' girls. It was a spaghetti bowl of tangled liaisons. When the news broke, chaos erupted. It's shocking that there were no fatalities. There's simply no going back after a mess that big."

"No doubt."

"The bright side is it gives me the opportunity to make amends at least. I'm sorry the timing is so poor. It's not fair to demand such short prep. My only other choice, though, is to cancel the project altogether and fail my class."

"Don't expect miracles, but I think we'll be able to pull something together."

"I can't tell you how grateful I am."

"Answer me this, though. How did you really feel about our audition?"

A broad smile crept over Steve's face as he recalled the moment. "The five of you were like a breath of fresh air. As if you belonged on the stage and knew it. If you hadn't told me you were newly formed, I'd never have guessed." His eyes lit up as the memory flooded over him. "And Heather. What a find."

"She is something, isn't she?"

"Let me tell you. This town is full of pretty faces who come from all over the world to be discovered," he said gushingly. "Heather has something most don't, though. Magnetism. The enchanting way she turns a phrase, the elegance of her every move, the effervescent way of expressing herself. She practically demands attention."

"The lovebug bit you deep, I see."

Steve ignored her comment. He was too lost in reverie to care. "You heard her sing. That vibrancy and raw emotion mixed with dynamic energy. And the way she bends notes rather than sing them directly. That's hard to categorize." He didn't stop there. "After you played "Sk8er Boi" by Avril Lavigne, she started telling me about the song's interesting modulations and how the verses, chorus, and bridge are all in different keys. Stuff I never noticed before. That's gold."

"She knows music"

"And when she said 'the trick with pop is to do more with less. That's what gives it immediacy.' Wow. You have no idea how starved I am for that kind of insight. My girlfriend Casey mistakes an adagio for a type of cheese."

Grace laughed. "Would you like some grated adagio with that salad?" she said in mocking contempt. It didn't matter to Grace if Steve picked Made in Heaven purely to impress Heather. She couldn't see the harm in it if the means furthered the end. However, Grace ended Steve's romp through the daisies with a business question to keep the discussion from veering too far on the Heather tangent. "You mentioned a possible cash prize. What are we talking?"

Steve snapped out of his daydream. "This is primarily for a class project. So, obviously, I can't pay you upfront, but at the very least, you'll get an EP and a music video out of the deal. However, I also intend to enter into a video competition. The top prize is $50,000."

Grace's eyes lit up, knowing her fledgling group could use that money. "Okay, but we need to talk music. What kind of songs are you looking for? We've only had time to write a few."

"I'd like a fast one for the A-side and the video. A ballad for the B-side."

Grace only had a few demos on her phone to pick from. She felt most sure about 'Celestial'. He loved it. Grace pondered whether the song's merit or Heather's attractiveness moved him. Again, did it matter? "We have a ballad, too, but no demo yet."

"That's okay. A-side is the priority. Polish 'Celestial' as best you can in the time you have. We were supposed to go into the studio this weekend, but I traded slots to buy us a couple weeks." They discussed further details over the rest of the meal.

While preparing to leave, Steve touched upon a topic Grace had hoped to avoid. "So four of you actually trained to be idols? I had no idea it was that involved."

"You don't know the half of it."

"So tell me then, if you spent all that time and energy training in Korea, what are you doing here?"

The corners of Grace's mouth turned down. It seemed counterproductive to lay into the entire saga. Plus, she didn't have the emotional energy to even try. "It's complicated," was her only response.

Steve side-eyed her, sensing a gripping tale waiting in the wings but possessing enough sense not to tread where uninvited. "Believe me, I get it."

* * *

Grace had salvaged the rehearsal. That feat seemed impossible hours earlier when, once again, the practice space they'd reserved fell through. Improvising, she suggested moving to her family's garage. Technically, her father, Ha-joon, had forbidden it. He worried their neighbor would file another noise complaint with the HOA. That wouldn't be an issue this evening. With a work party to attend, he wasn't due home for a while. They'd be done by then.

Made in Heaven was holding its third rehearsal in four days. Crunch time had arrived. Heather's ballad "Have No Fear" was sounding splendid. As a more straightforward song, it was easier to learn. The full-on rock song, "Celestial," though, had issues.

"Stop! Enough!" Heather shouted into the mic, waving her arm to get their attention. "Stop!" The cacophony died a merciful death.

"That was hard," complained Erin.

"It sounded like five different songs at once." Heather turned her attention to Grace. "I don't understand why you picked this. We need time to get it right."

"We *specifically* invited your input," responded Grace. "You were *specifically* too busy pouting. Remember?"

"I'm not happy with the way it's sounding."

"Can't they fix it in post?" suggested Mindy.

Heather shook her head. "We have access to a real studio with natural acoustics. I want the band to sound the same live as recorded."

"What are we supposed to do?" asked Grace. "Steve is expecting 'Celestial.'"

"Funny you should ask." Heather extracted several music sheets from a manila folder. "I've been working on another song that'll be easier."

"Great." Grace loved Heather but found her capriciousness exasperating.

"Truthfully, I've solved everything up to the rap break. I thought we could work on the rest together." Hearing no objections, she continued. "The song's called 'On Your Lips.' It's about meeting an exciting new guy and imagining your first kiss together."

"That sounds nice," said Sun-hee.

"It does." Heather smiled. "Erin, hand me your instrument." She borrowed it long enough to play a snappy, sneaky bass line. "The first two bars are bass only," she explained. "Drums will start on this measure. Can you learn it?"

"Sounds fun, but not too hard," Erin said as she retrieved her bass.

"I'd like us all to sing the chorus together. Could you do that, Mindy, while playing the drums?"

"Sure thing."

"Erin?"

"Let me concentrate on the bass."

"No problem." After a restart, Heather sang through the initial part and stopped. "See, I'm stuck at this point."

Grace found the song bright and catchy, with a faint vibe of surf rock. She noted the boundless optimism in the lyrics but felt it would benefit from more edge. "I have an idea for the rap, if you don't mind." She began jotting down notes as Mindy and Erin practiced the proposed opening together. Meanwhile, Heather and Sun-hee discussed a post-rap bridge propelled by and built upon the energy of the opening bass line.

Once they had sketched it, Heather continued her explanation. "This is where the break comes in. What do you have for us, Grace?"

In contrast, the rapper devised a verse that expressed skepticism about the relationship's viability. The opening half ran in time with the beat, while the second was in double tempo. She substituted patter for the incomplete lyrics to convey the rhythm she had in mind.

"That's masterly," Heather said. "Erin, here's my idea. Let there be drums alone for the first half of the rap. When it goes double tempo, join in with a running bass line." Erin nodded in agreement. Having heard this new idea, Sun-hee proposed modifications, which Heather approved.

As rework continued on this segment, Mindy grew bored and started wailing on her drums in an improvised solo. Erin watched as the drumsticks twirled between beats. "How do you do that?" she asked.

"Easy-peasy," Mindy replied. "I lived in a remote monastery in the Himalayas as a child. The temple master wouldn't let me leave until I perfected this technique."

"Really?" asked Erin, eyes wide in wonder.

"Yeah. I had to wax decks and paint fences for months before he'd even let me touch the sticks."

"That's amazing."

Grace rolled her eyes at Erin's naivete. "She's full of it. It's an optical illusion."

Mindy smiled slyly and showed the technique again, this time in slow motion. "I can do more complex stuff, too." She resumed drumming, tossing sticks upward and catching them before striking the next beat.

"It might be a trick, but it still looks neat," said Erin.

"I'm all about showmanship."

"Okay, pay attention, everyone." After finding a resolution to the musical dilemma, Heather interrupted the side discourse. "Sun-hee will sing the post-rap bridge over simple piano chords. The rest of you, no instrumentation at all. When I start the crescendo, let's have drum and bass return. During the final chorus, I want to hear full guitars as well. Everyone got it?"

All nodded except Erin. "We'll see."

"No pressure. It's only rehearsal."

They performed the song once more, beginning from the top. This time, the individual pieces blended into a coherent whole. Sun-hee improvised a lovely passage stemming from Grace's rap. She warbled a melancholy bridge that transitioned into the final chorus. Heather fashioned a bright climax punctuated by a full octave jump.

"Much better," encouraged Grace. "It's starting to sound like an actual song."

With that utterance, the garage door jolted open, causing the members to jump in surprise. Car headlights bathed the garage in a blinding luminescence.

"Appa's home," said Grace, motioning for him to dim the lights as he parked on the driveway. She jumped to her father's side when he emerged. "How was your day?"

"Sweetheart, I told you not to practice here. What will Mrs. Cavanaugh say?"

"She's in Omaha this week visiting her son."

"Oh," he said, appeased by the update. "Still, it's getting pretty late, isn't it?"

"We're almost done. Do you want to hear our song?"

"It won't take long, will it?"

"Three and a half minutes."

Mr. So placed his briefcase on the workbench and laid his

suit jacket on a stool that Heather brought forward. Umma joined to watch them play "On Your Lips" again. With growing ease, the members started infusing the song with more nuance.

Her parents applauded at the end. "I'm not familiar with that song. Who's it by?" Grace's father asked.

"That's ours, Appa," she responded proudly. "We wrote it. Just now."

* * *

With days remaining before their first recording session, Grace had booked a spare room at the SIU Music Building. Heather called to say she'd be late to the rehearsal. Her absence restricted the band's progress. Despite Grace's best efforts to deflect attention away from 37-G and their time together in Korea, questions persisted. As the members waited for Heather's arrival, Mindy inquired about their main singer. "What was she like as a trainee?"

Grace figured it wouldn't hurt to share general impressions. "Heather was the glue that held us together," she explained.

"How so?"

"Her approach was unique. Certainly, I was surprised at first."

"She doesn't strike me as a radical."

"I don't mean in a subversive way. How do I describe it?"

The intensity of trainee life remained fresh in Grace's memory. She recalled one time sitting on the floor of a dance studio at Seoul's 37-G Entertainment. Beside her was Heather. They faced a mirrored wall, practicing aegyo, the hand and facial gestures that all K-pop idols must master.

"You're getting close, but show more flair," Heather instructed. It was 10:00 p.m. Their classmates had all returned to the dorms, leaving them to work undisturbed.

"I feel like I'm overdoing it as it is," Grace responded.

"Personality is your selling point. Don't underestimate its value."

"Nothing I try seems natural. You make it look easy."

"Be yourself. Fans have biases. Let your personality shine, and your fans will gravitate towards you."

Grace had drawn the agency's attention by winning an amateur rap competition at a regional shopping mall in downtown Seoul. She occupied a unique position in the class. Before she arrived, the agency assigned rap breaks piecemeal, with varying degrees of success. They recruited Grace as a specialist. Her inclusion in 37-G's mix of talent made a powerful statement of intent and unlocked intriguing possibilities. Heather innately understood the potential.

Grace repeated the hand gestures in the mirror with which she hoped to forge a unique identity. Heather watched closely and suggested refinements, demonstrating by example. "Sweet. That has style," said Grace in response to one noteworthy variation.

"Fans notice subtle details. Producers, too."

"To be honest, this entire experience has been a shock."

"How so?"

"I expected more, I don't know, cattiness, I guess."

"That's the wrong mindset to have," Heather said. "Consider the big picture."

"But why is everybody helping me?"

"Trust is crucial to teamwork."

"We're competing for the same spots."

"Bettering yourself is fine, but always act with regard for others." Grace wrinkled her brow. "Trust demonstrates commitment," Heather explained. "As the team grows stronger, you grow stronger." The confusion must've remained evident on her face, for Heather clarified further. "Let me put it in musical terms. Think of an orchestra. Sometimes, we play solo, sometimes together. An individual musician's contribution is essential, but each must also mesh with the common design. Musicians must listen to each other to form a complete performance."

The pair related to each other. They were both born and raised in the U.S. to Korean parents before relocating to Korea. English was their preferred way of communicating, as it kept native language skills sharp. Heather had also learned many tough lessons over the past three years and was eager to share knowledge. Grace welcomed the advice and appreciated the companionship. In short order, they had become inseparable.

It was common for new trainees to experience isolation. With entrenched cliques and delineated hierarchies, each fresh addition sent ripples through the established order like pebbles thrown into a pond. Yet the regularity with which turnover happened kept every veteran trainee sharp. Security was a fleeting notion, even after a job well done. Everyone at the agency faced monthly evaluations for fitness, talent, personality, and performance, among other qualities. Complacency invited disaster. With hordes of eager young hopefuls waiting on the sidelines for their own stab at the opportunity, they dismissed anyone who showed less than total commitment. Heather acknowledged that today's awkward newbie could become tomorrow's fervent rival. The best defense, she argued, was constant improvement to show irreplaceable value at each opportunity. It paid to be mindful that all trainees were working towards the same goal: to form a group. While each member contributed their skills, their effectiveness as a team was paramount. Even the most talented member would fail without the ability to function as part of a cohesive unit. This was the lesson Heather hoped to impart to all new arrivals.

"My evaluation is in three days. I doubt I'm ready," Grace said.

"Pace yourself."

"I don't want to fail in my first month."

"Remember what I said. You're judged not only against others but yourself."

"What does that mean, though?"

"You want to strike the right balance. Compete. Yes. Avoid being the worst. Yes. But if you fail to show improvement from month to month, producers will dismiss you as lazy."

"So, I should try hard but leave room for growth?"

"If you're confident you'll be better next month, do your best today."

"Are you sure about this?"

"Balance, Grace. And trust."

A month later, on a lovely day in late summer, Grace and Heather visited Jamwon Hangang Riverside Park for a jog. The thought of shutting themselves inside a gym for their daily workout routine was disheartening. Chilly weather was around the corner, and they wanted to enjoy the sunshine while they could. After running ten kilometers, they spotted a food truck with a hand-painted sign advertising hamburgers. A refreshment break was in order.

Though the line ahead was long, it moved quickly. "Are you

heading home for the holiday?" Grace asked.

Heather sighed. "Unavoidably, yes."

Grace laughed. "Geez, don't be so enthusiastic."

"I can only imagine what it's like having parents who support your dreams."

"You've been at the agency for three years now. Surely your folks approve?"

"They're just waiting to see me fail. And spectacularly."

Grace snorted. "I doubt that."

"You haven't met them."

"You're bound to disappoint them then."

"Now you're catching on." They ordered banana milks and sat on a riverside bench, taking small sips. Rain clouds appeared on the horizon to the north. The gentle breeze grew stronger. "What attracts you to idol life, Grace?"

She tilted her head from side to side. "It seems fun, I guess."

"Everyone says that. But what specifically appeals to you?" Heather didn't wait for an answer. "For me, it's the feeling I get singing before an audience. I want to touch people with my music and make a difference in their lives. If I could do that…Oh, my." She shuddered with excitement at the thought.

"Do you suppose we'll ever get a chance?"

"I can't imagine what I'd do with myself otherwise."

"You're a model trainee. It's time the agency recognizes that."

"I want them to be proud of me, so I play my part." She stood and grabbed Grace's empty bottle to recycle it. "Let's go. We need to finish our run before that storm rolls in."

Heather's arrival at the practice room cut the story short. "Sorry, I'm late, How's 'Celestial' coming along?"

* * *

Grace answered the phone despite the incoming number being an unfamiliar one. The voice on the other end was gruff, with an indeterminate East Coast accent.

"Yeah, my name's Arnie Johnson. Calling 'bout the manager position you posted. When are the interviews scheduled?"

The ad Grace placed received so little interest that she'd forgotten its existence. "Um...what time can you get here?"

For the occasion, Heather met Grace on campus at The Lair. The day was beautiful. They sat at a patio table in the shade of an expansive umbrella, drinking iced Americanos.

"Glad you came. I didn't want to decide this alone," said Grace.

"Believe me, skipping out early on Precalc is a blessing," said Heather. "My brain was dying in there. Where is he?"

"He texted. Should be any minute." Curious, Grace asked, "How do you like Finance as a major?"

Heather rolled her eyes in desperation. "I can't wait until next year."

"What happens next year?"

"I get to take the Creative Experience class."

"Yeah." Grace laughed. "Your one chance to show them business majors who's boss."

"Sad but true."

A stubbly bearded, paunchy, white guy approached, wearing an oversized dress shirt with sleeves rolled up and one too many buttons undone at the collar. "Hey, either of you, Grace?" They introduced themselves and offered to buy him a soda. Surprisingly, he ordered two slices of pepperoni pizza as well. It was 3:30 in the afternoon. Heather volunteered to fetch the order.

The first part of the interview comprised Arnie responding to simple questions with long, rambling trains of incoherent thought. He spoke of his days spent touring with Sordid Gorgon, which he described as a thrash core band from Denmark. However, when Grace inquired about the abrupt end of their North American circuit, his demeanor turned cagey, muttering something indistinct about a hazmat team and a Welsh Corgi.

"How's your punctuality?" asked Grace as Heather returned with the pizza.

"I don't pay much 'tention to grammar or nothing. Does it even matter?"

Heather stifled a grin. Communicating with her eyes, she dared Grace not to laugh as she placed the food tray before Arnie. "Naw, it's overrated," agreed Grace, overcoming her friend's silent challenge.

As Heather got settled, Arnie stared at her a moment too long before folding a pizza slice and taking an enormous bite. He spent most of a minute chewing as he spoke. The next round of questions focused on K-pop girl groups, of which Arnie could not identify a single example. He mentioned seeing an all-female metal band once at a festival in Connecticut but couldn't remember their name. "It was Fist of Diana or Feast of Dinosaurs. Something like that."

"What are your expectations as a manager?" asked Heather.

"For a man of my talents, I'd need, like, a minimum of $70K per year."

Heather and Grace both waited for a punchline that never arrived. Heather switched to Korean. "Was that a genuine request?"

Grace responded in kind, saying, "Apparently so." And continuing with, "Okay, play along," before returning to English. "To be honest, we hoped to find someone who'd accept six figures."

Arnie's eyes brightened. "I'm okay with that," he said, head nodding.

"The position also comes with free use of a limo, VIP seats to twelve concerts of your choice each year, plus a monthly allotment of either coke or heroin."

Heather supported her friend's statement with an eager nod and an inviting smile. "Oh, and you also get first pick of groupies to do in the back of the tour bus."

Grace nodded and slapped her head in exaggerated slapstick. "Duh, how could I forget?"

Arnie bolted upright. "That's awesome!" It took a moment, but slowly, his skepticism sunk in. "Wait a minute. Are your groupies male or female?"

"Whatever floats your boat, Arnie," responded Heather. "We don't judge." Grace was forced to look away to maintain a straight face.

Arnie reclined back to assess the two of them. The hamster wheel powering his brain seemed to spin as he planned a response. "Hold on a sec. I don't get this kind of luck. What gives? This sounds too good to be true."

"It is, Arnie," concluded Grace, "but you started it. Care to cut the crap now?"

The girls spent the remainder of the interview tag-teaming their list of expectations, attempting to harness Arnie's tendency to run off on wild tangents. After 45 minutes, they had made actual progress. "We're willing to work hard to make this a success, and we need a manager who feels the same way.

Does that describe you?"

"I'll say yes if it gets me the job."

Heather was caught off guard by this response, disguising her reaction with a cough. Grace smiled awkwardly. "Okay, thanks. We'll contact you."

Once he departed, Heather inquired, "Was that last response acceptable?"

"I don't know. This is all new to me."

"He's enthusiastic. I'll say that for him."

"That's because Arnie's as desperate as we are."

Grace shared the news during a conference call with Steve later that day. "We have a new manager."

"Oh, that's great," he said. "How'd you find him?"

"Through Craigslist."

Lengthy silence.

"Hello?"

"What are his qualifications?"

"Uh, he applied."

"I see." Steve paused before adding, "Well, good luck with that."

8

MAIDEN HEAVEN

With unbound excitement, Heather looked forward to the first-ever meeting of Made in Heaven's dance unit and the new opportunities it promised. This represented a significant milestone in the group's development.

They had found their sixth member through a casting call. Her name was Julie Walker, a student of English background who also studied at St. Ignatius. She had an outgoing and dominant personality to go along with her abundant singing and dancing experience. Her slight frame fit the group's visual profile. Julie's major drawback was her inability to speak Korean, not a single word. This concerned Heather, but they couldn't afford to be too picky.

They co-opted an unused classroom in a neglected annex tucked away behind the university's physical plant. Grace stood amid a semicircle of mostly occupied chairs, reviewing their proposed schedule of activities for the weeks ahead. They reserved a vacant seat for Julie, who remained absent. "I know most of you are preparing for mid-terms," said Grace.

"Hopefully, tonight won't take long."

As she spoke, the door squeaked open. A petite girl with tanned skin entered the room. She wore brand-name orange workout clothes and tied her oak-colored hair in a ponytail. "Excuse me, is this the— Oh yes, I recognize you." Her loud voice echoed in the mostly empty room as Grace welcomed her with a broad arm wave. After a round of introductions, the group returned to their seats. Julie hesitated as she assessed the seating arrangement. "When will the rest arrive?" she asked.

This question prompted an exchange of puzzled glances. "Everyone's here. We're a six-pack right now," answered Heather.

"Why? What were you expecting?" inquired Mindy suspiciously.

Julie's pupils dilated. "I wasn't sure if there were...if I was the only..." she paused.

"Go ahead. Say it," blurted Mindy, her jaw clenched.

Julie opened her mouth as if to protest, but soon thought better of it. "Oh, no. I didn't know, is all."

"Don't worry. You'll be fine," said Sun-hee, placing her hand on the vacant chair next to her in a welcoming gesture. Julie took the seat and removed the scrunchy from her hair, letting loose abundant locks.

Grace encouraged each member to summarize their experience to break the ice. When it was Julie's turn, she flipped her hair and combed through it with spread fingers. "My parents own a navigation technology company. We live in Palos Verdes Estates. I won regionals with my cheerleader squad in high school and starred in *Carousel* during my senior year. Here at SIU, I've been a key member of two dance teams."

Throughout this checklist, Mindy tapped her foot on the ground, but stopped once it became noticeable.

With the formalities over, it was time for Heather to introduce their newest song. She distributed music sheets for "Feel the Heat." This was a hard-driving, up-tempo dance track regarding a girl's fast-fading patience with a low-effort boyfriend.

"Do we really need to learn the whole thing if we're only singing one part?" asked Erin.

"Lines will be distributed according to suitability," explained Heather. We first need to assess each singer's approach.

"Are we singing together or individually?" queried Julie.

"Everyone will get a turn in the spotlight."

"Are you the lead singer?"

"No, Sun-hee is."

"Really?" Julie jerked her head back. "That's surprising."

"Heather's the main singer," noted Grace.

"That's what I thought, but why did she say Sun-hee is?"

"She didn't."

"She did, too! I just heard her!" The volume of Julie's voice rose as she spoke. Dramatic arm gestures accompanied her words.

"No, she said Sun-hee is the lead singer," explained Mindy, trying to remain calm.

"And Heather is the main," repeated Grace.

Julie's frustration was obvious. She seemed displeased, like the target of jokes. "Why are you all messing with me?"

"We're not!" countered Mindy.

"Is this some sort of hazing ritual? The main and the lead are the same thing!" By now, Julie was shouting.

"Okay, time out," said Grace, forming a T with her hands. "You're using the two words interchangeably, but in K-pop, they're different."

"How?" Julie asked, hesitant to believe the explanation.

"Look at it this way," explained Mindy, jumping in uninvited. "The lead singer is responsible for a strong start, whereas the main singer kicks it up a notch during the most demanding parts."

"Why didn't you say that?"

"We did."

"No—"

"Enough," said Heather, regaining control of the proceedings. "Julie, I'm sorry. I should have explained it better." She put aside her copy of the music. "Let's move on to the level tests."

"What's the point of these rankings?" asked Julie.

"To show our relative strengths and weaknesses and identify improvement areas," explained Grace.

Heather and Grace performed "Feel the Heat" once through for demonstration. Members then had time to learn the song. Vocal assessments took place without accompaniment, not even a metronome. For Heather, this offered the truest insight into every singer's capabilities.

Sun-hee kicked off the test. Everyone knew about her talent, so this part of the exercise was somewhat superfluous. She set a strong benchmark for the others, though. Her bright sound was enough to warm the coldest winter. Mindy's singing voice was refreshing, like sunlight on water. Heather figured she'd make a strong harmonizer but lacked the power to be a full-time lead. Grace excelled at rap, but her ability was chorus-level when carrying a melody.

Heather paid the closest attention to the last two members, the most significant question marks. Erin had limited potential as a singer because her voice was thin and had scant power. Regarding raw vocal talent, Julie had enough to sing lead. Still, her style was more suited to rock than pop, limiting her effectiveness. A bigger problem was language. While they would sprinkle English lyrics into every song, Korean would be the predominant language. Both non-speakers would have to work on their pronunciation to sound the least bit convincing. While Erin was at least learning it, Korean was foreign to Julie. To facilitate a solution to this problem, Heather provided the lyrics in Romanized form. The hope was that they'd sing phonetically, if not naturally.

Julie handled the English parts with ease but fell apart beyond that. She looked intimidated pronouncing words in a foreign language. After three failed attempts, she lost interest in the process altogether. "Why do it this way? Nobody will know what we're saying." She refused to continue.

Heather tried to formulate a response, but Mindy beat her to it. "It wouldn't be K-pop, then, would it?"

"Why make it harder on ourselves?"

"We never said this would be easy," noted Grace.

"Who'll even listen to us?"

Nobody volunteered input. Heather didn't push the issue, reminding herself that she had recruited Julie primarily as a dancer. Hopefully, that role would suit her better.

With the singing exercise coming to an abrupt halt, the dance test was next. Grace demonstrated some simple steps Vanessa had dismissed earlier as 'cheerleading.' Heather observed as each member took their turn. Mindy proved a skilled mover, though she was less physically fit than the others. Sun-hee was not a quick learner, but her peak physical condition suggested she'd be more than capable as a performer. Grace had superior dance skills but had grown rusty since 37-G. While lacking formal training, Erin's lithe body was tailor-made for K-pop. Her line development needed substantial improvement, however.

Much to Heather's disappointment, Julie struggled here too. As a dancer, she had advanced skills. Upon further assessment, though, her style clashed with the other members of the group. With the bulk of her experience from the university's premier dance groups, Julie had grown accustomed to the high-energy, big-movement, hip-hop style prevalent there. She'd have to be broken of those habits and taught the subtler approach Heather envisioned for her group.

More troubling was Julie's attitude. Gone was the chirpy cheerfulness she'd shown at auditions. In its place was a constant torrent of whining and moaning. Julie consistently resisted all attempts to offer constructive feedback. The longer the evening wore on, the more irritable Julie became. "Wait, are you serious? That's impossible," she countered when Heather mentioned they'd perform in heels.

"It's common for girl groups," explained Mindy.

"No other dance team does that here. Why cripple ourselves?"

* * *

Heather assessed the studio where they'd be recording their first single. The facility within SIU's Music Building might not have been state-of-the-art, but it sure looked close. It was spacious, well-appointed, and sleekly designed. Heather was certain the band would excel in such a fantastic venue.

"Where's Steve?" asked Grace of the sound engineer positioned at the console, labeling channels for the session.

"Down the hall, getting psyched," he responded. "Name's Mateo, by the way." He shook Grace's hand and waved to everyone else.

Over the next half hour, the girls lugged their equipment inside and began setting up. Arnie arrived just before Steve did. In a fresh round of introductions, Heather tried to avoid eye contact with Steve. She remained upset with him for initially rejecting them. When her name was called, she looked up briefly, then returned focus to her guitar without saying a word.

The A-side single, chosen for the music video, was designated "Celestial." It was a supremely confident, catchy, and hard-driving tune with choruses sung by Heather and Sunhee and an aggressive rap by Grace in place of a guitar solo. The tune expressed overwhelming emotions felt in the presence of a crush. It was a proper rock song that kept the strong pop vibe the group wanted. Steve found it appealing when Grace played a rough demo at their cafe meeting. Much to his chagrin, the girls told him they had dropped it in favor of another option. "It wasn't coming together," explained Grace. "We thought going in a different direction would be more productive."

"I mean, this is like a bait and switch. We had an agreement," he said, unable to restrain himself.

"We did, Steve. I'm sorry. During our meeting, I should've considered it more. Given the timeline, we went with a simpler approach. Heather was right."

"Why didn't you join us? Your input would have been valuable." Heather kept staring at the floor as Steve addressed her.

"I wasn't feeling well," she responded.

"All that time wasted planning for a different song. You could have called me. I don't bite."

"Okay, I got it," Heather said. "Can we proceed?"

To ease tensions, Steve dropped his complaint. The replacement tune, "On Your Lips," was 60s-inspired pop-rock infused with modern flavors. Cheerful and catchy, it was the perfect summer beach anthem. Steve described it as having potential but wasn't sure it would work for his purpose. That they ignored his input still obviously bothered him. To aggravate matters, Arnie offered heaps of unsolicited advice as if trying to prove his worth. His constant interruptions chipped away at Steve's patience.

The recording process for both songs was similar. The sequence commenced with a drum and bass rhythm. Guitars and synthesizers established the chord structure. Melodies, primarily as vocals, followed. The last step was to add nuance through the background vocals and percussion/piano/guitar fills. The trial run of "On Your Lips" demonstrated the band's readiness. Their playing was tight. The peppy song lightened the mood. When the moment arrived to record, the professional disparity among the members proved challenging. Four had at least some prior studio experience. Mindy, for example, laid down a solid scratch track right from the start, but the process was unfamiliar to Erin. Her eyes darted back and forth, conveying uncertainty throughout. Mateo was a patient mentor, though, taking time to explain the multi-track process. To her credit, Erin absorbed the information with eagerness.

They progressed throughout the day, but at a much slower

pace than desired. Steve kept his eye on the clock, knowing they'd have to clear the room for another project by 6:00 a.m. While the initial results for "On Your Lips" sounded promising, the B-side proved an unexpected revelation. "Have No Fear" was a simple, uplifting ballad with thoughtful lyrics and soaring vocals. The song concerned a woman working up the nerve to reveal her genuine feelings of love. Its jangly guitar chords and simple rhythm established a country vibe, though it departed from pure country. Heather sang the opening verse while Sun-hee followed. This time, Grace delivered a notably different rap, choosing subtlety that harmonized with the ballad's calmer tone.

To Heather's surprise, excitement grew as the composition came to life piece by piece. The emotional climax of "Have No Fear" was extraordinary. Grace's rap transitioned into simple piano chords, over which Heather sang the bridge. This quiet moment was soon to pass. As her powerful voice rose to a sustained high note, Sun-hee took over the main chorus, leaving Heather's vocals sailing overhead like a cloud. Their singing contrasted with and complemented each other. Heather repeated the final refrain alone before the song came full circle with the return of the intro guitar.

After the song's first rehearsal, Mateo proposed a switch, which Steve volunteered to execute. When Heather saw him enter the isolation booth, her eyes widened. Lifting the headphones off her ears, she responded tersely, "Is something wrong?"

"Mateo thinks you'd sound better on this Shure." He disconnected the Electro-Voice from the microphone stand and placed it on a nearby desk. The pause must've struck him as an excellent time to thaw the tension. "Are you still mad at me?" he asked.

Heather looked at him sharply. "Seriously? That's what's on your mind right now?"

"Since we're working together, shouldn't we at least try to get along?"

"And people call me sensitive."

Steve seemed unsure of how to proceed. An awkward silence followed.

Mateo's patience ran out. "C'mon guys, what's the holdup?"

Heather gave him an OK sign through the window. "It'll be fine," she told Steve. "Let's finish this song. Okay?"

Steve plugged in the new mic and returned to the control room. Heather provided a brief test and then sang the song twice.

"Wow, that second take is a keeper," said Steve. The band waited while the crew fiddled with the controls for several minutes. Mateo transmitted a rough mix over the intercom. The group rejoiced upon hearing the results. Smiles were in abundance.

"Okay, let's get Mindy in for some vocal fills next," said Steve.

"In that case, we'll need that Electro-Voice again," said Mateo.

Steve re-entered the booth as Heather was listening to the playback. "We're going with that take. You're done."

Heather perceived sniffles as Steve switched mics again. It sounded like crying. She tried to take a closer look, but Steve turned away each time.

"Are you crying?" she asked.

"No."

She took hold of his chin to peer directly into his eyes. "You are, too. Why are you crying?"

Steve smiled in embarrassment. "That was beautiful, is all. I guess I get worked up when creative ideas come to fruition like that."

His response caused tears to well in her own eyes. The pair laughed at the silliness of their reactions. The relief of a job well done was evident on their faces.

Mateo's voice came over the intercom, "What's the deal, guys? Clear out. We've got work to do."

"Let me know when you're done with this crap," Mateo said. "I'm going for a smoke." Most of the band had departed hours earlier. Heather remained behind, eager to evaluate the final results as soon as they were ready. The pressure was on. Only an hour remained in their reserved time slot before the next crew arrived. They still needed the mix. The pleasant mood that had prevailed earlier had long since dissipated. Exhausted from the all-night recording session, Steve's increasing annoyance toward Arnie proved the primary cause for the breakdown.

"The ballad's too slow. People want a rock song," argued Arnie. "That was the plan."

"Now that I've heard both, I'm convinced 'Have No Fear' fits my concept better."

"So change the concept."

"I can't at this late date. It's money I don't have."

"You're exaggerating."

"It's not your video, pal."

"I'm not your pal, chum." Arnie thrusted a pointed finger in Steve's direction. "The fast song is stronger. That's what counts."

"Well, I'm sorry you think that way, amigo. Maybe it's more immediate, but 'Have No Fear' has more depth."

"Ballads have less potential."

"Lots of ballads are hits. Where are you drawing that conclusion from?"

"As manager, I havta maximize this band's performance."

"Dude, the day you pay for this project is the day we'll talk. What part of this do you not get?" The fracas continued for several more minutes as they repeated talking points ad nauseam in every imaginable variation. Steve at last acknowledged Heather, who had observed their entire argument without making a sound. "Where'd you dig this guy up from?"

"Which one do *you* prefer?" asked Arnie.

Heather frowned. "That's like asking me to pick a favorite child."

Before the bickering could resume, Mateo returned to the studio. He looked exasperated. "Guys, knock it off. We're running out of time. What'll it be?"

A moment of awkward silence passed. Steve shifted his eyes back and forth between Arnie and Heather. "I'm going with 'Have No Fear.'"

* * *

Heather received a phone call from Julie two days after the recording session. "I'm sorry to lay this on you, but I have some awful news."

"What's up?" asked Heather.

"I developed a viral infection in my throat, and my doctor recommended I stop singing for now." Heather wanted to sound sympathetic but couldn't muster much of it. Anticipating this very moment, she acknowledged Julie's clever excuse. "My friends say it's best if you go on without me. It may take a while to heal."

"Prioritize your health. Let us know when you get better." Heather spoke these words, knowing she'd never hear from Julie again.

* * *

Made in Heaven's rental van, packed with passengers and band equipment, made its way through the scruffy eastern reaches of Hollywood. Heather watched as two unhappy pedestrians puddle-jumped their way across the potholed street. It hardly ever rained in L.A., so of course, tonight, of all nights, it did. Angelenos treated mild showers like the end times, and this storm was decidedly not gentle. Arnie had promised them a club gig within a month and had delivered. Would their debut be a success? Heather wondered if anyone would bother coming to their official debut.

Arnie briefed the musicians as he drove. "We're running early. Showtime's at 9:00. Play for half an hour. Pretty sweet, right?"

Nobody said anything.

"Told your friends and family, right?"

A few muttered yeses.

"Tell them to drink a lot too. That's what gets ya called back."

Again, no response. Heather didn't have the heart to inform him all their friends were underage.

"C'mon, where's the energy? It's like a morgue in here."

Arnie slowed the van as it entered a somewhat desolate

stretch of Fountain Avenue, turning left onto a side street near their destination. He rolled down the window and shouted at a guy wearing a club jacket who had taken shelter under the marquee. "Back or front?" was all he asked.

The fellow pointed to the alley. Heather looked at the blinking neon sign and the tattered facade.

"The Wormhole?" she had noted incredulously when Arnie first revealed the venue earlier in the week.

"Ya think you can play the Palladium your first night?" he responded. She couldn't counter his reasoning at the time and let it go. Upon seeing the club firsthand, its reality fell far short of her imaginings.

With the van parked, Arnie slid open the side door. "Okay, grab something and head inside." The five band members struggled to 'grab something' without lingering too long in the downpour. Still, the effort to hustle only complicated the process. After they finally passed the burly security guard at the door, their outfits were soaked, their makeup streaked, and their coiffed hair lay limp.

Stepping into the harshly lit backstage area, the scene before them resembled a bunker from a Fallout game. The band faced perplexed stares from what seemed, initially, like a dozen members of an all-male motorcycle gang. A profusion of leather clothing, tattoos, facial hair, and piercings was on display. The girls huddled together like cornered prey.

One man with a soul patch, stringy black hair, and a Machine Head t-shirt looked at them, chuckled, and uttered, "What the fuck?" Heather noticed catcalls from across the room but refrained from glancing in that direction.

"Is this like Babymetal or some shit?" said a guy in a Slayer shirt with a bald head and a short, boxed beard. His companions laughed.

"Kono sukebe jiji me," whispered Mindy in Japanese under her breath.

Heather stifled a laugh. "Babymetal's Japanese," she whispered to Grace in Korean.

"Don't you think that's a little beside the point right now?" she responded in kind.

Arnie squeezed past the girls as they refused to budge. "What kind of club is this?" Grace whispered to him. Before he could answer, a beardless guy emerged from a side office. He appeared to be in his upper 50s and donned a long gray ponytail. Arnie greeted him with a broad smile and a bro hug. One look at the girls, however, and the beardless guy grew distraught. "What did you bring me here?" he asked, failing to put a positive inflection on his voice.

"Tim, this is Made in Heaven," Arnie said, presenting a copy of their band flyer.

Tim took one look at it and grimaced. "Dude, you made it sound like an Iron Maiden tribute band. What the hell is this?"

"You girls enjoy Iron Maiden, right?" Arnie asked. They stared at him in silence. "They're a K-pop group, but don't worry, they rock." This news generated snickers from among the 'biker gang.'

"A what? Dude, you're killing me here. What do I do with this?"

Arnie addressed his charges. "Don't worry. I got this." He ushered Tim into the office and shut the door. Heather could hear them locked in a heated debate. The girls lingered near the entryway as most of the guys lost interest in the newcomers.

Slayer guy, though, seemed intent on making amends for

his initial reception. He walked to a tattered leather couch, the most substantial furnishing in the room, and kicked the legs of its current sole occupant, a black-clad, scrawny teen. "Hey, dickhead, be polite for once." The teen grumbled but moved to a Marshall amp. With a broad sweep of his arm, Slayer guy motioned for them to approach the couch. Not wishing to cause a scene by resisting, Heather took the first tentative steps. The others soon followed. The five moved like a school of fish avoiding sharks. Scrawny kid shot them a resentful glance as they took tentative steps to occupy his former seat. Heather hoped that whatever substance stained the upholstery wouldn't transfer to their wet outfits.

The office door reopened after an interminable amount of small talk with Slayer guy. Tim approached. "Here's the deal. We're moving you off the 9:00 slot. You can start first or last. I'd recommend the former. The crowd won't be as drunk."

Erin looked to Mindy for reassurance but received none. After a brief discussion in Korean, the band conveyed their preference to go on at 7:00. All enthusiasm regarding their official debut had long vanished.

The primary advantage of the opening slot was the leisurely setup time it afforded. The house engineer conducted a soundcheck at 6:30, but seemed to prioritize chatting with his friends over ensuring the band sounded good. Once ready, the group congregated at the stage end of the bar, awaiting their call.

"We told everyone to be here by 9:00. What should we do?" asked Heather.

"We could text them," said Grace.

"Will anybody show?" inquired Erin.

"Do we want them to?" asked Mindy. "We might not *have*

any friends left after tonight."

The clock rolled to 7:00, then 7:15. No stage call came. A middle-aged female bartender in a sleeveless Sturgis t-shirt was wiping the bar near where the band waited when she spotted Sun-hee sitting on a stool, looking dismayed. "You sure do look like you could use a stiff drink," the woman said, "but if you're planning on sitting there, sweetie, I need to see some ID."

Sun-hee stood. "Sorry, I'm not old enough."

"What's wrong, honey?" asked the bartender. "You look like you've seen a ghost."

Sun-hee surveyed the room. "Are they going to kill us?"

The woman chuckled. "Who, these guys?" she said, indicating the clutch of muscled, leather-bound, middle-aged men gathered at the opposite end of the bar. "Nah. So long as you stay on their good side, you're in the safest place in America right now."

This statement did not seem to reassure Sun-hee. "So, how do we stay on their good side?" she asked.

"Keep doing what you're doing," the bartender explained. "Believe me, they ain't seen girls like you in this club since the Reagan administration." A customer called for attention at the far end of the bar, and she departed.

Once the woman moved beyond earshot, Heather wondered, "What do you suppose she meant by 'girls like us'?"

"From the looks of this place, I'm guessing girls who bathe regularly," said Erin. Unfortunately, the music ended on the PA system as she spoke, leaving the words hanging mid-air.

A blushing Mindy placed her finger over Erin's lips in a silencing gesture. "Just because you have an apparent death wish," she whispered, "doesn't mean you need to drag us all down with you."

At 7:30, Tim reemerged and instructed the girls to hit the stage. Heather counted 12 people in the main room, including staff. Not one of their guests had arrived.

The set opened with "Celestial." Heather thought it would be a wise choice since it was their hardest-driving song and stood the best chance of making a positive first impression with the 'crowd.' The rest of the band did not share this view. Erin lost the beat. Grace followed her into oblivion before migrating to Mindy's steadier rhythm after skipping a few bars. Mindy grew annoyed by the disjointedness displayed by her peers. Distracted by these observations, Heather missed one of her own lines, which caused Sun-hee to enter late.

The three audience members who were at least making a show of listening soon lost interest and instead joined in the general conversation. The sound guy sensed the vibe in the room and inched the volume toward zero. In less than a minute, their debut performance had been reduced to background noise. At the song's conclusion, nobody even acknowledged it. Heather looked at her dejected bandmates. This was far from the evening they had long dreamt about. She had to motivate them somehow.

Fortunately, Grace came to the rescue, stepping towards Mindy and motioning for the five to gather. "Believe it or not, it could be worse," she said.

"At least they didn't boo," said Erin.

"They'd have to care enough to boo," surmised Mindy.

"Okay, well, regardless, let's treat this as extra practice. From the sound of "Celestial," we could sure use it." Upon realizing their mistakes would go unnoticed, the band grew more at ease.

By the time their show ended, the club's patrons were greeting newcomers and oblivious to what marked Made in Heaven's first-ever gig. As if they weren't feeling beaten enough, the band that followed added insult to injury by not waiting for their equipment to be removed. Mindy looked ready to punch a guy shuttling her drum kit into a haphazard pile offstage without permission. Sun-hee calmed her so she wouldn't commit an action they'd later regret.

During the van ride home, the group argued, highlighted mistakes, and provided unsolicited advice. Arnie received the brunt of the vitriol for booking such a wildly inappropriate club.

"Show me a K-pop joint in L.A., and I'll book ya there," he responded.

The van stopped off at Grace's parents' house, where they unloaded equipment and went their separate ways, each vowing to do better next time. Their first club performance was in the books. Heather hoped for brighter days ahead, or her band idea would be short-lived.

9

NOW THINGS WILL CHANGE

On the morning of the "Have No Fear" video shoot, both dressing rooms at the Film & Television Building on campus were in bedlam. The women's room was overwhelmed by the need to prepare five female cast members simultaneously. In a pinch, they used the unoccupied men's room. The pungent aroma of ammonia and sodium hydroxide permeated the air in both spaces. It was a scent that brought back fond memories. Heather felt at home, at least to some extent.

To forget their lackluster club debut, she decided that a dramatic personal makeover was the ideal solution. To define the overall look of Made in Heaven, Steve brought on board Bryan Caprio, a promising fashion design student from Otis Parsons, who was of Brazilian and Italian descent. Three months earlier, they had met on the set of a Chanel commercial, where they discussed the possibility of collaborating. Bryan had brought assistants, João and Alejandra, fellow Otis students hoping to break into the industry as makeup artists.

The team was putting the finishing touches on Heather's

new short hairdo. Bryan had turned the chair away from the mirror for a dramatic unveiling after completion. Heather knew the transformation was dicey but proceeded anyway after seeing the quality of his portfolio. Even as an idol trainee, she made little effort to establish a distinct appearance. The designers would ultimately have their say, she reasoned. When the stylist presented his idea, Heather agreed, feeling the risk was worth the reward. If the concept failed, she could always wear a hat until it grew back.

Bryan's inspiration came from a dream he had of Anna Karina's pool hall dance scene in Jean-Luc Godard's *Vivre Sa Vie*. He proposed a modernized, voluminous, platinum-blonde version of Nana's bob from that movie. The style was a variation on the iconic Louise Brooks cut from *Pandora's Box*. Heather watched both films in the name of research and fell in love with the concept. "You need to understand. What you see today won't be the final color," Bryan explained. "You can't get from black to platinum in one session. But it will look fabulous for today's shoot."

"Okay."

"It'll take tremendous effort to keep it maintained. I'm warning you."

"Got it."

"The truth is not everyone can pull off this style, but the shape of your head and face are perfect for it."

"Oh my god," said Mindy as she entered the dressing room along with Erin and Sun-hee. The three stared, eyes shifting back and forth between the mirrored image and the live person. Their mouths hung open in surprised delight.

"Have you seen it yet?" asked Sun-hee.

"Not yet." Heather bit her lip in anticipation.

"Saejaelyae."

"You resemble a goddess," said Erin, only half-joking.

Heather's patience was crumbling. Tempted to defy her stylist's wishes by peeking, she decided not to anger him. Seeing the others' results only increased her excitement. Sun-hee's hip-length hair had been dyed the color of milk tea. The stylist crimped several strands to accent her face. Erin's long black hair now cascaded down one shoulder instead of mid-back. Mindy's hair, trimmed to her shoulders, featured a classic red dye with curled ends.

"You all look fantastic," Heather said. Her eyes shifted to and fro as she attempted to take them all in without moving her head. "Where's Grace?"

"Ta-da," her friend announced as she slid into Heather's view from the right. The boundless enthusiasm on display signaled complete satisfaction with the results. Grace received a flirty, fierce, chin-length, electro-purple bob with straight bangs.

"Wait 'til you see the outfits," said Mindy. "Honestly, they're better than the ones we had for WeR5."

Steve's friend Marielle Brodeur, an American of French-Canadian ancestry, had volunteered to help with costuming. Her day job at a prominent costume rental shop was a vital consideration. With the aim of becoming a costume designer, Marielle viewed Steve's music video as a chance to hone her skills. She had taken the girls' measurements the week prior but only hinted at the ultimate plan.

When Bryan finished with Heather's hair, the wait wasn't over. For maximum visual impact, Alejandra insisted on finishing her makeup first. Heather closed her eyes and held still to facilitate the process. As she neared the breaking point,

Alejandra uttered the magic words: "Are you ready?"

"Do you need to ask?"

Bryan turned the chair around.

She didn't recognize the person looking back at her from the mirror; the unfamiliar image was startling. True to Bryan's instincts, an inverted bob consummately suited Heather's small and delicate facial features. Rather than trimming the bangs straight across her forehead, he left them longer on the sides, akin to theater curtains on a proscenium. The bob's front edge flipped under and conformed to her jawline. Stacked layers in the back, trimmed to below the tips of her ears, adhered meticulously to the shape of her head, evoking an almost helmet-like effect. Dark liner made her bright eyes pop, especially in contrast to the light-colored hair. The result of this transformation was electric, being at once slightly old-fashioned yet excitingly modern. It both thrilled and terrified her.

"Marvelous. You should show it to Steve," suggested Grace.

Heather took that advice, leaping into the air as if electroshocked. It didn't take long to find him. He was on the loading dock supervising two crew members as they packed the equipment van. She stood in silence, wondering if the team would notice. Being immersed in their work, they did not. Clearing her throat also failed to gain their attention. Steve was placing a Fresnel lantern in the back of the van when she addressed him. "Will this work?" Heather adopted a cute pose and framed her face aegyo-style for maximum impact.

Upon noticing her, Steve's jaw dropped. So did the lantern, slipping from his grasp and shattering on the concrete floor. Neither Steve nor the two crew members reacted. They simply stared.

Heather stifled a laugh as the three remained in stasis. "Are you okay?" she asked, while pointing. "That looked expensive."

"What?" Steve glanced at the remnants of the lamp, which he doubtlessly would have to pay for. "Oh, yeah. No prob. Yeah, that looks good, Heather. Real good." Steve kept staring. Meaningful utterances escaped him.

"I'll just finish getting ready then," she said, pointing at the dressing room only steps away. Now embodying her borrowed Nana persona to the fullest, Heather sashayed away from the boys with the sound of Michel Legrand's "Swing! Swing! Swing!" playing in her head. She understood innately the effect she was having on the audience in question. Her confidence soared.

* * *

The caravan crossed the Mojave Desert north of Los Angeles in the heat of the midday sun. One equipment van, one passenger minivan, two cars, and 18 people made their way to a spot best described as the middle of nowhere. The destination remained unknown to Heather. Steve had a specific location in mind, but kept it a mystery to everyone else. The minivan carried the five musicians, Alejandra, Marielle, and driver Gil. With four crew members each and various supplies, the two cars were fully loaded.

Steve planned to light the set and block action in the afternoon while filming the bulk of the video during golden hour, the period of soft light before sunset. The cast and a skeleton crew would stay overnight at a nearby campground for early morning shots. The remaining team members would travel home the same day.

After miles of flat desert, Heather watched a small group of low hills appear on the horizon. In the center of this geographic landmark, two roads met at a T: one paved and one gravel. A collection of buildings sat at this intersection, looking as if someone had plucked them straight off Route 66 during its 1960s heyday. The caravan pulled into the unfenced lot.

As the cast and crew emerged from their vehicles, Steve announced in his best MC voice, "Welcome to Crossroads Movie Ranch." After receiving initial instructions, the production team expressed its approval and bolted into action. They unloaded the film equipment, erected a cooling station for the cast, and arranged food on the craft services table. As Steve monitored the activity, Heather approached. "How much did this place cost?"

Steve looked at her coyly. "You don't see a fee collector, do you?"

Heather's eyebrows arched. "Rolling the dice, I presume?"

Steve placed a hand on her shoulder and responded, "I like living on the edge."

When Gil requested keys to the buildings, Steve said. "We only have permission to film outside."

Heather stifled a giggle. "Permission, huh?"

"They'd have given it to me if I asked."

"And paid."

Shandi Perkins was the director of photography. Steve decided to film the entire video via drone, except for the opening and closing images, and she possessed the best piloting skills at the university. Besides making dramatic overhead shots possible, he believed this technique was most efficient for capturing various angles without wasting limited daylight on multiple camera resets.

As the production crew scurried about like ants, Heather assessed the film lot. Something told her she'd seen it before. "Hey. This is like that Red Velvet video!"

Sun-hee, who stood nearby, agreed. "You're right. 'Ice Cream Cake.'"

Steve approached them, his complexion paler than before. "What do you mean?"

"You've heard of Red Velvet, right?" asked Heather.

"Yeah," he responded, sounding about as unsteady as a drunk on roller skates.

"'Ice Cream Cake' was filmed here. I think."

Steve appeared vexed by this news and demanded proof. Several phones searched for signals, but the remote location made establishing a connection difficult.

"If I can get on higher ground, I might be able to pick something up on mine," suggested Heather. The team put up a ladder at Steve's behest to access the roof. Once there, Steve and Heather resumed signal hunting. What they found was weak, but sufficient to allow for a substantially buffered view of the music video. Sure enough, Steve could recognize the place. "That's the Four Aces Movie Ranch, not far from here. I swear I've never seen this video before. This is a disaster."

"What's wrong?"

"I'll be dismissed as a copycat. I'm screwed."

"K-pop groups steal from each other constantly," said Heather.

"Not me. Besides, if I wanted to be cliché, I'd have filmed at Vasquez Rocks. And what the hell is a Korean girl group doing in the middle of the California desert, anyway?"

Heather adored the irony. "As a matter of fact, I've been asking myself that all day."

Steve ignored the comment. "I designed this concept for Radial Elliott and didn't have time to change it. What am I going to do?"

"At least ours is a band, not a dance group."

"That's not enough," he responded. "I need a new wrinkle to make it mine." Heather watched as Steve paced what would have been the canopy of the gas pumps if the building had been an actual service station. The sun was taking its toll on her stamina. She opted to leave for the shade. As she descended the ladder, Steve cursed while stubbing his foot on some protrusion. Once back on the ground, Alejandra handed Heather a portable fan to keep cool. She found a spot in the shade to wait. Minutes later, Steve joined her. "I got it!" he said. "We have a drone."

This scant response offered no explanation at all. Before she could inquire further, Mindy approached, asking, "Where do you want us, boss?"

Steve pointed above his head, indicating the roof of the gas station.

Heather's eyebrows arched. "Up there? Are you serious?"

"Yup. Pretend you're the Beatles, but instead of central London, you'll sing to...I don't know...coyotes."

Heather looked baffled. "Do coyotes like K-pop?"

"They're surprisingly cosmopolitan, I'm told." Steve barked new orders to the crew. "Jason, get the band equipment on the roof. Have a team help you. I need inkies and diffusion there too."

Meanwhile, the crew erected a tent to serve as a makeshift green room for the musicians. Inside, the girls were gathered around a portable cooler as the stylists touched up their hair and makeup. When it came time to dress, Heather admired their new outfits. Marielle received a set of parameters to forge the group's identity. The goal was to project an image of confidence and control. Fun, flirty, and sexy without appearing either too trampy or cutesy. Balance was key. Other than that, she was free to be creative.

Her outfits comprised pieces borrowed from the rental house, but custom-tailored for each member. Sun-hee's presentation underscored her feminine qualities. It included a flared leather skirt extending to mid-thigh and a high-necked, short-sleeved top that exposed her slender midriff. Grace exuded confidence in skin-tight leather pants with a tank top and a studded leather jacket. Erin's garb was playful, with a flat-brimmed baseball cap, a leather raglan-sleeved princess-cut dress, and hose. Mindy's spirited outfit consisted of shorts and a cowl-neck blouse. Marielle used a faded blue denim jacket in tandem with a pencil miniskirt and black blouse to reflect Heather's charm. All five members wore unique pairs of heeled boots. The predominant material was black leather, with white and navy-blue cotton fabric splashes to tie the ensemble together.

Gil Parkhurst, an exchange student from England, had the task of photographing the band members for promotional purposes. He chose shaded areas around the lot to pose each member. The group shot took place near a magnificent Joshua tree.

As the sun dipped towards the horizon, the intense heat weakened. Steve ordered the band in place, which was easier said than done. Their heeled boots proved a hindrance to ladder climbing. "I didn't want to die this way," complained

Erin on her wobbly ascent.

"Wait 'til we climb down," said Heather.

Once on the canopy, Erin continued to find fault with the working conditions. "Eww, it's filthy here," she said as she approached her bass amidst the dust and debris.

"Welcome to glamorous show biz," responded Grace.

Steve stayed on the roof long enough to block the scene, then returned to the ground to discuss his options with Shandi. To capture the best light, there was just enough time for one practice run with the musicians in place. The plan was to go through the song several times, focusing on medium range and close-ups of each member. A wide-angle master shot would follow, encompassing the entire group. If timed well, this master would align with sunset, presenting the sky at its most opulent. The first rehearsal revealed a slight hitch. Because the members were all of different heights, Shandi had to adjust the drone's altitude each time she flew from one musician to another. Steve instructed the three shortest members, Heather, Grace, and Erin to stand on apple boxes to even out the cast. This adjustment delayed the first take by 15 minutes.

Since the on-camera mics were dummies only and not recording, Heather and Sun-hee could sing out loud in time with the music playback. This method, Steve felt, would produce the most natural-looking results. Mindy was told to play the drums live as her timing was spot on each take. Steve was less concerned with guitar and bass-playing accuracy since they would be less noticeable on camera. Instead, he encouraged those musicians to interact with the camera as much as possible.

Shandi used different flying patterns to give Steve plenty of editing coverage later. They managed to play through the song three times before a surprise visitor arrived. Upon finishing the close-up run, a cloud of dust in the distance signaled the imminent arrival of a vehicle. It was the first one they'd seen all day. The white Jeep Cherokee slowed to a crawl as it approached the crossroads. The driver stared at the crew, vehicles, and equipment covering the breadth of the lot.

"Looks like we have company," said Erin. The production team held its breath as the Jeep lingered at the intersection for an eternity before turning onto the paved road and speeding away.

"What do you suppose that means?" asked Grace as the band watched from the roof.

"That our luck's about to run out," Heather surmised.

"All right, let's finish this," shouted Steve from his chair at the playback monitor.

The showpiece master shot was designed as a single take, with the drone starting in a hover position directly in front of the band. During the song's crescendo, the drone ascended and retreated, exposing widening vista of surrounding ter-rain. Shandi aborted the first attempt because the propellers vibrated on ascent. The second attempt went smoothly, but after watching the playback, Steve remained unhappy. "The sun's still too high, and the sky's too bright," he explained over the walkie-talkie. "Relax for a bit, but stay in positions." As they waited patiently, the white Cherokee returned. This time, instead of driving by, the driver pulled into the lot and stopped near Meadow. The two exchanged words before she pointed out Steve's location.

A tall, overweight man in his mid-30s, wearing a trucker cap and a Houston Astros shirt, emerged from the vehicle. Peering past the roof's brink, the band witnessed the exchange out of sheer curiosity. The driver approached Steve and asked, "What prodvction company is this? I didn't hear of a booking this weekend."

"Miracle Pictures," responded Steve.

"Miracle Pictures?" the man responded with a smirk.

"You know what they say. 'If it's good, it's a Miracle.'"

The driver looked neither amused nor convinced. "I'll have to call this in." He dialed a number on his phone. As the guy waited for someone to pick up, Steve looked at Heather with a sheepish grin. The man shook his phone in frustration. "Damn service out here. Stay put. I'm driving into town to ask Freddy." He returned to his Cherokee and disappeared down the desert highway.

Before the dust could settle, Steve shouted, "Places, every-one! This is our last attempt."

A single run would have to suffice. The unexpected delay meant the sky would appear darker in the shot than Steve would have preferred. Shandi adjusted the exposure as much as she dared, and they went for it. The take wasn't perfect. By then, evening winds were stirring, which caused slight vibrations. However, the pullback was well executed, and the band suffered no miscues. During video playback, Steve concluded that the sunset would look radiant once color-corrected. Rather than risk lingering until the Jeep returned, he accepted the shot for what it was and called for a wrap.

The crew packed hastily, lacking the care with which they had started the day. Most gear and crew not needed for the morning shoot would travel back to L.A. in two vehicles. With the sun setting, two sets of headlights approached. "Meet you at the rendezvous point," shouted Steve, waving farewell to his L.A.-bound cohorts.

The groups fled in separate directions away from the approaching menace. Steve instructed his group to keep the headlights off as long as possible. Heather kept glancing out the rear window to check if they were being followed. When the pursuing vehicles reached the crossroads, she was relieved to see them follow the L.A. group without hesitation.

10

SOJU AND RAMEN

By the time the overnight group arrived at their campsite, the sun had long since set. Utter darkness pervaded; the moon would not appear for many hours. For lifelong city dwellers unaccustomed to the task, arranging camping equipment by flashlight was an exercise in exasperating futility. Steve claimed to be a former Boy Scout with plenty of desert camping experience. He tasked Jason with assisting. Steve also recruited Erin, whose sole qualification was a onetime family vacation to Yellowstone. They aimed to establish four tents for 10 occupants. While Gil built a fire, Meadow organized the cooking area. Shandi concentrated on cleaning and prepping the camera equipment for the following day. The remaining cast members pitched in wherever they could.

Mindy made herself useful by shining a flashlight on the work crews as needed. She watched Erin with amusement. The girl was a study in contrasts. Despite being graceful on the dance floor, she was comically awkward in most other situations. Wide-eyed and innocent, her default expression resembled a newborn kitten dropped by the side of a freeway. Erin grew discouraged after 15 minutes of trying to fit tent poles into fabric loops, only to find she had missed some each time.

"Why don't you rest?" said Mindy, struggling not to laugh. "You've had a long day." Erin's frown turned to delight. She wasted no time accepting her unnie's suggestion. Mindy had watched enough to comprehend the basic principles of tent assembly and got to work.

Sun-hee and Heather found some battery-powered lamps in the equipment van. The added illumination made everyone's job much more manageable. Tents were soon ready; the water for instant noodles boiled, and the warmth of the campfire staved off the cool desert air. The burning mesquite smell made Mindy yearn for barbecue before she knew the menu.

Even with rudimentary facilities, the volunteer chefs Meadow and Grace made their evening dinner a success. The crew's half-starved condition contributed to their positive reaction, but the meal also had some welcome inspiration. Grace brought extra ingredients to enhance the dish, following her mom's advice. The makeshift budae jjigae, or army stew, was a smash hit even among non-Koreans. To the instant noodles were added: Spam, Vienna sausages, pork and beans, enoki and oyster mushrooms, green onions, cheese slices, and, of course, kimchi.

Naturally, there was alcohol, too. As the unnie of the group, and at 22, the one member over the legal drinking age, Mindy brought along some bottles of soju to warm the party's spirits. She doubted authorities would check IDs anytime soon and heard no complaints when she revealed the treasure.

"What is this stuff?" asked Erin. "It's...interesting." The

four other Koreans stopped what they were doing and stared at her in disbelief. Erin looked embarrassed. "What?"

"You're Korean and don't know what soju is?" queried Mindy.

"I'm telling you, I lived a sheltered life," explained Erin. The looks she was receiving intimidated her. "Give me a break. I was the only Asian in my hometown."

"That must've been rough," said Heather.

"Uh, where do I begin?" She paused for a moment. "Don't take what I'm about to say wrong. My adoptive parents were wonderful. They'd have supported me if I wanted to embrace my heritage."

"But you didn't," said Mindy.

"Not then." Erin, delighted to be the center of attention for once, rambled. "My town had 3,000 people in it. I was an outsider. That's if people paid any attention to me at all. Truthfully, when they weren't making fun of my eyes and telling me I was ugly, I was basically invisible, which was better than the alternative. Outside of movies, I didn't see another Asian until I went to Oklahoma City when I was nine, so you can't blame me for preferring hamburgers and pizza, can you? The closest thing we had to Asian food was canned chow mein at the grocery store."

This comment produced an outburst of laughter. At first, Erin looked hurt by their reaction, but gradually saw the humor in the situation.

"A frog in a well can't know the sea," said Mindy.

"Sorry for laughing," said Sun-hee, "I can't even imagine."

Erin continued, "Seriously, I didn't want to have anything to do with Korea back then. I blamed my birth parents for abandoning me. My goal was to act as American as possible to fit in. If I embraced my culture, I would've been even more isolated."

"It'd have been way easier if you'd lived in California," said Grace.

"When I got older, my curiosity grew, but my options remained limited. I read every book on Korea at the library at least six times each. When I expressed an interest in attending university in L.A., my parents understood. I couldn't believe my luck when you invited me to join this group. It was like a dream come true."

Shandi left the table. "All right, guys, thanks for the stories, but I'm calling it a night. Keep it down, will you? We need sleep."

"What are we doing tomorrow?" asked Heather.

"The opening and closing shots," explained Steve. "You'll be walking down the highway, the sun rising behind you. It should look awesome. We'll need to wake well before dawn to get ready in time." He ignored their collective groans. Meadow, Jason, and Gil used that prompt to retire as well.

The five band members and Steve moved to the campfire, where Mindy gave the uninitiated a primer on proper etiquette for drinking soju. She noted that the maknae's job, as the youngest of the group, was to keep the glasses of her elders full. Erin expressed her displeasure at this news.

The drinkers talked into the night. As the one among them who had been a K-pop idol at one time, Mindy fielded many questions. Most were trivial, but some delved into weighty topics.

"Is it true that idols aren't allowed to date?" Steve asked.

"Are you serious?" exclaimed Erin.

"Deadly serious, especially for the younger, less-established groups," explained Mindy. "Idols must appear innocent yet desirable at the same time. The fantasy is shattered if they're seen dealing with messy love interests."

"It reminds me of the old studio system in Hollywood in how they controlled the image of their stars," said Steve.

"That's the goal, but the reality is different." Mindy was now basking in their undivided attention. "Think about it. You've got these gorgeous young people working together in the prime of their youth. Things are bound to happen. Hear what I'm saying? The fact is, they do sometimes date, but must hide it. If the news broke, it would cause a scandal, bring shame to the company, and result in dismissal from the group."

"For dating?" asked Erin.

"I've seen it happen," confirmed Mindy.

"The veil of perfection surrounding idols is inviolable," added Grace.

"How do they hide it?" asked Erin.

"With the whole world watching your every move, it's not easy. Also, young groups live in chaperoned dorms, meaning they have no privacy. Ever. Love hotels are off-limits too because they'd draw immediate attention."

"So, what do they do?" asked Steve.

"Get creative," said Mindy. "We'd borrow someone's car with tinted windows and find a private parking place."

Erin laughed. "We used to call those submarine races in high school." The statement caused the group to stare at her in surprise. Erin quickly qualified her observation, "That's what I heard." Once again, they burst into laughter.

"Sure, Erin, I bet you won your fair share of races," teased Grace.

"I'm serious," she said, laughing.

Mindy continued, "Honestly, I'd still advise discretion when posting your relationships on social media. Avoid trouble. Fans can be possessive. And boyfriends, too, come to think of it."

"Do you miss it?" asked Sun-hee. "Being an idol, I mean."

"Not to sugarcoat things," she responded. "Looking back, I'm glad I left when I did. At first, I was in shock. I refused to listen to K-pop for over two years after leaving. The industry is universally rough, but girls have it worst."

"How so?" asked Steve.

"Boy bands have been known to make mistakes and recover in the eyes of the public. If a girl group slips even once, that usually spells the end of their careers. The pressure for perfection is immense. You're under constant scrutiny. By the time WeR5 disbanded, we weren't enjoying it anymore. The stress was too much."

The group sat in silence. Heather was lost in thought. Mindy snatched a small branch from the ground to play with the fire.

"What brought you back?" asked Erin.

"I hope to re-spark my love of performing again."

"What did you mean leaving was a shock?"

"The way it ended."

"You had a contract dispute, right? That's what I read," said Grace.

"The agency tried to save face by spreading that story. The truth was much messier. Our company was young, with inexperienced backers. They felt substantial pressure to succeed immediately and didn't understand how long it takes to build a fan base. Our debut didn't go well. No matter how hard we worked, our numbers wouldn't increase. One day, they called us into the office for a meeting. We thought it was about our next album. Instead, we were replaced. Like that," she said, snapping her fingers, "Gone in an instant."

"Brutal," said Steve.

"We, of course, protested, but they insisted we'd never be popular. The backers didn't want to lose their brand investment, so they reformed the group with new members under the same name." She tossed a small branch she fiddled with into the fire and watched the flames pop before continuing. "For years, we were treated like family there. As soon as that meeting ended, security guards arrived to escort us to our lockers and then out the front door. Wouldn't even let us say goodbye to staff."

"Jeez," said Steve.

"As if that wasn't hurtful enough, we ran into our replacements on the way out. All were trainees we'd worked with before. They'd known for days but couldn't comment. We just stood there, eying each other. Out with the old; in with the new."

"Talk about awkward," said Grace.

"What happened to them?" asked Erin.

"They disbanded a year later. Not surprising. The few WeR5 fans who remained rejected the newcomers, and the complete overhaul confused everyone else."

As the logs in the fire cooled to a deep orange glow, Grace shifted them, reigniting the flames and brightening the campsite.

Mindy continued. "I remember the first day of idol training. The instructor told us to raise our hands if we were leads in our school plays or first chairs in our orchestras. Every single person did. Then he goes, 'You're here now. And in this place, you're nothing. Get used to it.'"

Heather, who had listened silently for most of the evening, shared her thoughts. "A trainer once told me, 'If you can imagine yourself doing anything other than being an idol, do it.' At first, I thought he was dissing me, but later, I understood it to mean I'd need that level of passion to succeed."

"I hope I'm not out of bounds by asking," Mindy said, "but why did you leave your agency? Grace said the truth should come from your mouth."

Heather grew distraught. While staring into the fire, she tore off tiny bits of bark from the stick in her hand and tossed them in. They only heard the sputter and snap of flames consuming the extra fuel. When she spoke, it was only to confirm her reticence. "This isn't the right time."

Mindy felt bad about touching a raw nerve. As a distraction, she called on Erin to pour another round. As the cumulative effects of soju took hold, the conversation shifted into Korean. Steve became a mere observer. Erin, too, looked perplexed as she struggled to keep pace with the frenetic conversation. During one pause, Steve interjected with a silly question. "What is this egg yolk I keep hearing about?" This caused an eruption of laughter.

"Aegyo, not egg yolk," said Heather with a smile. "How to explain it?"

Mindy offered her take. "Aegyo is the Korean art of cute flirtation. It's useful when you want to gain influence in a non-intimidating fashion. All idols learn at least some, and new aegyo often goes viral because of an idol."

This topic brightened the mood. The four veterans, Sun-hee, Mindy, Grace, and Heather, demonstrated some well-known examples, ranging from simple hand gestures like finger hearts to full aegyo songs for the benefit of their less experienced friends. This developed into a competition as each tried to elicit the biggest response from their audience. Mindy sang "Gwiyomi" while Sun-hee offered her version of the "Confession Song." Heather shared an original aegyo song. But it was Grace who dropped the mic with an excellent "I dreamt of a ghost" aegyo. Collective laughter greeted her performance, and everyone agreed she had won. Mindy found it endearing to see the ordinarily deadpan Grace become the life of the party.

Heather soon reversed the situation by issuing a 'Baby Shark' challenge to Steve and Erin.

"You mean that's an aegyo song?" asked Steve.

"Yes, and neither of you are escaping it," said Grace.

The crowd chanted their names in unison until both relented. Mindy provided a basic tutorial on how it worked, then turned her pupils loose to face their critics. Erin, as expected, was well-suited for aegyo. Though her execution was unpolished, she possessed an innately cute way of moving that complemented her latent talent. Conversely, Steve looked ridiculous, and his attempt to repeat what he had just learned sent the girls into fits. Heather was so tickled that she lost balance and toppled off her rocky perch.

Suddenly, a voice boomed from one tent. "Shut! The Fuck! Up!" Shandi was not amused.

This outburst doused all laughter. The six delinquents sealed their lips to comply with the demand, though not without a few giggles and pointing accusations.

"We should get some sleep," whispered Steve. "I'll be waking you in a couple hours anyway."

* * *

The following Wednesday, a school night, Erin double-checked the time. It was midnight. The light remained on in Mindy's apartment. Erin realized she had taken a gamble in driving from Westchester to Hollywood without knowing whether her unnie was awake. But she had a favor to ask and decided that an in-person visit was better than an impersonal text. She tentatively knocked on the door, hoping an angry roommate wouldn't answer.

Thankfully, Mindy opened the door. She looked unsurprised. "Sexiled again?"

Erin nodded without saying a word. The pillow and blanket she clutched must've communicated her plight.

"You're in luck. My immediate roommate's in San Diego visiting her folks. The other two are in Big Bear."

Erin beamed. "Oh, thank you. You're a lifesaver. I was so worried I'd be sleeping in my car again. It's cold tonight, and the thought of—"

Mindy cut her off. "I was making ramen," she offered. "Want some?"

Erin tried to nod without appearing too desperate. "I skipped dinner."

As Mindy went to the kitchen to finish preparations, Erin surveyed the apartment. The mismatched furniture comprised hand-me-downs in various stages of dilapidation. Mindy's drum kit sat in a far corner of the room, squeezed between a tattered armchair and an unwatered plant. The floor lay cluttered with clothing and other personal items, including boxes that remained unopened. The lack of shelf space explained why many objects were stored on the floor. Walls were bereft of decor beyond a few random music posters thumb-tacked in unexpected places. Apart from the kitchen, which was bathed in a cold and bright fluorescent light, the sole illumination source in the apartment was a shadeless living room lamp. The contents of a sewing kit spilled across the dining room table. Piled next to it was a red cloth.

"What are you working on?"

"Marielle was teaching me to sew," said Mindy, speaking from the kitchen. "I've always wanted to learn. Could come in handy for outfits. The tablecloth is for practice."

"Can I see?"

"Knock yourself out." Erin wasted no time clearing the table of items, unfolding the cloth, and smoothing out its wrinkles. Her attempts to line it up with the table edges were unsuccessful. Its corners had been cut at odd angles, preventing a match. "How's it look?" Mindy asked from the next room.

"Um...good," responded Erin.

Mindy entered the dining nook, carrying two steaming bowls of ramen. Upon spotting her handiwork, she marveled at its awfulness, then giggled as she set the meal on the table. "Marielle has no reason to fear me."

"True," agreed Erin, relieved to see her jovial reaction.

"It's harder than it looks." Mindy invited her to sit. "I added gochujang, some bok choy, a hard-boiled egg, and a dab of soy sauce," she explained. "Also, sriracha. Hope you don't mind."

"If I knew what half of that was, I'd let you know. Smells amazing, though."

"I keep forgetting you're a newb when it comes to Asian food." Erin attempted to eat noodles with chopsticks but kept losing them long before they reached her mouth. She discarded the unfamiliar utensils and chose a fork instead. "Don't give up. You'll adjust," encouraged Mindy.

Erin rolled her ramen spaghetti-style and took one bite. "Mmm, it's delicious. You made it so fast. Mine are always so boring."

"The key is quality noodles. Don't bother with standard grocery store crap. Go to an Asian market."

"I tried once. Saw a million different packages in an aisle a mile long. No clue what to do with any of it."

"We'll go shopping soon. I'll teach you Noodles 101."

Erin tasted the broth but found it too hot. "Are you still seeing that guy?" she asked. "What's his name?"

"You mean Bryce? No, that's over. What a coward. Not even the decency to tell me in person."

"How'd you find out?"

"His dog unfollowed me on Instagram last week. That's when I knew the jig was up." Mindy shrugged as if it were no big deal. "The kiss of death." She added a few sprigs of Thai basil to her ramen. "So, what's up, buttercup? Your roommate at it again?"

"Oh my god, it's getting worse." Erin's pent-up emotions got the better of her. Words poured forth in a torrent. "When this first started, it would be different guys once or twice a week. Now, it's out of control. Tonight, she had *two* with her at once. I stayed long enough to grab my stuff but saw things I never imagined."

Mindy at first smiled, then broke into a hearty laugh. "Seriously? Wow! Her sex life sounds so much better than mine."

"They always encourage me to stay, but would you be comfortable with all that going on?"

"Maybe they're hoping you join in," Mindy suggested. "Sounds like they could use a fourth."

"Mindy!" Erin scolded.

"I'm teasing," she snickered. "I agree, though. It's inconsiderate. Is this the same roommate you started the year with?"

"Same one."

"Didn't she take a purity oath of some kind?"

"She did, at her bible school in Kentucky. When she began the semester, she'd quote scripture to explain why she was staying a virgin until marriage. Boy, not anymore."

"What happened?"

"Who knows? When this became a problem, I confronted her and said, 'You used to call your body the temple of the Lord.'"

"How'd she respond?"

"She goes, 'It still is. I'm just letting as many worshippers in as possible.'"

Mindy choked a loud laugh and clapped her hands in delight, "Oh, that's classic. I have to remember that one."

Mindy's reaction surprised Erin, but she appreciated the humor and laughed, too. "Is my roommate bad?"

Mindy smiled at the question as if she found it precious, but answered it honestly. "Well, here's the thing. Guys can sleep around as much as they want, and nobody cares. When women do the same thing? Yeah, good luck with that. It's not right, but that's reality." Erin's reaction must've signaled to Mindy that her answer was incomplete, so she continued. "Listen, do what your comfortable with, but just realize people will talk. You know how to avoid pregnancy and STDs, right?"

Erin nodded.

"What are you planning to do?"

"I don't want to rock the boat. My roommate's pretty nice most of the time. I could sleep in the car. It's only for one year."

"Well, you can stay here if I have room."

Erin's broth had cooled, and she ate more vigorously. After they finished and cleaned the dishes, including those left behind by the roommates, they got ready for bed. Before retiring to her room, Mindy prepared the couch with an extra sheet and pillow. Erin, in the meantime, mustered the courage to present another revelation. "Remember the night of the campfire when we shot our video? You all discussed dating and stuff and teased me about my boyfriends in high school."

"I hope you didn't think we were laughing at you."

"Can I tell you a secret?"

"Of course."

"I've never, you know...I still haven't..." she hesitated.

Mindy extended a finger to stop her from continuing. "Okay, first of all, don't say, 'lost your virginity.' That sounds so negative. I prefer the phrase 'making your sexual debut.'"

Erin laughed, relieved that she wasn't being ridiculed. "My parents told me to wait until marriage, but that doesn't seem so important to anyone here. Everybody talks about sex so much. I wonder if there's something wrong with me."

"Keep this in mind. Before you know it, your parents will go from saying, 'Don't ever have sex,' to asking, 'Where are the grandkids?' Is that even remotely fair? Don't pressure yourself. When you're ready, it'll happen. Just make sure he's considerate." Mindy thought about it. "And avoid doing it for his sake. It should be your choice."

"I thought by coming to college, I'd master adulting, but

now I'm more confused than ever."

"Don't wish your life away. Enjoy the moment."

"You handle things so well. Meanwhile, smogging the car or doing the laundry without destroying my clothes kicks me in the butt."

"You give me far too much credit," Mindy said as she tossed her arms open wide. "Does this look like the home of a woman who has her act together?"

Erin scanned the apartment once more, despite knowing what she'd find. "Okay, I wasn't going to mention it," she said with a giggle, "but I see your point."

* * *

While driving to work the next day, Mindy pondered her life choices. If she was being candid, the past week had been a blast. It was exhilarating to create something in tandem with like-minded people. Also, she felt important. Since joining Made in Heaven, she noticed the subtle ways the other girls deferred to her experience. They valued what she had to say; they took her advice. That never happened with WeR5 or even the record store. But this sentiment came at a cost. In order to record the EP and film the music video, she'd have to request time off work, and on busy weekends. Being a regular employee meant days off were never an issue. Part of the upside of working in retail was its flexibility after all. Repeated absences no longer sat well with Brad. He was the one who had to pick up whatever duties she slacked on. And Mindy knew from experience that the band conflicts would only increase. Contrary to her expectations, the indie band possessed talent and ambition. The initial prediction that they'd quickly fold looked misguided now.

On the other hand, it seemed like the height of folly to reject the one career opportunity open to her in favor of an endeavor that amounted to storming the quixotic windmill. Made in Heaven was unlikely to provide an adequate living for seven members and support staff, let alone turn a profit. That wasn't a reflection on the group itself, merely a truth about the music business. Hard work and talent were only part of the equation. The rest came down to luck. Yet she couldn't help but love the idea that they were at least willing to try.

For one thing, she felt alive again. Not long ago, Mindy convinced herself that those feelings were dead forever. Heather's invitation changed everything.

After parking in the employee lot of Amorphous Records, Mindy studied her reflection in the rearview mirror. Under direct sunlight, she noticed faint wrinkles near her eyes for the first time. Emerging from the vehicle, her course of action became clear. Inside, she found Brad in his office, surrounded as usual by stacks of paper. She knocked on the open door to get his attention. He looked up but did not smile.

"Hi Brad, can we talk?"

11

ROLLING IN DOUGH

After weeks of fruitless modeling auditions, the first spark of hope June received came from the unlikeliest of sources: her own TikTok account. The direct message read:

"You have been shortlisted in our modeling database, and we would like to offer you the chance to come to our studio in the next couple of weeks for a trial photoshoot."

None of her tryouts had thus far resulted in even a callback. People warned her often that modeling was a tricky business to break into. Still, the constant rejection via silence was disheartening. Then, just when her spirits were at their lowest, this message arrived. Someone had finally noticed her! Enough to reach out directly, even. June wasted no time in responding. Within an hour, she received a phone call from someone named Jake.

"I sorry. English no good," she told him.

"That's absolutely no problem at all," he said in the friendliest of tones. "We work with a global clientele." June only recognized half of his words but could construct their rough meaning through context and repetition. Slowly, she extracted the most pertinent information. Jake proved patient throughout the entire conversation. He described Spectra Pacific as a scouting service for modeling agencies. June's lack of experience was not a hindrance, he assured her. The service made money by identifying new talent and guiding them through the process. "Your immediate need is new headshots," Jake said. "Once we do the shoot, we'll better understand your potential. If it proves successful, we'll help you build a portfolio of the highest standards."

June got an address with instructions to arrive in two days. She was to bring five or six outfit changes and leave hair and makeup undone, as they would be professionally handled. From her limited wardrobe, she could piece together just three decent outfits. Her arms trembled during the bus trip to the studio. However, the warm greetings she received upon arrival put her at ease. The photographer gushed throughout the shoot itself, calling June a natural. It took two hours to complete the entire process. Afterward, she waited in the sparsely furnished foyer while they selected the best shots.

A smiling white woman approached and introduced herself as Cathy. She led June to a small room with dimmed lights. A large monitor illuminated an array of photographs. "These are the rare days I look forward to the most," said Cathy. "We normally only pick 20 images, but yours are so good we wouldn't settle for less than four dozen." June flushed red with the barrage of compliments she continued to receive throughout the review.

Then came the unexpected news. Cathy advised June that only by purchasing a portfolio package would she be able to maximize her considerable potential. "The packages start as low as $399.00," she said. Cathy let that information sink in. June knew she couldn't immediately access that amount in cash and hadn't yet qualified for a credit card. When June failed to respond, Cathy continued. "It sounds like a lot, I know, but your potential is limitless. In fact, I wouldn't even bother with the lowest tier if I were you. Let me fill you in on a little secret. Fashion Week is coming up. If you upgrade to the deluxe tier, we'll showcase you for the most prestigious agencies."

"That so much," June said.

"All up to you. Can you really put a price on your future?"

June departed the studio, convinced this chance was too valuable to lose. Spectra Pacific saw her as above average. They had connections. As for the money, she requested an advance on her weekly paycheck and offered to cover double shifts. Her boss, Mr. Gardner, agreed without debate. June possessed a strong work ethic and was a favorite of the regulars.

When June returned to pay for the photos, she received a second shock. Cathy accepted the $599.00 due for the deluxe tier but referred to it only as 'a deposit'.

"What is depawzit?" June asked.

"We'll start on your portfolio once we have 10 percent down, which we do now, but can't release any photos until we receive payment in full."

"But that's—$6000?"

"Don't worry about it. Once you get a good modeling job, it'll pay for itself in no time. That price is a bargain when you consider your lifelong earning potential."

June went home in a dour mood. The amount they requested seemed out of reach. And it angered her that Cathy never once mentioned the total price beforehand. June pulled the signal cord three bus stops from her housing project. The public library there offered free internet access, which she used to research Spectra Pacific. What she found chilled her. Post after message board post warned of their scams and deceptive practices. June felt so foolish. She worked hard to set aside the deep distrust that had helped her survive in her home country, choosing instead to be more trusting in this new place. Now, she felt ashamed for being so easily duped.

June vowed not to rest until she got her money back. However, nobody responded to her calls and messages. Extended work hours prevented her from immediately returning to Spectra in person. Two weeks passed before the first opportunity arose. To her amazement, she discovered the suite that once housed Spectra Pacific was vacant. They left no forwarding address. A secretary in an adjacent office told June they knew little concerning the company beyond their signing short-term lease papers and vanishing unexpectedly.

A month of double shifts left June utterly drained. The apartment she shared with her aunt remained barely furnished. The wicker chair Aunt Ye-jin had snagged for five dollars at a garage sale was uncomfortable. June avoided it. A nest of blankets and pillows on the living room floor gave her a sense of calm. She opened the envelope of tips received from waiting tables at Hapa's Hawaiian, and sighed deeply after counting the day's meager haul. After the portfolio fiasco, there was hardly any money from her weekly haul to contribute towards living expenses. She took her socks off to massage sore feet. Paid work was fine, but she wasn't making any progress toward her modeling career.

A nearby stack of books beckoned. Despite being dead tired,

June knew the only way her English would improve was to continue working on lessons. The library was resuming free morning ESL classes next week, and she wanted to be ready. Her Saturday course at the local Baptist church was in its third week, with homework to finish.

June was reading through one assignment when the rattling of house keys signaled Ye-jin's arrival. "Eemo, let me get that for you," she said, rushing to meet her aunt.

"It's too hot to walk. I should have waited."

"I would have gone shopping for you." She grabbed the groceries and carried them to the kitchen.

"You're working. And how can I see what's on sale if I don't go myself?" They made a simple dinner of gaeran mari, a rolled egg omelet with spinach, carrots, and onions. "Could you get me some water, Jeong?" Out of habit, her aunt still referred to June by her Korean name. June grabbed the water pitcher from the kitchen counter, poured a glass, and set it on the table.

As they ate, June gathered the nerve to mention finances. "Eemo, I'm sorry I won't have much to give you this month."

Ye-jin looked at her and smiled. "It's okay. I understand you have expenses. We should manage."

"I want to help. You've done so much for me."

"How are your auditions?"

"They say I'm too short."

"But you're 171 centimeters."

"Here, that's not tall. Models need to be at least 5'8."

"Tell them how hard you work."

"I will, Eemo." June was hungry enough to take another piece of omelet, but left it for her aunt, seeing as only one remained.

"That music group that's interested in you, they're willing to pay, right?"

June, not wanting to appear disrespectful, restrained a laugh. "I'll ask, but they're new. It won't happen overnight."

"Well, don't let them take advantage of you. You can't work for free."

"Yes, Eemo."

Ye-jin took the last bit of omelet and ate it. "Be sure to research these agencies you audition for, too. I keep hearing stories."

"I do, Eemo." June didn't have the heart to share her own tale.

"It happened to my coworker's nephew. He paid thousands of dollars to an agency and got nothing for it."

"I'm sure it happens," said June. "I'll be careful." June reasoned that her loss of hundreds was easier to swallow than thousands. It made her feel better.

After eating, Ye-jin stood, grabbed her plate, and moved toward the sink., however, she knocked a water glass over. Shards scattered across the kitchen floor.

"Eemo, be careful! Are you okay?" Her aunt set the plate on the table but held her foot. Despite the applied pressure, large drops of blood stained the white-tiled floor. June retrieved a towel, alcohol, and bandages from the bathroom, then returned to dress the wound.

"Didn't you see that glass?"

"I don't understand what's wrong with me, Jeong. My eyes lately. They never bothered me this much before."

"How long has this been going on?"

"A few months."

"Have you seen a doctor?"

"We don't have money for that."

"You have to go. I'll work more shifts."

"You shouldn't do that."

"After what you've done for me, it's the least I can do. Promise me you'll go?"

* * *

Out of nowhere, an errant soccer ball bounced off the edge of the weather-beaten picnic table. It landed in a nearby bush, missing June's cherry pop by mere inches and chucking tiny wood splinters in every direction. The startling incident reminded her of the shattered glass from earlier in the day. She pushed the image from her mind to focus on the interview. A seven-year-old boy approached and spoke to her in Spanish. Without hesitation, June reached over to the bush, retrieved the ball, and tossed it to him.

As he scampered back to the playing field, Heather asked in Korean, "You speak Spanish?"

"I don't, but you pick things up after living here a while."

The afternoon was breezy but not cold. Unexpectedly, several members of the K-pop group she had auditioned for weeks earlier called to arrange a meeting. They even agreed to meet at her low-income housing complex in the Los Angeles Cypress Grove area. June faced mobility issues without a car. That they offered to visit struck her as thoughtful. Heather, she remembered from the audition. Grace could not attend the interview because of a prior commitment. Mindy, Sun-hee, and Erin introduced themselves.

June's guests looked uncomfortable in the unfamiliar surroundings, but at least they had arrived. Visitors usually canceled after realizing where she lived. Regardless, June, being shy among strangers, spoke little. She sat quietly, hoping her guests would take the lead. Unfortunately, they too seemed passive.

The silence broke when Heather asked, "You're comfortable singing in Korean. Can you dance in high heels?"

June found the question odd, but understood little about America. "Yes, that's okay."

More silence.

Mindy whispered to Heather, who nodded. "You don't dance hip hop, do you?"

"No, I'm sorry," she responded. The unexpected nature of the questions made her anxious. She kept the answers short.

That set the tone for the entire interview. Mindy and Erin watched videos together on a smartphone, occasionally glancing at June and smiling. June's shyness only increased when she realized the discussion was not going well. Erin asked no questions at all. Her Korean did not seem sharp.

After they departed, June returned to her room to replay the conversation. Lamenting another lost opportunity, she vowed to learn lessons from the disappointing experience.

Grace called later that evening. "Hi, June. Do you have a minute to talk?"

"I already know what you'll say. It's okay. I understand."

"Understand what?"

"Your friends didn't like me."

"Oh, no. You got it all wrong. They loved you. We think you'll make a terrific addition."

* * *

Perspiration filled the musky air in the starkly-lit Pilates room. "See you all Thursday. Be ready for a workout," announced the instructor, clapping to support her students. Vanessa waited for the class at the tattered Westside Gym to disperse. She had arrived only moments earlier, not interested in the lesson itself but in the woman who taught it. Though they only met sparingly these days, Danya Kay was a chief influence in Vanessa's life. The primary reason she had fallen in love with dance, to begin with, and the one person who encouraged her to pursue it as a career. As a young girl whose intense determination had frightened away both bullies and best friends alike, Vanessa could have become unmoored if it hadn't been for the free dance lessons offered by her neighborhood community center. Danya, then a young college student volunteering for experience, instructed that class. When it came time for Vanessa to attend university, Danya's recommendation played an instrumental role in helping her secure a coveted full scholarship at St. Ignatius. Without that help, her single-parent family would never have been able to afford tuition at the private institution.

When the studio cleared, Vanessa approached Danya with a simple, "Hey. Long time."

"Ness! I thought I saw you lurking in the corner." Danya pulled her disheveled hair into a ponytail and retied it. Drops of sweat lingered on her light brown skin. "You should have joined us. I wouldn't have charged you...much." She smiled slyly, knowing full well Ness could dish it out but also take it.

"I didn't come for a workout. I wanna talk," explained Vanessa.

"Everything alright? You still at university, yeah?"

"Yeah. No, things are going. In fact, I was hoping you'd help me with a project."

"What's up?"

"I need choreography."

"Oh, no. Too busy for that. This for a class?"

"No. Extra-curricular. A girl from school said she'd contact you."

"If I don't know the sender personally, I ignore their messages. Is this paid?" Vanessa shook her head in response, fearing to speak out loud. "Oh, hell no. I'm not doing charity anymore. I gotta pay bills. You think I stay in this place for stimulation?"

"I get it, but listen. I figured you'd reject them outright—"

"Got that right."

"—so, I thought I'd talk to you first. Hear our pitch. It would mean gobs to me. I'll repay you. Promise."

Danya shot her a sideways glance. "Are you okay?"

"Perfect," she said, less than perfectly. "What do you say I cover one of your classes, and you won't have to pay me?"

"This isn't like you, Ness. What gives? Why this?" As she spoke, Danya collected her belongings and packed them into an oversized tote bag.

"I'm taking a gigantic risk by committing to this major. You know the drill. I have to make it payoff somehow. The last thing I want to see is my mom making sacrifices on my behalf, only for me to end up flipping burgers in some backwater whistlestop."

"How's that play into this gig?"

"A gut feeling is all. There's no money in it now, but I can't sit around waiting for things to happen. Otherwise, four years will fly by..." Vanessa waved her hand in the air like it was a hard-driven golf ball "...and I'll be just another unemployed coryphée hitting the streets."

"I hear that."

"It's one more spaghetti strand to throw at the wall, hoping it'll stick. Could be an excellent opportunity for you, too. Unless you'd rather teach pilates the rest of your life."

"Cold," Danya said with a smirk. "You know I've got other things going on." She zipped her bag and slung it over her shoulder.

"Of course. You're the most talented choreographer I've ever met. I'd travel the world to be in your dances. That's why I want your help."

Danya thought for a moment. "What's your proposal?"

"We'll meet on campus. They have a presentation planned. You can stop by on your way home. Easy enough."

"Look, I'll be honest," Danya said as she headed for the studio door with Vanessa tagging along. "I'm not thrilled about this, but I'll listen if it means so much. You've been there for me in the past."

"That's all I ask."

"But I know some other people you can call. Should call." Vanessa reacted sourly to this less-than-subtle dismissal. "Don't give me that look, Ness. I'm grateful you thought of me, but we dancers have a brief shelf life. I gotta make the most of my limited time. That means I go with the highest bidder."

"Just come with an open mind, okay?"

"I'm open-minded about you covering my next three Tuesdays."

"Three?"

"Three."

"For one meeting—"

"Three."

"Fine," Vanessa said in resignation.

* * *

Vanessa offered to pick Sun-hee up on their way to the show. She otherwise could not transport her bus-unfriendly keyboards to the venue. The gig itself was experimental. The Wormhole fiasco illustrated a blunt fact. While audiences in the U.S. knew about K-pop (and followed the biggest acts in droves), there remained little in the way of an actual scene below the arena show level. This put smaller bands like Made in Heaven at a steep disadvantage. To make up for the lack of venues, Grace suggested booking a stage at a neighborhood park just to see what happened. With no recorded music to offer yet and no permission to sell tickets in a public space, the idea was to earn revenue through merchandise sales. Heather had sketched a cute wing-themed logo to silk-screen on T-shirts. Since the dance unit was still in its infancy, they'd only focus on the band. They didn't tell Arnie about it since he'd surely dismiss it as pointless.

"Grace is already at the park," said Sun-hee upon fastening the seatbelt. "Let me call to see how it's going." She talked with their leader to get a status update. Once the conversation ended, she reported, "Traffic's not too bad. I asked about the crowd."

"What'd she say?"

"'You're never gonna believe it.'"

"Believe what?" asked Vanessa excitedly.

Realizing that her response was misinterpreted, Sun-hee explained further. "I mean, those were her exact words.

'You're never going to believe it.'"

"Wow. Maybe there's some merit to this idea after all."

Of all the group members, Vanessa found Sun-hee the most relatable. This was surprising because they were opposites. Sun-hee was so easy to get along with, though, that even Vanessa's prickliness didn't seem to bother her. While never shy to state her mind, Vanessa kept her personal life at arm's length from everyone. Opinions were acceptable; feelings were not. With Sun-hee, things were different. The girl never gossiped about friends. Something said in confidence stayed that way. "I hope Danya says yes. I have no idea what we'll do without her."

"It'd be great, sure. But you could choreograph for us, too." When Vanessa didn't answer, Sun-hee continued. "Can't you?"

Vanessa bit her lower lip. "I've never done group stuff before. Only solo."

"Oh," said Sun-hee. Doubt tinged her voice.

"I was hoping to watch her first. To get some tips," said Vanessa as she turned off the Marina Freeway onto Slauson. "Don't tell anyone, though. I'm used to being considered the capable one."

In the Windsor Hills area of Los Angeles, Ladera Park sat in a residential neighborhood off southern La Brea Avenue. Among its features was an amphitheater big enough to seat several hundred people. "We won't be late, but it's gonna be tight," said Vanessa. They arrived to find ample parking along the street, making the gear lug a simple affair. Upon entering the amphitheater, they saw a solitary young Black man wearing a baseball cap sideways in the front row. The remaining seats were empty.

"Where is everyone?" asked Sun-hee. Believing they spoke to him, the stranger gestured toward the stage's flank where five companions waited. The shocked pair joined their comrades, who looked glum.

"Did someone forget the 'free beer' sign," asked Vanessa.

"Who is that guy?" asked Sun-hee.

"Said he was just walking by and saw the setup, so he stuck around," responded Grace.

"You advertised, right?" asked Vanessa.

"Yes, with the whopping $20 bucks available in the budget," she responded glibly.

"So, do we tell this guy the show's canceled?" asked Mindy.

"Absolutely not," objected Sun-hee. "Someone here wants music, and we're musicians." Her logic was persuasive. Though brief, Made in Heaven's second-ever concert was well-received by the stranger who dutifully clapped after every song. In the end, however, he had no cash to buy a T-shirt, so they simply gave him one.

"At this rate, we'll be rolling in dough in no time," said Vanessa.

12

SWIMMING THROUGH THE DAWN

Heather froze when she read her mother's text. Marked urgent, it read:

8:20 P.M. Ji-woo: Your father will be in L.A. tomorrow! He wants to meet for dinner.

That was it. The linked itinerary showed Appa would arrive on Asiana Airlines and stay for 26 hours. Heather called Grace to apologize in advance for missing rehearsal.

Despite heading against the flow of rush-hour traffic, Heather's drive to the Intercontinental Hotel in downtown L.A. was a struggle. She arrived 35 minutes late, during which three texts came in. Wishing to avoid a traffic citation (not to mention an accident), she ignored them until parked in the garage. Heather frowned at the series of messages requesting arrival updates.

No sooner had the elevator doors opened than Dae-hee shouted her name from across the marble-clad lobby. They approached. Appa's appearance was surprising. Not that he looked any different than usual. The realization that they hadn't seen one another for months shook her. It was the longest period they'd ever spent apart. The gravity of this revelation made her feel considerably older.

"I've been waiting an hour," he said brusquely.

"It hasn't been that long, Appa. And nice seeing you, too."

He grinned, embarrassed. "It's been a long day. Have you eaten?"

They opted for Koreatown. Dae-hee's business associates had recommended a new seafood restaurant there, and he was excited to try it. Heather found no reason to object.

The steamy scent of boiling chili-based stock welcomed them. The hostess chose an isolated booth in a remote restaurant corner with a broad view of Wilshire Boulevard. A pool of golden-orange light emanated from an ornamental lamp above their heads. Its warm glow pushed away the crisp cerulean and jade atmosphere of the eatery's minimalist décor. They ordered shrimp tempura, sundubu jjigae (a spicy tofu stew with oysters), ojingeo-bokkeum (squid stir-fried with vegetables in a chili sauce), and octopus with somen noodles.

Their conversation began innocently enough. Dae-hee explained that his trip aimed to secure a deal with a potential new client. Negotiations were dragging, and his boss thought a more personal touch would expedite matters. To his disappointment, though, the effort failed to produce tangible results.

"I won't be able to get more than a few hours' sleep before heading to the airport in the morning," he said.

"I'm sorry for keeping you up."

"No, I didn't mean that. Part of the reason I accepted this assignment was to visit you."

Heather looked pleased but viewed the declaration with skepticism.

"Your brother was accepted to Stanford. He starts next year."

Heather acknowledged the news positively, knowing it risked reinforcing her relative unworthiness. "That's wonderful. I'm sure you're proud of Andrew."

"He worked hard to get in," her father said, nodding. A long moment passed during which he analyzed her appearance. "What on earth possessed you to change your hair?"

Thus, it begins, she thought to herself. "I want a distinct look, is all."

"It's not professional. I hope you're taking your studies seriously."

"I'm in college, Appa, not applying for a job."

"There's more to college than attending class and completing assignments. You need to start networking to lay the groundwork for your career. Talk to your brother. He understands." Heather chose not to respond. She tried to recall Appa ever saying anything positive about her, but struggled to think of one example. "I talked to Kwan Byung-hoon this morning."

Who? she wondered while staring blankly at him.

"The internship I mentioned? I see you've done nothing to pursue that. Naturally."

She'd already forgotten about their earlier conversation. Her knee bounced as she hoped Appa would change the subject.

Unfortunately, he did.

"Be honest with me, Heather. Are you pursuing music again?" He stared into her eyes, daring her to turn away or, worse, lie. She was cornered.

"Yes, Appa," she said, crumbling under the scrutiny. "How did you know?"

"I saw photos on your social media. Who's Steve?"

"You were *spying* on me?" She crossed her arms in a huff.

"Can you blame me? You never tell us anything about your activities." His voice swelled with emotion, and his volume increased. "I'm so disappointed in you, Heather. I thought we had an agreement."

She responded in kind, no longer wishing to speak discreetly. "I promised I'd go to college, and I did."

"That's not even the point. What's your plan? To busk for quarters on the promenade?"

"If that's what it takes!" A white couple at a nearby table eyed them. She doubted they understood Korean but considered it wise to lower her voice. "Are you telling me you love your job so much you'd do it for free?"

"Of course, I work for money. Starvation and homelessness don't particularly agree with me. I can't believe you haven't realized that basic fact by now."

"Admit it. That's not why you're dead set against me singing. Is it?"

Her father appeared bewildered, as if he were seeing her in a fresh light. "Of course, I care for your well-being. Why else would I work so hard? Someday, you'll understand there's dignity in a quiet life." After an interminable silence, he continued. "I never told you about your grandmother, did I?"

"Halmoni loved music, but you didn't share the details other than she was a pansori singer."

"There's more to it than that. Do you know why it's called waterfall singing?"

"Sort of."

"They spend years training in isolation, singing in front of waterfalls to break their voices. That's how they learn their genuine tone."

"I find that level of dedication impressive."

"Do you know how she died?"

"You said she got sick."

"She drowned herself."

Dae-hee stated it matter-of-factly, sugarcoating nothing. His words chilled her to the bone. She recoiled in her seat, eager to create as much distance as possible between them without abandoning their shared booth. "Did that hit close to home?" he asked.

"Why?"

"Why did she do it?"

Why did he ask me that? She inquired of herself.

"Your grandmother was so obsessed with becoming the ideal pansori singer that she paid the ultimate price. Once her lofty standards of authenticity were deemed unattainable, the only escape in her mind was suicide."

Heather spent long moments processing this information. Their server came to clear plates, then returned moments later with tempura ice cream desserts, which Dae-hee ate, but Heather left untouched.

"There must be another reason," suggested Heather. "Did that ever cross your mind? You always blame it on singing because you don't understand. Have you ever chased a dream?"

"My dream is to raise a successful family."

"Why didn't you tell me this before?"

"You weren't old enough. At least that's how I felt. Your mother disagreed." Heather wished she'd known sooner, but news of that sort would always be hard to take.

"How does this relate to me? That's what I don't understand."

A look of dismay crossed her father's face as he recalled events. "I was only 12 when she died, but I remember it clearly. After performances, she'd be hailed as a living treasure; accolades poured in from across the country. Yet, at home, she'd head straight to her bedroom to cry herself to sleep. Nobody could console her for days." A tear came to Heather's eye. She considered wiping it away but let it run down her cheek. "How does that relate to you?" her father continued, paraphrasing her question. Heather nodded and waited for the answer. "I see similarities. This concerns me greatly."

"Appa, I'm not your mother. Why can't you understand? If I could sing, I'd be so happy."

"Do you think she sang from despair? She loved it more than anything. Go ahead, sing. But don't make it your career. Nothing positive will ever come of it."

Heather was incredulous. A hundred responses flooded her mind. "Do you expect me to sing into a mirror for the rest of my life? I want to make people happy."

"And what if you can't. What then?" Heather had no answer. She'd considered no other possibility before. Daehee continued. "Once people take what they want, they'll spit you out like a sunflower shell. Can you handle that? I doubt it."

"You got your wish when I left the agency. I'm playing by my own rules now."

"Your day has just begun. You have no idea what's coming. I already lost a mother to singing; I don't want to lose a daughter too."

"If music doesn't happen, I'll get a regular job. I'm passing all my classes."

His eyes protruded. Her father now spoke in a raised voice. "Whenever I try to talk some sense into you, you react with defiance."

"I'm not defying you, Appa. I'm making an adult choice. For myself."

"But you're not an adult! You depend on your mother and me completely. And frankly, I've had it. I'll not support this behavior any longer." His face reddened. "You want to make choices?" Heather nodded meekly. "Here's one for you. Come next year, if you continue to pursue your music career, you can do so without my help. Understood? No tuition. No room and board. No books. Certainly, no music. You'll finally know what being an adult actually entails." Having finished his outburst, he relaxed.

Heather's knee bobbed like a sewing machine. "Why would you keep me from doing what I want most? You like seeing me fail. Is that it?"

"I'm doing it for your own good," he said.

"And when do I get to determine what's best for my own good?"

"You have until the end of your freshman year. I suggest you choose wisely."

13

HARDER THAN IT LOOKS

Finals week at St. Ignatius offered student filmmakers the unique opportunity to present the fruits of their labor to teachers and peers. Every individual in a production class was required to screen their short films in public. Grades were one thing, but audience reaction affected everything from personal satisfaction to awards potential to post-graduate opportunities. After every movie, the creators of that project would face a gauntlet of questions and receive either praise or condemnation. The experience proved a nerve-wracking pressure cooker for those who endured it, but a source of endless delight and fascination for attendees who merely had to react to what they saw. Securing a seat in the 250-seat theater during screenings week was essential for anyone with a passing interest in the SIU film program. As always, Steve looked forward to it. He knew he had a strong project and was eager to present it. People had already packed the theater, anticipating the event.

Not all sailing was smooth, however. In a basement editing bay, Steve sat before a non-linear workstation, pleading with it to respond. Every click of the mouse resulted in an interminable wait. He reasoned that a last-minute crush of projects overloaded the system. *Such delay reaps this reward,* he thought. Rather than endure the tedium, he opted for a system reboot, hoping that would solve the problem. After initiating the process, Grace texted him.

5:33 P.M. Grace: We're here. This place is out of control.

5:33 P.M. Steve: Warned u. Did u find seats?

5:34 P.M. Grace: No luck yet.

5:34 P.M. Steve: I have a few minutes, where r u?

5:34 P.M. Grace: Theater doors.

5:34 P.M. Steve: BRT

Steve looked at the monitor and estimated he had at least five minutes before the machine was usable. That would allow him sufficient opportunity to settle his guests and return to finish the deliverable in time for the 6:00 p.m. deadline. He left his backpack and the USB drive containing his edited video master on the console. It would mark his territory should anyone desire to claim the station in his absence. The theater was on the ground floor, one level above. Steve took the steps two by two to get there. As he reached the main lobby, he saw his five cast members standing in a cluster amidst the chaos swirling around them.

"Hey," he said as he approached them.

"All seats are taken, and people are sitting in the aisles along the walls," stated Grace.

"Here, let me pass along some insider information." He motioned for Grace to follow inside and escorted her to the far side aisle, where they passed through two sets of curtains separating the inner theater lobby from the auditorium itself. As reported, the room was packed. Grace stood next to Steve as he scanned the hall. "There," he said, pointing across the room. "Do you see the group sitting halfway down wearing blue t-shirts?"

"Yes."

"They're not planning to stick around the whole evening. Their film runs before mine. If you stand near the curtains at the rear of the aisle and keep an eye on their departure, you can jump in and claim those spots before anyone else notices. Got it?"

"Yup."

"I have to finish my project," said Steve.

"Wait, I thought you turned it in already."

"I planned to, but the original mix is in stereo. Yesterday, I changed my mind and created a surround mix. Now I need to match it to the video."

"You're cutting it close."

"Yeah, but it'll be worth it. Gotta run."

The screenings kicked off at 6:00 p.m. sharp. Vanessa and June chose not to attend since they weren't in the video and had other matters of interest. Grace found it a blessing since they'd be lucky to secure five seats, let alone seven. The members who were present huddled between the double curtains. Grace wondered how many fire codes were being violated as people sat in any available space they could find.

The filmmakers of the opening movie, called "Derogatory Id," shot it in grainy, high-contrast black and white. It opened with a young man waking to an alarm clock. The next shot consisted of an egg frying in a pan for a full minute. A trio of off-key horns played random notes on the soundtrack. Meanwhile, an unseen radio broadcast uttered an endless chain of numbers in a monotone voice. The egg shot was replaced by images of a couch on a football field and then a wedding dress on a flagpole. A fly crawled across decomposing peaches. Slowly. Hooded figures ambled like tortoises through a creepy cemetery. The horn playing and the number counting grew more frenetic as the pace of edits intensified. A shadowy figure tossed a baby buggy down a wooden staircase before the image faded to black. The alarm clock shot repeated, but this time, the young man realized it was all a dream.

Grace found the whole thing tiresome. The resulting applause was polite, however. The filmmaker strode to the stage for his Q&A wearing a puffy black turtleneck sweater.

"Were those vuvuzelas?" whispered Heather to Grace, who could only shrug in response.

"What did we just watch?" asked Sun-hee.

"An art student splooging over the screen," responded Mindy, provoking laughter from some nearby.

Much to Grace's surprise, the audience comments were complimentary. One male pupil, wearing the type of tweed jacket found only in lower-end second-hand stores, praised the filmmaker's courage for 'not selling out' and 'telling it like it is.' A red-haired, goateed male in a Dia de los Muertos t-shirt suggested that adding honking cab horns would improve the soundtrack. Otherwise, he declared the film peerless and said it shined a 'much-needed light on the condition of man.'

Grace made a gagging gesture at the comment. "Did we watch the same thing?" she asked rhetorically.

Heather giggled in response. "I hope they're not all like this."

For a while, they were. Many films were forgettable because of sheer ineptitude.

"Filmmaking is harder than it looks," concluded Sun-hee in Korean. No sooner had these words left her mouth than the blue-shirt group exited. On the lookout for just this moment, Mindy jumped to the row of seats in time to claim them, but only after jostling with a girl in a tube top and Bermuda shorts who resorted to calling her an 'epic bitch.'

"We're next," uttered Grace as they took their places. The five held each other's hands, anticipating their video debut. But instead of the lights dimming, Grace noticed Steve arguing with one professor. It was hard to hear what they were saying. The instructor called for a brief break and left the theater. Grace caught Steve's attention in time to gesture questioningly. In response, he made a throat-slashing motion before following the professor outside. "That can't be good," she said.

"Easy come, easy go," said Mindy. The tube-top girl glared at them as they left before claiming the seats for her group.

In the lobby, the girls found Steve pleading with his teacher. "I can get the stereo mix from my dorm and submit that instead."

"That wouldn't be fair to those who complied, would it? You shouldn't have switched so late. I warned you."

"I don't understand what happened. My thumb drive just disappeared."

"I'm sorry, but you know the rules. A deadline's a deadline."

"Everything was under control."

"You'll still get a grade if you finish it, but it'll be marked late. I can't let you participate in the screenings tonight, though."

"But—"

"I'm sorry, my decision's final." Without further delay, the professor returned to the theater. Judging from the sounds emanating from within, the next film was ready to start, and it would not be "Have No Fear."

Steve looked distraught. "What happened?" asked Heather.

"After talking to you, I returned to my editing suite. The system was working by then, but when I went to grab the USB, it wasn't there."

"Did you double-check?" asked Grace.

"Believe me, I did. At first, I thought it might have gotten stuck in my backpack straps. Then I searched my pockets. Finally, I started dumping everything out on the floor. I even got on my hands and knees with my phone light to check every corner and crevice. Nothing."

"How does it just disappear?"

"I'm completely baffled. I swore I left it right on the console. So I could claim it."

"Maybe someone took it," suggested Heather.

Steve shrugged, then shook his head. "I wouldn't put it past some people here." Sun-hee proposed that they help look for it. This distraction occupied half an hour before they accepted the reality that the USB was gone. "I'm so sorry about this. I know you were all looking forward to seeing it."

"At least you'll still get class credit," said Sun-hee.

* * *

Later, Arnie minced no words when he heard about the failed premiere. "I had a hunch that guy was no good. All that work for nothin'."

"We only missed the screening," said Grace. "No biggy. The real goal is the festival prize. We can still aim for that money."

Arnie chuckled as he stroked his chin. "That's what I'm

getting at. You can't. By missing that screening, the film's disqualified."

"How come?"

"Because festival judges were scouting them."

Grace was incredulous. "How do you know all this? You weren't even there."

"Don't need to be. The sound engineer told me on recording day."

"That seems pretty tenuous, Arnie."

"Hey, if you don't believe me, ask Steve. See if he tries to lie his way out of it."

Grace took him up on the challenge. During the subsequent phone call, Steve confirmed Arnie was correct, but only after apologizing once more and promising to make amends. When she hung up the phone, Arnie smiled as if he had just won a wrestling match. "Guy's a waste of time, I'm telling you."

14

CROSSED WIRES

With his semester essentially finished, Steve relaxed in his dorm. Propped open on the armrest of his couch was a textbook for "Differential Equations." Girlfriend Casey studied for her one remaining final. She lay on her stomach, flipping through the pages to ensure nothing important had been missed. "This course turned out to be way easier than I thought it'd be," she said, closing the book.

"That's because you're so brilliant." Steve bent to kiss her, caressing her natural strawberry-blonde hair.

"Go on. These are words I love to hear." They kissed again, this time more passionately. Casey kicked her legs in the air, toes curled. They'd been friends since kindergarten but only started dating as seniors in high school. The decision to attend St. Ignatius together was easy. The university offered degrees in both of their preferred majors. For Steve, that meant Film and Television Production with a Recording Arts minor; for Casey, Mathematics. Steve hated the subject, geometry being the one branch in which he received anything higher than a

C. But he admired how easily it came to Casey. She lived and breathed it.

"This final's gonna be cake. Which reminds me, let's eat," she said.

"Yeah, in a minute." Steve sat on the floor next to the couch and opened his laptop. Always searching for something new and intriguing to showcase, he persistently attempted to spark Casey's interest in the arts. Despite all the effort, her tastes remained strictly pedestrian. She exhibited no understanding of what it meant to live a creative life and no willingness to learn. That didn't stop Steve from trying, though. He hoped someday they'd have deep conversations about the stuff he cared most about. Like, should "The Searchers" really be considered the greatest Western of all time? (The correct answer, in his view, was "Once Upon a Time in the West") "Let me show you something before we go."

"Again?" Casey asked.

"It's from a genius film director, Andrei Tarkovsky. You'll be amazed." Casey tried to disguise her displeasure, but Steve noticed the far corner of her mouth turn down.

The clip involved a man igniting a candle and then embarking on a delicate journey across a drained swimming pool. The scene unfolded with urgency as he endeavored to keep the flame ablaze while protecting it from the relentless gusts that assailed it. His first two attempts ended in failure. With dogged determination, however, he continued the trial. He triumphed during the third crack at it, reaching the opposite side with the flickering candle still aglow. Yet, his victory was short-lived as he gasped for breath and collapsed off-frame. Steve admired the director's technique of capturing the action in a single, continuous tracking shot that stretched for over nine minutes. Tarkovsky's unique vision, he concluded, elicited an emotional response that was both profound and inspiring.

"Is that not a marvel?" He asked as the scene reached its conclusion.

Casey looked annoyed. "I don't get it."

Disappointed once again, Steve's head drooped. Intent on displaying patience, however, he looked up and asked as nicely as possible, "What do you mean?"

"Why didn't he just go to the other side and light the candle there? It would have been much easier."

"You're missing the point."

"There is no point. It was stupid."

"It wasn't stupid." Steve checked his emotions to keep the conversation from developing into an argument.

"Besides, if *that's* the highlight, it's gotta be the world's most boring movie."

"The director is original, but certainly not boring."

"Give me a superhero flick any day."

Steve sighed in exasperation. "You're depriving yourself by not expanding your horizons."

"If that's the best you can do, I doubt it. And what is it with you and ancient history? How come all your references are decades old? Get with the times."

"I'd hardly call decades ancient. And good is good, regardless of what year it came out." Since nothing he said seemed to register, Steve decided on another tack. "Think of movies like nourishment. Sure, junk food tastes good, but you'd die of malnutrition on a steady diet of it. One Truffaut film contains more sustenance than a decade's worth of those digital Punch & Judy shows you like so much."

"Why are you always going off on superhero movies? What have they ever done to you?"

"You mean besides beating my brain to a pulp with their thunderous vapidity?"

"How snobby."

"Let me count the ways. There's no emotional resonance. No mystery. Collateral damage seems an afterthought. The characters' decisions never matter in the long run. There's always another gimmicky villain with a gimmicky weakness in a gimmicky costume waiting in the wings. I could go on. Besides, these people are super by definition. They're *supposed* to win. I'm much more interested in ordinary people exceeding expectations than extraordinary people meeting them."

"Meh. Life's too short to waste on stuff that slow."

"Tarkovsky used the poetry of images to depict the inner lives of his characters. This one scene encapsulates the entirety of a person's life struggle. It's genius."

Casey's head flopped to the couch as if fainting. "Well, genius or not, my corpse will be encapsulated soon if I don't eat something."

Steve slammed the laptop shut. "Okay, fine. Let's go." He wondered why he even bothered sometimes.

* * *

The thought of letting Made in Heaven down still ate at Steve a week after finals. He invited the group to his annual Christmas party to make up for it. This wasn't any old Christmas party, mind you. By tradition, the get-together, now in its fourth year, featured a 60s-era cocktail lounge theme. Steve maintained strong connections with the creative community in and around St. Ignatius; this get-together featured a stage for live performances. The guests always made good use of it. Any act was fair game, provided it had some link to the holiday season, no matter how tenuous. Steve promised to debut the "Have No Fear" video there and offered the band a key slot during the open mic event.

When Heather received the invitation, she bit. The band desperately needed live gigs, even non-paying ones. Aware of Steve's extensive knowledge of music, she sought advice on cover songs that would fit the party theme. Stoked by the thought that anyone would sit and listen to his record collection, he invited her to his place that very afternoon.

Perhaps it was overkill, but the three-wick candle worked wonders. Its mahogany and teakwood scent filled the room, creating a relaxed and pleasant environment. Heather arrived looking fabulous, wearing a loose-knit super crop-top sweater over a matching camisole. She paused for a moment to assess his dorm room. "Your style of décor is interesting," she said.

"People often substitute the word interesting when they really mean embarrassing."

"No, I mean it." She waved her hands across the walls for emphasis. "You have actual framed pictures arranged in coherent themes. Like you put some thought into it."

"It's cheap movie memorabilia collected at garage sales."

"But clearly a step up from what most guys have. Pyramids of empty beer bottles and taped-to-the-wall alcohol ads ripped from magazines do not impress."

"Not my style." He wondered how many guys' rooms she'd visited but banished the thought. "Then again, most people say I'm the weird one."

"Considering the state of what's deemed normal in the world, I find nothing wrong with that." It dawned on Steve that he could live to be 100 years and never hear Casey utter that exact phrase, even in jest.

While Heather visited for some setlist recommendations, she stayed long after. Rather than making a swift exit, she was captivated by their conversation on female singers, a theme that held a special place in Steve's heart. The intensity of his impromptu ramblings on the subject tended to scare people away. Heather, in contrast, was eager to absorb everything.

As a result, Steve was hopping back and forth between his collection of vinyl LPs (which he stored in pilfered milk crates by his desk) and the stereo system, which sat atop a closet dresser. As he selected music to play, he was careful not to step on records strewn over the carpet. Heather examined each cover when handed to her. When finished, she'd place them in one of several piles nearby. Her exact sorting method remained a mystery. When their conversation inspired new ideas, Steve would search for a corresponding record and set it alongside the turntable to be played next.

"Where did you get all these?" she asked. "I'm almost embarrassed to say I've never heard of most."

"They belonged to my uncle, who started collecting as a kid. We talked a lot about music and what it meant to us. He moved overseas three years ago but didn't want to haul them all along, so he passed the albums on to me, knowing I'd appreciate them."

"That was thoughtful."

"It's mostly 80s stuff, but there's some genuine gold in there. Uncle Fred always used to credit these songs as an escape valve when all else seemed lost."

"I know exactly what he means," Heather responded, almost under her breath. Steve awaited further explanation, but it never arrived.

"Many divergent music styles emerged that decade," he continued. "As did the growth of technology in music and the rise of a number of influential female singers. Take this song, "Metro" by Berlin. My uncle always lamented that the 80s promised a future that never came."

"Listening to this, I can see why."

"Don't get me wrong. The 80s has its share of haters, but in retrospect, I think it was a golden age."

"Apparently." Heather jolted in surprise, thrusting an album over her head. "Hey! An all-girl group."

"Yup, the Bangles were groundbreakers. This song, 'Eternal Flame,' is the biggest single by an all-female band ever." He watched Heather's face brighten as she listened to the record for the first time. When the backing vocals came in, she swayed her head, arms, and upper body to the beat. Her eyes were closed, envisioning a scene that Steve could only imagine.

"It's a trickier song to sing than it seems," she said. "A lot of registers to negotiate. Strong harmonizing, too. Maybe we'll cover them someday."

"You know Susanna Hoffs used to sing naked while recording in the studio. Claimed it was a freeing experience, like skinny dipping."

"Are you suggesting I try that next time?" Heather asked impishly.

Steve choked. "I...uh..." He looked for an excuse to change the subject. "Oh, look, Scandal." With no further mention of nudity in the studio, he played "Goodbye to You," comparing Heather's singing style to Patty Smyth's. "Besides her powerful voice, she strikes a perfect balance between cute and sexy with a little bit of edge. Like you." Steve stopped, aware that he was treading in deep water for the second time in less than a minute. Heather remained focused on the album cover, though she retained a sly smile. Whatever her thoughts, they stayed private.

"What is playing now?" she asked once the record changed again.

"'Destination Unknown' by Missing Persons. Check out this cover and tell me who the lead singer reminds you of." He handed her the *Spring Session M* album.

It took her less than a second to answer, "Lady Gaga."

"Yup. That's Dale Bozzio. She sang with Frank Zappa, too."

"This music is fun," she said.

"Exactly. That's what struck me about K-pop. It reminds me so much of what I like about that era. Good melodies, powerful hooks, and not afraid of a little fun. I know minimalism is the order of the day now, but pop has lost much of its former charm."

"I was so focused on K-pop for so long that I never took the time to listen to anything else. Go on."

"Are you sure you want to hear my diatribe? Once this train gets rolling—"

"I'm all ears," she said, interrupting.

Steve continued to share his observations, admiring the abundant harmonies and melodies, surprising chord changes, boundary-challenging song structures, genre-spanning appeal, and seamless blend of disparate vocal styles. "I haven't been this excited about pop music in ages. Too many record labels demand simplicity today. They must think we're too stupid to understand anything complicated. It's infuriating."

"I know what you mean."

"Korea reminds me of what we used to do well. Their songwriting palette is broader. There are so many more moving parts. Not just a reliance on the same four chords all the time. Bridges and melodies aren't taboo, either. If I were a songwriter, I'd consider working there."

"Reality is more complicated."

"How so?"

"It's hard for idols to have much control over their music."

Despite their early friction, Steve found talking to Heather as easy as running fingers through a cashmere sweater. But one question piqued his curiosity more than any other. He sensed it was a sensitive topic and approached it obtusely. "Do you miss Korea?"

Heather tapped the album cover she held with one index finger. The gesture seemed driven by annoyance and not timed to any beat. "That's a loaded question."

"Either you do or you don't, right?"

"I'm here now. L.A. is my focus."

Steve opted to quit probing lest he drive her away. Long after sundown, he ran out of records to play. "I have to hand it to you. For the first time ever, somebody outlasted me." He settled on the floor in front of the dorm room couch, resting one arm on the cushions.

"Thanks. You gave me a ton of ideas," Heather said as she moved to mirror Steve's pose. Their eyes met. His heartbeat quickened.

"Are you seeing someone?" he asked, surprising himself with his forwardness.

Heather built a slow smile before answering. "I gave up dating for Lent."

"Unacceptable," he teased. "This isn't Lent. Don't tell me you're observing the idol no dating rule, are you?"

"That has nothing to do with it. I have other goals right now. Nobody's interested, anyway," she said with a dismissive shrug.

"Oh, come on. I bet not a day goes by where some guy doesn't ask you out."

Heather laughed and held up a finger as if scolding. "Ha! Now, that's where you're wrong. You'd be surprised how many assume I'm taken and don't bother asking."

Steve cocked his head back. "If you met someone interesting, would you ask him out?"

"I already answered that. I'm not seeking a relationship right now."

He let the matter drop. They sat for a long moment until Heather grew uncomfortable and averted her gaze.

Then, the dorm room door burst open. Startled by this hasty intrusion, Heather sprang upright. Steve expected his roommate, Ken; instead, it was Casey. She made no eye contact with her boyfriend but glared at Heather with the heat of a thousand suns. "Oh, I'm sorry. Did I interrupt you two?" she asked, her cheeks flushed.

"No, sweetheart, we were finished. We've been discussing music." Steve stood up to greet his girlfriend. "Heather, this is Casey."

His guest stood and smiled, extending her hand in greeting. "Nice to meet you."

"She's the main singer of Made in Heaven."

Casey's nostrils flared like those of a Kentucky Derby winner. She refused to acknowledge the offered hand.

Heather regarded the couple. "I should go. It's getting late."

"I'll shoot you a playlist, okay?"

"That'd be great, Steve." Heather struggled to scoot past Casey, who exhibited no desire to accommodate her movement. As she departed, Heather waved toodle-oo with her fingers and sauntered down the hallway, singing "Goodbye to You" in a clarion voice.

When Casey closed the door, a draft slammed it shut. She didn't seem to mind. "So that's why you're always eager to see her, Steve." The way she emphasized his name mocked Heather's way of saying it.

"She was a key part of my video."

"You never told me she was so...striking."

His girlfriend would have been aware of this had she watched his video. Steve felt it unwise to mention this, as Casey's interest in this part of his life waned. He weighed a list of potential responses but chose distraction as the safest option. "Hey, would you like to listen to some cool music while it's out?"

Casey surveyed the mess on the floor with disdain. "Not really."

15

THE PLACE THAT SHAPED ME

The celebration was small but meaningful. Heather's Finance study group convened at The Shed, a local beachside hangout. They were celebrating the semester's end after earning an A-minus on their final project. The students, tasked with applying financial theories and concepts to real-world scenarios, studied a globally recognized payment-processing company.

Classmate Brad, without debate, named himself project lead. Type A personality, Katie, clashed with him over the unbalanced workload distribution. She felt all parties should share equally in participation. Gregg, who was typically quiet, gladly relinquished command to Brad in exchange for a good grade. Contrarian Maret contributed initial research but horsed around the rest of the time. They were all shocked to learn that Heather wasn't good at math despite being Asian, but she took charge of presentation aesthetics, thanks to Katie's inclusion campaign, a role in which she excelled.

Brad proposed the Shed outing to thank the group for staying out of his way. Heather had little interest in attending but tagged along to remain in the favorable graces of her classmates. Besides, if she wanted to be honest with herself, the likelihood that she'd enter a career in finance had increased now that the pitfalls of indie musician life were better understood. Regardless of her feelings, Heather spoke little. The conversation gravitated towards future classes, which professors to avoid, and national politics, none of which excited her. She silently ate half a hamburger and a quarter of the fries, waiting for an appropriate lull to excuse her departure.

The discussion then veered into a surprising new direction: music. Brad mentioned his streaming playlist, which triggered a sharing of song preferences. It was a topic Heather preferred to avoid. At no point had she revealed anything of her past to them. Katie, however, wasn't about to let her off the hook. "What about you, Heather?"

Shocked at their sudden interest in her, she faltered, then conceded, hoping it would end the inquiry. "I listen to pop."

"I hate pop music. It's so shallow," said Maret.

Chafing against her better instincts, Heather responded, "Isn't that the point?"

"How's that a good thing?"

"Accessibility is what makes it work. A pop song can teach the same basic life lessons as high-minded art but in a fun way. And if anything, the world needs more fun right now." This statement produced no further challenges. Merely looks of unease.

"Speaking of. Did you hear that new Travis Lenzo track that dropped yesterday?" asked Katie.

"I've been underwater this whole time," said Brad. "Is it any good?"

"I was shook."

"Bought it straight off," agreed Gregg.

"It's not lit like 'Baseline' was," said Maret, "but I'd still download it,"

"And Heather?" asked Katie. "What's your take on TL?"

She gauged their faces and considered outright lying, but then thought better of it. "He's okay."

"Just okay?" said Gregg incredulously. "He's the hottest thing going."

Their silent anticipation demanded a fuller response. Hers came, naturally, from the heart. "Well, despite being a baritone, his lower range is mostly underdeveloped. His falsetto is airy and lacks projection, while his vocal runs are often pitchy. Interestingly, the more volume he adds, the tenser he sounds. In his defense, though, his mixed voice is nicely relaxed." She stopped there. Her companions remained silent, now more out of pity than curiosity.

* * *

"Okay, is everybody ready?" Grace queried her group members as they stood outside the 1920s-era bungalow in Pasadena.

"Yes," they responded in unison. The sounds from the house confirmed that the Christmas party was in full swing. Over the PA system, a musician tuned his guitar while telling jokes. The crowd engaged in a riotous discord of conversations as they awaited the resumption of the entertainment.

Grace continued her briefing as her bandmates shivered in the chill December air. "Remember, as soon as we enter, it's effectively—" Her speech was cut short when a curly-haired blonde guy wearing a blue pinstripe seersucker suit and a 'Jerry

Mandering' nametag opened the door.

Heather didn't know his actual name but recognized his face from St. Ignatius. "I thought I heard voices out here," said the greeter with a welcoming gesture. "C'mon in."

"Well, anyway, it's showtime," Grace announced as she led the procession into the house. That was the signal to assume their idol personas.

Heather flashed the doorkeeper a cheerful smile and a flirty wink. "Merry Christmas, Jerry."

Most of the furniture had been removed, yet the space remained tight for the many guests. Floors, walls, doorposts, and cornices were trimmed in fine-grained wood according to a bygone era's fashion. A decorated platform stood before three enormous picture windows in the living room. The setting served as a makeshift stage. A full array of band instruments stood ready for general use. The house was lit with thousands of Christmas lights. Strategically placed period lamp fixtures provided subtle mood accents. The party was an annual event. Regular guests knew what to expect and came prepared. Three-fourths of the partygoers took the theme seriously, wearing a wild variety of 60s-inspired cocktail lounge attire.

"Hey, you made it," Steve said, welcoming them with open arms. "Let me grab your coats."

As their coverings came off, a young woman in a Jackie O suit whisked them away. Grace, Erin, Mindy, and Vanessa had improvised their 60s look using borrowed items. Grace's mother, Ji-woo, proved to be a godsend. Using her great-aunt's vintage jewelry and accessories, the girls showcased pieces hidden away for decades. Heather, Sun-hee, and June took a different tack according to plan. The three wore matching sleeveless black Twiggy-style shift dresses with white lace accents highlighting necklines and arm openings. Identical large buns sat at the back of their crowns, holding their hair. No bangs. Elbow-length black gloves and Mary Janes completed the outfits.

"Wow, you look magnificent," said Steve. "As soon as I got used to the blonde hair, you changed it again."

"Don't worry. These are wigs," Heather admitted.

"Well, I hope you're still planning to perform tonight."

"We have a set ready," said Heather. "If you have room for us."

"I saved you the best spot. The stipulation is you have to wear name tags." He held up a black Sharpie as though it were a baton. "Hit me with your lounge lizard names." He pointed to his own tag emblazoned with 'Norman Conquest'. "The more groan-inducing, the better." He grabbed a male passerby long enough to point at his 'Biff Wellington' nametag. "Case in point."

"Now we're talking," said Vanessa, who shot her hand into the air. "Dibs on 'Natalie Drest.'"

"That's the spirit." Steve moved to a small table with name tag supplies and began writing. "Keep 'em coming. Who else?"

Grace chose 'Yule B. Sorry,' Mindy chose 'Blake Deadly,' while Erin, perhaps putting too much thought into it, picked 'Amanda Rekonwyth.' Heather ordered a set of name tags for herself and her two 'sisters' for the evening: Sue Kim, Ai-ja Kim, and Mia Kim.

As this happened, 'Ella Vader' came by with a tray offering drinks. Heather grabbed one, sipping what tasted like a cranberry bourbon cocktail. It was delicious but packed a punch. Steve's girlfriend, Casey, approached the table, attempting to stand between Heather and Steve. Wearing red plaid capri pants and a white sweater but no nametag, she draped an arm over her boyfriend's shoulder. Steve peeled the backing off Heather's new tag. He hesitated to place it on her uninvited. Casey offered a solution to his dilemma. "I'll hold your drink," she said, more as a demand than an offer.

After handing over the beverage, Heather took the 'Ai-ja Kim' nametag from Steve and daintily placed it on her own dress. "Thanks," she said, retrieving the glass afterward.

"Don't mention it."

"Did you pick any of the songs we discussed?" asked Steve.

"Actually, two. We also prepared a tribute to complete our set, thus the outfits."

"You should walk around a bit," suggested Casey. "See if you know anyone here."

Heather found the apparent attempt to get rid of her amusing. "Yeah. I'll do that," she said. "Thanks...Tracey, was it?"

"Casey."

"Oh, yeah...Right."

A trio of musicians finished their rendition of "The Pina Colada Song" before plunging into a parody version of "Copacabana." Although she didn't understand most of the inside jokes, she enjoyed watching the crowd's reactions when spirited roastings targeted various guests.

By now, her own group members had spread throughout the room, practicing what Grace had assigned as homework. They were to hone the vital skill of fan service, which all idols learn as trainees. The techniques help make audiences feel special. K-pop idols, she explained, need to project warmth, modesty, positivity, and humility at all times in public. Made in Heaven's status as an indie group did not exempt them from this competence.

After over 90 minutes of mingling, Steve approached Heather. "You're next. You ready?"

"Most definitely."

Heather assembled her members. The prior act had performed a brief, ridiculous version of "All I Want for Christmas is You." The girls had little time to catch their breath before stepping on stage.

The MC spoke. "Now you're in for a treat. We have in-house the hottest K-pop group this side of the Pacific. Let's give a warm lounge lizard welcome to the newbies. Here's Made in Heaven."

In a departure from their standard setup, Grace stood at the center mic while Heather took the lead guitar. June and Vanessa shared one mic as backup singers, while the rest used the host-provided instruments. Sun-hee played the electronic keyboard on their cover version of "Christmas Wrapping" by The Waitresses.

During rehearsals, Grace doubted Erin's ability to handle the lively Tracy Wormworth bass line. Erin assured her she'd learn it on time. From the start, it sounded like their gamble had paid off. The audience caught on to her infectious groove, and soon everybody was dancing and singing along. The playing was super sharp, doing more than enough justice to the original. Grace ripped through the rap-like singing style without a hitch, enthralling the crowd. Their assured performance conveyed that Made in Heaven was not to be taken lightly. Once the enthusiastic applause diminished, Heather called Sun-hee and June to join her at the front while Grace reclaimed her guitar.

"You all know BTS and Blackpink, right?" Heather's query was met with near-universal shouts of agreement. "And how about the Kim Sisters?" One guy towards the rear of the room roared in the affirmative. Heather identified him as a pale, scrawny, near-giant with a head of unruly red hair. "Hmm, for some reason, I'm skeptical," she said, noticing his mischievous grin.

"I have a sister named Kim. Does that count?"

"Close enough." She explained how the first Korean wave started in 1959 when the Kim Sisters took both Vegas and the Ed Sullivan Show by storm. "They aren't household names today but heroes to us, and we wanted to share their song."

'The Kim Sisters' launched into a jaunty cover of the doo-wop tune "Mr. Magic Moon." The song's lyrics implored the moon to shine on their one true love. Steve, naturally, stood right in front of the stage. Heather locked eyes with him as she sang. Keeping in character, she keyed in on him as the object of her affection. He was transfixed. Casey, however, noticed their interaction and possessively kissed him on the lips, much to his surprise. She then stared at Heather as though celebrating a triumphant victory. At that moment, something unusual happened. Sun-hee flubbed a line. This never happened in Heather's experience. The girl was rock-solid. Despite that slight hiccup, the music ended with a bang, and the room roared its approval, calling for an encore.

Fortunately, the girls had come prepared. Their well-received set was to conclude with their most demanding number. As her two 'sisters' returned to their usual places, Heather asked Sun-hee, "Are you okay?"

"I'm fine," she responded unconvincingly.

"Remember your training. Always remain positive. No

matter what."

Sun-hee nodded, smiled weakly, and took her seat at the piano. She opened with a snappy, jazzy piano intro, accompanied by Mindy's delicate snare and hi-hat work. The band had prepared an extended jazz rendition of Aretha Franklin's "Kissin' by the Mistletoe."

Heather bit into the performance like a delicious steak, providing the audience with as much stagecraft as song. Toying with them from the opening verse, she offered a delightful blend of the sultry and playful. Various audience members were the target of her outrageous flirting, as the lyrics extolled the benefits of falling in love during the holidays. The room paid rapt attention.

Sun-hee's improvised piano solo lasted less than a minute in rehearsals. That night, though, she was on fire. The crowd's enthusiasm was infectious, but Heather assumed she had taken her advice to heart. Whatever the reason, Sun-hee went on a five-minute tear, transfixing the crowd. As the band strayed into uncharted territory, Erin nearly panicked. She glanced at Mindy, who reassured her with a calm expression as if suggesting, 'Just go with it.'

To the audience's delight, Sun-hee even channeled her best Vince Guaraldi impression, breaking into a spontaneous rendition of "O Tannenbaum" midway through the epic solo. It took everything the group could muster to build upon that energy and bring the number to a suitable conclusion.

"Let's hear it for the band," the MC said as the girls left the stage to wild applause.

Afterward, the group fielded many compliments and questions. People inquired about their outfits, the band, K-pop generally, and the Kim Sisters specifically. Eventually, another act took the mic, and the crowd's attention returned to the stage.

"We needed that," said Grace to Heather after things settled down.

"Now, if we could only get them to like our songs."

Steve spotted her from the rear bedroom window. Heather sat alone on a backyard canopy swing, lit by the warm glow of soft garden lights. Steve dug through the remaining pile of coats on the bed until he found the one she had arrived wearing.

The garden behind the Pasadena bungalow was cozy and bore the fragrance of lilacs and lavender. Dense plantings of goldenrod and milkweed embraced a small patch of trimmed grass arranged in the shape of a figure eight. A large oak tree and three smaller myrtles divided the space into smaller nooks, one of which embraced the canopy swing. Steve stepped off the cedar deck and onto the sandstone pavers. As the door closed behind him, The Skints' "This Town" faded into the background, replaced by the chimes of a bubbling fountain.

"I brought your coat."

"Are you hinting I should leave?" Heather asked, sitting upright.

"Oh, no," he stammered. "I thought you'd be cold, is all."

"I'm teasing. Come sit. There's plenty of room." She waved her hand invitingly and shifted to make space.

Heather leaned forward, a cue for Steve to drape the coat over her shoulders. When he sat down, their legs touched. She didn't move away. "Why are you outside?" he asked.

"This fountain relaxes me. How are the others doing?"

"Most everyone left. Erin and Sun-hee are crashed on the couch. Grace and Mindy are playing a drinking game with some others. Grace is winning, of course. Big surprise." Heather smiled knowingly. "Last I saw, Vanessa and June were on the front porch talking to some guys. I don't know their names."

"Where's Casey?"

Steve exhaled. "Ugh. Blacked out in a bedroom. Drank way too much tonight."

"Those cocktails were potent."

"She normally knows her limits."

A moment passed in silence. "How are things going between you two?" she asked.

"You know." Steve shrugged his shoulders.

Heather focused her gaze on Steve and smiled. "No. That's why I asked."

"They've been better."

"How long have you two been together?" As she spoke, her head tilted sideways and downward.

"We grew up in the same neighborhood but didn't date until just before college. She's changing, though. Or I am. It's confusing."

"We're all experiencing so many new things. It's bound to happen."

"It was much simpler when we were just friends."

"But you have a solid base to build on. That's good. Right?"

"I guess." An emergency vehicle passed, sirens blaring. Steve winced at its piercing shriek and waited for the noise to subside in the distance. "Do you think it's possible for men and women to just be friends?"

"Of course. We're friends, aren't we?"

"Yeah, but—"

"But what?" Steve noticed Heather suddenly move her

leg away from his. "If I wasn't with Casey, it'd be different. Right?"

"I don't see why."

"Maybe you're right." A burst of laughter erupted from the house. Grace was heard demanding a penalty from an opponent.

"This was a grand party," Heather said.

"Yeah, it always is. You guys were magnificent tonight, by the way. People spend weeks preparing for this. You pulled it together in two."

"The girls wanted it. The rough start shook our confidence."

"But you're a natural at this."

Heather smiled. "Singing allows me to connect with others. During those brief moments on stage, I'm a whole person." She chuckled and began stretching like a cat. "Are you going home for the holidays?"

"For a bit, but I'll mostly be working to pay for school."

"You pay for your own studies?"

"I'm the merit kid who aced the entrance exam. Work-study has been my salvation."

"My dad made it sound impossible."

"It is possible, but hasn't been easy. I went to a private high school, too. That was fun. My classmates constantly reminded me of my...shall we say 'commoner status.' They'd be getting Porsches for their birthdays while I'd arrive on transit. That was a source of endless amusement for them."

"Passive-aggressive bullying."

"Mostly straight-up aggressive. But enough of me. What was your experience?"

"I attended a performing arts academy aligned with my agency. Between school and training, I had little time for anything else. Thinking of all the fun things high schoolers did in the States makes me jealous."

"High school sucked. Don't let the movies fool you. You were doing what you wanted, though. Right?"

"Oh, definitely, but it wasn't easy. I'd wake at 5:00 a.m. and train at the agency until school started at 8:00. We'd learn the usual subjects, along with dancing, singing, and music. At 4:00 p.m., I'd go to the agency for more practice. Depending on homework, I'd return to the dorms at 9:00 to finish assignments. I rarely saw my family."

"That's insane. Did you at least have weekends off?"

She laughed. "No way. We trained even longer on weekends. If you didn't keep pace, you'd be cut."

"Jeez, no wonder you guys are fire." Steve sat up straight. "You know, I've been thinking. There's one more production class before graduating. I was planning to film a drama, but would rather take another crack at that film festival. Would you be up for it? We can design it together from scratch specifically for Made in Heaven. And we'll feature the dance unit this time."

Heather beamed with excitement. "We're in no position to turn down opportunities. And we could definitely use the money. There's prize money, right?"

"Quite a lot, depending on where we place. I think it's only fair that we split it 50/50. You all handle the music, dance, and choreography, while I handle the rest. Whaddaya say?"

"You sure you want to work with us again?"

"My industry philosophy has always been one for all and all for one."

Heather's eyes widened upon hearing this. She grabbed his arm in a tight grip with both hands. "Oh, my god. Me too!

People think I'm crazy."

"They're flat wrong. Listen. You know for a fact this business is tough. The odds of us making it alone are slim, and often, it's down to pure luck. But if we stick together, we increase our chances. If one makes it, they can lift all boats."

Heather's eyes softened. She tilted her head down but kept focusing on Steve. "It surprises me that more people don't see it that way."

Steve marveled at how far they had come in such a short time. Just weeks earlier, Heather wanted nothing to do with him. Now, they were bonding on a different level than he ever had with Casey. He thought the timing was right to ask something he had long wondered about. "Say, I've been meaning to ask."

Heather must've sensed an uncomfortable topic was about to be broached. Her shoulders tensed. "What?"

"If you trained as an idol, but you're sitting here with me on this swing...does that mean you—" Steve stopped mid-sentence, thinking he had already blown it with the insensitive wording.

"Did I fail as an idol?" Heather said, finishing his question. She slumped in her seat, her carefree manner gone. "Gapbunssa," she said, clenching her hands.

"Honestly, I should have found a better way to put it." He exhaled. "Look, forget it. I don't mean to pry."

"This was a fun party. Allow me to keep these positive feelings for one night at least."

"I'm sorry I mentioned it."

"The quick answer is no."

Steve looked at her, more curious than ever. "Then why—"

"I was offered a debut but rejected it."

"But that was your dream!"

"You're determined to bring me down, aren't you?" Her voice hinted at anger, but she turned his head to the side, and softened her tone. The brush of fingertips on his chin electrified him. Heather moved her lips to within inches of his ear. She spoke in an adamant whisper, words meant only for the two of them. "Someday, I'll explain it to you, Steve, but not tonight. Okay?"

16

THE COMPLICATIONS OF BEING HEATHER

The clock on the bedside table taunted Heather with its cool blue numbers. 3:06 a.m. Twelve minutes had passed since the last time she checked, but it felt like an hour. If she had continued with her usual belief that unaware is untroubled, she would already be asleep by now. Curiosity got the better of her, though. While browsing the internet that afternoon, an innocent-looking story on Korean folktales led her astray. Since starting college, she had tried to avoid entertainment news from Seoul. But there, in the suggested articles column, on the right-hand side, clear as day, in bright, bold, red letters, sat the headline and the article daring her to look away. She didn't.

She couldn't.

The South Korean online news platform Naver featured a cover story on 37-G Entertainment's major announcement. They were debuting their long-awaited new girl group, Glimmer Blue. The adjoining photo depicted the five members standing before an army of cameras. The image tore at her soul. She was intimately familiar with every one of their faces.

Even then, Heather might have limited the damage, but the temptation proved irresistible. Against every reasonable course of action, she made the opposite choice. The final straw came when she skipped a scheduled accounting class study group. By then, there was no turning back. Heather knew she'd be watching the live stream of Glimmer Blue's debut showcase. Fans eagerly anticipated their first mini-album, "Summer Sun." Everyone was talking about it.

She tried to convince herself to hate it, to find the music cloying and repetitive, the dancing robotic, and the outfits drab. Yet, the album genuinely impressed. The group had serious potential.

She wanted Mi-ok's performance to fall flat, proving that the singer was out of her depth. But that, too, was a stretch. Mi-ok had presence, both in the promoted music video and during live performances.

Heather wanted their ratings to tank, demonstrating once and for all that Glimmer Blue was over-hyped. But her heart beat a little faster when the title track shot to the top spot on four streaming services later that day. It was a genuine hit.

Reality had struck. Glimmer Blue was going places. Quickly. And they didn't need Heather Moon's help to do it, did they? No siree.

Keep focused, Heather. Grace's anticipated counsel had already reached her ears. *Remember your group. Breathe slowly. Don't let another one of your panic attacks set in.* Yet, she wasn't born yesterday. It would take a miracle for Made in Heaven to make the Korean music charts. Likely, the best they could hope for involved playing shabby clubs on slow weeknights, nursing paltry crowds who ignored or even despised them.

Meanwhile, Glimmer Blue was on track to perform in packed arenas before adoring crowds worldwide. That dream was dead to her. It was impossible to turn back. Maybe Appa was right. Time to grow up. It wasn't too late to succeed at something. Perhaps he'd notice for once.

It did Heather no good that the next day, during yet another rehearsal for a nonexistent gig, she overheard three Made in Heaven band members whispering about the debut. What was she supposed to say? Grace, of course, knew the truth of why they left 37-G on the cusp of Glimmer Blue's formal founding, but she remained silent whenever the question came up.

Heather endured a second long, restless night. She spent hours brooding over her last weeks at the agency, and found it impossible to forget her initial encounter with Mi-ok. The arrival of her nemesis marked the beginning of the end of Heather's K-pop dream.

37-G introduced Nae Mi-ok as a singer recently displaced from a bankrupt agency. The company's decision to include her in the pool of candidates at that late stage struck Heather as cruel. By then, scads of trainees had been kicked to the curb. Only a dozen remained. Given the agency's suggestion that only a small number would remain, additional departures were imminent. Saying goodbye to so many friends over such a short period had been tough. Still, that morning's announcement of an actual *addition* floored the remaining trainees. Despite the already brutal competition, things were bound to get worse.

Mi-ok's visage was unique. Featuring a long face and a broad mouth, she possessed vaguely masculine mannerisms without losing touch with her femininity. Heather stared at the newcomer in disbelief. When it was her turn to be introduced, she offered a graceful smile but was, in fact, shaken to the core. Mi-ok looked right through her, exuding an intimidating level of confidence. She seemed to sense Heather's status and was ready to challenge it head-on right from the get-go.

Heather's anxieties intensified following Mi-ok's performance. While lacking a powerful voice, she had impressive sustain and a bewitching presence. The other trainees clapped and cheered in genuine admiration. It was now obvious that Heather was no longer the undisputed star of 37-G. This sudden change was downright unnerving.

When needing an escape from agency tensions, the rooftop terrace at 37-G was her go-to spot. It offered a commanding view of the Sinsa-dong neighborhood. Nearby, the Hannam Bridge stretched lazily across the Han River like a centipede. Heather's peers rarely ventured here. She couldn't imagine why not. Apart from the persistent hum of traffic on Olympic-daero, the landscaping was pleasant and peaceful.

Heather heard honking and shouting from the street below while setting belongings beside a chaise lounge. Curious, she approached the rooftop railing and leaned over to witness the disturbance. A delivery driver had blocked the garage entrance with his truck. A furious motorist was giving him an earful. The scene amused her, but eventually, both men resolved their conflict and went separate ways without a fuss. Just as Heather was about to turn away, she heard an unexpected voice.

"Usually, trainees wait until *after* they're cut to jump."

Heather's muscles tensed as she faced the speaker. Mi-ok assessed her from the chaise lounge near where her belongings lay. *Did she materialize out of thin air?* she thought to herself. "The commotion is all," Heather explained, using her hands to indicate the street.

"I wouldn't blame you. This business gets to people."

Resisting the temptation to flee, Heather explained, "It's not what you think."

"Don't worry. It'll be our little secret. Okay?"

Heather's body flushed with heat. "Who said anything about secrets?"

Mi-ok smiled and held up a soda can. "I have an extra. Sit down." The invitation seemed genuine, but Heather sensed trouble. She had to learn more about this mysterious newcomer, even if it meant swallowing some pride.

Before Heather could settle into her own chaise, Mi-ok commenced with a recitation. "She started performing in front of audiences in third grade. By middle school, sang lead in *Alice in Wonderland* musical, earning plaudits from classmates and teachers. At 13, she moved to Korea, training for three years at 37-G. The first and only winner of the Three Bowl Challenge. Did I leave anything out?"

"Are you angling to be an historian?" Heather asked as she sat.

"No, but you can use me as a reference if you'd like."

Heather blinked. "I won't need references where I'm going." She popped open the can as if the sound would emphasize her sick burn.

"True. That'd be overkill." Mi-ok responded without skipping a beat.

The girl excelled at trolling, Heather had to admit. Skin tightened, causing her mouth to curl into a smirk. She took a gulp of cola, wishing it was spiked. "Is this how you win friends and influence people?"

"They say I'm difficult. Not my fault others can't keep up."

"That's one dysfunctional attitude."

"Da-som told me you'd say that. Always putting the team ahead of self. How noble. How...cute." Mi-ok wrinkled her nose as she said this. "Being hated was once upsetting to me. Sleep offered no solace, only tears and dread for the coming days. But you know what? I turned contempt to my advantage. Now it motivates me."

"Sounds lonely."

"I'm too busy watching others cry these days to care much."

Heather placed her half-empty can on the pavement next to the chaise. Oddly, she felt at ease sharing thoughts with this contentious stranger. "It used to bother me when I received more attention than the others."

"But not anymore?"

"Now I help them. I'm not their enemy."

"They're competition. Why concern yourself with inferiors?"

"Nobody succeeds in a void."

"Bah." Mi-ok waved her hand around as though shooing a gnat."Word of advice. Always keep climbing, or you'll find a knife in your back."

"That's a grim view."

"Is it? You're almost there yourself, I'd bet."

"I doubt that."

Mi-ok took a swallow of her own soda, maintaining a steady gaze that stung like lasers. "I know what you're thinking."

"Why do you say that?" Heather kept a blank expression, reluctant to hear the answer.

"We'd both be lost without this," Mi-ok twirled a finger in the air above her head, suggesting the industry. She then leaned closer to whisper under her breath. "The difference is

I'm a survivor. Are you?"

* * *

Amid the commotion at SIU's Tuition Office, Heather waited for her turn to come up. Her mind buzzed with thoughts about the future. The room was dreary, with obnoxious lighting and uninspired corporate artwork. She wanted to escape this bland reality and delve into her own musings. However, a pervasive threat loomed. Of course, it centered on money, or the lack thereof. With no cause to question Appa's sincerity, Heather knew she had only one semester left to shape her entire life. One path was deceptively easy. Take the free education and graduate with a "useful" degree in Finance. She never fantasized about a life in finance. The choice of majors was an appeasement strategy tempered by the knowledge that she could pursue her genuine passion on the side. But that was no longer an option, at least not with Appa's help.

Her thoughts then shifted to Made in Heaven. The members seemed to revel in the joy of creating music together. Still, Heather doubted their long-term commitment to the project. She understood the hesitancy. The group was a fun diversion, but they had lives to live. Who in their right mind would risk college for a fleeting shot at success with a band? But what if she *could* do both? Perhaps the ultimate act of defiance showed that what appeared to be impossible was actually just improbable. Perhaps she could follow Steve's example and pay for her education on her own terms. It would be madness not to explore that option, right?

That's why she waited in this office for her number to be called.

A blonde-haired white male sat in an adjacent chair, offering a playful grin and a wink. "Here for the annual bloodletting?"

Heather wasn't in the mood for tuition humor. Thus far, no student had left the office with a smile on their face. Needing to release nervous energy, she picked at the loose thread on her sweater. It was coming apart. "I'm getting a cost estimate for next year," she replied, hoping the lack of enthusiasm would send a message.

"Don't get too attached to your firstborn," he laughed.

Heather offered a friendly smile but didn't want to encourage more conversation. She had a lot on her mind.

"Where are you from?" he asked.

"Los Angeles."

"No, really. Where originally?"

Ugh, not this again. "Really. I was born here."

"Oh," he responded. "You speak good English."

Why in the hell shouldn't I? Before she could respond verbally, the number 23 flashed on the monitor. "That's me," she said, grateful for the timely escape.

The Latino counselor towered over her, even after they were seated in his office. After a few standard questions, he printed a document and pushed it across the desk for her perusal. Heather scanned the lengthy list of itemized costs: tuition, room and board, meal plans, books, fees, etc. Skipping the details, she settled on the prominent figure at the bottom right corner. Her blood ran cold.

"This information must be wrong," she remarked, handing over the datasheet.

The counselor reviewed it. "Nope, it's all there. Were you expecting something else?"

"I mean, $82,043? For one year? Are you serious?"

"You go here. Surely you know the cost by now?"

Heather had only a vague idea. Appa had taken care of the finances up to this point. "Okay, but there are scholarships, right?"

"That depends on your major and your skills."

"I'm hell at singing," she volunteered.

He looked at her blankly. "Okay, but you're not a music major. That's kind of key."

"If I switched, what would I be eligible for?"

"The best scholarships are reserved for the heavily recruited. Otherwise, we're talking maybe $5,000 to $20,000, depending on many factors."

"That still leaves an enormous gap."

"Are you good at sports by any chance?"

"Um." She scanned the room with her eyes, stalling for time. The counselor had a signed baseball in a clear plastic box on his desk. "I can tell you all about the sacrifice in baseball."

He rubbed the back of his neck, avoiding eye contact. "I'll record that as a no."

"What about Business? Surely, I qualify there?"

He scanned her file once more before issuing his response. "You need to raise your grades to be considered for the best of them. The Hallerschmid scholarship is a popular choice. It's competitive, though."

"I'm competitive. How much could I get?"

"The average is a thousand."

Heather laughed.

The counselor looked offended.

"For a second there, I thought you said a thousand," she said, explaining her reaction.

"I did."

Silence. "But…how do I secure the rest?"

"Most students engage in work-study for a chunk of it and borrow the rest through government loans. I can give you the forms if you're interested. And there are always off-campus jobs. You'd get some life experience."

"So, what are you saying?"

Heather's next stop was Colton Temporary Staffing. A gray-haired Black woman handled her 4:00 p.m. appointment. Before the interview started, one of her coworkers stopped by to complain about office policy. The pair spoke for several minutes, during which Heather's mind strayed back to the Glimmer Blue debut. *I bet Mi-ok isn't stressing over temp jobs,* she thought.

"It never changes," said the office worker afterward, dragging Heather back into the present reality. "Okay. Tell me what employment experience you have."

"I've never held a regular job. I was a trainee in Korea, though."

The woman's eyes narrowed. "Is that like a union apprenticeship?"

"No, like K-pop."

Perplexed, the woman peered over her bifocals. "You mean a soda company?"

"No, it's Korean pop music. I sing and dance and write songs."

The interviewer scowled in disgust as if Heather were wasting her time. "I'm asking about work, though."

"That was work. I spent a minimum of 80 hours a week on it."

"How much did you get paid?"

"I didn't."

"That's a hobby, then."

"No—" *This is like talking to Appa.*

"Never mind." The woman shook her head dismissively. "I'll ask a series of questions to determine your suitability for the jobs we service." She prepared her fingers to record Heather's responses on the computer. "How fast can you type?"

"About twenty words per minute."

The woman clicked several commands. "That eliminates those jobs." Heather watched in dismay as the woman's screen cleared a lengthy list of entries all at once. "Do you have experience with printed circuit boards?"

"I've operated an office printer," she responded, half in jest.

This attempt at humor produced another frown. "We'll take those off too." More listings disappeared. Two dozen questions later, the interview was done. One job remained on the screen. "Okay, I have an opportunity for you." Heather awaited her fate. "A catering company needs help. No experience necessary. It pays minimum wage, but the hours are flexible."

Heather did some quick calculations in her head. "Minimum wage doesn't even cover housing. I need to pay for college, too."

"You don't understand how this works, do you? When you have no experience, you start at the bottom like everyone else."

"But I can't get experience without a job, and now you're telling me I can't get a job without experience?"

"Rough, ain't it?"

"I need money."

"So does everyone else."

17

PRICKLY PAIRS

Sun-hee skipped class early to ensure she'd make the 4:00 p.m. meeting with Danya Kay. Grace had asked the group to assemble at the St. Ignatius Film & Television Building a half hour early to receive a briefing. The bus trip from UCLA to SIU seemed interminable, but the extra time allowed Sun-hee to conduct some research. She hoped to learn as much as possible about the woman. Driven by more than just curiosity, she was interested in what made Danya tick.

A quick browse of the choreographer's most recent social media posts revealed nothing. Upon deeper reading, however, a persistent theme emerged: connection. This point became obvious in Danya's interview for a performing arts magazine two years earlier. Blaming the problem on the rise of social media, she lamented the decline of intimacy in society. Live performances, including dance, she argued, helped counter that isolation. Sun-hee found this material useful.

The cinema was empty when Sun-hee arrived. She selected a prime seat in the fourth row and heard a knock from above and behind. Looking up, she saw Steve waving at her from the projection booth window. Her stomach fluttered as she acknowledged him with a wave and a smile.

Surprisingly, the theater then went dark. Heavy curtains parted, revealing an enormous projection screen. Sun-hee watched with curiosity as the black borders surrounding it transitioned from a near square to a long, thin rectangle stretching clear across her field of vision. A film clip appeared. She recognized it as the song "America" from the original *West Side Story*. She'd seen both cinematic versions before, but never in this way. The vibrant energy of the images arrested her attention. Funny but also insightful, the classic dance battle focused on groups of men and women arguing over the merits of life in New York versus Puerto Rico. The performances were terrific; the dancing was mesmerizing. Beyond its visceral impact, the imagery's grand scale guaranteed that minor elements profoundly shaped the experience. Elements that would have been lost in a home-based system now had an impact.

As the clip ended, the lights came on. Though brief, the presentation made a powerful impression. A few minutes later, Steve entered the auditorium. "Hey, Sun-hee. What d'ya think?"

"Brilliant."

"Yeah, impressive, huh? Vanessa and I prepared a brief presentation for Danya. Hopefully, it will inspire her to help us. I'm not so sure."

"It will." Sun-hee had so much she wanted to say to him, but her mind had suddenly turned blank. An awkward silence passed as they both waited for the other to speak. She struggled to find an engaging conversation starter. The longer she contemplated, the further her mind drifted from anything acceptable. Left with nothing to talk about, they both smiled uneasily.

"Have you talked to Heather?" Steve asked, breaking the silence. "She's planning on coming, right?"

Sun-hee's stomach clenched in disappointment at this question. "I assume so." This lack of a witty response illustrated the difficulty she faced in breaking free from Heather's inescapable gravity. Enthusiastic chatter soon heralded her group mates. As they settled into the theater, Steve's eyes sparkled as he greeted Heather. Sun-hee observed their body language as they embraced. They looked so comfortable together. It was a far cry from last semester when their main singer was as likely to spit Steve's name as say it. They'd known him for the same amount of time, but Sun-hee found herself eclipsed in his eyes by Heather's shimmering star.

Since there was little opportunity to waste, Grace turned the conversation to the upcoming meeting. Vanessa summarized their plan and briefed members on their expected roles. "To be honest with you, I doubt this will work," she said in summary.

"This was your idea to begin with," noted Grace.

"I know, but Danya can be picky. She may simply be humoring me." Groans met this statement. "I'm just saying," Vanessa said defensively.

A half-formed idea came to Sun-hee's mind. She stood and asked, "Where are the restrooms?"

"In the lobby, past the elevators, on your right," Steve explained. "Don't be long. Danya'll be here soon."

"What does she look like?"

"Mid-thirties, mixed-race, half-Indian," explained Vanessa. "Dark, wavy hair to her shoulders. There's a compass tattoo on her bicep. Why?"

"Just curious."

Sun-hee exited the cinema and surveyed the scene. During the next several minutes, a handful of students passed by. None met the profile. A clock on the wall showed five minutes past the hour. While at the drinking fountain, Sun-hee noticed a woman matching Vanessa's description amble into the lobby. The stranger paused to orient herself, noting the theater door but bypassing it to continue towards the women's room.

With that observation, the rest of Sun-hee's plan fell into line. She debated its merits before deciding to throw all the chips in. With a deep breath, she extracted her phone and used it to "converse" with an imaginary person on the other end. While entering the restroom, she spoke aloud, altering her voice in disguise. "I'll be right over after this meeting."

Sun-hee recognized Danya's shoes under the stall door but saw no others. They had the room to themselves. As she made her way to the sinks, the charade continued. "It won't take long. The choreographer we're waiting on is late, and I'm beginning to doubt she'll show at all." She gave her imaginary friend time to respond. "No, I have a feeling she'll flake."

Sun-hee turned on the tap to let some water run. "I don't know. We could probably do better." She ran her free hand under the stream to splash it around some. "Yeah, if she's as good as Vanessa says, would she be teaching exercise classes?" Sun-hee turned off the tap. "We'll see. Listen, I gotta go. I'll call you if this meeting is canceled."

Sun-hee pushed a button on her phone to produce a beeping sound, then left. Regret for her actions surfaced upon exiting the restroom.

"Nothing?" asked Grace as Sun-hee returned to her theater

seat.

"She'll be here soon."

A beat later, Danya walked in, wearing a half-hearted smile and failing to mask her displeasure. As Vanessa provided introductions, Sun-hee watched her body language. Danya listened intently to each member as they spoke. When it was Sun-hee's turn, she used a normal voice, which sounded distinct from her disguised one. Danya was flummoxed. The bathroom incident kept her unsettled for the entire meeting. Regret swept over Sun-hee as she witnessed the negative impact that her ruse had on the choreographer.

A half-hour later, the members of Made in Heaven exited the theater. Danya had already departed, and the group was free to share impressions.

"See, I told you it wouldn't work," said a sorrowful Vanessa.

"It was worth a shot," said Heather.

"We did our best, but I'm all out of ideas," said Grace. "That was our Plans A, B, and C walking out the door."

By this point, Sun-hee's pangs of guilt were overwhelming. Her remorse compelled Sun-hee to fix the screw-up she blamed on her own interference. "Sorry to run. I'm late for my bus."

"No prob, Sun-hee. I'll call you later."

She dashed outside the building and searched for the nearest parking lot. Down the mall and near the southernmost campus exit, according to the directory. It was a long shot, but if she ran, it might be possible to catch Danya in time. Students on the walkways scooted to one side to avoid her magnificent charge. Upon reaching the lot, she scanned it. Classes had let out, and many students were heading to their vehicles. But

Danya had a distinct hairstyle. By applying that filter, she could focus on the best prospects. A minute later, her target was spotted two aisles away, opening a car door. Sun-hee bolted once again.

The car was backing out by the time she reached it. Sun-hee motioned for her to roll down the window.

"Didn't I make myself clear?" Danya asked.

"Before you go, I'd like to say something. It's important."

Danya arched her eyebrows but instead of leaving, pulled back into the space. "Was that you in the restroom?" she asked.

Sun-hee nodded shyly. "I owe you a huge apology. What came over me? I was so desperate to make things happen that I didn't think it through."

"Go on."

"The truth is Vanessa adores you. And that's saying a lot because there are few things she admits to liking at all."

"I believe that."

"She's enormously talented but doubts herself. If she could only watch you work, I'm sure it would have a lasting impact."

"At some point, every choreographer has to stand on their own two feet. No pun intended."

"It's not about teaching us the steps. It's about understanding the intrinsic value of dance. And how it's more important now than ever."

Based on Danya's reaction, this statement piqued her interest. "And what is that intrinsic value?"

"That dance can communicate ideas that are difficult to articulate but which all humans can relate to. It transports us into new ways of seeing the world. It reminds us how important physical interaction is in our lives. That's what we want to capture."

Danya turned a side eye to Sun-hee in partial disbelief. "Vanessa said that?"

"We've talked about it."

The car's ignition shut off. Danya rested her arms on top of the steering wheel. "If I agree to do this for free, and I'm not saying I will, but if I do, it would have to be a one-time thing. Okay?"

"Teach Vanessa your process; she'll blossom in ways you always predicted."

* * *

Mindy had anticipated this recording session for a while. This marked the first of two days dedicated to recording music for Made in Heaven's forthcoming EP. It offered the group a chance to improve upon their debut release. The new songs were fun to play, and she expected excellent results.

They chose to record "From That Day On" first as the more straightforward song. As with their first album, they wrote the B-side as a contrast to the higher-energy promoted single. It was a rock-oriented power ballad about two people growing apart. Featuring a simple arrangement of acoustic rhythm guitar and muted synth, its understated beginning built to a soaring chorus before returning to a softer close. Rather than rap, Grace, this time, provided a reflective electric guitar solo.

True to its understated character, just the two top vocalists were needed. Heather had just finished recording her vocals when Steve approached. "You sounded great this time," he said as Heather emerged from the isolation booth.

"Are you saying I don't sound great every time?"

Steve blinked. "No, you do sound great every time."

"Then why don't you tell me every time?"

"Um...because...usually..." He pinched the skin at his throat. "Because usually, I'm overwhelmed by your artistry."

Heather's shoulders drooped. "So, you're not overwhelmed by my artistry today?"

He stared at her, his thought process disrupted. Finally, he admitted, "I can't possibly come out ahead in this conversation, can I?"

Heather stood straight. "There's hope for you yet, Steve," she said with a mischievous grin.

Mindy stifled a laugh. The poor fellow had no chance.

The recording session itself, unfortunately, became contentious for far less playful reasons. As manager, Arnie felt compelled to bring a distinctive rock edge to the EP. He had argued for the band to adopt this approach from the beginning. The EP was designed to connect the two parts of Made in Heaven. The idea was to have traditional rock music that the band could play while possessing enough of a dance groove to support the dance unit's activities. They could choose to perform either way, depending on the situation. As with any hybrid, achieving balance was vital. This proved difficult because Arnie and Steve bickered over where that balance should lie.

While the musicians took their dinner break, Mindy stayed behind to record drums for the B-side. She found herself in the center of this tug-of-war as it reached an apex. The tinderbox exploded when Arnie insisted on drums with a clean sound, like the classic rock recordings of the 70s. He requested thorough miking. Steve, conversely, sought to replicate the distinct 80s gated reverb drum sound. His approach called for more straightforward mic placement, featuring a compressed, gated talkback mic. They tried both options: first Arnie's way, then Steve's.

After the second attempt, Arnie stood his ground. "Okay, yeah, now put it back."

Mateo jumped to fulfill this request, but Steve blocked him as he approached Mindy's drum kit. "What do you think you're doing?"

"It does sound better," said Mateo.

"Sounds better? But does it sound right?" countered Steve.

Arnie dashed into the live room shouting, "Let him go. He's gotta reset mics."

"I don't remember making that decision," said Steve.

"I'm the manager!" countered Arnie.

"Who's paying for exactly nothing, I'll point out."

"We did it your way last go. Lookit what happened. Now we do it right."

"It's my project. And the music was sublime last time."

"We got nothing out of it."

"Quality had nothing to do with that."

"First, you blow the pick, then you blow our chance for the festival. Why should I trust you?"

"The project originated with me, and I'm paying for it. You agreed to help, is all."

"I was there from the start."

"What trip are you on? How is this in any way your idea?"

Mindy looked at Mateo, who could only shrug. The two watched as Arnie and Steve regurgitated weeks of bad blood. As the clock ticked on, the attacks became more personal. It hurt to listen to them.

"What do you say, Mindy?" Arnie asked after they had been

at it for a while. "Full sound is better, right?"

She threw her hands in the air. "Leave me out of this. I didn't write the song."

"We're wasting time by arguing," continued Steve.

"Then move out the way. Once I'm done, you'll have a hell of a track."

"I won't let you take over this project. It's not even your song. Can you even articulate the vision, or are you making this the Arnie Johnson show?"

"You should be so lucky."

"No, Arnie, I mean it. I'm done." He stood with his chest puffed and huffing. "This collaboration is not working. I'll kindly ask you to leave. We can hash over it later, but time's short tonight. This arguing is counterproductive."

Arnie stared coldly at him.

"Mateo, will you prepare the recording as we rehearsed it?" Returning to the control room, the engineer conveyed his displeasure with a head shake.

"Okay, give me another run-through," said Steve.

Mindy was glad to return to drumming. As she played, Arnie grabbed his belongings and left without uttering another word.

18

MODULATIONS

Despite their unresolved choreographer problem, Made in Heaven forged ahead with plans for filming the music video. Heather wished to prevent another instance of last-minute compromises to meet a deadline. If the dance aspect remained a sticking point, at least they had time to work on the music. The group held an internal discussion and decided to promote "Feel the Heat" as their second single. With the B-side track already recorded, the band focused on perfecting their A-side performance before heading into the studio again for the second session.

The song was an unusual bird. Conceived as a hard-driving hybrid of 80s synth-pop spiced with hard-rocking guitars, "Feel the Heat" was propelled by a constant dance beat and a melody exhibiting few peaks or valleys. Rich power-vocals were to be supported by strummed guitars through the bridge. The opening featured a chantlike chorus with distinctive whistling. Steve called the motif 'a refugee from a spaghetti western'. He predicted it would become the song's iconic hook.

The band sharply increased the number of rehearsals. For

one such practice, Heather had booked time at the Bird's Nest, a renowned campus hangout perched on the edge of the SIU bluff. The rehearsal itself ended early. She felt a sense of satisfaction with the progress of "Feel the Heat." The musicians had added nuance to the song; performances were tight.

Regarding the video, they scheduled a production planning meeting immediately after practice. Steve had news to deliver, and numerous aesthetic details needed settling. Heather figured the Bird's Nest's outdoor terrace, with its breathtaking city views and idyllic weather, would put everyone in a productive mood.

She noted with interest Vanessa's presence at the meeting. Danya still hadn't made up her mind, and thus Vanessa's status remained a mystery too. The dance major continued to take part in group activities, though, despite never having formally accepted the group's invitation. She even voted on key decisions. Nobody seemed to mind her presence. They recognized her value and didn't want to jeopardize matters by highlighting this minor technicality.

With Steve's appearance still moments away, costume designer Marielle arrived, toting new design sketches. Her task was to create three outfit concepts that fit the description: confident, flirty, powerful, charming, and playful. Seizing upon these cues, Marielle ignited the girls' imaginations.

"You know how to make us look thin and pretty," said Erin.

"I love how you take individual body flaws and turn them into strengths," said Grace.

Factions sprang up around two competing visions. Mindy, Erin, and Heather rallied behind the most feminine look. Vanessa, June, and Grace threw their weight behind the sportier option. The tension in the air was palpable, threatening to erupt into a full-blown argument. Sun-hee, however, came to the rescue with a clever solution. The idea suited Marielle, who agreed to adapt each outfit to the wearer's liking while retaining a harmonious theme. Crisis averted, for now.

"The material I have is predominantly black, white, and red. Do you prefer…"

Before she could finish her question, Steve arrived, hungrily munching from a bag of chips. "Mind if I join you?"

"Just in time," said Grace.

Steve placed the bag on the table, and the group immediately pounced upon it."God, I'm starving," said Erin. In the blink of an eye, nothing remained of the snack but crumbs. Steve looked bereft of all joy at the sudden loss of what amounted to his dinner.

"I hope you were done with those," a mischievous Heather said, licking the remaining seasoning from her fingers bewitchingly.

"No choice, it seems."

Steve wasted no time getting to work. Providing a broad overview of the project, he held his audience's attention while sticking to plain English, but once the technical jargon began, their eyes glazed over. "I plan to use a Red Helium sensor with Ultra Panavision 70 lenses to grab the image at 2:1," he explained. "Then, we'll crop it vertically to output at the 2:39 aspect ratio." Steve paused as if to gather accolades. A chorus of blank stares met his enthusiasm.

Grace leaned over to Heather. "You speak film nerd. Can you translate?"

"I'm not fluent," she responded.

"Oh, spare me," said Steve, dismissing their mockery.

He reminded them of the extra-wide-screen film clips they showed Danya at the theater. "That's what I'm aiming for. Plus, I want the colors to pop like music videos in Korea." This disclosure proved popular. However, the subsequent reveal that they'd have to embark on another road trip produced groans of protest.

"Again?" said Mindy.

"Not that awful roof?" asked Erin.

"No," he responded, "not exactly."

"What, exactly, then?" asked Grace.

"We'll be in the desert, but this time in an air-conditioned building. The Scottsdale Airpark, specifically."

"Where's that?" asked June.

"In Arizona," answered Grace. June remained perplexed.

"Why there?" asked Heather.

"My dad, much to my surprise, knows the owner of a private jet servicing hangar. Through him, I swung a deal to film over Easter weekend in exchange for promo services."

"Do we get to fly on a private jet?" asked Erin hopefully. "I've always wanted to fly on a private jet. Once my—"

"Um, no," he said, cutting her off. "But I bet they'd give you a tour if you ask nicely." Erin slouched into a half-pout.

Steve described the travel arrangements and previewed their daily schedules. Once Steve finished his report, Heather nudged Grace in the ribs. "It's time," she said in Korean.

Grace took the cue. "Um, Steve." Her manner of speech indicated a delicate matter was at hand.

He tensed, preparing for the worst. "Yes?"

"The other day, we discussed ground rules for our videos."

"And what did you decide?"

"Let's see. I have a list." She opened her phone and

began reciting terms. "First off, how women are portrayed in western music videos is unacceptable."

"I'm listening," said Steve.

Grace tallied their demands on her fingers. "Our videos must be told from our point of view. We won't be props for the fantasies of male characters nor depicted as weak, worthless victims. And don't you dare film us as fragmented, disconnected body parts either."

Steve shook his head and tsked. "Impossible. That'll destroy the whole video!" He slammed his palm on the table for effect. "I have a scene where a group of men throw slices of lunch meat at your thong-clad asses for target practice. You can't possibly expect me to cut that, can you?"

Despite his weighty delivery, the ruse was clear to Heather, who giggled. Grace remained intent on keeping a straight face. She snatched the empty chip bag, shook it in the air for a few seconds, then let it fall to the table. "Luckily for you, this is empty, or you'd be taking a crumb shower right about now."

With that resolved, Steve next turned to the thorny issue of choreography. There was no hiding from it now. "So, how's the dance coming along?" An uncomfortable silence met his inquiry. Members avoided eye contact with Vanessa, but Steve noticed. He addressed the dancer. "This concept relies heavily on the choreo," he said. "If the dance fails, so will the video."

Vanessa clenched her teeth. "I'm working on it." She began fidgeting.

"We're running out of time. I'll panic unless I see a rough idea soon." He assessed the members, but none had anything better to offer. "Sooner or later, you'll have to accept that Danya's a no-go."

Heather sought to ease the growing tension. "We'll have

something for you soon." Whatever the outcome, Steve seemed to find temporary peace in her assurance.

"I don't mean to change the subject, but the level tests are in." Grace's announcement produced instant anxiety. The idea had been to videotape each member's singing and dancing performances to be rated by an impartial judge from the professional ranks. They asked one of Sun-hee's former managers in Korea to do the honors. He happily obliged and proved acceptably unbiased.

First came the vocal rankings: Heather and Sun-hee were first and second, followed by Mindy and June, with Grace in fifth. Vanessa and Erin were tied for last place. This news shocked nobody, nor did anyone object.

The dance rankings went this way: Vanessa, June, and Mindy occupied the top three spots, with Grace and Sun-hee tied for fourth, and Heather and Erin tied for last.

"I'm tied for the worst singer *and* the worst dancer?" a deflated Erin complained.

"You're the best bassist, though," noted Sun-hee.

"Oh, whoop de doo. I'm the only bassist."

"That automatically makes you the worst bassist, too," said Mindy.

"A triple threat," added Vanessa, piling on the torment.

Erin responded with her trademark blend of feigned deer-in-the-headlights alarm and an I'll-get-you-back-someday-just-you-wait menacing stare. "Get out," she said, pointing to the parking lot. "I hate you all I'll have you know." Mindy put an arm around Erin and kissed her on the cheek. This gesture produced a sheepish smile from their beleaguered companion.

Heather listened to the rankings without participating in

the banter. "I'll work harder to become a better dancer, I promise."

"Ray specifically stated that these are not set in stone," explained Sun-hee. "They're merely a starting point based on raw talent."

"The last topic we need to address is fitness," stated Grace.

"Uh, oh. Now for the fun," said Mindy.

"Let me tell you from experience, a performance schedule can be hard on the body. I can't stress enough how important it is to keep in top physical shape. That includes eating right and exercising regularly."

"So, what are you saying?"

"Well, some of us are getting a tad...how to put it?"

"Big boned," volunteered Vanessa.

"Yeah, big-boned," repeated Grace. "We'll go with that."

* * *

It didn't sound right to her ears. Heather listened carefully to the final mix of "Feel the Heat." She wanted to be sure before objecting.

Nope. It wasn't her imagination. Something was wrong.

"Whaddaya think?" Arnie asked, holding his chin high as the playback ended.

Heather stared at the mixing console, searching for a way to express her dissatisfaction. "All the nuance is missing. What happened?" Arnie jerked his head back, surprised by her reaction. "My voice sounds small and thin," she continued. "I didn't sing it this way."

Arnie's demeanor changed. His voice thundered in the small room. "I told him it was dumb. Did he listen?"

"Are you saying this was Steve's idea?"

"It sounded good last time; he must've messed with it after I left."

"You guys way overused the editing tools. Now I sound like a robot."

"It was a bad idea to let Steve touch it."

"Can it be restored? This concerns me."

"We'll do another mix. You got time?"

Heather absolutely would make time even if she lacked it. The plan was to send previews to local radio stations within a week, and there was no way she'd allow the song to be released in its current form. After stepping outside to cancel a hair appointment and delay the band rehearsal, she returned to find Arnie tweaking controls on the console.

"Reset everything to zero for starters," she demanded. The next playthrough was an immediate improvement. At one point, she paused the playback to emphasize her complaint. "See, I didn't sing this part flat because I'm clueless. I intended this inflection." Under her guidance, they reviewed the song line by line and adjusted settings until Heather was satisfied. Gone were most of the impeccable timings and the precise pitches. Heather enhanced some areas to disguise the worst mistakes of the amateur members or to correct notes when they rubbed awkwardly against guitar chords, for example. The remaining changes were subtle and, by necessity. The time-consuming exercise restored the spirit of the performance. She understood this level of control would never have been possible at 37-G, and sought to make use of it before it passed.

"I'm surprised Steve went for this," she said after they finished the work. "We discussed our mixing options days ago."

"He don't understand nothing. He's not meant for this stuff."

A knot developed in Heather's stomach. "What do you mean?"

"His instincts are all wrong. Plus, he quits too easily and is unreliable."

These statements surprised Heather. She hadn't known Steve long but struggled to recall any incident where he behaved as Arnie described. "He's the producer. You have to work with him."

"The music biz needs a steady hand. You know that. I bet you saw rough times as a trainee."

Heather's pulse raced. Could Arnie have heard what happened in Korea? The way he worded it made her wonder. Had she let some sensitive information slip? She studied his face. No, she decided. He had to be guessing. "Can you elaborate on that exactly?"

"Someone living with regrets might overcompensate later."

Her jaw dropped. "Where would you get that idea?"

"You'd be surprised."

"Try me." She folded her arms across her chest, debating how much further she wanted this conversation to continue.

19

DROOPING FLOWERS

The long-awaited call came after Grace's last class on Tuesday. "I'll do it," were the only words spoken. Danya did not tend toward verbosity.

"Oh, that's great," Grace responded.

"But here are my conditions. This as a favor for Vanessa. She's been there for me."

"Got it."

"This is my only freebie. From now on, services are charged at full professional rate."

"Understood."

"And in lieu of payment, I want an end credit."

"That, I can't promise. Steve's funding the project for his class."

"Find a way."

Steve did not receive this caveat well. When Grace informed him of the condition later that evening, he responded, "No way."

"Steve, it's her one demand. And I think it's reasonable."

"Music videos don't have credits."

"K-pop videos often do."

Deep silence came from Steve's end. "If I allow that, the next thing you know, everyone's gonna want a credit."

"Is that so bad? It's not like any of us are getting rich off this. The alternative is a substandard dance. You said so yourself how important it is."

"Well, I don't like this one bit. However, I'll draw the line at crediting the honeywagon driver."

"We've never used a honeywagon. We can barely afford honey."

"I sincerely hope you meant that as a joke."

* * *

After much patience, the girls teased out of Grace a story related to their final days at 37-G Entertainment. Frankly, she had brought the problem upon herself. Grace had a habit of referring to lessons learned there. The frequent mentions were enough to stoke curiosity among her bandmates.

During one of Heather's rehearsal absences, Erin cautiously asked, "What was it like at 37-G before Glimmer Blue?"

Grace remained adamant about maintaining Heather's privacy. "I told you I wasn't gonna go there."

"Tell us what you feel comfortable with," objected Vanessa. "You were part of it too. What's *your* story."

They had a good point. Grace knew that distrust issues would arise if their curiosity remained unsated for long. Continuing to withhold her story risked doing more harm than good. "Well, as you can imagine, the last weeks before a debut are intense," she said. "Especially when it came to a high-profile group like Glimmer Blue." Once more, Grace found her thoughts racing back to the past.

Three of Grace's fellow trainees stood on the sidewalk in the passenger loading area outside Seoul's KBS studio. The 12-seater van was already full.

"Get another van," team leader Da-som instructed.

"They left already," a member of the isolated trio protested. "This is the last one."

"We have no more room."

Grace evaluated the situation. "It'll be tight," she suggested, "but if we squish together, they should fit." Da-som appeared vexed by the countermand but, lacking better options, let the strays in. After much mayhem and lighthearted teasing, the occupants settled and commenced their journey home.

37-G had treated the entire class of trainees to a taping of the network's latest music program. In what marked a rare break from their monotonous routine, the girls' adventure flushed them with excitement, and they chatted ceaselessly. Besides seeing Stray Kids perform in person, they witnessed a live television production, marking a first for most. Their producer justified the excursion as a learning experience, and it was hard to argue with the results. Grace had taken copious mental notes for later inquiry.

One long-haired girl sitting in the front shared an anecdote about touching singer Lino as he walked by. This prompted general debate over professional standards trainees must uphold, despite their informal industry status. Grace listened for a while, but soon lost interest. Enjoying a window seat, she preferred to watch the passing streetscape instead. The rhythmic purr of tires on the pavement made her drowsy. The sudden application of brakes jolted her back to consciousness.

Rose, a quiet young woman occupying the adjacent seat, used this opportunity to engage in conversation. "Exciting news today, huh?"

Grace wasn't sure she followed. Shaking off her drowsiness, she said, "You mean the taping?"

"Did you not catch word?" Rose appeared ecstatic at the opportunity to spread juicy gossip. "Baram overheard two executives talking on break. The rumors are true. They're debuting the new girl group next year. Can you believe it?"

Grace's eyes widened. "Who's in it?"

"They haven't decided yet," interjected Eui from two seats away.

"From here on out, all evaluations will be life or death," said Rose.

"We're sure about one of them, anyway," Eui added with a hint of resentment.

"Who?" asked Grace.

"C'mon. You're her friend."

"You mean Heather? I am confident we all have a chance."

"Puh-leeze. Little Miss Perfect's a guaranty. They love her. Don't be coy. I'm sure she'll put in a good word for you."

"Yeah, you're the best rapper here," said Rose. "They have to pick you."

The conversation grew too tantalizing for eavesdroppers to ignore for long. Soon, most of those seated in the rear benches offered assessments on which trainees had the best chance of making the group. They reserved their boldest opinions for those riding in other vans. Grace wondered if their viewpoints would hold if seating arrangements differed. The troop proposed full lineups, with each trainee naming five to nine candidates they felt would comprise the best overall group. Heather's status was abundantly clear. She made every list.

After a late dinner, most trainees settled in to finish their assigned homework for the next day. Grace went to pay Heather a visit, but her roommates said she had returned to the agency for practice. Despite being exhausted, Grace couldn't wait until morning. Fortunately, the building stood three blocks away. She made the short trek in the rain.

The front door was locked tight. A friendly night watchman recognized her face and allowed access. All rooms on the third floor were dark except for Studio C. An EDM track was playing from within. Grace cracked the door open and peered inside.

Most of the lights in the sleekly designed, wood-paneled studio were dark. The few that remained on were sufficient for the room's sole occupant. Heather practiced her dance performance, facing the one mirrored wall in the studio that didn't provide a direct view of the doorway. The music was so powerful that Grace's entrance went unnoticed.

"Looking good," Grace said at its conclusion.

Heather jumped out of her skin. "You scared the life out of me!" she exclaimed, clutching her heart. Before she could say anything more, the looped track began repeating.

"How long will you train tonight?" shouted Grace over the music.

"Why would I need one?"

"Need what?"

"It's five minutes away."

"What is?"

"The dorm."

"That's why I'm asking."

"I don't need a train," Heather said louder.

"What train?"

"I don't know. You asked."

"I didn't ask about a train. I asked how long you were training."

"Why do you keep asking? I have no idea how long trains are."

Grace was exasperated. She stomped over to the audio rack and switched off the noise. "That's driving me nuts." She turned to see Heather smiling devilishly and grew suspicious. "Were you doing that on purpose?"

"The music *was* loud," she responded slyly.

This supposed prank angered Grace, but Heather's nonchalant reaction forced her to acknowledge the humor in the situation. She calmed herself with a deep breath. "Haven't you practiced enough? It's midnight."

Heather grabbed a towel off a nearby chair and wiped the sweat off her head before sitting down. "Dancing is not my forte. To stay relevant, I must practice twice as hard as the others."

"You're already a better dancer than most," Grace said. Heather shrugged off the comment as she chugged water from a bottle. "And you're the best singer by far. Everyone on the ride home was talking about you."

"That's not new."

"They say you're a lock to make the debut."

"Remember our complacency discussion?"

"At some point, you must recognize where you stand, though."

"If you rest in this business, you become roadkill."

"You seem unenthused."

Heather replaced the cap on her water bottle, gathered her

belongings, and powered down the audio equipment. "I avoid dwelling on what might happen."

Grace tried to recall the last time she encountered such a jovial atmosphere at the dorm. The trainees looked ecstatic. Kimchi jjigae was precisely what they needed, and she was already enjoying seconds. Heather, who had concocted the dish for her roommates, glowed at the warm reception her improvised recipe had generated.

In recent weeks, the dorm's cast of characters had changed repeatedly. Permanent dismissals came in rapid succession. The process was taking an emotional toll on the surviving hopefuls. The agency's policy was to close dorm rooms as the trainee pool shrunk. This was to save money on housing. As a result, the agency consolidated survivors into fewer and fewer accommodations. The stress of adjusting to new roommates and their living habits made matters worse. Clearly, they warranted a morale boost. Thus, the recipe.

"Did you guys finish your Statistics homework?" asked Rose.

"We're doing it tonight," said Grace. "Are you joining us, Heather?"

"I have to finish my song."

"What's the rush? They never use our songs," said Rose.

"I want it ready, in any case." Heather had often shared her feelings on the matter. The agency's practice of assigning songs instead of encouraging latent songwriting skills irked her. The new group would need music, and she aimed to fill it.

Evaluation day had arrived. Positioned along one wall of the assembly hall, ten surviving trainees worried for their friends.

Three of their peers stood in the center of the room, facing the producers. Their heads hung in shame. Everyone knew what was coming. Soon, two more trainees would face permanent dismissal.

Grace's evaluation had not gone well, but she remained stoic, ready to meet her fate. Rose, a singer to her left, failed to stifle tears as she waited. Eui, the dancer, was silent but nervous. She grasped her wrist so tightly that it noticeably restricted her blood flow.

"The rest of the group is ahead of you three," Creative Director Park Jee stated. "Are you content with falling behind?"

"No," the trio answered in unison.

"There's little time left. Your lack of effort is disappointing. Perhaps you're not cut out for this business."

"We are," they responded in unison.

Park Jee huddled with the other managers, whispering in conference. Occasionally, they'd reassess the candidates before returning to discussion. The wait was excruciating. Finally, the summit ended.

Director Park stood and faced them again. "Grace, step forward." She winced at being singled out, but this alone meant little. The producers rarely handled dismissals the same way twice. However, if a second person was called forward, that was a sure sign her K-pop career was over. Another interminable pause began before he spoke again. "Rose and Eui, thank you for your service. We wish you the best in your future endeavors."

Before he finished speaking, Rose collapsed to her knees. "No! How could you?" She lowered her face to the floor and covered it with her arms. An overwhelmed Eui bent over and sobbed. Eleven trainees remained. Those seated along the wall rushed forward to comfort the dismissed pair. Heather's tight embrace prevented Grace's wobbly knees from giving out.

Back in the rehearsal space on the SIU campus, Grace's tale riveted the members. They seemed affected by it.

"Such a close call," said Mindy.

"I feel bad for the ones cut near the end," said Erin. "Can you imagine going through all that only to fall short?" As soon as the words left her mouth, she blushed in embarrassment.

"Yes," Grace responded with a grimace. "I can easily imagine that."

* * *

The seven members of Made in Heaven were in the dance studio practicing choreography for "Feel the Heat." They'd been at it for hours. Danya, their vaunted choreographer, walked back and forth, monitoring their performance while identifying mistakes. "Erin, you're late." "Sun-hee, too soon." "Mindy, you held position too long. Heather has to be there." Occasionally, she'd stop the music altogether. "Stop! Stop!" The girls were sweating. Several were bent over, wheezing.

"Heather did it wrong," said Grace.

"Is that what you think?" Six girls nodded. "Incorrect. Heather's the only one who did it right." Danya's explanation met with protests, but she tolerated none of it. "Heather, show them." They repeated the last few steps without music until Danya told them to stop.

"Do you see that?" Danya herself repeated the gesture with her right hand above her right temple. "Pretty lines, ladies.

That's what I want to see. Pretty lines. It's subtle but makes a difference. The rest of you make it look like rain-soaked petals, while hers is a glorious feather. Again."

They ran through the dance three more times. Danya stopped their third attempt to correct another error. "Not on the downbeat; on the upbeat. Listen. To. The. Music." She emphasized her intent by clapping in time with the beat. "Once more."

"We're exhausted," protested Grace.

"Exhausted? I can't imagine why. I count one of you who looks like she practiced before today." The girls stood with slumped shoulders and sad eyes as she continued her harangue. "Why are you wasting my time?" She was shouting, but articulated each word to emphasize their importance. "Listen to me. You have a week to pull your shit together. If I return next Tuesday and you're still learning the steps, I'm walking straight out of here, and you will never see me again. Do you understand?"

A couple of meek acknowledgments.

"What? I didn't hear that." Danya placed a hand against her ear. "I'll ask again. Do you understand?"

"Yes!" the seven of them shouted in unison.

"These sessions are for refinement. Remember, dance is an illusion. Your job is to make the difficult look easy. You should be long past the point where you're learning the moves. Vanessa, you need to step it up big time. They expect guidance." Vanessa nodded in shame. "By this point, you ought to be thoroughly familiar with this. By next week, make sure they do too. If y'all ain't taking this seriously, why should I?"

Danya collected her belongings and left the room without

saying goodbye. Despite her departure, the girls remained motionless for a time, hesitant to act or speak lest they provoke further anger. Grace called for another run-through. Nobody complained. They continued for another 90 minutes until they had given it their all.

As group members reclined on the hardwood floor, regaining energy during the break, Grace whispered to Heather while pointing in June's direction. "Okay, I want to get to the bottom of this dialect thing once and for all." On several occasions, they had discussed the peculiar way June spoke. Because of their relative unfamiliarity with the regional dialects of Korea, however, they could not identify hers. Grace peeked over Heather's shoulder again to observe June sitting on the dance floor near the backpacks.

"Hey June, inside my bag there, I have some caramels." She spoke in Korean using the borrowed term for the candy, kae-reo-mel. "Could you distribute those to whoever wants some?"

"I do," said Erin, raising her hand.

June fished around in the bag but appeared puzzled. After a second look, she extracted index cards and displayed them to Grace.

"No. What else do you see?" asked Grace.

June responded, also in Korean, "Some clothes, a water bottle, snack bars, and gi-reum-sa-tang."

As expected, her description was odd. "Show me those," ordered Grace.

June extracted a resealable baggie of caramels. Heather glanced at Grace; eyes wide with curiosity.

"Yeah, those. Hand those out, please." Grace returned her attention to Heather. "See what I mean?"

"Oily candy?" questioned Heather, using the literal interpretation of gi-reum-sa-tang. "That's an odd term. Is that some sort of old-fashioned usage I'm not familiar with?"

"She has a strange vocabulary but I have a theory."

Moments later, as the members gathered in a circle on the floor, drinking water and sharing caramels, Grace pushed her experiment. The members typically handled band activities in English despite June's lack of fluency, because it was the one language common to all. "June, you haven't told us much about yourself. Where did you live in Korea before coming to the U.S.?"

June froze. It took a moment, but she recovered enough to say, "Near border." Her chin trembled.

Grace found the response unsatisfactory. "Well, that doesn't narrow it down much, does it? What city exactly?"

"It village. You not know." She looked stressed, even beyond the demands of the rehearsal.

"Try me," said Mindy, now equally curious. "I toured the entire country as an idol."

June squirmed. Her hesitation focused their attention on her answers. When she realized she couldn't avoid the question any longer, she cast her gaze downward and shyly said, "Kimjongsuk."

The gasps were audible, as most in the group realized what her answer meant.

"I thought so," said Sun-hee.

Unacquainted with Korea's history and geography, Vanessa asked, "What's wrong?"

"Kim Jong-suk was Kim Jong-il's mother and Kim Jong-un's grandmother," explained Grace.

"And?" Vanessa was still not getting it.

"If she came from a town named after her, that means June is from North Korea," noted Mindy, "not the Republic of Korea like the rest of us."

Once the truth of the matter dawned on Vanessa, she uttered, "Oh."

The air conditioner blower clicked off, leaving the members to ponder the conclusion in silence.

"My accent too poor. I try lose it."

Heather responded, "It's okay, June, but why were you afraid to tell us?"

"You not understand."

"That's right, we don't. Help us."

"When I say I North Korea, that all people see. To they, I refugee only. Not what I do can change minds. That be me always."

"It's unfair," said Sun-hee.

"How did you escape?" asked Vanessa.

"I will say, but no mention again, please. I want behind me."

"We promise," said Grace. "Do we all understand that?" She stuck her hand in the center, inviting the others to join in the pledge, which they did. "We won't mention it again after tonight."

June appeared moved by the gesture, even if she remained hesitant. However, with continued encouragement from the others, she grew comfortable enough to share her story as the girls listened intently.

"Kwan Jeong is my Korea name," June said, beginning her tale.

Jeong moved to Kimjongsuk at age eight to live with her uncle and aunt after her mother died from a chronic respiratory disease. Her father disappeared before she was born.

"Government said U.S. great enemy and Korea in South slaves, but my eyes said not true. When I little girl, foreign music and movies common but forbid. We go in danger to see. Yet, secret we watch and listen to all. North songs cold, but South and from America songs fill hearts. We know not in paradise like government say. We know they lie, but we not speak against."

She began receiving compliments on her looks as a child. As a teenager, her beauty attracted the attention of high-ranking provincial ministers. They often inquired about her, and Jeong's relatives grew fearful.

Her aunt recalled an event she had witnessed when only 15 years old. Once, a group of administrators walked into her classroom unannounced, told the boys to wait outside, and lined the girls along a wall. After assessing them, the most beautiful one, Hei-Ran, was taken from the school and not seen again by her family or peers. Ten years later, people learned that she had gone to Pyongyang and that the Chairman of the Control Commission had forced her to pleasure him. Wanting to spare their niece from a similar fate, Jeong's relatives triggered an escape plan they had prepared for just such an emergency.

"How is that allowed?" asked Erin.

"Authorities there have the power to do whatever they want," Grace responded.

"I cannot refuse," June explained. "They punish whole family for crime of one. They scare people to force. Sex crime is daily life. The pretty suffer most. I would, too, if save family."

"I can't imagine being in that position," said Sun-hee.

June explained that her uncle's factory job only paid enough for a meager living. To supplement their income, he smuggled contraband across the border from China. Despite recurring risks, he built dependable connections throughout his career. He knew which guards to bribe and what crossing points to use.

The night they fled was less than ideal. A storm hit, providing them with much-welcomed cover, but gradually conditions became hazardous. They had no choice but to carry through with the plan. To abandon it at that stage would reveal their intentions to the authorities. During the crossing of the Yalu River, a swift-moving current knocked Jeong over. In a timely maneuver, her uncle grabbed the jacket she was wearing. But tragedy struck. Just as Jeong entered the safety of her aunt's waiting arms, the branch her uncle held onto for stability snapped. The river current carried him away.

"Oh, my god. Was he okay?" asked Sun-hee.

"We know not. Too dark," explained June. "We hear splash in the far. We hide in bushes waiting, but dawn come, and we leave or be catched. We go to search, but broker said dangerous."

"What happened to your uncle?" asked Erin.

"We know not. Broker warn us leave."

"What did you do?" asked Heather.

"That was start of trouble." June shared her memories of the terrible two years they spent as refugees, making their way across China to eventual safety in Southeast Asia. First, they had to make a living despite not speaking the language. Few Chinese wanted to risk their well-being to help them, while many exploited their vulnerable condition. They lived in constant fear of being discovered. If caught, the Chinese officials would deport them to North Korea, where they would be detained in a hard-labor camp. Even if government officials didn't find them first, the criminal underworld often ensnared female refugees to be sold into sexual slavery or as brides for poor farmers.

When they received a tip that their employer had betrayed them for a price, they fled again, leaving behind what few possessions and money they had accumulated. They were homeless and at the mercy of fate, unable to trust anyone. Jeong made herself look as plain as possible to avoid unwanted attention. This wasn't hard to do, as they ate rarely and bathed less.

Then, in a moment of extraordinary fortune, they encountered a U.S.-based missionary group dedicated to rescuing North Korean refugees. With the church's help, they entered Thailand via an underground refugee network. Upon reaching safe ground, they applied for asylum in the U.S., but their struggles were not over.

"Life here difficult," said June in conclusion. "Everything different. We have little money. My Aunt works as sewer lady?" June was unsure of the correct English word and repeated it in Korean.

"Seamstress?" volunteered Heather.

"Yes, seamstress," said June. "I work in restaurant but want to be model. When I be famous, I go to China to find uncle and friends."

"What friends?" asked Sun-hee.

June grew more distressed. "Not like to remember," she said with a deep sigh. Sun-hee put an arm around June's shoulder to comfort her until she could continue.

"After come to U.S., I speak two best friends in North. I wish not to do this now."

"Why?" asked Grace.

She spoke fondly of Hae-won and Young-soon, both talented singers she had known since childhood. The three would often perform together at official functions. When they heard June's stories regarding the entertainment industry and her dreams of stardom in the West, they desired a similar life. They attempted to escape, but their plan failed because they lacked her uncle's connections and expertise.

"I later hear government watch them," said June. "Once plan clear, friends arrest and sent labor camp. Their fate is to me."

"No, no," said Sun-hee. "You can't blame yourself."

"What happens in these labor camps?" asked Erin.

June was too distraught to reply. She leaned into Sun-hee's shoulder and sobbed.

Grace took it upon herself to answer. "Nothing good, Erin. Hard, dangerous physical labor, long hours, lack of food, no medicine, exposure to the elements, torture, abuse, you name it." Heather discreetly urged silence for June's sake. Grace complied, but not without finishing her thought by miming a throat-slitting motion to indicate death, taking care to prevent June from seeing her gesture.

"That's a perfect example of how birthplace can determine your fate," said Sun-hee.

Rehearsal was over for the night. Grace offered rides home to anyone who needed one. "Remember, we have the music festival this weekend."

20

SO PUNK ROCK

To his credit, Arnie had landed a major booking. Made in Heaven's most notable thus far. That he kept the details to himself should have raised red flags, but Heather was too excited to care. Their manager reported they had signed to play a festival 'somewhere in the desert.' Heather initially conjured up visions of Coachella, but was relieved to hear Arnie describe it as 'smaller than that.' Still, she hoped their destination would prove more substantial than a few amateurs in a city park.

Heather had lobbied for an early departure so they'd have plenty of time to settle their nerves before going on stage. However, traffic through the Cajon Pass was heavier than expected, and their rented van had only reached Victorville. They had another forty minutes to go before their destination.

With plenty of time to think, Heather grew apprehensive about the challenges they faced. For the first time, the band and the dance units would perform one after the other. While waiting for the later dance, June and Vanessa were slated to sing backup for the band. Heather worried about switching

"

from wired mics to a wireless set. They lacked the proper equipment to practice such intricate transitions, and the sound crew would be unfamiliar with their act. Plus, their only two dances were rudimentary and imitative. "Feel the Heat" was not ready yet, and dance rehearsals had been sparse for the other songs. Plenty could go wrong.

As the van approached the festival grounds, traffic slowed to a crawl. From appearances, it seemed like a family affair. Pedestrians walked alongside the road carrying backpacks, portable chairs, and coolers while shepherding their children away from traffic. Vehicles were being herded onto vast expanses of grass that rose from the parched desert soil as if by a miracle.

"So many people here," remarked Erin.

"This is exciting," said Mindy.

"Yeah," said Heather dryly.

The van reached the parking entrance, where Arnie sought directions. As they made their way to the designated artists' area, Steve, too, grew anxious. "What type of music festival did you say this was, Arnie?"

"Who cares? It pays." Arnie no longer made much of an effort to hide his contempt for Steve, who, in turn, grimaced whenever Arnie spoke.

They passed by a large sign which Heather read aloud, "High Desert Lighthouse Festival."

Steve, now alert, assessed their surroundings. "Arnie, when did you last see a lighthouse in the desert?"

The manager looked at the group in the rearview mirror. "I dunno. It's sort of poetic, doncha think? Why you gotta get on my case for? It's a festival, ain't it?"

Erin and Steve seemed to share the same wavelength. Their

nervousness increased on the way to their assigned parking area. "Are you thinking what I am?" she whispered to him.

"I'll let you know once we're inside."

After parking and unloading, they were met by a volunteer who directed them to the staging area. A large tent had been erected as a makeshift general ready room. Inside, a host of musicians were engaged in tasks ranging from rehearsals to prepping equipment to napping. Limited interaction occurred between groups. Large floor fans blew at both ends of the structure to improve air circulation, but it remained warm. Curious stares met the "Made in Heaven" troop as they settled into their assigned area near the aromatic porta-potties.

"Diverse assemblage, I see," said Mindy.

Heather analyzed the room, noting a sea of white faces. "We're not in L.A. anymore."

Steve left to scout the scene. While waiting, Heather reviewed the setlist and monitored her bandmates' well-being. Mindy demonstrated a series of breathing exercises to calm the girls. Her experience was precious in moments like this. When Steve returned, he motioned for the group to gather in a circle. Speaking in hushed tones to deter eavesdroppers, he said, "Uh, we have a problem."

"This is Made in Heaven; were you expecting anything less?" said Mindy.

"I had a feeling something was off when we arrived," Steve continued. "This isn't your average, everyday music thing. It's run by a shady televangelist operation that's been sued for fraud. Apart from normal stuff like placing a high premium on family friendliness..." He paused to let a group of officials pass without raising suspicion. "They also milk the prosperity gospel for fun and profit. Tax-free, I might add."

Grace sighed.

"What have we gotten ourselves into?" asked Mindy.

"Whattaya worried about? You don't have any offensive material," countered Arnie.

"You're missing the point, genius," said Grace. "Let me spell it out for you. We're not a Christian music band. What do you think's gonna happen when we start singing about cheating boyfriends?"

"Not to mention we'll be helping millionaires beg social security checks out of retirees," said Vanessa.

"Can't we leave before anyone notices?" suggested Erin.

"No way," said Arnie. "And forfeit the money? You're in no spot to chuck a payday, let me tell you."

"That's easy for you to say. You're not the one making a fool of yourself in front of hundreds who question why you are here at all," Grace stated.

"More like thousands, from the looks of it," said Steve.

"Thanks for the reassurance."

"Mountain out of a molehill," said Arnie dismissively. "Here's what you do. You've got love songs, right?"

"Yes," said Heather.

"You're called Made in Heaven, right?"

"Um, yeah," said Grace suspiciously.

"Okay, halfway there. Each time you sing 'baby' or 'sweetheart,' just replace it with 'Jesus' or 'Lord.' And vee-o-la, instant Christian song."

More groans. "Arnie, we can't do that," protested Erin.

"Why not? I bet you half the hacks here do the same thing already. They know a meal ticket when they see one. Besides, how many Korean speakers do ya see?"

"Five," said Vanessa, looking around at her bandmates.

When Erin scoffed, she added, "Okay, five and a half, tops."

Steve entered the debate. "I hate to admit this, but Arnie's right with the money thing."

"See," responded Arnie.

"Sure, it's cynical and not ideal, but his plan could work in a pinch, and this is looking like a tight one. Besides, the more money we take from their pockets, the less they'll have available to expand their time-share schemes in Boca or whatever."

"We'll have to scrap the dance portion, though," Grace said. "I'm not sure how we'd change that at a moment's notice."

"What? No way," protested Vanessa, "I didn't come all this way for nothing."

"Sorry, Ness, but she's right," said Heather. "You and June will still be backup singers."

"And the outfits?" asked Mindy.

"Uh, I didn't consider that," said Grace.

"You should tone it down a bit," said Steve. "The miniskirt look will mark you as prostitutes with this crowd."

Heather took offense. "Now, you sound like one of our trolls."

"I'm not saying I agree; I'm telling it like it is. I was raised in this kind of environment. Tell you what. I spotted a thrift store on the way into town. You have 90 minutes until showtime. Let me get your sizes, and I'll hop over to see what I can find." Lacking a better option, the girls agreed to Steve's plan.

"I suspect we'll burn in hell after this," said Heather.

"I wouldn't worry," said Vanessa. "The thought of spending eternal life with these grifters is not the selling point they make it out to be."

Heather rechecked the time. They were less than a quarter-hour from showtime, and Steve hadn't returned yet. The festival implemented a backline setup, which meant the band would simply have to plug in instruments and run a mic check. Unfortunately, the operators were competent, so the performances ran on schedule. They'd enjoy no slack.

As they stood shoulder to shoulder in a line near the stage awaiting their turn, a blonde, muscular, middle-aged male with a trim beard approached, looking irate. His monogrammed yellow dress shirt and black slacks identified him as a member of a large choir from Huntington Beach. His booming voice carried to the others as he spoke to Erin, who stood nearest. "Someone spilled a tub of ketchup over by the generator. Instead of standing there useless, why don't you do your job? Pronto! People are tracking it everywhere."

Erin stared at him with her mouth open, pointing to her chest to ensure he was talking to her. The rest remained speechless, except for Vanessa, who was having none of it. She shot back from the far end of the line with a pointed finger, "Hey, Chuck Norris, I have a better idea. How 'bout you go lick it up yourself?"

The man was horrified by her audacity. He gestured as if pushing them away in disgust, then skittered back whence he came. June looked perplexed. "Why did he say that?"

"I'll give you one guess," said Mindy. Before anyone could respond, a harried stage manager implored them to remain in place. They were up next. "It's sweltering. I'm glad we don't have to dance after all."

Heather scanned the updated song list to divert her attention from the wait. It was radically different (and shorter) than the one they had practiced. She quietly rehearsed the improvised lyric changes until Steve arrived at last carrying two bags of clothing.

"I bought jeans. You can wear them with your current tops, and they'll match. Let's get to the dressing room." He continued his explanation on the way. "Some sizes are bigger than you'd prefer, but I bought safety pins. You can wear our belts too. Arnie, give them your belt." Their manager complied, but not without grumbling.

"Where are you going?" the stage manager asked when he saw them jogging away from the stage.

"We'll be right back," said Grace.

"You better be, or there'll be hell to pay."

"Too late for that," chimed Vanessa.

Minutes later, the girls emerged from the dressing room wearing their improvised outfits. Mindy and Sun-hee looked distraught. "Must we do this? I look awful," said Sun-hee.

"This belt's big enough to fit three of me," added Mindy. Arnie glared at her with steel in his eyes.

"Don't sweat it. Nobody'll notice. You'll both be in the back, anyway." Steve helped pin the loose material as best he could. "How 'bout the rest of you?" There were no further complaints.

"Okay, let's go," said Grace.

When they returned to the stairs, the stage manager admonished them. "You're cutting it close, don't you think?"

"Sorry," said Heather, using her aegyo skills to extract a smile from him. She had already assumed her onstage persona and was raring to go.

The MC finished his stage announcements. "You'll love our next group. Visiting all the way from Japan, let's welcome Heaven Sent."

Heather looked at Grace and shook her head in resignation. They didn't have time to protest.

"Okay, you're on," said the stage manager.

"Rock the house!" shouted Steve.

The girls emerged to a smattering of applause. The stage was stifling. Despite the metal roof offering direct protection from the sun, both sides were enclosed, a design flaw that cut potential cross breezes down to a minimum. A massive, metal-bladed ceiling fan turned furiously above their heads but was woefully insufficient. The band members took their places, plugged in their gear, and plunked out a few chords. Mic checks followed. Heather assessed her group. Their smiling faces told her what she needed to know. Grace gave a perfunctory greeting, and they began.

The first number was "From That Day On." Heather chose it because the song's mellow vibe allowed the band to ease into the venue. It also didn't hurt that the singing burden fell to Sun-hee and her. In terms of tone, the song could pass as a Christian one to those not fluent in Korean, even without a change of lyrics. Grace's guitar solo sounded better than ever. When it ended, the applause was polite, if not enthusiastic. The audience looked confused by the foreign words.

The heat was getting to them all. Sweating, Heather wiped her hands on her jeans, then resumed.

"Celestial" was next. She rewrote the English lyrics to imply the song was about an angel instead of an attractive crush. The Korean parts remained unchanged. Her confidence grew when she realized their crazy plan was working. The song's harder-driving pace meant more work from the band. This time, their performance was not sharp. It bugged Heather that "Celestial" often sounded better in rehearsals than it did live. She encouraged Grace to extend their next intro to buy precious time for the girls to grab some water.

The third tune was their newest one, "Back Off." It required the most extensive alteration because it was a breakup song. Heather couldn't settle on original lyrics she could accept and therefore took a straightforward approach by singing it entirely in Korean instead. The girls attacked the notes with gusto. Easier to play than "Celestial," their new music rocked. It was an enjoyable experience and was proving to be the best live performance they'd ever given.

Indeed, their moment of euphoria was the ideal time for disaster to strike.

The drumming stopped abruptly, followed by a loud bell-like clanging, then wood clattering on metal. Heather watched as Mindy's drumsticks skittered past, stopping just shy of rolling off the front edge of the stage.

"Goddammit. Fuck this bullshit!" shouted Mindy, forgetting the live mic positioned directly above her drum kit. The multi-thousand-watt PA system ensured every man, woman, and child in the amphitheater heard the outburst.

As a result, the band's playing ground to a disheartening halt. Heather looked over her shoulder, shocked to see the ceiling fan wobbling as it worked to regain equilibrium. Mindy jumped from her seat and stomped to the front of the stage to retrieve her drumsticks. She was furious. The ridiculous need to prevent oversized jeans from slipping off compounded her walk of shame, adding insult to injury. The crowd watched silently, unsure how to respond as the sound of heavy footsteps on metal magnified. When passing the mic stand, she shot Heather a sideways glance as if daring her to utter so much as a single word of admonishment.

Heather turned to face the audience with a weak smile. Parents had covered their children's ears, and some were even ushering them from the venue. Most gave disapproving looks. A few people laughed.

"Say something," urged Grace, leaning away from the mic in Heather's direction.

"*You* say something."

"*You're* the leader."

"Oh, so now *I'm* the leader. Gee, thanks."

Before they could say something, Mindy returned to the drum set and, without warning, resumed right where she had left off. Her swift motion caught the band off guard, making it difficult for them to reorient. After eight measures, they regained their form, but it didn't matter. The house engineer zeroed the PA volume. Mindy's unamplified drumming continued until the MC came on stage with his arms waving, forcing her to stop playing.

"All right, ladies, pack it up. Show's over," he said before stepping to the center mic as the engineer restored its original level. "We apologize for that. We're having some...ah... technical difficulties, but we'll be back in a few minutes. Please stick around. I guarantee you're going to love our next act."

Heather was livid. She unplugged her guitar, threw the cable onto the stage floor, and skulked away, feeling like a pariah under the watchful eyes of the MC, the stage manager, and the crowd. *Why does everything I touch turn to crap?* she wondered.

"What the hell was that?" demanded Grace when they stepped off stage.

"I was sweating. They slipped," Mindy responded.

"She was doing her stick-flipping thing again," charged Vanessa. Mindy shot her a dirty look.

Arnie rushed over to them, panting. "Argue later! Let's go *now* before they want their money back!"

With Steve and Arnie's help, the members gathered their belongings. As they hastened from the tent, a musician from another group applauded and voiced his approval, "That was so punk rock. I've been wanting to say that for years."

Upon reaching the van, they tossed their gear inside without care. Heather remained ever vigilant should officials try to intercept them. Within minutes, Arnie was maneuvering the vehicle off the lot. They dared relax only when the festival grounds were well out of sight.

Yes, Arnie had inflicted another one of his tone-deaf bookings on them without warning, but their manager saved his own skin the following day during dance practice. The news he shared was big enough to deflect all attention away from their disastrous festival appearance. "How'd you like to go on tour?" he asked.

"You want to book us on tour?" asked Heather skeptically.

"It's all set. You'll open for Dim Fandango. Just give the word."

"What's Dim Fandango?" asked Grace.

"A new Paisley Underground act. Indie too. Five guys. Could be fun." He winked.

"Ha, I bet," Heather smirked. "How much does this thing pay?"

"Zero," he responded.

"You really know how to sell your ideas, Arnie," said Grace.

"And pay your own expenses. But merch sales are yours to keep."

"We have no merch."

"Time to change that." Sensing their hesitation, he added, "The exposure will be good."

"We're broke, Arnie."

"You gotta start somewhere. It's a three-week tour. Sixteen cities. Starts in two weeks."

"Two weeks?" protested Heather. "But we're filming the video then."

"This tour's more important."

"What about Steve?"

"To hell with Steve. I warned you before. No offense, but that video ain't winnin' nothin'."

"But we've been working our asses off to perfect the chore-ography."

"Use it on tour. No loss there."

For months, "Made in Heaven" had too few options; sud-denly, they had too many. And given the conflict between their two main collaborators, neither choice came consequence-free.

21

LEAVES UNTRODDEN BLACK

Steve was anxious to witness the choreography for "Feel the Heat." This long-anticipated piece would complete the puzzle. Much of his class grade (and subsequent chances of winning the festival prize) would depend on what he'd see in the next few minutes. He possessed full autonomy regarding the filming and editing aspects of the music video, but held no sway over the dance performance, despite its importance. Choreography was something he enjoyed watching but did not know how to create himself.

Steve had placed great trust in the girls holding up their end of the bargain. They needed to produce an outcome impressive enough to carry the video. Amateurish content would waste even top-quality filmwork. Over the past semester and a half, he recognized that Heather's passion for music matched his own for cinema. This eased his mind somewhat. He hoped by the time the presentation was over, he could stop worrying and start planning the best way to capture it on film. His greatest fear was having to tell the truth about a project that would not work and scrap it altogether.

"Danya couldn't stay," reported Vanessa the moment Steve walked into the dance studio. "She said you better not think about changing a single thing anyway."

"We'll see," Steve responded. "Let's hope I won't have to." Stressed from constant pre-production headaches, he was in no mood to argue with anyone. While leaning against the mirrored wall, Steve steeled himself for the worst while hoping for the best. The seven performers took positions in a single line across the middle of the room, standing arm's length apart.

The music commenced, and the group transitioned into a constantly changing set of patterns. Their goal was impactful choreography without strenuous movements that would detract from singing, which they intended to do live. The choreography focused less on broad, showy, athletic, and improvised gestures in favor of small, concise details. Careful coordination allowed movements to be performed in unison or as individual parts of an overall tableau.

The root formation was the entire group in a delta, with the three tallest dancers, Mindy, June, and Vanessa, taking the three top spots front and center. In contrast, the shortest ones, Erin and Heather, formed the ends further back, creating a forced perspective illusion. A series of subsidiary patterns emerged from this core set. Some were symmetrical, while others exploited the odd numbers to isolate one, two, or three dancers from the main group. Each member would occupy the center when it was their turn to sing. Regularly, the pattern reset.

The quick pace allowed just enough time for one flourish to finish before moving on. Shifts were expertly planned. A step or two was all it took to alter the look of the formation.

The ever-changing visual impact appeared effortless. A single mistimed move would spell disaster, but they handled each change with aptitude. Synchronization between the dancers was top-notch. Steve concluded that the practice time needed to coordinate it all must've been staggering.

Three and a half minutes later, he had his answer. The results were masterful. The gracefulness of the dance complemented the rhythmic emphasis of the song. His concerns dissolved in an instant. The girls had provided him with quality material.

After the music stopped, the dancers remained frozen in final positions for several seconds. Steve said nothing, but dropped his head and covered his eyes with his hands. This reaction prompted an alarmed response. The clattering of seven pairs of heels on wood signaled their approach as they encircled him. "What's wrong with it?" demanded an alarmed Vanessa.

Now realizing that his body language was sending the wrong message, Steve raised his head and addressed the group standing before him. "What's wrong with it?" he repeated. "That's the most awesome thing I've ever seen in my life."

* * *

Heather found it challenging to present the dance without mentioning the possibility of a tour to Steve. The group lacked any opportunity to discuss the dilemma beforehand. Once their director left the studio, Grace called for a dialog. A decision of this magnitude required consensus.

"It seems obvious by now that Steve and Arnie are never gonna get along," said Mindy. "They're like oil and water, those two."

"We're at a crossroads," said Grace. "We can't be in multiple places at once. We have to choose. Video or tour? Keep in mind that whoever we turn down will likely quit. From my personal viewpoint, sure, Arnie's been a problematic manager at best."

"That's putting it mildly," said Vanessa.

"But he does make my job easier. Before, I was doing everything," continued Grace.

"We can always help," offered Erin.

"That's what you said last time, but everything falls to me in the end."

"And it's not like Steve hasn't caused us problems," noted Mindy. "We're resubmitting a new video because of his screw-up. But remember, our goal all along has been to enter the *Soundscape Showdown*. We have two of the four requirements. But we're still missing radio airplay and gigs. This tour would check one more box off that list."

"I vote video," said Sun-hee. "I can't miss three weeks of school for a tour."

"We worked so hard on the dance, I want to see it on film," said Vanessa.

"For the video to make any money, we need to win the prize, though," said Mindy. "What are the odds of that?"

Erin, looking like her usual nervous self, said, "This tour could be expensive, and merchandising is no sure thing. What if the Dim Fandango fans hate us? What then? Imagine going from city to city being booed the whole time."

"So, are you voting video?" asked Grace. Erin nodded. "Okay, June. Your turn."

Their newest member acted sheepish. Only with considerable prodding did she state her preference. "Travel sounds fun."

"Alright, chalk another one up for the tour," said Grace. "That makes it three to three. Dead even."

And so it came down to Heather's tiebreaker. From a career perspective, both options had merit. Mindy's view was perhaps the most forward-looking, offering a valid point about the *Showdown*. But more people might view a music video over time than would ever see Made in Heaven on a Dim Fandango tour. Yet Heather relied more on intuition than reason for big decisions like this. True, Arnie and Steve had both made crucial errors. But in her view, honor mattered. She had promised Steve a video. Leaving him in the lurch at this stage would represent an epic betrayal. He'd have no time or money to reimagine his class project, never mind the film festival. Whatever other considerations were in play, personal integrity mattered most.

Heather attended the subsequent phone call. Despite Grace leaving the door open for Arnie to continue as their manager, he took the decision personally. Heather winced as Arnie's rage was audible from afar. Grace faced his tirade for what seemed an eternity. He resigned and the call ended, causing Grace to sigh. Once again, they had no manager.

* * *

The caravan to Arizona left at dawn on Good Friday. Traffic was heavy. The vehicles soon became separated. Opting to ride in Steve's car instead of the passenger van seemed like a good idea. Sun-hee now regretted it. Her sense of adventure evaporated in less than two hours. This desert trek lasted far longer than the previous one. Traversing the endless suburbs east of Los Angeles proved arduous. A thermometer on the Redlands Bank sign showed a temperature of 99 degrees. She steeled herself. It was only 10:00 a.m. They still faced hours before entering the hottest region.

Steve cracked open the windows of his 1973 Gran Torino Sport to allow for better circulation. This produced a maelstrom inside the vehicle. Sun-hee shut off her streaming playlist midway through NCT U's "Baby Don't Stop." There was little point in continuing when she couldn't hear a thing. Steve's past-its-prime muscle car kept a sporty look despite its faded blue metallic paint. However, the former brawn it once possessed had atrophied in the throes of infirmity. Among the car's many deficiencies was an air conditioner that blew only warm air. The alternative to this meager remedy for heatstroke was suffocation.

As they snaked their way through the long, narrow valleys of the Inland Empire, trees became sparser and smaller. Two giant dinosaur sculptures rose alongside the freeway, marking the entrance to the desert proper. The first wind turbines appeared soon after that, their giant blades turning lazily hundreds of feet in the air. Sun-hee counted them to pass the time but gave up once they appeared in multitudes. Vanessa and Heather had the right idea by opting to sleep through this experience. Sun-hee grabbed a pillow and stretched her legs. For all its many flaws, Steve's car had an expansive and comfortable rear seat, at least. Fifteen minutes passed. Perhaps sleep would set in if she pretended long enough.

No chance. By the time they reached the journey's halfway point, the three girls were wide awake and fanning themselves relentlessly to keep cool.

"I need to get gas at the next exit. If you're hungry, we can grab a bite to eat," offered Steve. "It's covered in the budget."

"You stop, or we riot," demanded Vanessa.

"I'll get some ice water too. We need to stay hydrated." The nameless rest stop they pulled into featured four lonely buildings: a combination gas station/convenience store, a diner, an abandoned motel, and a boarded-up radiator shop. "What'll it be?"

"The convenience store should be fine," said Heather.

"Diner sounds better," said Vanessa.

"I wouldn't mind leaving this car for a while. The diner it is." Steve dropped them off at Dale's Grillorama and proceeded to the gas station. "I'll be back soon."

The chilled air inside the restaurant was exhilarating after the sweltering automobile. A young, gangly teen with curly black hair greeted them with a meager smile and escorted them to a booth at the front window.

"Not there, Mark," an unseen woman's brusque voice said from the kitchen grill area. The young man grew nervous. He led them to an adjacent booth in a dark corner instead.

Heather surveyed the dining room. There were few customers. "Why can't we sit there?" she asked.

The busser shrugged. "It might be broke or something. I'll get your water."

"Can you bring four? We have a friend coming."

While waiting for menus, they heard the kitchen woman reprimand the boy for reasons unknown. Vanessa noted several rips in the booth's red Naugahyde upholstery and pulled a bit of stuffing out to play with. Faux wood paneling from the 1970s and dusty plastic flower arrangements dominated the décor.

"What's with the atmosphere in here?" asked Vanessa.

In a playful mood, Heather launched into an impromptu imitation of a museum tour guide. "I'll have you know, Ness, people come from miles around to take in this signature artwork." She pointed at the wall over their booth. "Behold, a faux wagon wheel strewn with barbed wire for your viewing pleasure." Shifting her gaze to another wall, she said, "Or if prints are more your style, here's John Wayne's disembodied head in a cowboy hat floating above a covered wagon for no apparent reason." Her friends laughed at the art critique.

"We shouldn't overeat right before the video," said Sun-hee, "but if I don't get something soon, I'll faint."

"I wish they'd bring menus," said Vanessa. "It's not like they're busy."

"I bet this is the height of the lunch hour rush," said Heather.

Just as they considered leaving, a pear-shaped white woman approached, her sandy brown hair piled into a disheveled topknot. With a scowl, she slapped the menus in a pile on the table's edge. As if speaking to small children, she over-articulated each word, saying, "We don't serve Chinese food here."

The girls stared at each other, daring anyone to laugh first. Vanessa's silence surprised Sun-hee, who attributed it to shocked disbelief. Only when the woman returned to the kitchen did Ness speak. "Should I be more offended by the baby talk or the assumption that all Asians are part of a single monoculture?"

"Don't be a snowflake," scolded Heather sarcastically.

"Do people who use snowflake as an insult realize the irony?" Vanessa asked rhetorically. "Do they know it came from "Fight Club," a satire written by a gay man about male fragility causing men to radicalize?"

Steve rejoined them just as she finished. "Ah, toxic masculinity. My favorite subject."

"How did you turn out so normal?" asked Heather.

"Relatively speaking," added Vanessa.

Steve stared at Ness for an uncomfortable moment but ignored the comment. "I tried to hang out with so-called 'regular guys' for the longest time, but the conformity-masked-as-rebellion bullshit got old quick. Plus, the notion that fear and anger are the only acceptable emotions for men is repulsive. And can anyone explain to me why feminine traits are supposedly less valuable than masculine ones?"

Before they could answer any of these questions, the top-knot woman returned to take orders. This time, her mood seemed warm and welcoming, the polar opposite of earlier. She was especially responsive to Steve.

"She's nice," he said once she was out of earshot. The girls burst into laughter. "What's so funny?" he asked.

"Remember to invite him along whenever we want to enjoy the perks of privilege," said Vanessa to the other girls.

The taquitos and chicken strips they ordered were merely serviceable but much appreciated under the circumstances. A white, middle-aged, long-haired guy in a plaid flannel shirt entered the restaurant just as they finished the meal. He sat at the table by the window, unmolested by staff.

"Amazing how quickly that booth got fixed," said Vanessa under her breath.

As they waited for their bill to arrive, the guy in flannel turned to address them. "You musicians?" he asked. Their surprise prompted an explanation. "I saw your Korg bag in the car outside." He introduced himself as Matt and said he once toured with a grunge rock act in the 90s. He seemed friendly and interesting, so they invited him to pull up a chair. They spent most of the next half-hour conversing about band life.

Sun-hee was most intrigued by Matt's answer to one question. "How did it feel to sign your first record contract?"

"At first, it was great, but I soon came to hate it."

"Why?"

"'Cause you lose all control," Matt warned. "You'll sign away your rights for peanuts. Then they'll bring in some 'top guys' (he emphasized these words with air quotes) to loan you a hit because they'll never like your stuff enough. They'll pick your chord progressions and hire studio musicians to record them. Your job is to tour on that record. So, you end up doing all the legwork on the road. Meanwhile, they're collecting a hefty cut on everything that comes in. In the process, you'll struggle to make enough to pay them back for the recording costs. Then, if you want to remain relevant, you have to repeat that cycle every few years. It was no life for me. No thanks. More power to ya if it works, though."

22

THE SACRIFICE

Full from the restaurant meal, Heather napped a bit in the car despite the temperature. She woke as they were passing through a tunnel in downtown Phoenix. Upon arrival in Tempe, Steve helped the cast settle into his parents' house before leaving with Dalton, his cinematographer friend, to do some prep work on the set. Stocked with sleeping bags, pillows, and blankets, the girls counted on a good old-fashioned slumber party.

Since recent rehearsals had gone so well, and seeing how there was scant space available to practice anyway, Grace granted them the night off. Armed with directions from Steve's father (who seemed enamored with his unexpected guests) they set off on an evening walking tour of the university town. After dinner at a Mill Avenue Thai restaurant, they found themselves at Tempe Beach Park admiring the desert's imposing night sky and its myriad stars reflected on the water.

After strolling the promenade, they discovered a wide expanse of lawn by the Tempe Fine Arts Center and settled into a broad circle, facing one another. Discussions turned to all topics: school, family, and, of course, the band. Excited by the prospects of the impending video shoot, Heather felt exuberant and chatty that evening. The warm breeze tickled her skin, charging her with energy. Perhaps sensing that the timing was right, Mindy raised an issue their main singer had long avoided. "Do you feel like talking about 37-G?"

Heather knew the day would come when she'd have to face the truth of the situation. Made in Heaven had proven resilient enough to reach this point. They were on the eve of their biggest-ever undertaking. If all went well, the video could win a festival prize and maybe even earn some money. Perhaps the increased exposure would spark something big. Would it be anything like the fame Glimmer Blue was enjoying? No, not even close. But the seven of them were building something all on their own. Nobody could take that away from them.

Heather believed she owed the members an explanation as collaborators and now friends. The incident in Korea had scarred her deeply. The pain of that memory continued to hold her back. By refusing to acknowledge it, she'd never heal. And to heal, she had to talk about it. Would she find a more perfect moment, embraced by friends in a serene setting, distant from the scene of trauma? Probably not. After Mindy asked, silence prevailed. The girls waited patiently, sensing that they would soon unravel the mystery that had long intrigued them.

Heather took a deep breath and recalled the events of that fateful day.

"This is the day we've been waiting for!" shouted Da-som as she barged into the lunchroom at 37-G Entertainment. "Rehearsals are canceled. Get dressed. We're going to Amethyst tonight."

Jaws dropped. An explosion of delight followed the news as the message hit home. "Is this it?" asked dancer Minjung.

"We're meeting a group of company investors," answered Da-som. "That means final selections are coming soon. Be sure to show off your best self. Your future depends on it."

Grace smiled. "This could be the day," she said, hugging Heather.

The guest list included all 12 remaining trainees. These were the A-listers. The ones who had survived culling after culling to make it this far. Many tears had been shed in previous weeks, but 37-G had plans for only one girl group. Those who failed to debut would have to start again elsewhere or abandon their idol dreams altogether.

That afternoon, the dorms were chaotic. Given the time crunch, there weren't enough showers and mirrors for privacy. Preparations became a group effort as trainees coordinated bathing schedules, advised on dress selections, and did each other's hair and makeup.

Heather selected a long-sleeved, straight-necked, form-fitting, red dress that extended to mid-thigh, with sheer black hose and red pumps. She chose the material because it shimmered in the moody lighting expected at the restaurant. Grace wore a backless, gray tartan plaid frock with long sleeves and a turtleneck. Her outfit was the same length as Heather's, but flared at the hem. Black knee-length boots completed the look.

At the dorm entrance, the girls found a small bus waiting. The overwhelming sense of excitement dwarfed any nerves they experienced.

"Remember to show these VIPs your appreciation," said Manager Chi-won during the ride. "They're financing your debut."

"How big will the debut group be?" asked Da-som.

Chi-won looked sheepish. "Don't put me on the spot."

"Come on, we won't tell anyone," Grace said. Her entreaty was joined by a chorus of others who piled on the pressure.

"I believe they're considering five," he said, relenting.

Minjung whistled. "Those odds are worse than I thought."

"You didn't hear any of this from me, by the way."

Amethyst was one of Seoul's most exclusive restaurants. Prior to this, no trainee had visited because of its prohibitive expense. The restaurant catered to a crowd more familiar with signing multi-billion-dollar business deals than paying mortgages (or living in dorms). Rumors also abounded that arrangements of a more clandestine nature transpired there. As they walked through the crowded dining room, the elegantly dressed young women encountered disapproving stares. Heather experienced embarrassment for herself and her colleagues. Had these folks known the real reason for their presence, she mused, they would judge less.

Tucked away at the end of a long corridor, a heavy wooden door opened onto a richly decorated chamber. Water cascaded over an imposing granite face comprising one entire wall. At its base was a pool stretching beyond the floor's edges. The effect of this unique arrangement was akin to dining on a floating platform. Around an impressive oak table sat seven men. They wore finely tailored suits, but some had removed their coats. Ages ranged from the early 40s to the late 60s. Heavy cigar smoke filled the air. The smell of alcohol was pungent. Dinner service had concluded, though banchan of watercress namul and oi muchim were being served as the trainees entered.

The girls soon understood that they had to tend to the VIPs' needs. This comprised pouring drinks, laughing at terrible jokes, and making these men, two or three times their own age, feel desirable. Achieving this feat demanded that the trainees use their not-yet-fully formed acting abilities. They handled themselves with aplomb, though. No one complained if a joke targeted them or if they experienced unwanted touching. They understood what was at stake and knew their idol dreams could crash and burn with an adverse reaction.

Soon, Mr. Lee invited Heather to sit beside him. His respected status was evident in how the others deferred to him. He acted cordially towards her, inquired about her interests, and avoided improper behavior. Considering what some of her peers experienced, she had it easy.

The night was long, and the bus didn't return home until 2:30 a.m. The trainees felt disillusioned and confused. No further news had emerged regarding the debut date or the selection process. Despite a late bedtime, they were expected to observe their regular class schedule, starting bright and early the following day.

Heather's mind raced with worried speculation throughout the night. Sleep avoided her. She spent the next morning in a daze and intended to skip lunch to nap, but Chi-won intercepted her. He had other plans. "Heather, you're excused from afternoon practice."

"Did I mess up?"

"Mr. Lee requested you meet at his office regarding the debut. Get dressed. A car is being sent."

"Right now?" Heather could not contain herself. Grace, standing nearby, overheard the news and insisted on accompanying her. Chi-won granted the request after much joint needling. Heather had but two dresses refined enough for such a momentous occasion. As she had worn the red dress the previous night, she only had one option left: a black, off-the-shoulder pullover. It was more risque than she preferred, but a matching overcoat allowed some modesty.

"What time is the ride coming?" asked Grace an hour later.

"Should be soon," responded Heather, rechecking the clock on the marquee of the bank building across the street.

"Look." Grace pointed at an approaching raven-black town car with inky windows. It stopped directly in front of them. An impeccably dressed driver emerged and stiffly walked around the vehicle. Without offering a greeting, the towering hulk opened the rear passenger door. Heather, amused by his aloofness, grinned and entered the automobile. Grace attempted to follow, but the driver's massive outstretched arm impeded her.

"Chi-won said she could join me," protested Heather.

"I was sent for you only," the driver said gruffly.

Heather looked perturbed but relented. "It's okay, Grace. I'm sorry you had to get dressed for no reason."

"That's not the issue."

"I'll be fine. Don't worry. We'll talk later." The car door shut unceremoniously. Heather waved and smiled to reassure her friend, but the tinted windows wasted that gesture.

The town car left Gangnam-gu and pushed into the hills overlooking the district. A serpentine road coiled through the mountains, arriving at a secluded, stone-walled compound. Without slowing, the vehicle slipped through iron-jawed gates that opened as if by magic. The driver stopped in a stately courtyard bricked in the hue of ash and surrounded by a hulking mansion. Heather peered at the splayed staircase designed to deposit guests at ornately girded double doors. Thorny vines enveloped a glass canopy like pythons. "What is this place?" She asked the driver when he had opened her door.

"Mr. Lee will see you at his residence," he answered.

A woman with soot-colored hair stood in the doorway, waving her arm. Confused over this change in plan, Heather climbed the stairs and approached the woman, stating, "I was supposed to be at Mr. Lee's office."

"It's here," she said brusquely. The woman took her coat and handed it off to a lanky, square-jawed male, where it disappeared down a labyrinthine hall. She then guided Heather past a grand staircase, through a short corridor, and into an expansive great room that offered a stunning view of Seoul stretching toward the horizon below. "Oh, wow," Heather gasped as the full extent of the panorama became apparent. The lights of the magnificent city were shimmering in the gloaming.

"Impressive, isn't it?" said a dignified voice from behind.

Heather faced Mr. Lee, who approached as a king would in his palace. Compared to the previous night, he seemed younger than she recalled. His clothes were of the finest quality, evident even from where she stood several feet away. The great room's furnishings and décor appeared magazine-worthy. Everything was in its place, perfectly neat.

"I've never seen a house like this before. It's beautiful."

"I prefer to handle my business dealings in domestic environments. More gets done this way."

"That's understandable," said Heather.

"Please, shall we sit outside? Seoul is preparing a spectacle for us, and we'd be foolish to miss it." A resplendent table had been set under a fairy-laced gazebo near the edge of the terrace with every manner of china plate, silver utensil, and crystal glassware Heather could imagine. Sublimely scented flower and candle arrangements, likely costing a fortune, surrounded the dining area. "Dinner will be served soon. I understand you're from the States. Perhaps you'll find some of our offerings to your pleasure?"

"Um, sure," said Heather, unimpressed with her unartful response.

Mr. Lee whispered instructions to the staff before inviting Heather to sit at the table. Unexpectedly, he chose a seat next to hers rather than sit across the way. Over the next half hour, various piquant appetizers, salads, and beverages were served. Heather enjoyed Korean steak tartare, taro root tacos with shrimp, and Moroccan-spiced Wagyu short ribs. The main course was a delicious, wild-caught, cedar-plank-grilled sockeye from Copper River, Alaska, spiced with the perfect amount of pepper and lemon. As a trainee, Heather would avoid eating on some days to keep her weight below the maximum allowed. On this occasion, she abandoned her usual caution. Tomorrow, she'd squeeze in an extra workout, she decided. Today was a rare opportunity for guilt-free indulgence. She deserved it.

During the meal, Mr. Lee peppered Heather with questions regarding her family background, interests, and goals. Whenever she inquired about Mr. Lee, however, he would deflect her questions away as though hardly worth a moment's thought.

With the meal and desserts gone and more drinks served, Heather's inhibitions faded. She shared unfiltered thoughts concerning the struggles of life as a trainee. At one point of carelessness, she touched Mr. Lee's arm in response to a humorous comment. In return, her host smiled and explained that while he rarely involved himself in the daily running of entertainment ventures, little happened in the industry without his knowledge.

"You're obviously doing well for yourself," said Heather.

"I have the connections to open doors and the finances to keep them open. But enough of me." He took a long sip from his champagne glass. "I see tremendous potential in you, Ms. Moon." His lips parted invitingly as he stared at her.

She didn't know how to respond except with a simple "Thank you."

"I'm sure you've heard about our new group. We're aiming for an international release, including heavy promotion in America. Your background and talent are assets. You're a candidate, possibly even for the center."

Considering the deluge of recent stimuli, she took a moment to collect her thoughts. Heather found concentrating in that moment difficult. Two words stood out. *The center.* An idol's dream position, handed to her on a silver platter. Or was it? He described her as 'a candidate'. She wondered whether that bit of news, unhindered by a firm commitment, warranted such an elaborate presentation. "Mr. Lee, excuse me if I sound lightheaded. The drinks may be affecting me. But I must ask, why did you invite me here?"

He smiled, tenting his fingers under his chin as he spent long minutes assessing her. She caught his prurient gaze roaming down her body, coming to rest on bare legs. She shifted them under the tablecloth. "Are you a baseball fan, by any chance?" Mr. Lee asked.

Uncertain of the question's relevance, she indulged him. "I don't follow it, but watched my brother play some."

"But you understand the basics, correct?"

"More or less."

"I'm a romantic when it comes to the sacrifice bunt. Are you familiar with the term?"

Heather thought for a moment. "That's when you hit the ball a short way on purpose?"

"A bunt allows baserunners to advance."

"Yes, I remember that."

"I can't recall another sport that employs such a concept. Can you?"

"I've never considered it."

"Of course not." He offered a bemused grin. "I find the practice of bunting intriguing, perhaps because of its meaning, being symbolic of the greater good. Do you see what I mean?"

Heather shook her head.

"Sacrifices are not valued like they once were, I'm afraid. The game has become overly analytical. 'Why drop an out?' critics argue ad nauseam. Yet, it persists. With the sacrifice, you can earn a base hit or a well-timed squeeze play, beat over-shifted defenses, or even move runners into scoring positions. By paying these small prices, you win games, and series, and championships."

Heather wrestled with the metaphor, but its meaning continued to elude her. "Excuse me, Mr. Lee, but why are you telling me all this?"

"Have you noticed what separates you from the rest, Ms. Moon? Truly thought about it?"

Heather pinched her bottom lip as she struggled to find an answer that didn't sound arrogant. "I'm good at singing?"

"In my field, one has to excel at reading people. Perhaps it's bold of me to say, but I understand you better than you know.

Do you believe that?"

She shrugged her shoulders.

"You're not like your classmates, I suspect." She listened intently. "They trained because they wanted to become idols. *You*, on the other hand, did it because you *need* to become an idol. For you, there is no alternative. For you, all other endeavors pale in comparison."

Heather clenched her jaw and awaited his following words.

"Sure, you might attempt to fake your way through a normal life for a while, but eventually, it would consume you. The ongoing dissatisfaction with your mundane existence would ultimately lead to your demise. Am I right?"

Heather's knee bounced beneath the table. She wondered how someone she'd met less than 24 hours earlier could see right into her. His ultimate point remained a mystery, however. The effects of the alcohol and the hard-hitting nature of Mr. Lee's commentary left her head spinning. Her confusion must have been evident.

"Like bunting in baseball," he continued, leaning close. "A batter makes a minor sacrifice to gain a more favorable outcome. A nominal price to be paid for the team." He sat back in his chair, much to her relief. "You care for your group members, right?"

"I do."

"Like any good teammate, you want their success to com-plement yours?"

She nodded.

"And if you were called upon to make a small sacrifice for their benefit, you'd do it?"

"I sacrificed my youth to be a trainee."

"The price of admission only, I'm afraid." He tsked. "If you want to be in the big leagues, Ms. Moon, you have to play big-league ball. I'm offering you the chance to put your old life behind you. An opportunity like this comes once in a lifetime. Consider your position carefully. I had options, but I chose you."

"What are you saying, Mr. Lee?"

"We each possess something of value the other wants. I have plenty of ways to make your life more comfortable than you ever imagined. Look around. You know of what I speak. Let's say we both make minor sacrifices for the greater good?"

Heather's mouth fell agape as the true nature of his request became apparent. The pause was awkward.

"Your hesitancy vexes. Perhaps you're not as driven to succeed as I suspected."

"Not this way," Heather responded.

"Don't exaggerate your naivete," he said. "Blushing violets don't dally the way you do. And for what purpose? To preserve your childhood fantasies regarding the pristine life of a pop idol?"

"This isn't how I imagined it."

"You won't make it far in this world by clinging to outdated values."

"Talent. Hard work," she replied. "Those mean something." The awkward way she spoke those words made her sound unconvincing.

"Pssh," he scoffed. "Do you have any idea how many talentless, lazy people become stars because they know how to game the system?"

"I've earned this opportunity. I've done all that's been asked of me without complaint."

"And yet I simply ask for one more. There's no such thing

as a free lunch, after all."

"Wouldn't that make me a...?" The thought made her shudder.

"I prefer the term 'motivated collaborator.'"

She contemplated the absurdity of his response. "Who's to say I can't succeed on my own?"

"Perhaps you can. But why bother with the tedium of a long season if you can jump directly to the championship?" As he took a bite of his salmon, his stare dug into the exposed flesh of her shoulders. She wished she had chosen a less revealing dress. "Also, you'd be wise to consider the following." He turned his fork around, pointing its tines at her like stabbing knives. "My preference is to further your career, but should I be pushed, I could also hinder it."

Her jaw hit the floor. "Are you threatening me?"

"Not at all. Merely stating a fact. Thousands of girls would kill to be in your shoes. Their choice would be easy."

Heather was in stasis. Could this be happening? Might years of effort and pain condense into this singular, defining instant? Had her struggle to reach this point been for naught? What would her father's reaction be? Likely reject her as a failure despite having poured every ounce of energy and talent into this endeavor.

Conversely, was the asking price so terrible? Mr. Lee wasn't repulsive, unlike some of the other VIPs. She'd be the envy of countless society girls and idol wannabes. Her living arrangements would go from a crowded, disheveled dorm, lacking even the basics of privacy, to some of the most exceptional living accommodations in the country. Most importantly, the path to her dream life and all its associated rewards would be wide open.

But that's not who you are, Heather. Besides, if he possesses the power to turn lazy, talentless nobodies into stars, as he claims, what does that say about you? Would success depend on your merits or his?

"I'm sorry, Mr. Lee. Your admiration flatters me, but I must decline your offer. Please understand. I'd prefer to do things the normal way. I believe I can."

Mr. Lee failed to disguise his anger. It took him a moment to recover. "Fine," he said through gritted teeth. He summoned his staff to serve the best champagne. "You are indeed a formidable challenge, Ms. Moon, as I had been warned. Let's recognize we see things differently and allow no hard feelings to linger on this exchange."

His muted reaction pleasantly surprised her. The fluted glasses came, and they toasted to bright futures.

Gulping down that delicious beverage was the last memory Heather had of the evening.

23

TODAY WON'T BE LIKE YESTERDAY

Grace woke early the next morning, excited for the upcoming video shoot and relieved that Heather had finally opened up about what had happened with Mr. Lee. Heather appeared more relaxed, returning to the pleasant demeanor she had long ago displayed. Grace knew it would be a long road to full recovery (and the constant reminders about Glimmer Blue didn't help), but it was a good start. The news saddened the girls, but they were not surprised. Heather welcomed their unconditional support.

Steve's mother, Vivian, drove the cast to Scottsdale Airpark. Her son and the rest of the crew had woken predawn and were already well into their workday as the procession of dancers arrived. The excitement was palpable as they got their first glimpse of the 16,000-square-foot space. Five executive jets formed a broad semicircle against the open hangar doors, silhouetted by the McDowell Mountains rising in the background. The scene looked magnificent in the morning sun. It was hard for Grace to believe that this was their set.

Everyone reacted at once.

"Wow."

"Look at this."

"Am I dreaming?"

"This is awesome."

"How'd you find this place?"

The girls scattered to the four corners, scampering around like kittens in a leaf pile. During the facility tour, Vanessa stumbled upon their choreographer sitting in a chair tucked away behind the wheel strut of a Gulfstream. "Look, Danya's here!"

Danya remained seated, leaning against one arm of the chair with her legs draped over the other. "Damn straight," she said. "You think I'm going to let y'all ruin my dance?" The members gathered around to greet her.

"How'd you get here?"

"I flew in this morning."

"That's not fair. How come she gets to fly?" asked Erin.

"Bargaining power," explained Steve.

He gave his cast a brief tour of the facility and then escorted them to the conference room, which served as a temporary green room. Steve asked them to get dressed so he could critique their outfits one last time. As they changed, Grace noted Heather's pale look and glassy eyes.

"Are you okay?" Grace asked.

"Yeah, I'm fine. Just a lot's at stake is all."

"Tell me about it."

When the dancers emerged a half-hour later, it was evident that Marielle had again conjured magic. Based on feedback from the prep meeting, she had adjusted the outfits by incorporating bits and pieces of existing costumes. In their new form, they appeared unrelated to their previous use but retained a streamlined sense of their former magnificence. "You look like the Powerpuff Girls grew up and joined the Federation," Steve said approvingly.

A genuine scare emerged before the cast took positions for a lighting test. Erin's scream signaled the trouble. All attention turned in her direction. There, she struggled to hold Heather upright. Sun-hee came to assist, and together, they eased their collapsed star into a nearby chair. By then, the rest of the team had gathered around the stricken singer. Heather was hyperventilating and clutching her chest. Grace took control, leaning in to calm her while encouraging slow breathing.

"I can't breathe," said Heather. Terror was evident in both her expression and tone. "My heart. I'm dying." She kept repeating these phrases in rapid succession.

"Is she having a heart attack?" asked Vanessa.

"Somebody call an ambulance!" said Toby.

"No. It's a panic attack," explained Grace. "She gets them sometimes. Everybody, back up! Don't crowd her."

Heather kept insisting she couldn't breathe. Her hands trembled as they grasped her throat.

Steve paced nervously, concerned about her condition. He barked an order to Malcolm, a grip, requesting three ice cubes. His command was met with confusion. "Now, please!" Steve repeated more forcefully. Malcolm abided without further hesitation. With the cubes secured, Steve told Grace to stand back. She resisted at first, but soon thought better of it.

"Heather, listen to me. I want you to open your mouth. I'm going to give you some ice. Okay?"

"I can't breathe." Her rapid intake prevented him from getting any ice into her mouth.

"Heather, please do what I ask. Open your mouth. It will be okay."

"Do what he says," added Grace. Soon, others were offering encouragement as well.

Eventually, Heather kept her mouth open long enough for Steve to place one cube inside. She wrapped her lips around it. Soon, her hands stopped shaking. Arms then dropped to her side as her breathing slowed. The redness faded from her face. As the ice cube melted, Steve provided a second and a third. The cast and crew sighed in relief as Heather's health improved before their eyes. Before long, she was talking normally again. Mindy gave her a glass of apple juice, and Heather gulped it down. She was smiling now. Fifteen minutes later, Heather felt well enough to stand. The girls hugged her. So did Steve.

"What happened?" asked June.

"Sometimes it's brought on by stress. Other times, it simply happens," said Grace. "Fortunately, not often." As Heather got her makeup retouched, Grace pulled Steve to the side. "Where did you learn that ice cube trick?"

Steve smiled. "A kid in my high school suffered from anxiety. It worked for him, so I thought I'd give it a shot." They waited another 20 minutes before Heather confirmed she was well enough to continue.

With the crisis behind them, attention returned to the matter at hand. Both the cast and crew needed rehearsal time, and Steve provided plenty of it. The hangar doors were closed to better control the lighting. Danya ran the members through their dance routine once more, correcting minor errors in execution. Stan, the gaffer, tweaked the lighting setup while his camera crew practiced moves with the crane dolly.

Dalton Lim, Steve's cinematographer, was a UCLA graduate

student from Singapore. Not only did he possess an impressive demo reel, but he also offered to bring along an entire camera crew as a package deal. This unexpected perk was a boon. They were skilled and familiar with each other. After many run-throughs, the team operated like a machine. Each test ran smoother than the last. Happy with the progress, Steve opted to release the cast and crew to a lunch break.

The number of hangar employees on the scene grew throughout the meal break. The men ambled around the facility, trying to seem busy. They spoke excitedly, opened drawers randomly, and gesticulated wildly at the parked jets, pretending their observations were of utmost importance. Grace was pleased they weren't part of the cast; their ruse was unconvincing. She knew precisely why they were there. The girls noticed this, too, and conferred within the dressing room while receiving touch-ups. Grace felt something needed to be said. When they reemerged onto the set, she approached Steve, who was supervising last-minute lighting adjustments. "Do you have a second, Herr Director?"

"Sure, what's up?"

"A couple of the newer girls expressed concern about having an audience. What are those guys here for?"

"They work here."

"I know, but today's supposed to be an off day."

"It is."

"So why are they watching us?"

"A couple of them are babysitting the facility, but the rest forgot stuff and dropped by to pick it up."

Grace scoffed, finding it unbelievable that Steve said those words without a laugh track. "Oh, please. Eighteen guys just happened to forget something and coincidentally appeared right as we're about to shoot? You're telling me that with a straight face?"

"Hey, don't shoot the messenger," Steve said. "I'm renting the place. At a below-market rate, I might add. I can't tell them how to run their own business. Besides, if y'all are too shy to perform in front of strangers, you probably got in the wrong line of work, don't you think?"

Grace turned her back on him with a "humph" and rejoined the group. She couldn't argue with that logic. They'd have to deal with it and move on.

To capture the dance, they planned to film it multiple times from different angles. The first take was a stationary shot using a wide-angle lens, the goal being to capture the group's choreography in full. When Steve yelled "cut," the pop-up audience offered a round of applause. He reminded them that the film set was live and requested silence. Their vocal support, however, galvanized Made in Heaven. No longer were they nervous about the spectators. In fact, they looked eager to perform again.

For the second setup, Steve used a 70-200 f2.8 lens for close-ups, focusing on the center of the formation. This allowed him to capture fine details in choreography, such as the hand and facial gestures that gave the dance character.

The final two setups featured the crane. The first move was more complicated, as it included what Dalton called the diving board maneuver. As Steve conceived it, the action comprised a group overhead shot that dropped to a tight portrait of Mindy, who occupied the center at that point. The scheme required close coordination between the camera crew and Mindy, who had to hit the same spot each time to be in focus. Perfect synchronization proved the most challenging, but everyone agreed it looked excellent on playback when finally achieved.

As an insurance run, Steve opted for a separate crane shot without the maneuver to ensure he had basic coverage in the editing room if the need arose. The many run-throughs took a physical toll on the dancers, whose energy flagged. The hangar employees, too, became disillusioned by the long waits between takes as the crew made countless adjustments to equipment, costumes, and lighting. By the time they were ready to attempt the second crane shot, most of the superfluous looky-loos had found excuses to return home.

Since it was a half-hour before the scheduled wrap time, Steve opted to take one more wide-angle shot, this time with smoke machines.

"I was wondering what we brought those for," said the gaffer.

"It's an experiment. I'm not sure I'll use it," said Steve.

Everyone took their positions one last time. Nobody complained despite the fatigue. The two machines began pumping away at Steve's command, filling the hangar with an atmospheric cloud. The smell of the fog fluid hitting the heating element caused Grace to sneeze.

"Okay, that should be enough," Dalton said moments later.

"No, a bit more," Steve said. "Keep 'em running!"

Dalton seemed anxious. "If you add much more, it'll reduce the light—"

Steve cut him off before he could continue. "Don't worry. I like how this looks."

Someone, possibly Erin, coughed as the smoke cloud grew. The density made it difficult to see anyone. "Okay, shut them off," Steve demanded.

The machines kept pumping with no signs of stopping.

"I said, cut!" The poor visibility made it impossible to distinguish the coughers, but the smoke was now affecting multiple people.

Malcolm's discarnate voice said, "I can't find the machines."

"Unplug the damn things," commanded Steve.

"There are cables literally everywhere!"

"Find them!" A tinge of panic colored Steve's voice. At this desperate order, chaos erupted. Nobody knew where to go, yet everyone wanted to be somewhere else. Grace dropped to the ground, intending to help search for the power cable, only to discover the fog was even thicker at floor level. As she crawled around on all fours, searching for any type of plug, a sneaker nearly crushed her hands, as did a high heel. Then the hangar went dark. The chugging of the smoke machines ceased. Someone must've tripped the breaker box, she reasoned.

"Thank god," said one male voice.

Their relief was short-lived. A harsh-sounding alarm began clanging.

"What is that?" an exasperated Erin could be heard asking.

"Fire alarm!"

A beat later, the sprinkler system triggered. The hangar soon became drenched with water. Puddles formed on the floor. Somebody cursed as they slipped and knocked over the craft table, producing a tremendous crash of splattered food and shattered dishes. Amid this deluge, one employee had the wherewithal to locate and open the hangar doors. Cast and crew members staggered outside, holding each other for support. A few remained subject to violent bouts of coughing. Once exposed to fresh air, the afflicted could breathe more freely. Now unconfined, they could also better hear the approaching sirens of the Scottsdale Fire Department.

Twenty minutes later, paramedics were checking patients for lingering respiratory problems. Firefighters had shut off the sprinklers and reset the alarm. Police had arrived to take reports and check for violations. Meanwhile, the fire marshal combed the building to ensure it was free of any conflagrations.

Made in Heaven's members, once lighthearted, now huddled glumly, resembling scolded puppies. Their smeared makeup suggested a troupe of deranged clowns. Their once carefully tended hairdos hung limp. Marielle's lovely costumes dripped puddles onto the airport tarmac. Danya frowned in disbelief at what she had gotten herself into. Heather looked miserable.

"I should learn to quit while I'm ahead," Steve said to her with a chuckle. His awkward attempt to lighten the mood failed.

"Ya think?" responded Heather icily.

No serious injuries or ailments resulted, fortunately. Once the business was done, the hangar employees tasked with safeguarding the facility issued their edict. Everything would have to be returned to standard operating condition by noon the next day. Steve called for an all-hands-on-deck effort, cast and crew included.

Grace requested that the talent be allowed to sleep in the following day because they had danced all evening. Steve granted the request on the condition that they buy breakfast for the crew members arriving pre-dawn to begin the cleanup. He handed her a prepaid debit card to cover the purchase and provided an address for a bakery.

"There's just enough on it to pay for the order. I'll see you at 9:15 a.m. Don't be late!"

"Aye, aye, captain," she saluted.

* * *

"It doesn't open 'til 9:00," said Grace. The next morning, she and her fellow group members stood outside Sprinkles Bakery, ogling the dazzling confections on display in the window.

"I knew it was too early," complained Vanessa. "Nothing opens early on Sunday, especially Easter."

"You should have double-checked. I thought we could head home sooner by getting a head start."

"What should we do?" asked June.

"We wait," said Grace. "What else is there?"

Sun-hee, Erin, and Mindy claimed spots on the one bench outside the shop. Without better alternatives, Grace, Heather, and June returned to the Shepard family minivan they had borrowed from Steve's parents, who were at church. The doors and windows were flung open for circulation. It was early, but the Arizona sun shone brightly, heralding the searing heat it would dish out later that day.

Vanessa paced. At one point, she walked away.

Though Grace was relieved to be free of Ness' annoying behavior, she didn't want the group to disperse too far, even for a few minutes. "Where are you going?"

Vanessa spun quickly, shouting, "Just looking around."

"Don't go far, or we'll leave you behind."

Vanessa laughed. "You wouldn't dare."

Not five minutes later, she was back. "Guys, guess what I found?"

"A million bucks?" guessed Erin.

"No."

"A pirate treasure?" suggested Mindy.

"Close. A bike-share station's 'round the corner."

"And?" said Grace.

"Let's get off our asses and live a little instead of sitting here like a buncha slugs on reds."

"Vanessa, chill," said Grace. "We're recovering from yesterday."

"Check out this weather. It's gorgeous. The sun's shining early. There's a greenway half a block away. When'll we ever be back? Come on. It'll be fun."

"The shop's opening in 45 minutes," countered Heather.

"It's a dollar for a half hour. I'll gladly pay a few bucks to avoid watching you mope around all morning. Thirty minutes tops. We'll be back before it opens."

"I mean, it *is* boring just sitting here," said Erin.

"I want to see too," said June.

Grace ignored her better instincts, but had to admit that Vanessa's idea held merit. "All right. Who am I to defy the will of the people?"

Without further resistance, Vanessa led the way to the bicycles. Before long, the seven rode along Greenbelt, imitating the "Do-Re-Mi" bicycle scene from *The Sound of Music*.

"Tea, a drink with jam and bread," sang Mindy out loud.

"Why do you get to be Liesl?" asked Erin.

"I'm your unnie, that's why. Besides, you look more like Kurt anyway." The other girls laughed.

"I do not."

"Don't feel bad, Erin," said Grace. "Liesl's the one who fell for a Nazi."

More laughter. This time, Mindy was the one reacting. Gritting her teeth, she kicked the action into high gear, taking off racing to see who would follow. Vanessa was game to give chase, and soon the others struggled to catch up. It didn't take long for Vanessa to reach Mindy. As the group's most athletic member, with years of intense weight training, her developed leg muscles allowed her to leave the others in the dust with little effort. She'd spur them toward a new destination each time they caught up. "Let's see if we can reach that red mountain over there," she said, pointing to one of the iconic peaks encircling Scottsdale.

"That's too far. It'll take too long," said Sun-hee.

"Naw, a few minutes. Besides, Steve said we could come late. Before anyone could offer a reasonable response, she took off again. Heather could be heard shouting from the rear, "We're supposed to be resting."

After 20 more minutes of riding, the mountain they saw in the distance was much farther away than it had first appeared. Vanessa, at that point, was far ahead. Only when Grace got the remaining members to shout out her name did the mischievous one abandon her quest and return, though not repentant.

"It's 9:30 already," Grace noted. "We need to get to the bakery."

The return trip was much less enjoyable. Now warmer, the girls were also under pressure, unlike before. Heather led the vanguard on the return, but there was far less enthusiasm to charge forward. Vanessa sullenly brought up the rear. At one point, the group stopped to debate options.

"Which way?" asked Heather.

Vanessa considered the fork and selected the rightmost path. "This way."

"Are you sure?"

She didn't answer, preferring to let her legs do the talking. The others followed. After another 30 minutes, it was evident she'd chosen incorrectly.

"Dammit, Nessa, you got us lost," said Grace.

"We're not lost. Just go back and pick the other side," said Vanessa.

"It's too hot. I need to rest," said Erin.

"I saw a smoothie place nearby. Let's stop on the way back," suggested Mindy.

"With what money?" asked Heather.

"Grace has the debit card," she responded.

"That's for breakfast."

Grace once more yielded to group influence. "We can, I suppose. Just don't order anything expensive."

"Kale-infused, artisan kombucha in a mason jar?" observed Grace when Heather joined them with her drink. "There's one in every group."

"If no one volunteers to be different, I will," responded Heather.

"These smoothies are super-duper delish," stated Mindy.

"I know, right. Exactly what I needed," agreed Erin.

"I thought I'd melt out there," said Sun-hee.

"Does the card have any money left?" asked Heather.

Grace's lips stayed glued to the end of her straw as she sipped hands-free with the cup resting on the table before her. Her eyes darted around to assess each member's appetite for the truth. "Um."

"Spit it out," demanded Heather.

Grace made a quick set of calculations. "Well, we're gonna have to pay extra for the bike rentals because we're late," Grace said.

"Yeah, and?"

"And you all ordered expensive drinks even though I told you not to."

"Grace, get to the point."

"I need to borrow a phone to check. Mine's charging at the house."

Heather turned on her phone. It started bing-binging frantically as a series of texts came through at once.

"We're dead," said Heather as she scanned through them. "The boys are *not* happy."

"What are they saying?" asked Sun-hee.

Heather read some messages aloud. *'Where are you?' 'We're starving.' 'Are you okay?' 'We need help.' 'You're still not here!' 'What the hell is going on?' 'We'd be done by now.' 'Thanks a lot.'*

"We didn't trigger the alarm; why should we clean up that mess?" said Erin.

"I mean, I do feel guilty. We're out having fun while the guys are working," admitted Sun-hee.

"We're just blowing off steam after a long shoot," said Vanessa.

"It's not like they didn't work hard, too," noted Heather.

We must make amends somehow," Mindy said.

Grace grabbed the phone from Heather's hands and dialed the number on the card to check the balance. "Great," she said upon dropping the connection. "After we pay off the bikes, there'll be $5.37 left."

"We need to bring food. If we arrive empty-handed on top of everything else, the guys will force us to walk back to L.A.," advised Mindy.

"What can we buy with $5.37?" asked Erin.

"I have an idea," offered Sun-hee. "We need to find a grocery store, though."

24

TRICKS ARE FOR KIDS

Steve watched nervously as the minder from the jet hangar company inspected the facility. The film crew spent the morning hours rectifying the previous day's disorder. Fortunately, some quick-thinking grips covered sensitive film equipment, preventing terrible damage in that department. Prospects for the facility seemed poorer.

The minder continued to tally up numbers on his checklist. "Good thing the sprinklers only activated in the hangar itself," said the minder. "If the office had gone too, we'd be looking at a whole lot worse." He photocopied the list and handed it to Steve. The bill totaled $1,846. It was not a cataclysmic amount, but another expense that took away from the rapidly depleting budget. That prize money looked more appealing by the day. Steve complained about their missed breakfast as the minder left to process the payment. "I am sorry for not feeding you guys. The girls dropped the ball big time."

"Did you ever get a hold of them?" asked Dalton.

"I've been texting all morning. No answer," said Steve.

"Maybe something happened?" said Toby.

"No idea, but I'm starving," said Stan.

"Food was supposed to be here hours ago. Sorry guys, I was counting on their help." Just then, his phone vibrated, showing an incoming text. "It's from Heather." Steve read it, then groaned. "You're never gonna believe this. They went bike riding."

"Bike riding? Is this a vacation to them?"

"That really pisses me off," said Malcolm.

"That's what the message says," explained Steve.

"They did it on purpose, I bet," added Dalton.

"We toil while they go on a joyride," said Toby. "I'm ballistic."

Steve shut off his phone. "I say screw it. Once I get my card back, let's grab lunch."

Steve arrived at his parents' house later that afternoon. The minivan in the driveway signaled that the band members had returned from their escapade. His crew had eaten their fill at Miguel's Taqueria. The meal improved their spirits, yet forgiveness for the girls' negligence remained elusive. "Okay, here's the deal," he explained. "We need to present a unified front. Be tough. Don't let them off easy. They need to know their behavior was unacceptable."

"You got that right," said Malcolm.

"They left us in the lurch," said Dalton.

"They're not getting away with this," added Toby.

"Listen up," Steve said. "We go inside, pack the equipment, and load the vehicles for the trip home. Don't say a word. Give them the ol' silent treatment. Make them worry. Force them to respond. Capiche?" The crew nodded. "My parents are out Eastering, so the girls won't be able to use them as a shield.

This is our best chance. Let's roll."

As they bounded across the driveway and through the front door, initial reconnaissance suggested they were in the clear. The crew set to work on their assigned tasks. Steve kneeled on the floor, separating the cables according to size and type. Dalton and Toby tended to the camera while Stan and Malcolm packed the grip equipment. As Steve pondered the girls' whereabouts, the girls sprung an ambush.

"You're here!" said Grace as she entered the living room, followed soon after by her group mates. Steve refused to look up, relying instead on peripheral vision to note that they came bearing gifts. He focused on the task at hand to avoid paying his adversaries any undue attention.

Despite only glimpsing her from the knees down, he recognized Heather as she approached. "Are you mad?" she giggled, though not mockingly.

Steve was determined to send a message and refused to respond. Unfortunately, his band of merry men proved that their bark was worse than their bite. Exposed to the heat of battle, they withered instantly.

"Where were you?" asked Toby from his position near the living room window. *Toby, you idiot. What's wrong with you?* Steve wasn't sure who Toby was talking to, but judging from the tone of his voice, it didn't sound promising. Cracks were already forming in their supposedly ironclad façade.

"We made you treats," Sun-hee said brightly. Steve couldn't resist any longer. He snuck a glance out of the corner of his eye and observed Sun-hee presenting two wrapped confections of some sort, one in each hand, shown to both Dalton and Toby. *Don't you dare take those, you morons!*

When Dalton pointed at him, Steve averted his gaze to avoid

being sucked into the vortex. Heather, meanwhile, was pulling on Steve's left arm to get him to acknowledge her. He feigned ignorance. A terse "What?" is all he mustered in response.

"We want to apologize for our behavior this morning. We made you dalgona. It's a Korean sweet candy. Taste one."

"No."

"Why not?"

"I'm not hungry. We ate."

"Take a bite. It's splendid."

"I'll have one later."

"They'll be gone later."

His mates were being worked over by the other girls. Their assault was total and unforgiving. His beleaguered crew was faltering. Sun-hee communicated in Korean to Heather, who released the sweet from its crinkly envelope. She leaned towards Steve and placed it near his mouth. Its baked, sugary scent filled his nostrils. *Resist, Steve. If you take their gift, you're done for.* He pushed her arm away. Heather laughed like a mother dealing with a petulant child.

"Well, since you went through the trouble of making them, the least I could do is sample one," he heard Malcolm say. *That damn backstabber.*

Stan was now complimenting June. "You must've worked hard to make these. They look beautiful!" *These guys are hopeless.*

"Wow, these are delicious," said Dalton. *Et tu, Brute?*

One by one, they fell to the Made in Heaven charm offensive. Soon, an armistice was called. Heather opted to seal a formal peace agreement with another offering of freshly wrapped dalgona. This time, Steve relented, too. He didn't want to upset Heather. Besides, his entire crew was already enjoying their treats. Discussions of key ingredients and preparation techniques had replaced all talk of silent treatments and unified fronts.

Gold-colored cellophane wrapped Heather's dalgona, secured by a red twist tie. It resembled a sizable, thin lollipop the color of a pancake. A heart-shaped pattern had been carefully pressed into it.

"If you eat around the heart without breaking it, I'll give you another." Heather issued this promise with a flutter of her eyelashes. Further resistance was futile.

The moment had arrived to return to L.A. "Thanks, Steve," said Vanessa, "but Sun-hee and I decided we'd like to live a little longer. We'll take the van this time."

"No, I understand. I recognize my car has some serious shortcomings," he said. "I don't blame you."

"Will you go by yourself?" asked Sun-hee.

"I can ride with him," said Heather. "I don't mind."

Sun-hee offered a meek "Thanks," now appearing to regret her decision.

The seven members gathered around Steve's parents to thank them for their hospitality. Mr. Shepard received extra-special attention.

"We're glad we got to meet Steve's father," said Erin.

"Yeah, now we know where he got his handsome looks from," said Grace.

In succession, they kissed him on the cheek, sometimes two at a time. When June took her turn, Mr. Shepard nearly melted into a puddle on the sidewalk. Heather and Steve walked to his car as the rest of the group climbed into the waiting van.

"What the hell was that all about?" Steve asked.

"Your dad's been so sweet," Heather admitted.

"He's still shocked that I brought seven girls on this trip. Y'all almost gave him a heart attack." He shook his head in disbelief.

They entered a Torino that had been sitting in the Phoenix sun for several hours. "This is how Hansel and Gretel must've felt," Heather said.

Rolling down the windows helped a smidge, so long as the car kept moving. "Do you know how Phoenix got its name?" asked Steve as they struggled through the late holiday traffic.

"From the mythological phoenix, I assume."

"That's what most people think, but in reality, it's from all the birds bursting into flame mid-flight due to the relentless summer heat."

This elicited a laugh from Heather. The exchange helped take her mind off the weather, however briefly. Waiting at traffic signals stung the most. Steve responded by turning the fan on full blast. That merely transposed the inferno from the outside to the inside.

As they were being broiled alive, Heather asked a sly question. "You guys didn't think it would be *that* easy to resist a K-pop girl group in full charm mode, did you? We're professionals. We have standards to maintain."

Steve thought about this for a while. "You know, for a second there, yeah, we kinda did."

"Silly rabbit."

Steve looked askance at Heather, who wore an impish grin. He had fallen into her trap. And a movie-related one at that. "Oh, no. I'm not taking the bait. There's no way in hell I'm allowing myself to be out movie-referenced by a K-pop singer."

Steve stopped at a convenience store to gather road trip provisions. After they had stocked enough sodas, chips, and candy for the journey, he asked her if she was "Ready to roll?"

"Let's do this."

After roaring past downtown Phoenix, the Torino punched its way through the western suburbs. Miles of nondescript mini-malls and cookie-cutter subdivisions pummeled them before they finally reached the untouched desert. "Full tank, cold drinks, open road. Whatta you say we crank some music?"Steve turned on the radio and encountered static. The first clear signal he found was a classic rock station emerging from a commercial break. The distinctive opening guitar chords signaled the song that would start their trip, AC/DC's "Highway to Hell." Steve smirked at the irony.

"What do you think that means?" Heather asked.

* * *

As they approached Arizona's border with California, Heather's phone vibrated. "Are we taking I-10 the whole way?"

"Yeah, why?" Steve asked.

"I just received a traffic alert." Heather read the message on her phone. "Rollover accident reported on I-10 east of Indio. All westbound lanes closed. Expect delays."

"East of Indio? Great." Steve hit the top of his steering wheel in frustration. "That will add hours to our trip."

"Can we make it to L.A. before midnight? I have a class tomorrow morning."

"I doubt it. Traffic will be jammed for miles. Who knows how long it'll take to clear?"

"Isn't there another way?"

"I-10's pretty much the one route connecting Phoenix and L.A." He considered it a moment longer. "Unless..."

"You have an idea?"

"Once, when I got bored driving the same route back and forth, I took an old road north of Joshua Tree. It runs parallel to the I-10, but it's way...I mean seriously in the middle of nowhere. I doubt anyone would even bother with it. We could try."

"If it'll work," said Heather.

"At least we won't be stuck in a monster traffic jam having our insides grilled to a crisp."

Steve's description of the route was apt. After detouring at Blythe, the only sign of civilization they encountered along the way was tiny Moya Junction, comprising a gas station and an agricultural inspection site, both of which were closed. Beyond that point, the open road stretched into the distance. Not one structure appeared in view. Along the entire stretch, they ran across one other vehicle heading in the opposite direction. The experience profoundly contrasted with Heather's time spent in densely populated Korea. She found it a marvel to behold, even if a bit intimidating.

The heat became impossible as the afternoon wore on, even with open windows. The super-heated air blowing in from the vents was withering. Heather fanned herself with a wadded tourist brochure she had pilfered from the lobby of the jet plane hangar.

"My air conditioner doesn't work well, but it's gotta be better than this," Steve admitted.

"Please. Oh, please."

They shut the windows and experienced a gentle sensation

on their faces. The result was mildly refreshing, but Heather questioned whether it was worth using, considering the windows had to be shut tight to notice anything.

After 20 minutes had passed, an oily, burning smell filled the enclosed compartment. "What is that?" she asked.

Steve didn't respond, but he, too, noticed something amiss.

"It smells like—" she could not finish her sentence before the Gran Torino shuddered with a bone-jarring thud. The dashboard lights blinked on and off in quick succession. Smoke entered their lungs, forcing them to reopen the windows. Steve swerved into a wide spot of gravel beside the road.

"Get out!" He shouted. His voice conveyed urgency. They both fled, doors flying open as they jumped. Heather watched flames lick from the engine compartment as the car rolled to a halt yards away.

To her horror, she watched Steve return to the burning vehicle. "Be careful!"

He reached behind the driver's seat, extracted an extinguisher, and popped open the hood. Steve ducked to avoid the flames as they shot towards him. Five long blasts from the extinguisher, and the fire was out. Residual smoke wafted from the engine for several more minutes.

When it looked safe to approach, Heather peeked under the hood to assess the damage. Hoses and wires had melted. The engine was pitch-black. "I guess we won't be home soon?"

"That's a safe bet." Steve expressed his anger by tossing the extinguisher high in the air. It landed with a dull thud in the desert soil not far away.

It's your fault. You pushed him to turn on the AC. Good job, Heather. She hoped to remedy the situation by searching for a local area map on her phone. "There's a town ahead called

Gage. It doesn't look far. Let's walk."

"Waste of time. Gage is a ghost town." Steve looked exasperated. His shoulders slumped. "Let me put it this way. We're standing in one of the candidate sites for the world's first atomic bomb test. Don't expect much in terms of civilization." He double-checked his phone, but wasn't getting any signal. Heather offered hers instead.

Steve called the only two service stations found anywhere within 100 miles. Not surprisingly, they were closed for Easter. He texted Dalton, who responded 12 minutes later. "Dalton and Toby say they can detour at Desert Station and swing round to pick us up," said Steve.

"How long will that take?"

"His GPS is saying three hours without traffic. We have some waiting to do." Heather didn't complain. Her conscience was already heavy enough.

Steve rigged a flimsy sunshade using an old blanket from the trunk to avoid heatstroke. Some C-stands from the video shoot held the contraption in place. He encouraged Heather to drink lots of water for hydration. They huddled together in the meager shade, awaiting rescue.

"I have enough battery left on my phone to play one song. What would you pick?"

Heather pondered his question for a moment. "That's impossible for me to answer," she said. "I love so many; I could never settle on one. How about you?"

"Easy." He pressed play. The music itself was deceptively simple; its performance aged like fine wine. Musicianship was unparalleled. She didn't understand the Spanish lyrics but understood the singer's intent. The song was a hauntingly beautiful expression of desire, reflecting a lifetime of struggle and pain. Set against the stark landscape in which she found herself, the experience created a visceral image that stuck with her long afterward. When it ended, Steve's phone beeped a depleted battery warning.

"What was that?" asked Heather.

"A Cuban song called 'Chan Chan' by the Buena Vista Social Club. That single piece encapsulates the experience of living life like no other. Music in its purest form. The trumpet part slays me every time."

Heather smiled as she contemplated Steve's ability to appreciate beauty. "I can see why you'd pick that. Thanks for sharing." He looked pleased with her response. Without saying another word, he leaned against the car, and within minutes was fast asleep. The experience of the weekend had pushed him to the edge of exhaustion.

The highway remained deserted.

Heather was left in solitude.

Now, at rest, she could assess the desert as never before. The sweet fragrance in the tranquil air drew her attention to the abundance and variety of wildflowers nearby. From the vantage point of a speeding car and set against the grand terrain, the tiny blossoms blurred with the passing scenery. What she had so recently dismissed as desolate now teemed with life upon closer inspection.

The pervasive silence of the desert, too, struck her as profound. It was at once ominous and comforting. City life was cacophonous in comparison. She spent long minutes listening for a single sound, any sound at all, but heard little more than Steve's irregular breathing and the beat of her own heart. That moment brought her cathartic peace.

The distant rumbling of an approaching freight interrupted

her long reverie. As it drew closer, the dull roar of its four linked locomotives woke Steve. The rail line it traversed lay yards away, allowing them to feel the vibrations of the diesel engines as much as they could hear them. On and on it passed, at one point stretching so far in either direction that they could see neither end. A train hopper in a flaxen-hued bucket hat rode the well of an intermodal railcar. They waved as he passed, but the traveler seemed too preoccupied with his beer to acknowledge them. The desert's tranquility gradually returned as the clickety-clack of the eastbound freight faded into the distance. With that moment of entertainment over, Steve attempted to resume his nap.

By that point, Heather had experienced enough silence. With knees tucked under her chin and arms wrapped around her legs, she spoke. "Remember at the Christmas party when you asked me why I didn't become an idol?"

Steve aborted his sleep attempt and sat upright. "Yeah," he said eagerly.

"The first time I met him, the executive, was the evening of our investor meeting."

25

AFTERMATH

Heather's tale of being drugged by Mr. Lee left Steve in shock. "My God, what happened next?" he asked.

"I woke the next morning alone in the most luxurious bed I'd ever seen. The sunlight poured through the windows of this magnificent bedroom, with a lovely garden right outside the glass walls. It seemed like a dream at first."

Heather remained silent for a long moment. Steve had no desire to rush her as the memories came flooding back.

"From the sun's position, it must've been early afternoon," she continued. "I found myself naked under the covers. Mentally, I felt exhausted, not like I would have after a full night's sleep. I was dizzy. Sounds echoed. The garden flowers were blooming, but I was emotionally detached as if viewing a painting on a wall. It's difficult to explain, Steve, but my whole body seemed to vanish. My head felt detached, adrift."

"How did you escape?"

"Eventually, I forced myself up. It took every ounce of strength I had. I wanted to stay in that bed, yet dreaded what would happen. I couldn't find my clothes anywhere.

A terrycloth robe had been placed on a nearby chair. It fit perfectly; I remember that. The agency didn't allow us phones, and there wasn't one in the room, so I had no choice but to venture out. When I saw a maid in the hallway, I called to her. 'Where are my clothes?' She left without saying a word but returned with her supervisor, the gray-haired woman who had greeted me at the door the previous evening. She asked if there was anything wrong. Can you fathom that? Anything wrong?"

"How did you respond?"

"I demanded the return of my belongings and a ride to the dorm. The woman told me the closet had garments of all sizes. To take what I wanted. She also said my belongings could be transported to the house whenever I wished."

"They expected you to stay there after that?"

"Crazy, huh? Mr. Lee was nowhere in sight that day. After much insisting, I finally convinced the woman to call a taxi. When I returned to the dorm, the girls burst into tears. They were worried sick. I was given permission to skip the evening rehearsals, but the agency's CEO insisted I meet him in the morning."

"What did he say? What did you say?"

"The first words out of his mouth were, 'You, stupid, stupid girl. Do you want to bring this company to ruin?'"

"'Sir, I'm not ruining anything,' I responded. 'I was assaulted.'"

"Then he goes, 'What proof do you have any of that happened? Nobody will believe a word you say. Mr. Lee has been a godsend to this company. You're nothing more than an overrated trainee with an inflated opinion of herself. If you dare press this, your family will pay the price.'"

"What did he mean?" asked Steve.

"I assumed he meant Mr. Lee would use his connections to ruin my father's career somehow."

"Brutal. What was your reaction?"

"I didn't. I knew I had lost. My spirit was destroyed. I felt beyond worthless. Besides, I was in no physical condition to resist. My body still suffered from the effects of the drug, aching like the flu, only worse. The whole first day, I vomited. I was nauseous for a week. Sleep provided my sole remedy. They cut me after missing several rehearsals, glad to be rid of a nuisance, no doubt. Grace left in solidarity. Effectively banished from the industry, we returned home to live with our parents until college started."

"That's a shocking story, Heather. I honestly don't know what to say other than I'm sorry."

Heather laughed, which surprised Steve. "You had nothing to do with it. Why be sorry?"

"It's awful that such terrible things happen to good people."

"That's life, Steve," Heather concluded. "That's life."

"Did he, you know..."

"Rape me?"

Steve nodded.

"At first, I thought so. I still can't remember anything after that drink. The next day, Grace and a non-industry friend snuck me to a clinic under a false name. They found no physical evidence of sexual assault but gave me an HIV prophylaxis and the morning-after pill to be sure. I didn't report it to the police. My wish was to stay anonymous."

"You must've been scared," Steve said.

"I was terrified. Mr. Lee is connected. Someone like me stood no chance against him. Plus, there's the victim-blaming.”

“You mean people saying you deserved it?”

“Exactly. ‘Why did you go to his house?’ ‘Why were you dressed that way?’ ‘You knew what you were doing.’ Or, worst of all, ‘You were trying to get money out of him.’ There’d be nothing to gain from reporting it. And my sanity to lose.”

“If he didn’t rape you, what was that all about?”

“I’ve spent many months contemplating that very question. My conclusion is Mr. Lee was after power, not sex. Men like him aren’t used to the word ‘no’ and don’t react well when they do hear it. They prefer to keep their play toys complicit. Making me believe I was raped was a power-play move. He’d have the final say regardless of my response.”

“That sounds plausible.”

“And in a perverted way, maybe he figured I’d be more receptive to a sponsorship arrangement if he could convince me I already paid the price. I don’t plan on asking for details.”

“What do you mean, sponsorship arrangement?”

“Rumors abound that less reputable agencies float secret lists containing the names and asking prices of idols amenable to sponsorships. The more popular the idol, the higher the price.”

“God.”

“Dark stuff. See why I didn’t want to discuss this at the Christmas party?” She found a rock the size of a quarter and carved a circle in the dirt beside her. “I wanted to hate my old group when they debuted, but I didn’t. Why do you think that is?”

Steve shrugged his shoulders. “Your influence had a lasting effect on them even after you left.”

“If you say so.”

"Honestly, Heather, consider this. Grace specifically mentioned how you created a nurturing environment for the other trainees when, most times, it's a cutthroat experience."

"But I lost."

"You did what you thought was right. You have nothing to be ashamed of. If that's not winning, what is?"

"That's not how the world usually views it."

"It's how it should be. And look at the big picture. Those gestures ripple far and wide. I, for one, will never forget you standing up for me against Arnie when you didn't have to."

Heather smiled. "I'm glad I did."

Steve placed a hand on Heather's shoulder. "It wasn't long ago this happened. How are you doing now?"

"Some days are okay; others are a struggle. Pouring myself into music staves off the worst. Grace doesn't leave me alone with my thoughts for long. Always keeping me busy."

Steve reflected on what Heather had just conveyed to him? "Honestly, I wouldn't have known," he said. "You're so positive."

"An idol's job is to make people happy. I take that role seriously."

"I couldn't do that."

"Laugh on the outside; cry on the inside." She paused, then lifted her head. "That didn't come out right. It makes me sound disingenuous. Honestly, I have both sensations at once." Heather drew a face in the dirt; its mouth formed a straight line, and its eyes were X-shaped. "Most people view depression as an illness you recover from like a cold." She tossed the rock away. "'Just be happy,' they say to me as if that'll cure it. But it's more so a dreadful sense of isolation. Thoroughly crippling at times." With her free hand, Heather erased the drawing. "By the way, this stays between us, okay? I only told the girls two days ago." She looked to Steve for reassurance. He provided it with a nod.

"Your parents? Did you ever tell them what happened?"

"Never." She shook her head. "In my family, emotional problems are taboo. To seek professional treatment is to invite shame. As hard as it was to let my family regard me as a loser, it was miles better than telling them the truth."

Minutes passed. Remarkably, a small quail hopped from under a shrub to peck at a seed. The bird looked at the stranded pair with curiosity before scurrying away.

"Thanks for listening," she said. "It means a lot."

Before he could respond, they heard tires on gravel and a horn honking. Peeking over the car's hood, Heather saw Dalton's Tacoma barreling towards them. Toby leaned out of the passenger window, waving. "They're here! We can go home."

26

A VISION IN LUCID COLOR

Having learned their lesson from the prior semester, the members of Made in Heaven now occupied prime seats at the student screenings. This was not mere happenstance. Steve had vowed to compensate for his earlier fiasco. As the designated student manager of the facility, he snuck the party down a locked stairwell in advance. Steve timed the clandestine maneuver to coincide with the official opening of the lobby doors, thus avoiding suspicion. The remaining seats filled in under five minutes.

Heather texted Steve, who by then had returned to his theater duties.

5:37 P.M. Heather: I hope you're ready this time ;-).

5:38 P.M. Steve: Most def. I have 3 backup copies cached nearby. Intentional overkill.

5:38 P.M. Heather: Can't wait to see it!

Once again, the screenings kicked off at 6:00 p.m. sharp. The lights dimmed after brief opening remarks, and a hush fell over the audience. As before, the event began inauspiciously.

"The Inoculation of Turnip Boy" was memorable for all

the wrong reasons. While it displayed quality production values, most of its length consisted of bombastic main titles or interminable end credits. This was an obvious ploy to artificially inflate the production's grandeur. Its incoherent plot featured a midget mime on a unicycle and a clown weeping over a decapitated stuffed bunny. The dialog was asinine.

"Next," Heather whispered to Grace. Despite the theater being too warm for such attire, the filmmaker took to the stage wearing an oversized white pimp hat and a knit scarf. He answered a host of questions, most of which seemed fawning. Relative to Heather's expectations, the audience's praise eclipsed the few minor criticisms. She learned, to her considerable surprise, that the dreary mess was intended as a comedy. So said the filmmaker. Heather concluded that an overzealous fan base was more important at these screenings than a quality film. Perhaps that was true of many things in life.

Fortunately, some movies justified the wait. "The Legends of Pew Pew" was a funny, short mockumentary covering the fictional career of the last great "disco laser virtuosi." It was well-acted, tightly edited, cleverly conceived, and precisely long enough to tell a humorous, tongue-in-cheek story without overstaying its welcome. The crowd laughed at the plentiful jokes and enjoyed the abundance of disco hits from the 70s.

"Finally, a good one," said Heather. Erin gave a thumbs-up, and Sun-hee applauded. The twin brothers who co-directed the film shared humorous anecdotes about their production travails. The professors lavished much praise on the work and offered supportive feedback.

"I'm glad we don't have to follow that," said Grace.

What did follow was "Sapi," a showcase of time-lapse photography shot at night and set to a New Agey soundtrack. The film was ten minutes long but passed in a flash. Each image was a minor marvel to behold. During its running time, the appreciative audience expressed its approval as one spectacular shot followed another. The student who filmed it, a skinny, nerdy male with sandy-brown hair, fielded a series of technical questions. Professors raved about it and suggested "Sapi" had strong awards potential.

The proceedings returned to the mean with "Does Anybody Remember Laughter?" This film consisted of one long, 360-degree panning shot across an empty field. The soundtrack featured ambient noise mixed with children playing, despite no people appearing in the movie at all. During the subsequent Q&A, the audience roasted the filmmaker (an emo girl with pink hair) for lack of effort, amateurish photography, and an incoherent theme. Heather believed many other films suffered from these same problems.

"Figures they'd crap all over the female," Vanessa whispered.

At last, it was their turn. "Next, we have 'Feel the Heat' music video by Steven Shepard." Some people groaned, but others applauded. The seven group members held hands as the lights dimmed.

A black screen hushed the crowd. The Made in Heaven logo emerged gleaming. Heather had sketched the concept on a napkin, and Steve got it animated. This was her first glimpse of its finished state. The logo faded away to a wing-fluttering sound. A beat passed in darkness before the video opened on a brightly lit, wide-angle shot of the airplane hangar. There stood the seven of them in a glorious line. The formation filled the screen, stretching across an entire wall of the theater. They looked heroic, posing before the five sleek jet aircraft arrayed in the background. During the whistling intro, the camera inched closer. By the time the dance started, their visages towered over the heads of the audience members. Heather sat with her mouth open in wonder, hardly believing how magnificent they looked on the immense screen.

The video was a powerhouse. Everything came together just right. Thrashing guitars, an incessant dance beat, choreography, cinematography, and editing worked harmoniously to produce an impressive result. Heather wouldn't have imagined this possibility only a few weeks earlier.

Steve kept to his strategy of filming in wide shots to capture the scope of the choreography, but also inserted strategic close-ups to highlight specific visuals. Heather happily noted that the members enjoyed equitable screen time. They looked tremendous in their outfits, especially Erin's A-line princess dress and Mindy's prettified Harley Quinn-style hair. She was the complete picture of the consummate idol. June, too, proved her value right away. Exhibiting no nerves, she looked radiant in her first on-screen performance. Marielle's outfit complemented her slight shoulders and well-defined hips.

And just like that, it was over. As the wing logo's reprise faded, Heather felt part of an actual girl group for the first time. When Steve walked buoyantly to the stage for the Q&A session, she heard someone nearby whisper to her friend, "Now I'm questioning my sexuality." Her friend responded, "Remind me to go on a diet."

The post-screening comments were mixed. Reviewers lauded the technical aspects, yet found the 'story' lacking. Nobody mentioned the music or the dancing.

A South Asian student spoke. "It looked professional," he said, "but there was no depth." Heather found this comment pointless.

Steve responded as if expecting this line of questioning. "It's a pop song. We just wanted to brighten people's day."

One comment derailed Heather's mood entirely, though. "I'm not sure we needed to see another male filmmaker objectifying women," one female reviewer said.

Extensive murmuring, some claps of support, and more than one boo followed this opinion. Steve looked astonished and laughed nervously. He hesitated to formulate a response. "I...it's not..." He took a deep breath to calm himself. "You have the wrong idea."

The audience filled the awkward silence with more murmuring. Heather felt terrible, but it would have been inappropriate to intervene on his behalf. Steve gathered his thoughts, though, and then spoke. "I helped develop the concept, but the music, choreography, design, and performances were all handled by women. They had specific ideas, and I helped express them." Steve looked frustrated. Applause was more robust after this comment.

Several students raised their arms to be called on next, but the professors requested a break. Further discussion would have to wait.

Following the film screenings, an open reception occurred on the soundstage. Made in Heaven huddled together in one corner, sharing impressions of the video while sipping soft drinks from red party cups. Heather remained silent, preferring to fume over the criticism. Nobody else seemed to be bothered by the speaker's remarks. A fact that irked her.

"Good call, Ness, getting Danya to do the choreo," said Grace.

"Told you. She's ace," said Vanessa.

"That was us," said June, still in awe.

"I sprained my neck looking from side to side," responded Erin.

"We looked like giants," said Sun-hee.

A young white male with thick black rim glasses and a porkpie hat approached. Introducing himself as Elvis, he stated, "Hey! Your video was fire."

"Thanks," six of the seven said in unison.

"Do you perform anywhere?"

"Rarely," answered Grace. "It's like pulling teeth to find gigs."

"I hear you. Can I get updates at least?" Grace pulled him aside to share the band's website and add him to the newsletter.

Sun-hee observed Heather's mood. "Why so quiet? Didn't you like it?"

"No, I did. Apologies, but I am unwell."

"What's wrong?"

"She's still mulling over that comment, I bet," said Mindy.

"Forget her. That was rude," said Vanessa.

"Why did she have to say that?" asked Heather, sparking to life. "Who are the victims supposed to be?"

"Don't overthink it," advised Grace, upon returning to the group. "She was uninformed."

"Just because we prefer makeup and cute clothing doesn't make us less empowered. It's our choice." Her face was becoming flushed. She fanned herself with a napkin.

"Heather," Grace said, "you need to stop dwelling on every

little negative comment. It's not healthy."

But Heather did keep talking and dwelling. "I don't see what she expects us to—"

"Heather. Enough."

"—do, instead, and—"

"We'll never please everyone, and there's no point in even trying," advised Mindy.

"—when did feminism become a weapon to beat other women?"

Grace put an index finger to Heather's mouth, "Calm down."

After taking a deep breath, Heather couldn't resist continuing, "I'm the one being calm. It's you all who are—"

"I'm serious. Just ignore it," said Grace.

"It'll be okay," said Sun-hee as she put her hand on the singer's shoulder.

"She sounded like a bitch anyway," said Vanessa.

"Hey, Tiffany Young's appearing at the Fonda on Saturday," said Sun-hee, eager to change the subject. "Anyone wanna go?"

"I'll go," said Mindy. "Loved 'Magnetic Moon.'"

Steve soon joined them, balancing a napkin of cookies in one hand and a soda in the other.

"Congratulations, Mr. Spielberg," said Grace.

"God, I'm glad that's over," he said. "What a semester."

"Thanks for making us look good," added Erin.

"We couldn't be prouder," said Mindy.

Two females approached and introduced themselves as Mei-ling and Ya-wen from Taipei. "We liked your video," said Mei-ling.

"Yeah, we stan boy groups mainly, especially TXT," said Ya-wen, "but that was a real bop. You should be proud."

"Are you planning more?" asked Mei-ling.

"That's the goal," responded Grace. "But the indie scene here doesn't quite know what to do with K-pop, we're discovering."

"I can imagine. Never thought I'd see a video like that here," said Mei-ling.

"Hopefully, doors will open soon," said Mindy.

"Or we'll open them ourselves," added Vanessa.

"When Dalton told us about this project, we had to come. Glad we did. Are you on streaming?" asked Ya-wen.

Grace provided the details and bid them farewell. "We now have three fans."

"Don't give up," Steve said. "K-pop's about to blow up in this country. Once it does, you'll be positioned to capitalize on it."

"What are your thoughts on the screening?" asked Sun-hee.

"I'm happy, for the most part," he responded. "The comments could have been more positive, though."

"Oh, no," said Grace.

"Oh, my god, yes!" exclaimed Heather, grabbing Steve's arm. "See, he agrees—"

Vanessa rolled her eyes. "Now you've really done it."

* * *

After their Marketing Analytics class let out, Heather and Grace walked to their cars discussing the latest news. During class, Grace slipped Heather a note informing her that the video had been accepted for inclusion in the festival. That was all it said. Time for details. "Steve said we qualified for the music video category, as expected, but also for Best Director,

Best Editing, and Best Cinematography," explained Grace.

"What about choreography? And the music?"

"He didn't say. I think we have a good chance to win something, though."

"We need to. Besides the money to stay afloat, we are still far short of the *Showdown* requirements."

"Yeah, and the deadline's June 1."

"Exactly. I doubt we're gonna make it. Thanks to Steve, we have two videos and two singles. But we've had no regular gigs and zero radio airplay. What hope is there we'll get them in time?"

"There's always next year, I guess." Grace shrugged. She didn't sound optimistic.

"Do you really think the girls will stick around that long?"

"I'd like to think so. Really haven't considered it much."

"I have. And that's my biggest worry. I'm afraid they'll lose interest without some tangible sign that this band will work out. Besides, their commitment level is at a bare minimum. You know how hard we worked in Korea. We'll need to kick things up a notch to make a serious run, and that could scare them away."

"I see your point."

"My other consideration is school. If the band doesn't pan out, I'll likely pursue the free business degree my dad wants."

"What if we do stay together? Will you drop out?"

"I'm thinking of doing both, but on my own terms. Paying for it independently and studying what I want."

"Is that even possible?"

"I may be deluding myself, but if I can make it through next year, I might win a music scholarship for the last two."

"Good luck. I'm rooting for you."

"Whatever happens, I'm gonna need answers. And soon. I just wish I knew how the girls felt."

* * *

Heather cursed her printer. The ink cartridge ran dry again. It always seemed to fail when she needed it most. The financial aid deadline for the next academic year had arrived. She was paying a steep price for procrastination. As she was about to upload her application, the university's website went down. This left only one option, an in-person submission. She'd have a small window to do so right before the philosophy final. Financial Aid would be closed by the time exams let out. This gave her 15 minutes to print the documents before heading to campus.

The nearest office supply shop was two blocks away. Time constraints made pickiness imprudent, despite the higher cost compared to chain stores. Heather snatched the old cartridge from the printer and dashed from the apartment in flip-flops. Moments later, a quick scan of the shelves told her that the ink type she needed was out of stock.

A long-faced employee was on the phone dealing with another customer. He raised a finger, signaling he'd be done soon. Heather's look of exasperation must've influenced him to take action. He motioned for the empty cartridge while continuing to answer the caller's questions.

With little better to do than wait, Heather paced nervously near the front window. The L-shaped mini-mall, in which AVCO Office Systems was located, contained several other small companies. Three people emerged from the portfolio services firm next door. A young woman in business attire escorted two middle-aged clients to their car. Heather studied her face as they conversed. She wondered if this was a preview of her life in five years. Did that woman's expression reveal any true feelings? Was she happy exploring these formative stages of her career, paying off debts, and becoming an adult? Hard to say. As the couple bid farewell, the woman smiled, which meant little on its own.

"Miss, I have your ink." Fifty-five dollars poorer and convinced that the printer cartridge racket was the biggest scam going, Heather rushed home to finish her application and prepare for the final.

The Acura Integra rumbled to life. Heather let it warm for several minutes as a mother and child passed on the sidewalk. No older than six, the girl wore a tutu and carried a pink microphone similar to one Heather had used as a child. She remembered it being her favorite prop, a regular feature of singing sessions in front of the mirror.

That microphone had somehow survived Umma's purging of Heather's childhood belongings. She remembered tucking it away in a box shortly after that humiliating day she returned home after being banished from 37-G. Her mood had plunged to its lowest point ever. For at least a week afterward, she'd wait until Appa left for work before daring to emerge from her locked bedroom. The thought of facing him knifed her heart. He kept quiet, at her mother's behest, but his dour expression spoke volumes.

On the drive to campus, Heather preoccupied herself with the insurmountable task she had set for herself. How would it be possible to pay for and attend school while leaving time for music? The more she pondered it, the more ridiculous it seemed. Even if she did pull it off, the debt load would force her to accept the first job offer that came along.

"Oh, Heather, what are you doing?" she asked out loud as she waited for a traffic signal to change. A free education was being offered on a silver platter. Other students would kill for such a gift. Why discard that for a silly dream, particularly one contingent upon others' whims? Were her members even serious about Made in Heaven? She had no way of knowing. True, they shared brief moments of triumph together, but those were far outweighed by the many disappointments. She wouldn't blame them if they dropped the group for better opportunities. And if they did, where would that leave her? Out of a dream and out of school.

SIU's Financial Aid Office wasn't busy at that hour. She simply had to submit the paperwork at the desk. Before she could depart, however, a clerk called out. "Excuse me, you forgot to sign it." Heather returned to the desk, accepting a pen from the woman. Torn by indecision, she hesitated. The clerk pointed to the signature line. Just then, the office phone rang. "I have to get that. Leave it there when you're done."

Heather stared at the document as she tapped the pen on the counter. The empty line mocked her. By the time the phone call ended, Heather still hadn't signed.

"Is something wrong?" the clerk asked.

"Could you please shred this for me?"

The woman looked baffled. "You want me to shred this now?"

"Yes, please."

"You won't qualify for financial aid then. Today's the deadline."

"I understand."

The clerk, her expression troubled, uttered "Okay" while feeding the document into the shredder. Heather winced as the voracious machine devoured the application she had spent so long preparing. Freed from that dilemma but still uncertain of her ultimate choice, she stepped outside.

The alarm on her phone warned that five minutes remained before the final started. That was just enough time to text Grace.

3:56 P.M. Heather: Cancel Thursday's rehearsal. Time for a road trip.

27

HEATHER, ERIN, SUN-HEE, MINDY, VANESSA, AND JUNE DRIVE OUT IN A CAR TO SEE A VIEW; GRACE DRIVES THEM

Grace tapped the brakes of her Subaru at the first sight of beachfront. "Is this it?" she asked.

"No, this is Zuma," explained Vanessa. "Ours is ahead."

As they approached Point Dume State Beach, Heather, in the front passenger seat, turned the radio down to a conversational level. Grace had suggested Malibu for their outing after Heather requested a heartfelt discussion on the group's future. Along the way, they stopped at a Korean BBQ restaurant for takeaway. The plan was to eat an early dinner and watch the sunset from the shore.

"You better park soon, or there won't be any fries left," complained Mindy.

"I was hungry," protested Erin.

"You're always hungry."

In the rearview mirror, Grace watched Erin scowl at Mindy, before offering a fry. Mindy accepted the gift with an open mouth.

Since it was a weekday, parking at Point Dume was abundant. Grace backed her Subaru Tribeca into a superb spot, steps from the beach and well clear of any other guests. The seven members spilled onto the sand. Heather spread a blanket as the girls gallivanted in the sunshine. Grace left the SUV's rear hatch open to access supplies as needed.

They claimed spots along the edge of the blanket as Heather arranged the food. The feast included Korean fried chicken, popcorn shrimp, kimchi fried rice, and a remarkably small number of sweet potato fries.

"I thought three orders of fries would be plenty. They were huge," said Heather.

"You didn't plan on Erin," said Mindy.

"Seriously," exclaimed Vanessa. "How can you eat so much and stay so skinny? It's not even remotely fair." Erin smiled, but said nothing.

"Thank you for the food," they said in unison. The meal disappeared quickly. As they ate, they teased each other mercilessly over the flirtatious guys they'd encountered since the video debut. Once satiated, they split into groups and wandered off to explore the beach.

Grace stayed with the SUV, stretching her legs on the blanket, while enjoying the scene that unfolded before her. The radio DJ promoted an upcoming concert, but the roaring surf drowned out most of what he was saying. She watched Sun-hee, June, and Vanessa splash in the ankle-deep water nearby. Erin and Mindy climbed rocks a short distance to the south. Heather took a solitary stroll along the beach to the north, lost in thought. She sometimes let the incoming water advance to her toes but went no further.

A light but warm breeze kicked up as the intensity of the late afternoon sun diminished. Grace took a deep breath of the salty ocean air. She reflected on the events of the past school year and the girls who had become valued friends. What lay ahead for Made in Heaven? Had their time together come to an end? She had no idea what they would say in the next hour, but she hoped they'd find a reason to stay together. Besides the camaraderie, Heather's outlook had improved drastically since the group's formation. Grace worried she'd regress into self-destructive behavior without a creative outlet to channel her energies.

Once Heather returned from her walk, the group gathered. Grace suggested a photograph for posterity. Was this their last opportunity for one? Seven cheerful faces assembled in a tight circle. Heather sat in the middle, basking in the warmth of companionship. The glorious California coastline, lit by the sun's golden rays, trailed off in the distance. Grace scanned the three images she had taken and selected one to show the others. The image was the best they'd ever taken together.

"I hope years from now, we can recall this day fondly," said Sun-hee.

Grace invited the girls to sit in a circle on the blanket. They would soon know their fate. "We need your input," she said without delay.

Heather took a moment to spread her knee-length skirt over the blanket. She folded her hands on her lap, looked at her cohorts, and spoke. "I'll get right to it. I'm thinking of leaving school."

Everyone but Grace gasped at the news. "Why?" asked Erin.

"Nothing's certain yet, but I want your thoughts on Made in Heaven before I decide."

"Why ask us?" asked Vanessa.

"The reality is I can either continue my studies or pursue an idol career. I can't do both. The finances are not there." Heather's situation required no elaboration. Heads nodded in understanding. "Being an idol remains my dream, but I can't do it alone."

"You carried us this far, Heather," said Sun-hee to the agreement of the others.

"I believe in you all, but I'm afraid we'll hit a wall without progress." The girls fell silent and listened intently. "The good news is we're in the running for the festival prize but are falling short of qualifying for the *Showdown*. My question is, how committed are you to taking this to the next level?"

"What's wrong with our commitment?" asked Erin.

Mindy jumped in with her own response. "We've been living off the charity of others. That'll only carry us so far."

"That's right," said Grace. "Steve's been making our videos for his class projects. Danya and Marielle worked for free. Same with the film crew and the recording crew. Even Arnie, bless his heart, didn't get paid a cent for what he did. Nobody has mentioned legal issues, contracts, and all the boring but important stuff. The cost of promotions, traveling, albums."

"That's true," said Vanessa, shoulders slumped.

"Two singles and three disappointing shows. The sum of our hard work," said Mindy. "That won't make much of an impact, I'm afraid." The members looked distraught at this realization.

"How are the videos doing?" asked Erin.

"Last I looked, 'Have No Fear' reached 600 YouTube views in

four months. 'Feel the Heat' cracked 1,500 yesterday." Grace winced as she delivered her report. "We've made a grand total of $12.14 from streaming and have no physical CD sales to our credit because we only printed enough to give away as promos. The merchandise we commissioned cost more than we made back. If Ness' family hadn't bought a bunch, we'd be in an even bigger hole."

"That's humbling," said June.

"BTS videos can hit 100 million views in two days," Mindy added.

"Way to set a high bar there, Mindy," said Grace.

"600, though. That's friends and family," said Vanessa.

"Pretty much. Heather's point is that we need to take this much more seriously if we hope to make it as a professional group. That means practicing more, getting and staying in shape, and perfecting our technique. Not to mention committing to more live performances, promoting ourselves, and raising money to pay the bills. It's not all sunshine and unicorns, people."

"I want to stay in school. I'm not losing my scholarship," said Vanessa.

"That's understandable," responded Heather. "My example is not something I expect anyone to follow."

"Image, too," Grace said. "We'll have to agree on a code of conduct. It doesn't have to be as severe as what agencies demand in Korea, but we must cover the basics. We have to set an example of how to act in society. That includes no foul language."

All eyes darted to Mindy, who feigned surprise. "Why is everybody looking at me?" Her faux-innocent question provoked general laughter. "It was *one* time," she said with a guilty smile. "Even monkeys fall from trees. But seriously, we're doing this alone. No agency, no connections, and no expertise. That's the price of independence. We can't expect miracles."

"We're not in Korea either," added Sun-hee.

"True. Let's be clear. Being small fish in a vast seas means the chances of succeeding beyond a bit of fun are tiny."

"But what does success mean?" asked June.

"It's when people say they like what we're doing," said Sun-hee. "That's what makes the struggle worthwhile." The others agreed.

Before matters could spin out of control, Grace wrangled the conversation back to her agenda. "Remember, we set a tangible goal: qualify for *Soundscape Showdown.* Well, the bad news is we'll miss the deadline this year. We can't qualify in time. We need a lot more live shows, for sure. Which brings up Heather's main point."

"What do you want to happen? Do we break up now or forge ahead?" added Heather.

"A year is sure a long time," said Erin.

"I just wish people would pay attention. Sometimes it's like we're shouting into a void," said Mindy.

"Just one success would make a huge difference."

"And the prize money would help," said Vanessa.

This exchange triggered a torrent of opinions. Grace sensed they had enough to consider. She let the discussion take its own course. All formalities broke down. Members sometimes spoke in small groups and sometimes shouted over each other. They argued, traded compliments, and expressed various views on their experiences together and possible futures. They shared their fears and dreams. In the end, it was difficult to discern whether they had reached consensus. She could tell from Heather's expression that the primary question remained unanswered. Was Made in Heaven just as important to the other girls as it was to her?

The sun had set, and the beach was closed. Nobody shooed them away, though. As Mindy shared another entertaining story about idol life, Grace noticed a curious look on Sun-hee's face. She cocked her head as if distracted by a noise in the distance.

"What's the matter?" asked Grace, a hint of alarm coloring her voice.

Sun-hee responded with a question of her own. "Do you hear that?" All Grace perceived was an immense wave thundering onto nearby rocks before subsiding into the sea. As if sensing confusion, Sun-hee clarified further. "I thought you said your phone couldn't connect to the stereo."

"It can't. The socket's broken."

"Then how are you playing our song?"

Nobody else caught this exchange, but Grace discerned Sun-hee's point. Standing and gesturing with her arms outstretched, she shouted. "Quiet!"

Startled by this sudden outburst, the group stopped talking and beheld her.

As the chatter ceased, two sounds clearly registered in their ears: the continued crashing of waves on the shore and the iconic whistling of "Feel the Heat," barely audible from the car stereo.

Sun-hee bolted from the blanket and dashed to the nearby Subaru. She tore open the door and climbed into the front seat. "It's on the radio! Our song's on KIGN!" she yelled, before increasing the volume as loud as it could go without distorting.

The rest of the group sat wide-eyed for a moment until they realized what was happening. Ecstatic shrieks burst forth without warning. They jumped around in sheer joy, tears flowing. Hugs abounded, as did laughter. Each fresh song passage renewed their enthusiasm.

Grace's rap started. "That's me. I'm on the radio." She vaulted in place like a baby girl, not caring one bit if it diminished her reputation as a level-headed leader.

June, Mindy, and Vanessa picked up their dance routine midway through the song but erupted into laughter so often that it soon went awry. Meanwhile, overwhelmed by the emotions pouring forth from everyone, Heather dabbed tears with a leftover napkin, sharing a piece once Erin began sobbing too.

During the commotion, a middle-aged white man in a faded red tank top and camouflage baseball cap ran to the parked Subaru. Two teenage boys dressed in similar beach attire soon joined him. They appeared alarmed and ready to fight. "Are you okay?" he asked as he struggled to catch his breath. "There was screaming!"

"Oh, my god!" Sun-hee exclaimed in response. "We're fantastic." She grabbed the man's hands and started dancing with him. Mindy and June hugged the boys, who looked befuddled by the scene they had encountered.

As the celebration continued, Grace assessed the situation. The unexpected development invigorated Made in Heaven's members, bestowing upon them fresh vitality. This was a big deal. Radio airplay signified that someone outside their circle was paying attention. It also moved them one step closer to the *Showdown*. But most importantly of all, it revealed the girls' true feelings. Made in Heaven *did* mean something to them. Given the right motivation, they *would* commit to the work.

Heather leaned against the Subaru with a dazed look. Grace touched her friend's shoulder and asked, "Does that answer your question?"

-To be continued-

Afterword

This book briefly touches on the subject of suicide. If you're thinking about suicide, are worried about a friend or loved one, or would like emotional support, the 988 Suicide & Crisis Lifeline network is available 24/7 across the United States. The 988 Lifeline is available for everyone and is free and confidential.

Dial 988

https://988lifeline.org

Cast of Characters

Made in Heaven: The main focus of our story. Conceived as a hybrid act, the all-girl indie K-pop group features a seven-member dance unit, five of whom double as musicians in the band unit.

Heather Moon (18): Made in Heaven's main singer, songwriter, and rhythm guitarist. Known for her vibrant and charming personality, she has a powerful voice despite her diminutive stature.

Grace So (18): With a dominant personality, she is the group's rapper, lead guitarist, and de facto leader. She often feels compelled to bolster Heather's shaky confidence.

Sun-hee Ahn (18): A Korean native, Sun-hee is the group's talented singer and keyboardist. Her sweet voice contrasts beautifully with Heather's powerful vocals.

Mindy Ito (22): Mindy is the talented veteran drummer for Made in Heaven. The daughter of a half-Japanese/half-Korean father and a Ukrainian-American mother, she is a former member of the disbanded pop-rock group WeR5.

Erin MacLeay (18): Recruited as the band's bassist, she's a Korean American from the tiny town of Harper, Oklahoma. Her sheltered upbringing left her underprepared for life in the big city.

Vanessa Nguyen (19): The group's dance specialist, Vanessa, is a Vietnamese American from Garden Grove, California. Her dance excellence landed a full scholarship to St. Ignatius, a fact she often brings up.

June (Jeong) Kwan (19): Made in Heaven's main visual and talented dancer, June dreams of becoming a top model and has the looks to achieve it.

Other cast members:

Glimmer Blue: Formed at 37-G Entertainment, they've achieved global fame as one of the top girl groups in K-pop.

Mi-Ok Nae (19): Main singer of supergroup Glimmer Blue, who beat out Heather Moon for the position when the group was first formed.

Steven Shepard (21): Originally from Mesa, Arizona, he is a student filmmaker at St. Ignatius University. Tapped to direct several of Made in Heaven's music videos, he befriended them in the process.

Dong-jun Lee (50s): A prominent and wealthy investor in 37-G Entertainment, also known to abuse his position of influence.

Arnie Johnson (30s): Made in Heaven's boorish manager. Formerly a thrashcore musician, he is not known for possessing a refined appreciation of K-pop culture.

Dalton Lim (21): A Singaporean film student from UCLA who serves as cinematographer on several Made in Heaven videos.

Marielle Brodeur (30s): An aspiring fashion designer from Quebec City, Canada, who works for a costume rental house and creates outfits for Made in Heaven on the side.

Dae-hee Moon (40s): Heather's father, with whom she shares a turbulent relationship. To accommodate his never-ending career ambitions, he has relocated his family from Korea to Los Angeles and back again.

Ji-woo Moon (40s): Heather's mother who strives for family harmony despite the challenges.

Andrew Moon (17): Heather's immature, if brilliant, younger brother.

Danya Kay (30s): Professional dancer and friend of Vanessa's. Tapped to choreograph Made in Heaven's first dance-oriented music video.

Casey Revere (21): Steve's childhood friend from Arizona and current girlfriend. She majors in Mathematics at SIU.

Ye-jin Kwan (40s): June's aunt, who fled as a refugee with her before they settled together in the U.S.

Preview of Book Two

If you enjoyed
DEBUT
watch for
COMEBACK
Book Two of the Idol Pursuits trilogy
By Robert Rioux
In the meantime, enjoy this brief preview.

* * *

A vibrating phone in the middle of the night woke Heather. For a long while, she ignored it. Insatiable curiosity, though, compelled her to rise from bed and traipse across the cold linoleum floor. She didn't recognize the sender's name, but the message was personalized in a way that suggested familiarity. Whoever sent it wished to remain anonymous, at least for now. Most intriguingly, the text was in Korean.

2:30 A.M. Regal1: The Getty's lovely this time of year. Have you seen the Cactus Garden? Saturday, noon. I'll be there. Intrigued?

The answer to that question was yes, indeed. But who was the asker? Heather racked her brain to remember anyone using that tag but drew a blank. She couldn't wait to find out, though.

2:34 A.M. Heather: Who is this?

2:36 A.M. Regal1: Trust is crucial to teamwork. Your words, not mine. Go to sleep.

Heather texted several more probative questions, but they remained unanswered. Fifteen minutes later, she returned to bed. Sleep evaded her. Staring at the ceiling, struggling to clear her mind, she came close to slumber. Each time, though, a new thought forced her eyes open at the last minute. Whoever sent the text knew her, but that didn't narrow the list much. Yes. She often said, "Trust is crucial to teamwork," but it was just one of her many catchphrases. Who would remember that one specifically?

The other mystery preoccupying her thoughts was the sender's furtiveness. Why would they go to such great lengths to remain anonymous? She reasoned that an old friend eager to catch up would want to identify themselves from the start. Heather imagined many possibilities, but none emerged as more plausible than the others. The sender's fluent Korean likely ruled out any association with Bertrand. Despite a full Saturday schedule, she knew she'd be making time for that meeting.

The view from the Getty's West Pavilion was arresting. Heather paused a moment to soak the scene in. A thin layer of clouds hung over the city, but downtown Los Angeles remained visible to the east. To the west, the Pacific shoreline beckoned with tantalizing waves dancing in the golden sunshine. The brochure map she received at the museum's entrance identified the Cactus Garden as the backward P–

shaped platform jutting southwards one level below. From her vantage point, it appeared empty. She'd never forgive herself if this proved an elaborate practical joke played at her expense.

But then she noticed movement. Someone stood there. On the terrace below the stairs, Heather spotted a petite shape moving. A planted bed of towering euphorbia and aloe trees concealed her from full view, but the stranger wore a tan-colored long coat. Was this the mystery texter?

Heather proceeded down the stairs from the pavilion to the garden. Upon reaching the terrace, she saw a slender, youthful female standing at the wall, facing away towards the west, towards Korea. The girl stood several inches taller than she did. From the rear, her long, straight black hair revealed little. Her clothing was couture, highlighted by a luxurious shearling coat that probably cost thousands. The garment's subtle details suggested a design of Korean origin. Her own utilitarian ensemble looked dowdy in comparison. Shrugging off waves of insecurity, Heather moved forward, having progressed too far to turn back now.

As Heather drew nearer, the mysterious girl tilted her head, acknowledging the approaching footsteps without fully showing her face. Despite the subject hiding behind dark sunglasses, Heather could tell they were the same age. She addressed the stranger in Korean, using appropriate honorifics.

"I had my doubts you'd come," the stranger responded.

Heather's spine chilled. She recognized that voice, but it couldn't be. Could it? Why did it have to be her?

About the Author

Upon graduating from Loyola Marymount University in Los Angeles, Robert Rioux spent two decades working in the Hollywood entertainment industry, rubbing shoulders with struggling dreamers and top-level achievers. A year spent circumnavigating the globe ignited an intense admiration for the world's varied cultures. Now married and living in Cascadia, Idol Pursuits marks the author's first attempt at trilogy form.

Thanks for reading! Please add a short review on your favorite book site and let me know what you think! It means a lot.

I enjoy writing and see no point in using AI to replace something I love doing. Rest assured that this book was 100 percent human authored.

You can connect with me on:
- https://www.rprioux.com
- https://www.youtube.com/@IdolPursuitsTrilogy/featured

Also by Robert Rioux

As Robert Rioux
    IDOL PURSUITS TRILOGY
    Book One: *Debut*
    Book Two: *Comeback*
    Book Three: *Legacy*

As R. P. Rioux
    Swimming Through the Dawn
    Morning Finds the Breeze
    Arrows Pierce the Sun

For more information, please visit www.rprioux.com

For links to YouTube playlists of music referenced in this series, please visit: www.rprioux.com

Or link there directly using this handy QR code:

9 7 9 8 9 8 8 8 5 6 5 0 4